KING'S LAND RANCH

THE LEGACY

BY:

MARIONDEES

Copyright Case ID: 1-15088890291

LCCN: 2026903037

E-book: 978-1-291-82875-7

Paperback: 978-1-291-82872-6

Hardcover: 978-1-291-82869-6

Acknowledgment

First and foremost, I want to thank my Lord and Savior, Jesus Christ, who makes all things possible. My wife Deborah, my son, and my grandchildren for inspiring me to keep going when things get hard. I always tell people I'm not a polished writer, but I think I tell a pretty good story. I hope you think so, too, after reading my book. I hope you enjoy the journey while reading it. God bless you and your family, and thank you!

Table of Contents

Introduction

In 1850, after saving every penny they could for years, Matt and Sara Evens, with their three children, left the hills of Northern Kentucky. To join other families for the journey of a lifetime and the dream of a better life. They were headed West to Oregon. Jim's dad had bought a covered wagon, and now, all their belongings were packed down inside it. Water barrels were strapped to the sides of the wagon along with bundles of ropes and canvas. Matt Evens had been saving up the money for this trip for a long time now. They had sold all their livestock, except for three laying hens, a milk cow, and three horses. The two draft horses, and Jim's father's riding horse. Jim was the oldest of three children. He was sixteen years old at the time; he had two younger sisters, Hanna and Lizzy. Ages ten years and fourteen years old, Hanna was the oldest of the two girls, and she was her mother's helper. She worked as hard as her mom; Lizzy just did whatever Lizzy wanted to do most of the time. Hanna spent most of her time with her father and brother, taking care of the livestock when she was not helping her mom.

"Lizzy," yelled her mom, Sara, "get in this wagon now," "we're leaving." Lizzy came running from the barn holding a kitten, "You are not bringing that dang cat," said her sister, Hanna." "Oh, yes, I am," said Lizzy, as she climbed into the wagon. "Momma tell her, "Said Hanna, "Oh, let her be," said Sara, "it will probably run away in a day or two anyway." "Or be eaten by a Wolf," said Hanna in a scary voice, staring at Lizzy. Lizzy just stuck her tongue out at her sister Hanna. "Get up," said Jim as he popped the horses with the reins. The wagon jerked forward as the horses started walking. Matt led the way on his horse as Jim followed behind him with the wagon. Sara's heart was racing, partly because of the excitement of the trip and partly because of the fear of the unknown. They had lived there for the past seventeen years; their three children were born there.

But now all their kin had either died or moved away. They were to meet up with a group of other wagons in Kansas City, Kansas, about thirty wagons in all. A diverse group of people from all over, most from the Eastern parts of the United States, but some were from the South as well. The year was 1850, and the day was March 2nd. The Evens family had to be in Kansas City by April 10th. Hundreds of other people had already successfully made this trip, so the trail was well mapped. However, many had failed to make it all the way to Oregon, and some did not make it at all. Some were buried along the way, and some just disappeared, while others simply gave up and settled along the way. It was not an easy trip by any means. Matt and Sara knew this, but their hopes for a better life pushed them onward.

Jim got off his horse and tied it up to a tree. He took his rifle and ran up the trail. The screams were getting louder as he stopped by a big rock for cover. He eased around the rock and saw the Indians and the girls in an open area just off the trail. He got down onto his hands and knees to get closer. He could see Hanna and another girl sitting by a big rock; their hands were tied in front of them. Two of the Indians were standing guard over them with rifles in their hands. In the middle of the small opening, the other three Indians were terrorizing what looked to be the oldest girl with blond hair. Grabbing at her and pulling at her clothes. She was trying her hardest to fight them off, even with her hands tied. Jim got in a good spot for cover where he could see them all. Then one of the Indians ripped the girl's dress off her, exposing her undergarments. One of the other Indians threw her to the ground and jumped on top of her. Jim knew it was time, he took aim, shooting the two men guarding Hanna with his rifle, then turned and shot the Indian on top of the girl. "It's Jim," yelled Hanna, "stay down." The last two Indians ran for their horses, as they jumped on their horses, Jim shot one of them. The last one rode off. Jim couldn't get a clear shot at him through the brush. "Damn," said Jim. He ran down to Hanna and the other girls.

As Jim walked out from the Saw Mill, one man fell from the roof of the Land office with an arrow in his back, another man shot at Jim from the restaurant roof, and Stew shot that man. A shot rang out from a window in the hotel. Jim falls to the ground, hit in the leg. Hanna yells, "JIM!" Hanna hears a shrill whistle; Anna's horse came running by Hanna, who had just made it to the street. The horse ran down the street, and Anna ran out to Jim. The horse stops at Jim, "grab the stirrup, Uncle Jim," said Anna. Jim reached up and grabbed hold of one stirrup. Anna dragged him into the alley with the horse. Then, she helps Jim up onto her horse, and Anna puts a pigging string around Jim's leg above the wound. "He got you good," said Anna, "don't worry, I'll get you out of here." "They will be coming, Uncle Jim, you be ready," "I'll try to find them before they get here," said Anna, as she ran to the other end of the alley and disappeared. Jim waited. Hanna, Missy, and Kate all started trying to work their way to Jim and Anna in the alley before the other men got there.

Chapter One: Pulling Up Stakes

One early spring morning, Jim's father, Matt Evens, told his son Jim to hook up their team of four horses to the wagon. The Evens family was leaving their small two-room shack in the hills of Northern Kentucky for good. They were heading West to Oregon. Jim's dad had bought a covered wagon for a long trip, and some repairs were made before all their family's belongings were packed down inside the wagon. Water barrels were strapped to the sides of the wagon along with bundles of ropes and canvas. Matt, Evens had been saving up all the money he could for this trip. They had sold all their livestock, except for three laying hens, a milk cow, and five horses. Their four draft horses, and Jim's father's riding horse. Jim was the oldest of three children. He was sixteen years old at the time; he had two younger sisters, Hanna and Lizzy. Ages ten years old and fourteen years old, Hanna was the oldest of the two girls, and she was her mother's helper. She worked as hard as her mom; Lizzy just did whatever Lizzy wanted to do most of the time. Hanna spent most of her free time with her father and brother, taking care of the livestock when she was not helping her mom.

"Lizzy!" yelled her mom, Sara, "get in this wagon now," "we're leaving." Lizzy came running from the barn holding a kitten, "You are not, bringing that dang cat," said her sister Hanna. "Oh, yes, I am," said Lizzy, as she climbed into the wagon. "Momma, tell her," Hanna said, "Oh, let her be," said Sara. "It will probably run away in a day or two anyway." "Or be eaten by a Wolf," said Hanna in a scary voice, staring at Lizzy. Lizzy just stuck her tongue out at her sister Hanna. "Get up," said Jim as he popped the horses with the reins. The wagon jerked forward as the horses started walking. Matt led the way on his horse as Jim followed behind him with the wagon. Sara's heart was racing, partly because of the excitement of the trip and partly because of the fear of the unknown. They had lived on that hill for the past seventeen years; their three children were born there. But now all their kin folks had either died or had also moved away.

They were to meet up with a group of other wagons heading West in Independence, Missouri, at the courthouse there. About thirty to thirty-five wagons in all, a diverse group of people from all over. Most of the eastern parts of the United States, but some were from the South as well. The year was 1850, and the day was March 2nd. The Evens family had to be in Independence by April 10th. Hundreds of other people had already successfully made this trip, so the trail was well mapped. However, many had failed to make it all the way to Oregon, and some did not make it at all. Some were buried along the way, and some just disappeared, while others simply gave up and settled along the way. It was not an easy trip by any means. Matt and Sara knew this, but their hopes for a better life pushed them to leave the home they knew.

There was still some snow in places in the Northern Kentucky hills as they made their way down the mountain, but the wagon road was clear. Other than it being wet and muddy from the snow and ice melting away. Jim was holding the team back as they eased down the steeper parts of the road; his father had taught him well. Jim kept the wagon wheels in the bottom of the ruts in the road so the wagon wouldn't try to slide side to side. "Why are we going so slow?" asked Lizzy, "We won't get there." "Hush, child," said Sara, "you let Jim drive." Lizzy could hear the worry in her mother's voice. Sara was afraid of what could happen if Jim didn't stay alert. Finally, they made it to flat ground in the valley after about two hours, "Stop up here," said Matt. Jim got down off the wagon. "You ok, son?" asked Matt. "Yes, sir," said Jim. "You did a good job, son," said Matt. The two men check out the wagon wheels to make sure there is no damage anywhere, and they check the ropes holding the barrels. Hanna jumped down and checked on the milk cow tied to the back of the wagon.

"Ok," said Matt let's get moving, Jim climbed back onto the wagon and yelled, "Get up," as they started moving again. They headed to the nearest town to buy supplies for the long trip ahead. Bloomfield, Kentucky, a small town on the east fork of the Simple Creek, is best known for its produce and the tobacco it grows. The town also had a flour mill, that's where Matt could buy flour in 50 lb. bags. But they would not make it there on the first day; that night, they would camp on "Simple Creek," a little over halfway to town.

Just before dark, Matt found a good spot to set up camp near the creek for the night. Jim unhooked the wagon team and led them to the edge of the creek to drink water. Sara and the girls went out to find some firewood while Matt unloaded the cooking supplies from the wagon. Matt went to the creek and got some stones for a fire pit. Jim hobbled the team and Matt's riding horse, then turned them out to eat grass. Sara and the girls came back with firewood, Jim cut the wood up while Matt built a fire. Sara and Hanna started prepping the food to be cooked, while Lizzy sat by the wagon playing with her kitten. After they ate, Jim brought the horses up to the wagon and tied them close by. Sara and the girl climb into the back of the wagon to sleep while Matt and Jim spread out their bedrolls by the fire. Jim and his father both had their rifles by their sides, just in case.

The next morning, Jim watered the horses and fed them some grain, while Hanna milked the cow and got the eggs from the chicken cage that was tied on the side of the wagon, while Sara started cooking breakfast. Matt saddled his horse and then helped Jim hook up the wagon team. "It's going to be a beautiful day, Son," said Matt. "Yes, sir," said Jim. "Looks that way," said Jim. Matt always tried to have a positive attitude around his kids. After breakfast, they packed everything back up into the wagon, Jim poured water on the fire, then climbed up onto the wagon. "Get up," said Jim, as the wagon started rolling again. The Evens family made it to the town of Bloomfield midafternoon. They tied the team and the horse in front of the General Store while they went inside to get their supplies. Matt handed Hanna a coin, "Get you and Lizzy some hard candy for the trip," said Matt. "Yes, Poppa," said Hanna, with a big smile. They got all their basic supplies, lard, flour, sugar, meal, coffee, beans, potatoes, and fat back. Jim and Matt would have to hunt for wild meat along the way. They left Bloomfield just before dark and crossed the Simple Creek bridge, headed West out of Bloomfield. A couple of miles from town, they stopped and camped again for the second night.

On March 12th, they crossed over into Illinois. That night, Matt told Jim, "Son, you've done a great job with the team; they're pulling a heavy load."

"But we've got to pick up the pace some,"

"We need to get started earlier in the morning and cover more ground." "I didn't want to push the horses too hard starting off, "but the team should be used to the load by now." "Just keep your eye on them, but try to find a steady pace a little faster than we've been going," "Yes, sir," said Jim. "I'll tell your mom to find a way to cut down on the bathroom stops for her and the girls," said Matt. "What's Oregon like, poppa?" asked Jim. "Well, Son, I really don't know. They say it's a beautiful country." "But this here is not that bad either," said Matt, "No, sir, it's not," said Jim. "But in Oregon, the government is giving away free land, thousands of acres for the taking," said Matt. "All we have to do is get there with your mom and sisters safely," "then pick a spot and build them a house to live in." "One day you and I will buy cattle and start a ranch, a big ranch with grass as far as you can see," said Matt. "Son, you have to think about the big picture. Other families are going there too with their sons and daughters." "Those sons will meet other families' daughters and marry them, just like you will one day." "Your sisters will meet other families' sons and so on, and so on." "Son, your mom and I are doing this for you and your sisters." "It's going to be a hard trip once we leave Missouri," said Matt. "But with you helping your mom and me, and God watching over us all, we'll make it just fine," "Yes, sir," said Jim.

Jim lay in his bedroll that night with a sense of pride. He realized now that there was a bigger purpose than he knew for this trip. It wasn't just an idea that his father came up with one day, and his mom just went along with it. Together, they had made plans for the futures of their children; they could have just stayed on that mountain, getting by day by day. But Matt and Sara Evens wanted more for their children, more opportunities, a better chance in life. It would be an adventure that none of them would ever forget. The next morning, they were all up before daylight, getting ready to travel. Sara and Hanna whipped out breakfast, they ate, and were on their way by sunup. Jim found his pace as they traveled along the dusty road headed to Missouri. Each time they stopped at night, Matt tried to find a place near some water. Lizzy would always wade around in the creeks, finding rocks she thought were pretty, and then hide them somewhere in the wagon. "You're going to make this wagon so dang heavy with rock these horses can't pull it," said Hanna. "Those rocks are no heavier than this kitten," said Lizzy. "Well, that kitten needs to be thrown out, too," said Hanna. "You just leave my rocks and kitten alone," said Lizzy, getting in the last word.

March 20th. They made it to the Mississippi River, near St. Louis. They would have to wait until the next day to cross over on the barge. There was a line of wagons of all kinds waiting to cross the river, freight wagons, buggies, people on horseback, and covered wagons like theirs. Matt rode ahead and counted the wagons up ahead, "Thirty-eight wagons ahead of us," said Matt, "it's going to be a while." The barge could only carry two wagons and a few horses at a time. It took two hours to load, cross the river, then unload on the other side, and then come back across. The barge stopped crossing the river at dark, each evening, because they couldn't see the floating logs coming down the river at night. It would be midday tomorrow before the Evens would get to cross the river into Missouri. The rest of the day, they only moved a few feet every two hours. In the dark, they could see the river up ahead. Matt pulled Jim to the side, "Son, these horses have never done this before." "They may get spooked by the moving water," said Matt. "I'll lead them onto the barge; you stay on the wagon." "Once we have the wagon loaded on the barge, I'll cover the horse's eyes with these clothes," "you lock the brake on the wagon," yes, sir," said Jim. "Look, Son, we don't know what kind of people we have here. Tonight, we'll let the girls sleep in the wagon." "You stay in the seat of the wagon with your rifle," "I'll stay on my horse in the shadows and keep an eye on the back of the wagon." "We will have time to take a nap after sunup," said Matt. That night, they ate leftover biscuits and bacon. Matt handed Jim some jerky, "if you get sleepy, just chew on that," said Matt.

The next morning at daylight, the barge started loading again, and the Evens moved up a couple of wagon lengths. By noon, they were fourth in line. Jim and his sisters were in awe of the massive body of water in front of them. There were people, wagons, and horses on the other side of the river waiting to come across on the return trip. When it was finally their turn, Sara and the girls left the wagon and walked onto the barge, then Matt led his horse aboard, and then went back to lead the team. Jim popped the horses and made them pull the heavy wagon up the ramp onto the barge. Matt covered the horses' eyes, then hung feed bags on their heads. Jim locked the brake on the wagon. As the barge slowly started moving across the river to the other side. Jim was scared and excited at the same time. The horses did fine, and it was mid-afternoon once they reached the other side. After unloading from the barge, Sara and the girl got into the wagon. "Jim," said Matt, "let's find a place upriver away from all these people and set up camp." "Yes, sir," said Jim, as they followed an old wagon trail up the riverbank for a couple of miles. Matt found an open spot with easy access to the river, "Stop here, son," said Matt. "We'll camp here for the night, Jim started unhooking the team from the wagon. Matt opened a box on the side of the wagon and pulled out a tin can. "Who wants fish for supper?" asked Matt. "Me," said Lizzy, "sound good," said Sara, Matt, Sara, and the girls walked down to the riverbank, Matt cut some Willow limbs and tied fishing string and hooks on them. Then he went to look for some fish bait under the rocks and logs along the bank. Jim led the team to the river and let them drink water, then took them back to the wagon and tied them up. He then led the milk cow and Matt's horse down to drink, also, Jim always did what needed to be done without being told.

Hanna had caught two catfish, and Lizzy one, by the time Jim came to where they were. Sara caught one as Jim walked up Matt was baiting hooks. Jim cut himself a limb and rigged it up he caught two right away, then Lizzy caught another one. Then Sara caught a large one, and Matt helped her get it in. "Ok," said Matt, "that's enough, that's all we will be able to eat." "Aw, Dad," said Lizzy. "We only take what we need," said Matt. Jim took the fish and dressed them while Matt built a fire, Sara and Hanna peeled potatoes to fry. All but one of the fish were fry whole size; the last one Sara had caught, Jim flayed it out and cut it up into small pieces with no bones. They all ate until they were about to pop; they even let the kitten have some to nibble on. They sat there looking up at the stars. "Well," said Matt, "now we've just got to make it across the Missouri River, then on to Independence to meet the others." "Which way are we going?" asked Jim, "straight through St. Lewis," then on to Independence," said Matt. "Are we stopping in St. Lewis?" asked Sara, as she looked at Matt with begging eyes. "We need a few things; there may not be anything left in Independence once we get there," said Sara. "Ok," said Matt, "make me a list of what you need, we will re-stock there." The next morning, they packed up their things, Jim watered the animals, then hooked up the team. None of them had any idea how big the city of St Lewis was; they knew it was a port city and that there would be a lot of people coming and going. As Jim drove the wagon down the main street, they were shocked; it was like somebody had taken every town they had ever seen and put them all in one place. They could not see the other end of town as they rolled down the main street.

Matt saw a sign that said "Matty's Dry Goods", then another that said, "Hardware Supplies," next to it. "Pull over their son," said Matt as he pointed. Matt needed a new axe handle and some horseshoe nails. "Jim, you stay with the wagon, son. We won't be long," Matt, Sara, and the girls went inside the dry goods store. "Oh, Matt," said Sara, "look at all the clothes." "The girls need new night gowns, and you and Jim need new pants." "Ok," said Matt, "I'm going next door to the hardware store." Matt stopped and checked on Jim, "You ok, son?" asked Matt. "Yes, sir," said Jim. "You need anything from the hardware store?" asked Matt. "Well, nah, I'm fine." "What is it, son?" "Well, I could use a good skinning knife," said Jim. Matt smiled. "I'll look and see what I can find," said Matt as he walked off and went inside the store. As Jim was sitting there thinking that he might be getting a new knife, and what kind it could be. Sara and the girl were finishing up their shopping in the store. Then Jim heard something rattle in the back of the wagon. He pulled back the curtain to see a man in the wagon with a bag of sugar and their salt pork. Jim jumped down from the wagon and ran to the back just as the man was climbing out of the wagon. Jim grabbed the man and threw him to the ground, then grabbed the sugar and the pork. The man got up and hit Jim in the face with his fist, knocking Jim to the ground, but Jim held on to the sugar and pork. Then the man jumped on top of Jim and started hitting him some more, "let it go," said the man as he tried to pull the things from Jim's arms. Matt came out of the store and saw Jim on the ground with the man on top of him. Matt kicked the man in the face, knocking him off Jim. The man got up,

Matt pulled his gun out, and the man ran off holding his face. Sara and the girls came out after hearing the commotion in the street, as did Matty, the store owner. Jim was covered in blood and mud, but he had the sugar and pork under his arms. Matt helped him up. Matt put the sugar and the meat back into the wagon. Lizzy crawled into the wagon behind him, "That man better not have touched my rocks," said Lizzy. She dug behind the flower sack and found her bag of stones. Lizzy came out with her bag as Sara was wiping blood off Jim's face and lips.

"What kind of rocks do you have there, sweety?" asked Matty. "Oh, she's always picking up rocks every time we stop by a stream or creek," said Hanna, "they're just old rocks." "Lizzy handed Matty her bag. Matty looked inside," Oh, my God," said Matty, as she looked around to see if anyone was nearby. "Those are some nice rocks," said Matty. She had a shocked look on her face. Let's go back inside my store, sweety. Sara and the girls followed Matty. Matt pulled out a knife, "a hunting knife," and handed it to Jim with a smile. Then he turned and followed the girls back into the store. "How much do I owe you?" asked Matt. He was ready to leave town. But Matty was focused on the rocks, "I think I'm going to be owing you, Sir," said Matty. As she poured the rocks out of Lizzy's bag onto the counter, Matt and Sara's eyes got big as they saw the rocks. "Lizzy," said Sara, "Lizzy had eight gold nuggets, the size of marbles and bigger, three turquoise stones, a ruby, some Safaris, and some stones that were just pretty rocks." "Lizzy, those are nice rocks. Would you be interested in selling me some of them?" asked Matty. "I can't afford to buy them all, but I'll buy what I can." "For money," asked Lizzy, "yes, sweety, for money or for these clothes," said Matty. Lizzy looked at her rocks. Matt was in shock; he wasn't sure just how much they were worth, but he knew it was a lot. Lizzy slid four of the gold nuggets, two tuques, the Ruby, and two of the Safaris over to Matty. "How much for these?" asked Lizzy. Matty took out her scales and weighed each one of them, then took a pin and paper. Matty wrote out the weights, then put numbers beside them, and then subtracted the cost of the clothes. "I can give you $ 40.00," said Matty. Sara's eyes got big. Matt almost choked on his chew. Lizzy looked at her dad, "Is that a good price, Poppa?" "Yes, I think so, Lizzy," said Matt. "ok," said Lizzy. She started putting the rest of her rocks back into the bag. "Now, how much do I owe you for the clothes?" asked Matt. "I deducted them from the price of the stones," said Matty. Lizzy stuck the money in her bag with the other rocks. "Now you keep that in a safe place sweety," said Matty," "those yellow rocks are worth more than the others, you keep all of them you can find," "oh, I will," said Lizzy. As they walked back to the wagon, Lizzy asked her dad, "do I have enough money to buy me and Hanna some more rock candy." "You and Hanna go on and get into the wagon," said Matt, "I'll go get you some candy." Matt crossed the street to the general store and came back with a big bag of candy and four soda pops. He handed it all but one soda pop to Sara with a smile, then gave Jim the other soda pop. "Are you okay, son?" asked Matt. "I'm good," said Jim. "It doesn't hurt much," said Jim. "Let's ride," said Matt as he got up onto his horse.

They rode out of town, headed West. Sara looked at Jim's busted-up face, "Oh, son, I'm so sorry." "If I hadn't wanted to stop here, that wouldn't have happened to you," Jim said as he hugged his mom. "Don't worry, I'm a big boy now, Mom. I can take it." Matt was riding along smiling, his son had done his job protecting the wagon, and his little Lizzy had surprised them all. It had taken Matt five years to save up the money for this trip, and he wasn't sure it would be enough. But Lizzy had just helped, and now they would all spend more time looking for rocks in the creek and rivers along the way. They traveled until just before dark that day to get as far as they could away from St. Lewis. After all the animals were fed and Sara and Hanna had started cooking, Matt sat by the fire drinking his coffee, while Jim sharpened his new hunting knife. His father was giving him pointers about putting a good edge on it. Jim knew how to use a rifle and take care of it, but he had never had his own knife before. Somehow, just having the knife on his side made him feel a little safer and more prepared for trouble if it came along again. Jim was no longer a boy; his birthday was in two weeks, and he would be seventeen. He was somewhere between being a man and a boy; his father knew that by the time this trip was over, Jim would be a full-grown man.

Each day that they traveled West, it was getting warmer; in the afternoons, they rode straight into the sun. After traveling for almost two weeks, one afternoon, they found a shady spot under some trees, and Matt told Jim, "Pull up under those trees." As always, Jim did as he was told, but asked, "Why are we stopping now, Dad?" "Your mom wants to take a break," said Matt, "I saw some deer tracks in that last mud hole we went through. We need some meat, son." "You think you could track that deer down and kill it for us?" asked Matt. "I can sure try," said Jim, as he got off the wagon with his rifle. "Here, you take my horse," said Matt. "But don't wander off too far," "I'll take care of the team and watch over things, while you get us some meat," "Yes, sir," said Jim. Jim got on his dad's horse and rode back the way they had come. Matt unhooked the team, then built a fire. "Come on, girls," said Sara, "we've got work to do." "What are we doing, Momma?" asks Lizzy. "Today is Jim's birthday, we've got to make him a cake." "Oh, goodie, I love cake," said Lizzy. Hanna and Sara started to get the ingredients out of the wagon, while they had Lizzy spread lard in a big iron pan. Hanna measured out the flour and sugar and put it in a bowl, then added a pinch of salt. She mixed the dry ingredients together, then went and got some fresh milk from the cow. Hanna added two eggs, then the milk, until it was like she wanted it. She gave Sara the leftover milk, and Sara was working on the icing for the cake. Hanna adds a couple of drops of vanilla, then mixes it up some more. Sara took over, she teased the batter, then added some butter and poured it into the greased pan. Sara put the pan on the fire with a lid on it, then went back to her icing. Hanna and Lizzy piled potatoes, then Hanna cut off some dry-cured ham.

Jim was gone for a little over an hour; he came back with a small young buck deer draped over the horse behind him. "Good job, son," said Matt. Jim had always been good at trailing and hunting animals. Matt helped Jim hang the deer up and skin it, then they cut the meat off the bones and wrapped it in cheesecloth. After washing up, Matt and Jim walked back to the wagon. As they got close, Jim saw the food all laid out with the cake. "Happy Birthday," yelled his mom and sisters. Jim was surprised. He had completely forgotten about his birthday. After being on the trail for so long, every day just ran together. He walked over and hugged his mom and sisters. Matt stepped up to him, then reached out and shook his son's hand. "Happy Birthday, Son," said Matt, "here I got you something else." Matt handed Jim something wrapped in brown paper. Jim slowly unwrapped it. It was a 30 Cal. Colt Revolver with a leather holster and belt, it wasn't new, but it was to Jim. "I think you're grown up enough now, son," "but there are some rules that go along with that gun." "We will talk about that later," said Matt, "I'm hungry, let's eat." They all sat around the fire and ate mashed potatoes, gravy, bread, and ham, then Hanna cut the cake and started serving it to everyone. No, candles or fancy writing, just a white campfire cake with white icing, "yummy," said Lizzy as she took a bite.

That night, Matt told Jim as they sat by the fire, "that a gun is a tool, not a toy." "It's for protection, and protection only." "I will teach you how to use it and clean it, and help you practice aiming with it." "I want you to learn to use it well and safely. Once you've done that, I hope you never have to pull the trigger on it again." "But if you do, don't hesitate, if you pull it, you shoot it, it's that simple," said Matt in a serious tone. Matt and Jim practiced with the gun in the afternoons before dark, after they had set up camp. Jim seemed to have a natural knack for pulling and shooting the gun and could hit most anything he aimed at. That bothered Matt somewhat, but knowing the dangers that lay ahead of them on this trip, he was also glad. After all, it was up to him and his son to get Sara and the girls to Oregon safely. April 8th. They made it just outside in Independence, Missouri; they were two days early. It was time to rest the animals and themselves for a while now.

The next morning, Matt rode into Independence, Missouri, to talk to the trail Boss, a Mr. Tom Wagner. Mr. Wagner had already made this trip four times; this would be his fifth. Matt found him inside the courthouse at a corner table in the lobby, where people were lined up paying him their money and filling out the sign-up sheets. Matt waited for his turn, which took a while; he then stepped up and introduced himself. The man looked down the list, "Oh, there you are, Matt Evens," "Glad you made it, Matt," said Mr. Wagner. "Here, read this contract, and sign it," said the man. Matt did, and then pushed it back to him. "That will be three hundred dollars," said Tom. Matt handed him the money. Mr. Wagner handed Matt a flyer, "Pin this to your wagon so everyone will know that you are traveling with me." "We are living at sunup on April 10th. from the West side of town," said Mr. Wagner. "I see here you have a wife, a son, and two daughters with you," "Yes, sir," said Matt. "Do you need any supplies?" asked Mr. Wagner. "No, sir," said Matt. "That's good," said Tom. "Don't bring your family into this hellhole of a town." "Take your wagon North of town until you see where the Kaw River runs into the Missouri River." "Cross there, it's a good hard bottom, you'll see the crossing, then follow the Kaw River Northwest about five miles." "Wait there, we will be along about mid-morning on the 10th. "This town is about to explode with all these people here." "I've got men guarding the camp North of town. There have already been a rape and two murders in the past week here."

"You should be far enough away from town there, but keep your guns close, you never know," "Yes, sir," said Matt, "Thanks!"

Matt went back to where his family was camped, "Jim," yelled Matt, "let's move, Son." Jim jumped up and got the team hooked to the wagon again, while Matt was loading the wagon back up. "Where are we going?" asked Sara. "We need to cross at the Kaw River northwest away, to stay out of Independence." "I'll tell you about it tonight, but Independence is not a town we want to visit with our girls." "Ready, Dad?" yelled Jim. "Let's ride then," said Matt, as he rode up the riverbank, with Jim following him. Matt found the crossing Mr. Wagner had told him about; he crossed first on his horse, then waved Jim across with the wagon. Once Jim made it across, they headed along the Kaw Riverbank. It was a smaller river, not very wide or deep. They followed the river until it was almost dark, then stopped under some trees and set up camp. Tomorrow, they would have a whole day to rest up before they started their long journey West. Well, the girls would anyway, Matt and Jim would need to pull the wheels off the wagon and grease the axles, then check the shoes on the draft horses' feet. Every spare minute Jim had free, he sharpened his knife or threw it at a tree. Jim would mark a spot and then throw the knife at the mark; he was getting very good at hitting the mark. With his Colt, he was already very fast on the draw and never missed what he shot at, but being this close to town, Matt told him. Gunfire might draw the wrong kind of attention and bring someone looking for their camp. That night, they would eat deer meat, gravy, and biscuits, but Sara had given Hanna the afternoon off so she could go exploring with Lizzy by the river. They were to bathe in the river before coming back to camp. Matt was on guard duty near the girl. Jim stayed close to the wagon while Sara was cooking supper for the family.

Matt and the girls came back to the wagon after a while. Lizzy had found more yellow rocks in the river, smaller than the ones before.

Hanna had found a couple, too, but mostly just pretty rocks that caught her eye. After they ate, Matt told Jim to get some sleep, that he would take the first watch but would wake him later. Jim didn't mind; he was tired anyway. He climbed into his bedroll, and within minutes, he was asleep. After the girls had gone to bed, Matt told Sara about what Mr. Wagner had told him in Independence, about the crazy things going on in town. "We've got to be on our guard until the others catch up to us," "ok," said Sara. "Here, take Jim's rifle into the wagon with you tonight," said Matt, "turn the lantern down low but leave it burning." "Now you're scaring me," said Sara. "Well, I think we need to be careful," said Matt. "At least caucus, that's why Jim and I are standing guard tonight." Sara went to the wagon and crawled inside with the girls. She opened her Bible and read softly to the girls as they fell off to sleep. About 3:00 a.m., Matt woke up Jim, "Your turn, son," said Matt. "Keep a close eye out, wake me if you hear or see anything." Matt crawled into Jim's warm bedroll; Jim stoked the campfire, then walked away from it. The night sky was clear, the moon and the stars were shining bright, and away from the fire, Jim could see off in the distance. He slowly walked around the camp, keeping his eyes away from the fire. There were no sounds, just dead quietness, all around him. One of the horses let out a moan; the sudden sound startled Jim. His heart raced for a second until he realized what it was, "dang horse," thought Jim as he walked on. Finally, the sky started to lighten up slowly in the eastern distance, and whippoorwills started to sing forlornly. Then frogs started croaking in the river nearby; it was like watching and hearing the birth of the new day.

At sun-up, Jim heard Lizzy say, "Momma, I'm hungry," "You're always hungry," said Hanna. "Ok, girls, get up, I've got to go pee," said Sara, "me too," said Hanna, "morning Jim," said Sara as she climbed out of the wagon, "morning mom," said Jim. Sara scurried off to the bushes with Hanna and Lizzy following her. When they came back, Sara said, "ok, girls, wash your hands. Let's get breakfast going. Lizzy walked over to the fire, "You need to put some more wood on this fire," said Lizzy," in a bossy tone. "No," said Jim, "Momma just needs the coals to cook on, then I'll put more wood on it." "Go put you some clothes on if you're cold," said Jim. Hanna was milking the cow. "Come overhear Lizzy," said Hanna. "Let me show you how to do this," "No, thanks, you're doing a great job, sis," said Lizzy. Matt had his eyes open. "You awake, poppa?" asked Lizzy. "I am now," said Matt," Here come on," said Matt as he raised up the blanket. Lizzy crawled into the bedroll with her dad. Jim was feeding the stock; Hanna brought the milk to her mom. "Where is that Lazy Lizzy?" asked Hanna. Sara pointed at her and Matt under the wagon. Lizzy and Matt were both sound asleep again. Hanna eased over to them and reached under the end of the blanket. Grabbed Lizzy by one ankle and dragged her out from under the covers. The fight was on, hair-pulling, name-calling. Matt grabbed them both and started tickling them. They screamed and squealed until Sara said, "Ok, you three kids get up and get dressed, breakfast is almost ready." "Get off me," "you oh big cow," said Lizzy to Hanna. "I'd rather be a cow than a pig like you," said Hanna. Matt popped them both on the butt, not hard, "mind your momma, now get up." Matt crawled out from under the wagon, walked over to Sara, gave her a kiss, then popped her butt. "Morning, dear," said Matt. "We might have to go hunt for berries after breakfast," said Matt. Sara smiled, "We just might," said Sara.

Jim came back to the wagon. Sara was through cooking, so he put more wood on the fire, then poured himself a cup of coffee and sat down. Matt was already sitting there drinking coffee. Sara brought Matt a plate, and then Jim, "Girls, come fix your plates," said Sara. After breakfast, Sara had the girls clean up everything, while she and Matt went down to the river to take a bath. Jim stayed at the camp with the girls. When they came back, Matt and Jim started working on the wagon, pulling one wheel at a time and greasing the axles. After that, they work on the loose boards on the wagon, then the teams' feet. Later that afternoon, Jim took Matt's horse and crossed the river to go hunting. This would be his last chance for a while; tomorrow, the other wagon would be coming through. Jim eased along the tree line, looking for signs. He saw some deer tracks, but nothing fresh. Then he saw footprints in the sand by the river, well, shoe prints anyway, small shoe prints like a woman's shoe. Jim stopped and got off the horse to get a closer look; sure enough, they were shoe prints. How in the world did a shoe print get way out here, thought Jim. There was nothing around for miles. Jim followed them along the riverbank, then they turned and went into the woods. There was an old wagon trail leading into the woods; he could also tell a wagon had crossed the river there lately. Then he saw horse tracks leading back across the river the other way, something strange here, thought Jim. Then Jim smelled smoke, like a campfire's smoke coming from the woods.

Jim tied his horse and followed the shoe prints up the old trail away; the smoke smell was getting stronger. Then he saw a wagon up ahead and the smoldering fire. Jim slowly got closer as he eased down the trail. "Hello to the camp," yelled Jim. He had his rifle ready, but there was no reply. Jim eased on into the camp, "Anybody here?" said Jim, but nothing. It looked like the wagon had a broken axle on it; there was a busted wheel lying on the ground nearby, but where were the people and the horses? Jim heard a soft whimper coming from inside the wagon. "My name is Jim Evens. I'm not here to hurt you. Come on out," said Jim. "I just want to help you if I can," Jim saw the barrel of a gun sticking out of the back of the wagon, then a young woman followed out behind the gun. "You stay back, you hear?" said the girl, then she climbed down out of the wagon. Jim sat down by the fire to warm up and laid his gun down. The girl was shaking, "What are you doing here?" asked the girl. "I was hunting deer when I saw your tracks at the river, then smelled the smoke," said Jim.

“Where is your family?” asked Jim. Tears filled the girl’s eyes, “I’m not sure,” “the wagon broke down after we crossed the river.” “My dad went to find help with one of our horses, leaving Momma and me here.” “After a week, my mom took the other horse to go find him,” “that was over two weeks ago,” said the girl. Jim dropped his head. “You’ve been here this whole time alone,” said Jim. The girl nodded. Jim looked at the girl from head to toe. She was filthy, her dress was torn, and her hair was a mess.

Jim stood up, “Well, get your things, you can’t stay here alone,” said Jim. “But my parents will be coming back soon,” protested the girl. Jim knew that if they were coming back, they would have already been there by now. “Where were you and your parents headed?” asked Jim. “Oregon,” said the girl, “but my father wouldn’t pay the guide in Kansas City, my dad said he could find Oregon on his own.” “But then the wagon broke down, I think he was lost,” said the girl. “I think so too,” said Jim, “Look, my family and I are meeting up with a wagon train tomorrow, going to Oregon.” “You can go with us, maybe you will find them in Oregon, or along the way.” “Just leave them a note and tell them that you will see them there.” The girl thought about it a minute, “No, I'd better stay here and wait,” said the girl, “my daddy will be mad and whoop me something fierce if I leave.” “You come with me,” said Jim, “I want to let nobody ever whoop you again, I promise.” “It’s up to you,” Jim turned to walk away, “wait,” said the girl, as she ran to the wagon. She came out with a bag of clothes. “Bring your gun too, and I’ll teach you how to load it,” said Jim. The girl smiled, “How did you know?” asked the girl. “The breach is still open,” said Jim, “bring the bullets too,” “I’ll show you how to use it.” The girl grabbed the gun and put the bullets in her bag, then followed Jim back to his horse. Jim got on the horse, then pulled the girl up behind him. “Hold on,” said Jim. She wrapped her arms around him as they rode off back along the river. When they rode up into camp, Lizzy said, “That's no deer he’s got,” “That’s a girl," Matt and Sara turned to look. What in the world, thought Matt, "Oh my God," said Sara, as she walked over to them. Jim helped her down. "Mom, this is," "what is your name?" asked Jim. "Ezy," "well, Elizabeth," said the girl.

Sara took the girl's hand and led her to the fire and set her down. "How long has it been since you've eaten anything?" asked Sara. "Yesterday or the day before, I found some berries," said Ezy, "before that, I had the last of the grits. "Jim, go get a bucket of water from the river," said Sara, "Hanna get my scissors and a hairbrush from the wagon." Sara put some salt pork in a biscuit and gave it to Ezy, then gave her a cup of milk. Jim came back with the water, "pour it in that pot on the fire," said Sara. "Matt, you and Jim go off down by the river or something while we bathe this child, said Sara in a tizzy." Jim and Matt walked down to the river and found a place to sit down. Jim told his dad the story of how he found her. "I had to do something, Dad, I couldn't just leave her there," said Jim. "I know, son, you did the right thing," "I think you're right, though. I don't think her parents are ever coming back; they are probably dead by now." "What are we going to do with her dad?" asked Jim. "I think we will let your momma decide on that," said Matt. While Sara and Hanna were washing Ezy off with warm water, rags, and soap, Lizzy was in reporter mode, asking nine hundred questions. Then they washed her hair out and brushed it. Sara trimmed her hair while it was wet, while Hanna dug through Ezy's bag of clothes, she laid out under pants, socks, a top, and another dress for her to put on. Sara threw the old, torn dress of Ezy's into the fire. "Don't worry, honey," said Sara, you and Hanna are about the same size." "She has a lot of dresses you can wear," through Lizzy's questions, they had found out Ezy was seventeen years old, an only child, and her family was from Pennsylvania. Here, father was not a very nice man to her or her mother; he was a drinker and hit them both often. Ezy had brushes on her arms, legs, back, and bottom.

That night, after the bath and some food, Ezy was feeling a lot better. Jim could not believe what came out from under all that dirt and matted hair. She was beautiful, with long brown hair, hazel eyes, and a sweet smile. He couldn't stop looking at her. When Sara and Hanna started supper that night, Ezy jumped right in to help them. Sara could tell she knew how to cook and was a worker. When supper was ready, Sara took a plate to Matt, and Ezy took one to Jim, while Hanna fixed Her's and Lizzy's plates. After supper, the girls cleaned up and then climbed into the wagon. It was a little crowded, but they managed. Jim took the first watch; they would be heading out the next morning, so Matt relieved Jim at med-night so he could get some sleep. Matt woke everyone up just before daylight the next morning. Jim hitched up the wagon while the girls cooked breakfast. Matt saddled his horse, and as soon as breakfast was over, the girls cleaned up, and Matt and Jim loaded everything back up into the wagon. They pulled out from under the trees and into the opening near the main trail. Mid-morning, they saw a cloud of dust coming their way from the east; they knew it had to be the wagon train. Matt rode through the dust to make sure Mr. Wagner was leading the way. "I see you made it," said Wagner. "Yep," said Matt. "Well, try to pull in line behind the fourth or fifth wagon," said Wagner, "get ahead of them Oxon's, you don't want to be in the back with all this dust," "Yes, sir," said Matt. Matt rode back and told Jim, be ready to cut in behind the fourth wagon." "Yes, Sir," said Jim. As the wagon train came up, Jim started rolling along beside them. As the fourth wagon passed him, Jim moved over in front of the fifth wagon. Ezy looked out the back of the wagon as they moved away from the area where they had been camped. In a low voice, she said, "Bye, Momma, I love you, wherever you are." But down deep, she knew her mother was gone, and she would never see her again. She also knew that if it had not been for Jim, she would not have survived much longer herself. She owed him her life, and she planned to spend it with him wherever he went.

Chapter Two: Oregon Bound

The first night, the wagon train stopped along the Kaw River and set up camp. It was meet and greet time; Mr. Wagner called all the men together for a meeting about the trip. Matt and Jim both went to the meeting. Mr. Wagner started off by saying, I have four men and four wagons on this trip, plus I have three other men pushing cows behind us, about thirty head. The four wagons in the front, being pulled by horses, are loaded with supplies; they do not belong to you yet! They belong to me, so don't take anything out of those wagons; I will not tolerate a thief. Out here, I am the Law, the Judge, and the prosecutor. If you think someone has stolen from you, tell me. I will find out who, and I will make it right. For the next few months, we will have to get along and protect each other. Your family is your most valuable possession; keep them close and protect them. We will all take turns at night, standing guard over the wagon train and your families. Out there is the roughest land a man has ever crossed, there are Indians, outlaws, snakes, wolves, and bugs that most of you have never seen before. Storms come up in minutes without notice, lightning causes brush fires, and wagon breakdowns. People get sick, accidents happen, and Horses and Oxen die, and there is nothing we can do to stop it. So, we must be ready, no matter what; there is no turning back for this train. If you turn back, you do so alone, and I promise you, you're not going to make it fore, a lone wagon is always a target for the Indians and bandits out here. Our only safety is in our numbers and keeping our eyes open for any danger. Now go back to your wagons and pray, because we need all the help we can get. Matt told Wagner, I have an added member to my party, he told him about Ezy, Do I need to pay you more money. "No," said Wagner, but she is your responsibility, make her stay with your wagon." "One more thing," said Wagner, "only two riders per wagon, everybody else walks from here on." "You can swop out or take turns," "I don't care," "if you've got a spare horse, ride it."

Jim and Matt walked back to their camp. The girls had supper ready, and they all sat down and ate. Jim looked at Ezy, then his mom and sisters. He knew it was up to him and his father to protect them all on this trip. For the first time in his young life, he felt the weight of his responsibility heavy on his shoulders. But tonight, he and his father would get a full night's sleep while other men were standing guard. Matt spoke up, "Mr. Wagner said only two riders per wagon, everybody else walks," "walk," said Lizzy, "it won't hurt you," said Hanna, "you don't do anything else. After everything was cleaned up and put away the girl climbed into the wagon to get ready for bed, Ezy gave Jim a long stare as she climbed into the wagon, "good night, Ezy," said Jim with a smile. Ezy smiled back at Jim, Matt noticed but said nothing, at first. After a few minutes, Matt said, "Jim, you know you probably saved that girl's life." "Yes, sir, I know," said Jim. "But she won't be any trouble, I'll share my food with her, she will help Mom and Hanna." "Yes, she will, son," said Matt, "and I'm happy to have her in our family." "I'm sure she feels indebted to you for helping her," said Matt, "some men might take advantage of that, but I know you wouldn't." "Oh, no, sir," said Jim, "I only did what I thought was best for her; she is all alone in this world now." "No, son, she has you, even if you don't know it yet, and she has our family," said Matt.

The next morning at breakfast, Ezy brought Jim and herself a plate and sat down beside him. Sara looked at Matt and smiled as she handed him his plate and sat down by him. Jim had already fed the animals and hooked up the team before breakfast. After they ate, the girls cleaned everything up and put it away. Let's go, yelled Mr. Wagner as everyone fell in line. Ezy, Hanna, and Lizzy walked beside the wagon, starting out. After midday, Sara swapped with Hanna or Ezy, and Matt let Lizzy ride with him. Hours turned to days, and days turned into nights as the Kansas winds blew across the prairie. The nights were still cool, but the days were getting warmer, and afternoon rains were common, some light, but some heavier as they got closer to Nebraska. While they crossed the Kansas plains, they only saw a few bands of Indians, but they just sat on their horses and watched the wagons pass by. According to Mr. Wagner, the Kansas Indians knew the wagons were just passing through. It was the tribes in Wyoming that they would have to worry about. But it was the bandit in Nebraska that Wagner and his men worried about the most. Ezy and Sara had started taking turns riding on the buckboard with Jim. Sara knew Ezy wanted to be close to him. Sara believes God sent Jim down that wagon trail to find Ezy and bring her to them, a match made in heaven, thought Sara. It had been six days since they met up with the wagon train, and they had just crossed over into Nebraska.

The first night in Nebraska, Matt was chosen to stand guard with some of the other men from the group. That night, after Sara, Hanna, and Lizzy were asleep, Ezy eased out of the wagon and went to Jim underneath it. She pulled his blanket back and crawled under it with him, "What are you doing?" asked Jim in a whisper. "I just wanted to sleep close to you, Jim," said Ezy. Jim rolled over onto his back, as Ezy lay her head on his shoulder and snuggled up close to him. She went right back to sleep; Jim lay there feeling her breath on his neck and face. The warmth from her body radiated over to him. She smelled like flowers in the spring, and she was so soft. It was a wonderful feeling having her so close to him as he drifted back off to sleep, too.

The next morning, as always, Jim was up before daylight. He crawled out from under the blankets and then tucked them tight around Ezy as she slept. Jim was already dressed as he strapped his gun and started his day, first by stoking the fire, then by feeding the stock. As he put a little wood on the fire and started the coffee, Sara crawled out of the wagon. She went straight to the bushes, then came back to the fire. Sara looked under the wagon and saw Ezy as Jim poked at the fire. Sara looked at Jim and just smiled, "Nothing happened, Mom," "I know, honey," said Sara, as she hugged him up close to her. "Well, I'd best get the biscuit started," said Sara. Jim went to get the team hooked up to the wagon. Sara got her lantern lit, "Ezy, honey, get up." Ezy rolled over, "No, I want to stay rolled up in his smell forever." "I know," said Sara, "but we got work to do." Ezy got up and ran to the bushes, then came back to the wagon and got dressed. As she climbed back out of the wagon, she said, "Hanna, Lizzy, get up." Ezy started helping Sara. She put the iron skillet on the fire to fry bacon. "Coffee ready," asked Matt. "Should be," said Sara. Matt poured a cup and sat down by the fire. It was getting light now. Jim had the team ready. "Girls, get out here," said Matt. "We're coming," said Lizzy. Jim came back to the fire, poured himself some coffee, and sat across from his dad. "We are in Nebraska now," said Matt. Mr. Wagner is worried about bandits. Keep your eye open," "Yes, sir," said Jim.

The wagon train moved on, headed to Fort Kearny. They would stop there for one night. They should get there around noon, two days from now, according to Wagner. Between Fort Kearny and Fort Laramie is where they will be most likely to have run-ins with bandits. They come out of Northwest Kansas and cross over into Nebraska to steal cows, horses, and anything else the settlers might have that they can sell back in Kansas. So, the plan will be, after leaving Fort Kearny, to travel as fast as possible to Fort Laramie. After they leave Fort Laramie, it will be straight into Indian territory, from there into Idaho. That night, Jim was one of the men picked to stand guard; Matt had been sleeping in the wagon most of the day from being up the night before. The next morning, Jim came back to camp at daylight, and Matt was hooking up the team. Jim got coffee and sat down by the fire. Ezy, Sara, and Hanna were cooking breakfast. "Tired, son?" asked Matt. "Yes, sir," said Jim. "Well, after you eat, climb into the back of the wagon and get some sleep," said Matt. "I'll tie my horse to the back of the wagon and drive the team while you sleep." "I can drive the team," said Ezy, "I've been handling a team of horses and mules since I was ten years old." "Wagons, buggies, hay racks, and plows, you just ride your horse." "I'll take care of the wagon until he wakes up," said Ezy. "Sound good to me," said Jim. "Well, yes, ma'am, then," said Matt, "We'll give it a try."

Ezy brought Jim a plate, handed it to him, then leaned over and kissed his forehead, and went to get hers. Sara brought Matt his plate, he took it, then raised his head up and smiled. Sara laughed, then kissed Matt's forehead. Matt looked at Jim and smiled, "Son, if you knew what I know, you would be running as fast as you could right now." "Where's Jim running to poppa?" asked Lizzy. Sara and Matt just busted out laughing. "To bed, Lizzy, I'm running to get into bed," said Jim. Jim walked by Ezy at the back of the wagon, took her hand, pulled her around to the other side of the wagon, and kissed her on the lips. She melted into his arms. "Good night," said Jim, I'll see you after a while, Ezy couldn't talk; she was shocked. She just stood there with her mouth open. She slowly reached up and touched her lips with her fingertips, then giggled as she walked to the fire. "What's the matter with you?" asked Lizzy, "Why is your face so red?" Ezy still couldn't talk; all she could do was smile. "Probably from cooking over that hot fire," said Hanna, "you should try it sometimes, Lizzy. Matt leaned over to Sara. "I hope there is a preacher at Fort Kearny, I don't think they can wait much longer," said Matt. "We need to find one by tonight," said Sara, "Is there one in this wagon train?" "I'll find out," said Matt, "I hope so."

After everything and everybody were loaded back up on the wagon, Ezy took the reins and yelled, "Get up, horses." The team started moving, Sara walked with the girls, Ezy guided them in line with the others, and they were on their way again. Matt watched for a while; after seeing that Ezy was in control of the team, he rode ahead to talk to Mr. Wagner. He found him at the front of the line,

"Tom," said Matt. "Is there a preacher in this group?" asked Matt. "Did somebody die," asked Tom, "no' Matt laughed, "but my son Jim and that girl he found," "well, I think we are going to need a wedding soon." Mr. Wagnor laughed, "well, I could say the words, but it wouldn't be legal," "I don't remember there being a priest on the sign-up list," "just try to keep them apart until we get to the fort tomorrow." "I'm sure there will be one there," Tom laughed again. "Ok," said Matt, "thanks, I'll try." Jim woke up midday and stuck his head out of the front of the wagon. "Hello, sleepy head," said Ezy. "Did you get some rest?" "Yes, ma'am, a little," Ezy smiled at Jim, and he smiled back." "Looks like I lost my job," said Jim with a grin. "Oh, no," said Ezy, "I'll help you, but I'm not driving this thing 2,000 miles." Jim laughed, "Well, I've got to go walk for a while," said Jim. Jim climbed out of the back of the wagon and went to the river to go to the bathroom. He came running back up to the wagon in a little while and climbed on the buckboard with Ezy. "You ready for me to take over?" asked Jim. "I'm good," said Ezy, "just sit here with me for a while."

That night, after they set up camp and ate, Hanna and Lizzy went into the wagon while Matt, Sara, Jim, and Ezy sat by the fire talking. Matt spoke up, "I talked to Mr. Wagner today," "he said there should be a preacher at the fort tomorrow when we get there," "that is if anybody needs one." Ezy looked at Jim, wondering what Matt was talking about, then it hit her. She dropped her head and looked at the ground, while Jim poked at the fire. Everybody got quiet. Jim stood up and walked around the fire, poking at it. Jim was half scared, because he knew what his dad was hinting at. As he passed by his mom, she reached out her hand and dropped something into her son's hand. Jim looked at it, "That was my mother's," said Sara, with tears in her eyes. "I was saving this for Hanna," "but I think Ezy might like it more." Ezy was still staring at the ground in front of her. Jim looked at his dad, and Matt just smiled. "You're a man now, Jim, you make your own choices, me and your mom can't make them for you anymore, son." "We will stand by you no matter what," Jim paced around a little more, then eased over to Ezy. He dropped down on both knees, reached out and took Ezy's chin, and raised her head up. He looked into her eyes, "Ezy, you know I love you." "Do you want to get married?" asked Jim. "If you want to," said Ezy in a soft tone. "I've been yours since the first time I saw you," said Ezy. "Will let's get married then," said Jim. Ezy fell into Jim's arms, and with a muffled voice, she said, "Yes, Jim, I'll marry you." Matt and Sara both had tears in their eyes. They got up, went over, and hugged them both. Jim took Ezy's hand and put the ring on her finger, then kissed her lips. "Ok, it's bedtime," said Sara, "come on, Ezy, you're not married yet." Ezy lay there with her other hand over the ring, like she was afraid someone would take it. It means the world to her, as does the boy who gave it to her. She closed her eyes and prayed to God, thanking him for sending Jim to find her.

The next day, they made it to Fort Kearny around noon, as Jim and Sara were setting up camp outside of the fort, Matt rode into the Fort to make the arrangements. They made Ezy stay in the wagon away from Jim. Matt found the fort commander, who sent for the preacher, then together they drew up the marriage license and set a time for 4:00 p.m. that afternoon. Matt also made the arrangements for Jim and Ezy to stay in a cabin there in the fort that night. Matt rode back to the wagon and told Sara about the plans he had made. Sara, Hanna, and Lizzy went out to pick wildflowers for a bouquet, then went to the fort to look for lace. They found enough lace to make a veil, then went back to the wagon to get Ezy ready. Matt took Jim to the fort to meet the preacher and to wait for the girls to get there. At 4:00 p.m., the girls walked in with Ezy under the vale. There was no music. Matt walked to the door as the girls walked up front with Jim. Ezy took Matt's arm as he led her down the aisle. It was not a fantasy wedding, but it was special just the same, and now

Ezy was truly part of the Evens family. Matt took them to their honeymoon suite for the night, Jim picked Ezy up outside the door, she threw the bouquet over her shoulder, and Hanna caught it. Matt then gave the couple strict orders to be at the wagon come daylight. Jim hugged his dad and mom, as did Ezy. Matt took Sara's hand, and they took the girls, Hanna and Lizzy, to the fort commissary to eat supper. "No, cooking tonight," said Matt, "it's not every day your son gets married, we eat steak tonight."

The next morning, Jim and Ezy walked up to the wagon holding hands, just before daylight. Jim fed and watered the horses before hooking them up to the wagon. Ezy jumped in to help Sara and Hanna cook breakfast. They all just looked at each other and smiled, saying nothing. It was a day that they would all remember, but there was no time to dwell on it. They had to get back on the trail and keep chasing their dreams. Two days before reaching Fort Laramie, Jim was on guard duty again when out of the darkness came two men on horseback moving slowly. They rode up to one of the other men near Jim, and he overheard them ask if this was Tom Wagner's wagon train. The man said yes. The hair stood up on Jim's neck. Something just didn't seem right about these men. Jim went around behind the wagons and got closer, "Where is old Tom?" asked one of the men. The guard pointed at Tom's wagon, "Up there sleeping, I'm sure," said the guard. Jim ran up to Tom's Wagon, "Tom, get up," said Jim. "What?" said Tom. "Get out of that wagon now," said Jim. "Hurry," Tom jumped up and climbed out of the back of the wagon. "What is it?" asked Tom. "There are two men looking for you," said Jim, as he handed Tom his rifle. "Be quiet," "I don't think they are here to visit after midnight." The two men eased up to Tom's wagon, took their rifles out, and started shooting through Tom's wagon. When they ran out of bullets, Tom and Jim stepped out from behind the wagon next to Tom's. "You missed," said Tom as he shot one of the men off his horse. The other man went for his sidearm, but Jim drew first and shot him off his horse. "Bandits," yelled Tom, "cover your wagons." Two more men came out of the darkness, riding at them fast. Jim shot them both; they could hear other horses living riding away from them. By now, all the men were up and out of their wagons. Jim grabbed the reins of one of the bandits' horses, then looked at Tom. "I'm good," said Tom, "go, check on your family." Jim jumped on the horse and rode back to his wagon. "It's me, Dad," yelled Jim as he rode up. "Is everybody ok?" asked Jim. He could hear the girls crying in the wagon. "Yep, we're all good," said Matt. Jim jumped off the horse and ran to the wagon. "It's ok," said Jim, "they are gone now." Ezy jumped into his arms, "calm down, it's ok, baby," said Jim. Matt was putting more wood on the fire to light things up, as were all the other men at their wagons.

At daylight, Tom came riding up to the Evens' camp. Sara and the girls were cooking breakfast, Matt was sitting at the fire drinking coffee, and he still had his rifle in his lap. "Morning, Matt," said Tom. "You want some breakfast?" asked Sara. "I might take a biscuit and some coffee if you don't mind," said Tom. "Where's Jim?" asked Tom. "he's watering the horses," said Matt. "Why do you need him?" "No, just checking," said Tom, "here I want to give him back his rifle," said Tom as he handed it to Matt. "That boy saved my life last night," said Tom, "did he tell you that?" "Nope, he hasn't talked about it," said Matt. "What happened?" "I'll let him tell you when he's ready," said Tom. "Well, tell Jim I said thank you," said Tom, "and tell him that he can keep that horse, the man that was riding it won't be needing it anymore." "I will," said Matt, "thank you for the biscuit, Ms. Evens, and y'all have a good day." "We might be a little late leaving this morning, so take your time and enjoy your breakfast," said Tom. He got on his horse and rode off; in a few minutes, Jim came back with the horses. "Just tie them up for now," said Matt. "We'll hook them up after breakfast," Tom said. "We would be leaving a little later this morning." "Here," "he brought your rifle back," "oh, and he said to tell you thank you, and to just keep that horse," said Matt. "I was going to anyway," said Jim. He poured some coffee and sat by the fire. "Did he say who those men were?" asked Jim. "Nope, he didn't say," said Matt. Ezy brought Jim's and her plate over to him and sat beside him by the fire. Jim kissed her. "Ewe," said Lizzy, y'all stop that, Jim kissed her again, then Sara brought Matt his plate and kissed him. "Y'all are making me sick, stop it," said Lizzy. Hanna just smiled. Something had changed in Jim, Matt could see it, he was quieter, more alert, always seemed to be scanning his surroundings. Matt couldn't put his finger on it, but the boy in Jim was gone, it was like he had aged five years overnight.

Two days later, they made it to Fort Laramie, which was a bigger fort with a treading post and even a doctor there. It was like a small town inside a fence. After setting up camp, they all walked to the fort. Lizzy dug out her bag to bring along. Matt said, "Maybe you don't need to take all of that with you, Lizzy." "But I might want to buy something," said Lizzy, "ok, well, you let me carry it for you, I'll keep it safe." "Ok," said Lizzy, "but don't you lose it," "I want, I promise," said Matt. At the gates, Matt, Sara, and the girls walked inside the fort. Jim and Ezy followed behind, holding hands. They went into the treading post to look around. The place was full of people from the wagon train getting more supplies. Everything was going fast, Sara had a basket with her, in it was butter she had made from her cow's milk. She finally made it up near the counter. The trading post owner's wife saw her, "What have you got there, dear?" asked the lady. "I have fresh butter I made," said Sara, "I was wondering if you wanted to buy it." The lady took one of the blocks of butter, opened the cheesecloth, and ran her finger across it, then stuck her finger in her mouth. "Umm," said the lady, "yes, I want it all, let me weigh it up." The lady came back, "You have six pounds," said the lady. She handed Sara a silver dollar and some change, two bits. Sara's eyes got big. That was a lot of money back then, nothing like what Lizzy got for her gold, but Sara was happy. Sara tried to give it to Matt, but he said no, that's your money.

Lizzy and Hanna had picked out all kinds of rock candy, Matt had gotten a smoked ham and more salt pork, and he and the girls got up to the counter. They put their things on the counter, "Give me my bag," said Lizzy. Matt looked around the room. "I'll pay for your candy," said Matt, "you and I will settle up later." "Ok," said Lizzy. Sara was looking at a nice, big quilt with beautiful stitching on it. The owner's wife came up behind her again. "I just finished that quilt last week," said the lady, "you're going to need that where you're going." Sara smiled, "It's beautiful," "give me two bits and it's yours," said the woman. Sara opened her hand and gave the woman the two bits; they folded the quilt, and the lady tied a string around it. The Evens family made their way out of the trading post and then outside of the fort. Once back at their camp, Sara put her new quilt inside the wagon and then started prepping for supper. The trip to the fort had been fun, but now it was time to get ready for the next long leg of their journey, and possibly the most dangerous part.

Matt stopped at Mr. Wagner's camp to get an update on the trip. Tom told Matt that they were having a meeting tonight with all the men about crossing Wyoming. Tom asked Matt, "Did Jim ever tell you what happened that night?" "You mean when the bandits hit us?" asked Matt. "Well, turns out they weren't just bandits," said Tom, "they were looking for me." "No," said Matt, "Jim never talked about it," "what happened." "Well, if it hadn't been for Jim, somebody else would be leading this train," said Tom. "Two riders came up after midnight and asked Emet, one of the guards closest to Jim, if this was Tom Wagner's wagon train." "The crazy fool said yes," and pointed at my wagon," Jim said the hair stood up on his neck, and he sensed something was wrong." "So, he ran behind the wagons and came to my wagon." "He woke me up and made me get out of my wagon." "We hid behind the next wagon." "The two men rode to my wagon and opened fire, emptying their rifles. Jim handed me his rifle." "I stepped out and told them they missed," "the two men went for their side arms," "I shot one and Jim shot the other one." "As we stood there, two more men rode out of the darkness, and Jim shot them both before I could raise the rifle." "Fastest draw I've ever seen," "and I've seen a lot," said Tom. "Are you that fast?" asked Tom. "Nope," said Matt, "not even close." "Well, two of the men had worked for me on my last trip, and I fired them both for stealing from the travelers." "I didn't know the other two men," "but Jim saved my butt, and probably the whole wagon train too, that's for sure," said Tom.

Matt walked onto his wagon. He never asked Jim about that night, and Jim never said anything. That night after supper, all the men met up at Tom's camp. Tom said, "We are in Wyoming, we've all got to be on our toes." "The Indians and the white men in Wyoming are at war over the land here." "There has been a lot of killing on both sides. We are going to try to ease across without being noticed." "So, no shooting your guns unless you have to, no yelling, and no talking loud," keep your children quiet." "If the Indians see us or hear us, they will come after us, and take horses, guns, and supplies; they may even try to take your women or children." "So, stay alert, at night we will circle the wagon with the people and stock inside." "If they attack, get under your wagon and fight back. If we kill enough of them, they will leave." "Now go back to your wagon and move all your things to the right side of your wagon. When we circle them, it will be to the left, putting the right side to the outside." "Your women and children can hide on the left side behind your things." "Pray that we can slip through without being noticed; if not, it will be a fight all the way across." "The last trip we lost five wagons and three people out of fifty wagons." "That's why this time I only agreed to take thirty or so wagons, I'm hoping we won't be noticed."

All the men went back to their camps and did as Mr. Wagner said, moving their things to the right side of their wagons. The next morning, they left, leaving the Fort behind them as they headed into the Wyoming territories. Ezy was driving the wagon as Matt and Jim rode alongside the wagon on their horses. Sara sat beside Ezy on the buckboard. The sky was beautiful as they slowly moved along, big white clouds hovering over them, with a blue background. God was surely smiling today, thought Sara, only a few miles from the Fort, without notice, they crossed over the Platte River. In the far distance, they could see the peaks of the mountains. At this point, they only looked like snow-covered hills, not very big at all. Lizzy and Hanna were walking at the back of the wagon; they had met a lot of little friends on the wagon train. Other girls and boys who were their age, but they only got to see them or talk to them while walking, and sometimes in the late afternoons, after they camped each night. Like any small community, nearby wagons visit with their neighbors, and by this time, most everybody knows each other, or at least where they are from. Jim is well known as the young man who stopped the bandits, the only difference is that this community moves every day to a new location.

Three days after leaving the fort, the rain started, and for two days it didn't let up for more than a few minutes at a time. Jim let Hanna ride with him, and Lizzy rode with her father; the others had to walk through the mud. For two days and two nights, there were no fires to cook on; everybody had to eat from canned food they brought along or eat cured meats. After two days, the sun came out, Mr. Wagner stopped the wagon train for the day, and had them secure the wagons. He ordered everybody to pull the canvas off the top of their wagons and spread it out on the grass to dry. This would also give the inside of the wagons a chance to dry out. Wet boots, shoes, clothing, and bedding were also hung on lines between the wagons to dry. No, fires were allowed until after dark, because the smoke might be seen by the Indians. By nightfall, most everything had dried out, and the canvases were put back on the wagons. Once the sky was completely black, fires were allowed to be built for cooking. This was the first time anybody got a chance to see what was in Tom's supply wagons. People started telling Tom, we need this, or I need that, but Tom said No! "Asked your neighbors," said Tom, "you see those mountains over there," "that's what this food is for." "I'm telling you, by the time we reach those mountains, most of your supplies will be gone." "Without these extra supplies, we want to make it over those mountains and to the other side." "So be sparing with your food and make it last until then. I'll shoot anyone who takes from these wagons or anyone else's without asking.

Each day, they moved a little further across the plains, so far, no Indians had been seen. But they knew that the Indians were there by the burned-out wagons and the horse skeleton left behind by previous wagon trains. Some days, they saw no signs that others had come through, other than the wagon wheel routes in the trail. Then on other days, they passed through an area littered with clothing, wagon parts, and signs of death. The wagon train had been following along the west side of the Platte River for the last few days. Each afternoon, while Sara and Ezy were cooking supper, Hanna and Lizzy would explore the riverbank looking for rocks with some of the other girls from the wagon train. On the third night after crossing the river, just before dark, Lizzy came running back to their camp, crying and yelling, "Indians." Matt and Jim both grabbed their rifles. "Where's Hanna?" asked Jim. "They took her," screamed Lizzy. "Oh, my God," said Sara. Jim, Matt, and some of the other men ran down to the river. Three girls had been taken. All around the same age as Hanna, from 14 to 16 years old,' "NO," yelled Matt. The men started searching the riverbanks for signs. Jim went off on his own, following the river, staying in the water until he was out of sight from the others. After dark, Matt went back to his camp to console his wife and Lizzy, "he was heartbroken."

"Where is Jim?" asked Ezy. "Still looking," said Matt. About that time, Jim came walking back up to the camp, wet up to his knees. Ezy ran up to him, Jim hugged her, and Matt was holding Sara and Lizzy by the fire. Everyone was crying except for Jim; he was just mad. He walked over to his mom and dad. "They came out of the river about a mile upstream," said Jim, "five horses with no shoes." "I marked the spot," "I'm going after them!" said Jim, "No," said Ezy, "I don't want you to go," Jim hugged her, "I've got to," said Jim, "if it was you, you would want me to come after you." Ezy dropped her head. "I need you to help mom and dad," said Jim. "You drive the wagon; I'll be back as soon as I can." "Don't wait on me, just keep traveling. I'll find you." Matt looked at his son; he wanted to go with him so badly. But he knew he had to keep the rest of his family moving with the wagon train. Jim went to the wagon and got extra bullets, then he saddled his horse and tied his bedroll on. Ezy put some food in a sack, Jim walked over to his mom, "I'll bring her back, Momma," "I promise," said Jim. Sara hugged her son, "You be careful, Jim, I don't want to lose you, son." "You want, and we haven't lost Hanna, I'll bring her back." Jim hugged Ezy, "I love you, Ezy, "but I've got to get my sister back before something happens to her," said Jim. Ezy smiled through her tears, "I love you, Jim." "Hurry back to me."

Jim mounted his horse, then said, "Dad, you just keep moving, I'll catch up to you." Then he disappeared into the darkness of the night. Later, the fathers of the other two girls came to Matt's camp. "What are we going to do?" asked the men. "Are we going after them?" Matt, still upset about his own daughter and now his son, looked up at the men. "How," asked Matt, "are you going to leave the rest of your family here, while the wagon train moves on?" "The wagon train can just wait for us until we find them," said one of the men. Matt, trying not to be mad at them for not knowing any better, "Are you willing to get all these people here killed, just on the chance we might find three girls?" The men dropped their heads. "My son Jim has gone looking for our girls." "If they can be found, he will find them and bring them back, or die trying," said Matt. "Just go back to your wagons, and be ready to travel tomorrow. We've got to get out of here, or more will go missing." The next morning, the wagon train moved on without Jim and the three missing girls. They were hoping to make it to Fort Bridger before running into any more Indian trouble.

Hanna told the other two girls the first time they stopped, "Just keep quiet, Jim will find us." "Who is Jim?" asked one of the girls. "My brother," said Hanna. "I bet he has already found our trail." "I want my daddy," said the other girl. It was daylight now; the Indian's had stopped to rest their horses by a small creek. They didn't stay long before they moved on. Hanna just kept praying to herself, asking God to guide Jim to her. After three or four hours, they rode over a ridge and stopped in a clearing with big rocks surrounding it. The Indians set the girls down by a big rock, and two Indian's stood guard over them. While the others watched the trail they had been following, after a while they came back to the clearing. They told the other two something, Hanna didn't understand the words, but felt they were saying that the coast was clear. They came and took one of the girls into the opening. This is not good, though, Hanna.

Chapter Three: Finding The Girls

After leaving his family's camp, Jim followed the river until he found the marker he had left, marking the trail that the Indians had taken with the girls. Jim got off his horse and followed the trail by the light of the moon, leading his horse behind him. There was just enough light to see the ground, but not enough to see any tracks. He did find a few broken limbs on the brush as he eased along the trail slowly. Jim followed the trail all night, only stopping to look for signs. As the sun came up the next morning, Jim could see the trail across the plains the Indians had taken. Jim knew he didn't have much time left; he figured the Indians probably rode all night to get as far as they could away from the wagon train. But even with the Indians knowing the trail, Jim knew they weren't moving very fast in the dark. Jim mounted his horse and rode in a gallop occasionally, stopping to check the trail along the way for tracks. Jim could tell he was getting closer; he had to find the Indians before they reached their main village. But either way, he was getting his sister back; he could still see the look on his mother's face and the sadness in his father's eyes, so he rode on. Around midday, with the sun high in the sky, Jim heard a scream. He stopped his horse, and he heard it again, this time louder.

Jim got off his horse and tied it up to a tree. He took his rifle and ran up the trail. The screams were getting louder as he stopped by a big rock for cover. He eased around the rock and saw the Indians and the girls in an open area just off the trail. He got down onto his hands and knees to get closer. He could see Hanna and another girl sitting by a big rock; their hands were tied in front of them. Two of the Indians were standing guard over them with rifles in their hands. In the middle of the small opening, the other three Indians were terrorizing what looked to be the oldest girl with blond hair. Grabbing at her and pulling at her clothes. She was trying her hardest to fight them off, even with her hands tied. Jim got into a good spot for cover where he could see them all. Then one of the Indians ripped the girl's dress off her, exposing her undergarments. One of the other Indians threw her to the ground and jumped on top of her. Jim knew it was time; he took aim, shooting the two men guarding Hanna with his rifle, then turned and shot the Indian on top of the girl. "It's Jim," yelled Hanna, "stay down." The last two Indians ran for their horses, as they jumped on their horses, Jim shot one of them. The last one rode off. Jim couldn't get a clear shot at him through the brush. "Damn," said Jim. He ran down to Hanna and the other girls.

Jim cut their hands loose; all the Indian ponies had run off but one. A bigger white horse with Indian war paint on it, this horse seemed unfrighten by the shooting and the commotion. "Grab that horse," yelled Jim to Hanna. As he went to check on the other girl on the ground, he cut her hands loose. Hanna and the other girl walked over to Jim, leading the white horse. Jim helped Hanna onto the Indian's horse, then put one of the other girls on behind her. Jim looked Hanna deep in her eyes, "I let one get away, sis, more will be coming." "Keep the sun to your right side and ride as you've never ridden before, don't look back, just keep riding." "When you find the river, cross it. The wagon trail won't be far. Turn into the sun and ride until you find the wagon train. Don't stop until you find them," said Jim. Jim climbed onto his horse and pulled the other girl up behind him. "I'll be right behind you," said Jim. "Now ride Hanna, ride," he popped the Indians horse's rump, the horse took off. As Jim followed behind Hanna, he yelled, "Faster, Hanna." The other girls were hanging on for dear life to Hanna and Jim as they crossed over hills, valleys, and open plains. Jim looked behind him and saw more Indians coming over a ridge. Jim yelled, "Don't stop Hanna," as he turned his horse around and pulled out his rifle. Jim shot two of the Indians, then turned and rode off after Hanna again, "Ride Hanna, ride," yelled Jim.

Jim heard rifle fire coming from behind him. He turned and rode up into some big rocks nearby. He let the girl with him down, then jumped down off his horse. Jim looked at the girl, "Can you ride a horse?" asked Jim. The girl nodded, "Then get up there," said Jim. Jim helped her up on his horse, "Go catch Hanna and don't you stop," said Jim, as the girl rode off on Jim's horse, leaving him there. Jim hid behind the rocks waiting for the Indians to come by him. As they rode past, Jim started shooting. One Indian fell off his horse, then another one. Jim aimed at the last one and pulled the trigger. All Jim heard was a loud chick; the Indian heard it too. Jim's rifle was empty. The Indian pulled his tommy hawk, thinking Jim was defenseless. He rode at Jim with his tommy hawk raised, yelling his Indian yell. Jim just stood there as the Indian came for him. Once the Indian was close enough, Jim pulled his pistol and shot the Indian in the head. Jim grabbed the rope on the Indian pony as the Indian fell off to the ground. Jim swung himself onto the back of the Indian pony and let out a loud yell of anger and frustration, then rode south after Hanna and the other girls. Hanna crossed the river, then reached the wagon trail and turned onto it. The other girl, not far behind her on Jim's horse, saw her turn. She did the same, when she finally caught up with Hanna, Hanna asked, "Where's Jim?" The girl said, "he made me leave him and follow you. There were more Indians coming," said the girl. Hanna stopped her horse; it was covered in sweat and breathing hard. Hanna said, "I'm going back for Jim." "No!" said the other girl. "He said not to stop," said the girl on Jim's horse. "I could hear shooting behind me as I lifted your brother," said the girl on Jim's horse.

Hanna kicked her horse and took off down the wagon trail to the West into the sun as Jim had told her. After about an hour or more, the horses were giving out and had slowed to a trot. As the girls came over a ridge, they could see the wagons dust up ahead. They all three started crying with joy, and they tried to make the horses go faster. But the horses were spent; they had given all they had. As the girls got closer to the wagon train, Hanna could see Matt, her father, riding along on the outside near their wagon. "Dad," yelled Hanna. "Dad, she screamed. Matt heard something; he heard it again. It was Hanna's voice. At first, he thought it was wishful thinking. "Dad, it's me," yelled Hanna, Matt turned his horse around, it was Hanna, her and the other two girls. Matt couldn't believe his eyes, "stop the wagons," yelled Matt, as he rode to them. Ezy yelled, "whoa horses," and brought the wagon to a stop, the other wagons behind them stopped too. Matt rode up to the girls with tears in his eyes, Hanna jumped over into Matt's arms and curled up crying. Matt took hold of the ropes on the other two horses and led them to the wagons. They stopped at the girl's wagon that was riding Jim's horse. She jumped off and ran to her folks, then at the other girl's wagon, they did the same. Ezy asked Sara, "What's wrong?" Then Matt rode upholding Hanna and leading the other two horses, "Look what I found," said Matt, tears pouring down his face. "Hanna," yelled Sara as she jumped from the wagon. She ran over and pulled Hanna down from Matt. "Ezy, just pull to the side of the trail," "we camp here tonight," said Matt. The other girls' families did the same. Lizzy, Hanna, Sara, and Ezy all grabbed each other into a big group and hung on the ground.

After a few minutes, Ezy asked, "Where's Jim?" Everybody got quiet. "Oh, no," said Ezy, "where's my Jim?" Then they heard a familiar voice as Jim walked up leading the small Indian pony, "Sorry I'm late for the reunion," "I had some catching up to do." Ezy screamed and ran to Jim; he gave her a big kiss as she cried in his arms. "Is supper ready?" asked Jim. "I haven't eaten in a while." "Not yet," said Sara, "but I bet I can whip something up for your son." Jim hugged his mom. "Oh, thank you, Jim," said Sara. Jim turned and shook his father's hand; Matt pulled him into his arms and gave him a long hug, "Thank you, son," said Matt. "Well, let's get a fire going," said Sara. Jim led the Indian pony that he had caught back up to Lizzy. "Here you go, Lizzy, Hanna caught her own horse, this one's for you, baby girl." "No more walking. Lizzy hugged Jim, "My own horse," said Lizzy, Wow!" Ezy looked up at Jim, "What about me?" "You ride with me, baby. I'm not ever leaving you again," said Jim. While Ezy and Sara were cooking, Jim unsaddled his horse, then he and Lizzy led the horses down to the river. The horses drank and drank and drank, then Jim and Lizzy washed the horses off to cool them down, also to get the war paint off them. Lizzy's new pony was a pinto, colored black and white, a smaller horse, but strong and gentle. Hanna was sore and could hardly walk from her desperate ride away from the Indians. But it was worth it; she was back with her family, unharmed and safe.

Jim and Lizzy led the horses back up to their camp and tied them up, then they went over to the fire. Jim had gone by his saddle bags and took something out of them. Hanna came over to Jim and crawled into his lap. Matt smiled. Hanna said, "Thank you, Jim, for coming after me. I knew you would." "I wasn't scared, I kept telling the other girls just be quiet, Jim will find us, and you did," said Hanna, with tears in her eyes. "I'm proud of you, sis," said Jim, "you were very brave," "you did just like I said." "You got the other girls back here safe," then Jim pulled out an Indians knife and shiv. He had taken it from one of the Indians. "I want you to have this," said Jim, "I want to wear it always, and remember where it came from." "Let it remind you to always be ready to protect yourself." "I'll teach you how to use it." "As dad told me when he gave me mine, it's a tool, not a toy, keep it sharp, and it will keep you safe." Matt smiled as Jim looked at him. They all ate supper. Jim ate two helpings; he had not eaten while looking for Hanna, who was all he cared about at the time. The next morning, the fathers of the other two girls came to Matt's and Sara's wagon to thank Jim for bringing their daughters back. They shook Jim's hand and told him they were indebted to him for saving their girls. Then they went back to their wagons to get ready to go; they had to catch up with the main wagon train. Jim's horse and the other two were still tired from their long, hard run yesterday, so Jim tied them to the back of the wagon and told Hanna to climb onto the buckboard with Ezy. Jim walked holding Sara and Lizzy's hands, they didn't know how long it would take to catch up with the wagon train that had moved on without them. Matt was leading the way; Jim was not happy about what he had done, killing those Indians. He took no pleasure in it, but he knew that he had no choice at the time. He had almost gotten over killing the bandits, and then this happened. He had to kill eight Indians and three bandits at the age of seventeen, which weighed heavily on his soul.

That night, they caught up with the wagon train after dark, and the next day, they made it to Fort Bridger in Wyoming. Jim asked Lizzy if she wanted to spend some of her money on a couple of saddles for Her's and Hanna's horses. "Sure, if I've got enough," said Lizzy. "Oh, you have enough," said Jim. "Just give me twenty dollars, and I'll get everything you need." Lizzy gave Jim a twenty-dollar gold piece, then took out a ten-dollar gold piece for herself to spend. The Evens family walked into the fort. Jim went to the livery stables to look for used saddles and tack. Then, after meeting his family back at the Treading Post, he still needed a small saddle for Lizzy. "Jim," yelled Matt, "overhear son." Matt was standing there talking to a man in the corner. Jim walked over to them. "Jim, I want you to meet an old friend of mine," "this is Jim Bridger," "we worked together for a while, he's from the hills too." "Nice to meet you," said Jim. "You too, son," said Mr. Bridger. "So, you're the man who went after those young girls and brought them back," said Bridger. Jim looked at him, surprised. "Oh, Tom Wagner talks a lot," said Bridger. "Sometimes too much," said Jim. "Well, he means no harm," said Bridger. "he's a good man, and he likes you a lot, says you saved his beacon."

"Did you get everything you need at the livery?" asked Matt. "No, Sir, I still need a small saddle for Lizzy," said Jim. "I might have what you need," said Bridger, "come back here." They walked to the back of the store, hanging on the wall was a small child's saddle with a matching bridle and chest strap. "How much?" asked Jim. "Five dollars," said Bridger. "Sounds good," said Jim. He paid him for the rig and took the saddle and tack. Jim walked over to Lizzy. "You get my stuff," asked Lizzy. "Yep," said Jim, "here you have eight-dollar change left." "You keep it," said Lizzy, "go buy Ezy something." "Well, thank you, Lizzy," said Jim. Lizzy just smiled. Jim found Ezy with Sara and Hanna. "Here, honey," said Jim, as he handed her two dollars. "Get what you need," said Jim. Ezy looked at the money; she didn't know what to say. "I've never had my own money before," said Ezy, "fills good, doesn't it?" said Sara. Sara had just sold more butter, plus she still had money from selling milk, eggs, and butter to the other families on the wagon train, but she just didn't see anything she really needed.

Jim bought himself some more ammo for his guns, then found a small silver heart necklace. He got it for Ezy. Jim then carried the saddles and the tack back to their wagon, sat by the fire, cleaned them up, and replaced some leather ties for the girls. After a while, the others came back to camp. Lizzy had two big bags of rock candy, and Matt was carrying more coffee and a bag of dry beans. Everyone sat around the fire while Jim saddled the two Indian horses and then his own horse. "Come on, girls," said Jim, "let's go for a ride." Jim helped Lizzy get on her horse as Hanna mounted her horse very slowly. Jim got on his horse, then pulled Ezy up behind him. "You ok, Hanna?" asked Jim. "Just a little sore still," said Hanna. Jim yelled at his dad, "will be back in about an hour," with a smile, "I suggest you two take advantage of the free time." Then he and the girls rode off. Matt looked at Sara. Sara jumped up and ran to the wagon, with Matt following right behind her. Jim and Hanna coached Lizzy on using the reins on the horse, which she had ridden before, but not a lot. Hanna was the cowgirl of the family. She loved to ride, but not when running from Indians; she was still a little sore from that. They made a big loop around the outside of the fort, then stopped under a shade tree. Jim and Ezy made out under the tree while Hanna and Lizzy picked wildflowers. It was a lazy afternoon, and the weather was perfect, a cool breeze was blowing across the plains. After about an hour, they rode back to the wagon, Jim unsaddled the horses and brushed them down. Ezy and Hanna started prepping for supper, and Matt and Sara came out of the wagon. "Why were y'all in the wagon asked Lizzy. "Taking a nap, sweety," said Sara, as she leaned down and kissed Lizzy's head. "Oh," said Lizzy, "I rode my pony." "You did," said Sara, "yelp, he's a good horse."

The next morning, the wagon train was moving on, and Jim saddled all the horses. Matt and Jim knew that once they reached the mountain trails, everyone, but the wagon drivers, would have to walk or ride horseback up the steep slopes. They wanted to get the girls used to riding for longer periods of time. That afternoon, after the sun started to set, he had them lead their horses until they set up camp. That night, as Jim and Matt sat by the fire, Matt asked Jim, "How bad was it, son?" "What?" asked Jim, "When you got Hanna and the girls back?" "What do you mean?" asked Jim. "Well, how many Indians were there?" Jim shuffled his feet, "There were five that took the girls," "I shot all but one, he got away." "Then that one came back with three more as we were trying to get back to the wagon trail." "I sent the girl riding with me on my horse to catch up with Hanna," said Jim. "What did you do then, son?" asked Matt. "What Mr. Wagner told us to do," said Jim. "I killed them until they stopped coming," Jim said, with tears in his eyes. Matt didn't ask any more questions; he could tell Jim was still dealing with it. After two more days, they reached the foothills of the mountains; on the other side of the mountains was Idaho. That night, they had another meeting. Mr. Wagner told them that they would take the next day to check their wagons and make any repairs needed. That the next leg of the trip over the mountains would be the hardest. Nothing but rocks and steep climbs for the horses and wagons. Wagner warned everyone to stay on the main trail, not to pull to the side, not to pass anyone, and to stay alert.

Thereby, the camp was a mountain spring, and everyone was filling their water barrels with cold water. Mr. Wagner made them all stop, "only half full," said Wagner, "there is more water at the top and the other side." "You don't need to add any more weight onto your wagons." Lizzy and Hanna were looking for more gold. Lizzy had figured out the best places to look for the yellow rocks, based on the kind of rocks they were around. That day, Lizzy and Hanna had filled up a two-pound coffee sack with nothing but gold nuggets. They hid the sack in the wagon and told no one about it. They just looked at each other and giggled. The next morning, the wagon train started the long and arduous climb up the mountain pass. Ezy was riding Jim's horse, Matt and Sara were on Matt's horse, and the two girls were on their horses. Jim would drive the wagon over the mountains; the traveling was very slow. After a long day, they only made it about five miles the first day. After six more days and nights, they finally made it through the first pass. They camped in a small valley by a stream, and Lizzy and Hanna found even more gold. The next pass was even stepper than the first; they were moving slowly, but they were moving. Each night it was getting colder as they went higher up into the mountains. As Wagner had predicted, people started running out of supplies. After over two weeks, they had made it to the other side of the mountain range into Idaho. They stop for a day to rest the stock by another small river before heading across the Idaho plains. Wagner had his crew butcher another steer from the herd. They divided the meat among all the wagons, along with other supplies. Lizzy and Hanna found more gold in that river, too. Unknown to their family and themselves, the two Evans girls were rich beyond their dreams. What started out as a game to kill time along the way will one day surprise them all and help build a legacy for the Evens family.

The worst was over, so they thought, with the mountain range behind them. There had been no major breakdowns, and no one had died, getting across the mountains. Wagner warned the travelers that night about the dangers ahead from this point on. Mostly bandits, but some of the Indians in that area were even more dangerous than the ones in Wyoming. But he forgot to mention another danger that most had never seen. The "Grizzly bears," unlike the brown bears and the black bears, which ate mostly berries and fish, Grizzlys were carnivores. Meat eaters, and they were fattening up for the long winter ahead. Without even thinking, Wagner's crew had just created a bait pile for the Grizzly's. Fresh blood on the ground and in the air from butchering one of the cows was all it took. That night, as most were sleeping, a big grizzly bear found the scrape pile. Unsatisfied with the scrapes left behind, the bear wandered into the camp. One of the night guards, hearing a loud grunting sound, went to investigate the noise. He found it, seeing the giant creature, he froze in place as the bear stood up. One swipe from the bear's big paw broke the man's neck, and he fell to the ground. The bear ripped a chunk of meat out of the man's arm, but that was not the taste he was looking for. The bear could smell the beef in the air as he went to one of the nearest wagons and stuck his head inside the back flap. The bear started to climb inside, the boards creaking. The man inside the wagon shot at the bear, wounding it. The bear went into a rage, killing the man and his wife, then took the cow meat hanging inside the wagon. The others heard the woman's screams as the bear attacked the two travelers in their wagon. All the men came running to see what was wrong, but it was too late, the bear was gone, and three people had been killed.

The next morning, after burying the bodies and saying a few words, the wagon train moved on, all but one wagon. As they crossed the Idaho plains, they were even more eager to reach their destination, Oregon. They were close but there was no time for celebration; they still had a long way to go. The wagon train followed alongside the Columbia River for over a week to get around the Cascade Mountain range. Then, it went south to reach Oregon City, Oregon. The big open valley was beautiful with the Columbia River behind it to the North, the Cascade Mountains to the East, and the Pacific Ocean to the West. On September 19, 1850, it had taken far longer to make the trip than Wagner had planned, but Mr. Wagner had left on April 10, 1850, with thirty-four wagons and thirty head of cattle. He had made it there with thirty-three wagons and twelve heads of cattle. He only lost three people along the way; it was not the fastest trip ever made, but it was the safest by far. The next day, everyone lined up outside the land office, hoping to receive their land grants. Matt, Sara, Hanna, Lizzy, Jim, & Ezy all went inside as it became their turn. Matt and Sara stepped up to the desk as Jim and Ezy stood behind them holding hands. "Marriage license," said the man. Sara stepped up and handed theirs to the man. Most of the land being granted was farther south, away from Oregon City, as much as a hundred miles or more. The man looked at Matt like he was studying him, then looked at his family, "Ok, Mr. Evens," said the man as he stamped a deed and a map, pointing at the map. "This is your section right here, good luck, sir, you've got four years to make something out of it." "Next," yelled the man. Jim and Ezy cowardly stepped up; they were nervous because of their ages. "Marriage License," said the man. Ezy handed theirs to the man, "How old are you, son?" asked the man. "Seventeen," said Jim, "is that your father there," asked the man, "yes Sir," said Jim "Your eighteen years old," said the man, as he stamped a deed and a map, "Mr. Jim Evens, this is your lot right next to your father's, they both run right up to the river, good luck son," "Next yelled the man." The Evens found out later that only four families with their group had been given land near Oregon City; the rest still had miles to travel.

Once the Evens got outside into the street, they looked at their papers, 640 arches each, totaling 1,280 arches. Their land was about three miles Northeast of Oregon City, and they were going to need supplies before they left town. "Well, we're here," said Matt, "we finally made it, we've got our ranch land." "But first, we've got to build a house for the winter. We'll need tools. Let me see how much money I have left." Lizzy pulled at her daddy's shirt, crooked her finger, and Matt leaned down to her. Lizzy handed Matt the cash and coins she had left from selling her goal at the start of their trip. Around twenty dollars in all, "I don't need it," said Lizzy, "Hanna and I found more gold along the way." "I just want a real house with my own bed," said Lizzy. "Deal," said Matt. Matt and Jim went and bought hammers, nails, axes, saws, shovels, and other tools. Matt sent the girls to buy food supplies and bedding materials. The livery station had a used wagon for sale for ten dollars that had just been reworked.

Matt bought the wagon and harnesses; Jim hooked his horse up to it. Tom came walking up to Jim, "Hello, Mr. Wagner," said Jim, "Hello, Jim," said Tom, "Looks like you and your family got your land grants." "Yes, sir," said Jim, "we are headed out to find it now." "That's great," said Tom, "so, what's next for you?" asked Jim, "Are you headed back to bring more people up here next spring?" "No, I think I've made my last trip down this old trail. This place is filling up fast." "I think Jake, Paul, and I are going to go to California for the winter and see the ocean." "I hear they're finding a little gold down there. Besides, I want to help the people headed South reach their land," said Tom. "I sold my wagons, all but one, we're taking it to haul supplies in," "we'll get these people to their land, then move on to California." "You see that carol over there?" asked Tom. "Yes, sir," said Jim. Tom handed Jim a bill of sale, "There are twelve head of cattle there." "They are yours now." "I don't know what to say," said Jim, "Thank You!" "No," "thank you, Jim," said Tom, "now go build that ranch," "I might come see you one day." "You're welcome anytime," said Matt. "Thanks, I'll keep that in mind," said Wagner as he walked off.

The Evens loaded everything into the wagons. Ezy and Sara got on the covered wagon, while Jim drove the other one. Matt and the girls rode their horses over to the carol, opened the gate, and pushed the cows out as they left, headed to find their new home. They got to their land by the Clackamas River just before dark. Matt found a level spot to set up camp for the night. The next morning, after breakfast, Matt and Jim went out to survey their new land. They found their corner markers; over half the land was covered in timber, with a wide-open area near the river on both sections. Jim marked a spot on his section not far from the river, as they rode back to the camp, Matt did the same on his section within sight of Jim's spot, also near the river. They would build a big barn between the two sections on a hill. Jim would help Matt build his house first, then Matt would help Jim and Ezy build a cabin. The land was beautiful, and the air was fresh, like a small piece of heaven on earth. The next few days, they cut timber from the wooded areas, White Oak trees first, then some of the Ponderosa Pine trees. Matt and Jim worked for two weeks cutting, skinning, and notching logs, some as long as forty feet. They had cut some smaller fir trees to build a shed frame, then covered the top frame with canvas. They covered the side walls halfway up with fir poles to block the wind. They set up the cooking area under that shed, for Sara, Hanna, and Ezy to cook under out of the weather. After setting the foundation stones for the main cabin, a 40' x 30', Matt, Jim, and the girls started stacking the logs. Using the draft horses, they rolled the logs into place; they stacked the side wall up fourteen feet high. Then they used the pine logs to frame the roof, then ran fir poles crosswise for the roof shingles, which were made from Seader logs. Matt had ordered them before they left Oregon City, as well as lumber for the floors, which would be coming from the Mill in Oregon City next spring.

To get through the winter, the Evens would build lean-to sheds off both sides of the main structure for bedrooms with sod roofs and dirt floors. Time was running out fast, as the weather was getting colder every day, Matt made a trip back to town to buy a wood stove and two small wood heaters. On one side, there would be three rooms, two ten by fifteen feet, with one room in the middle, ten by ten, for storage. Jim and Ezy will have one room, then Hanna and Lizzy will have the other room. On the other side of the main structure will be a ten-foot by twenty-foot room for Matt and Sara, with the wood-burning stove in it for heating and cooking. The remaining shed on that side will be for the milk cow and the horses, with an open carport attached. Doesn't seem like much, but after living in a wagon for five and a half months on the trail, it will be a welcome change. By mid-October, the rooms were finished, other than the chinking of the walls. Jim and Matt started building the bed frames and chairs for the rooms, while the girls were doing the chinking. By the end of October, they had already had their first snow as Matt and Jim made a final trip to Oregon City for supplies. They brought Lizzy along with them after an hour of pleading and begging to go.

Unknown to her father and brother, Lizzy had filled up one of her pockets with some of her gold rocks from her first bag; she had a plan. As they reached the town limits, Lizzy said, "Just drop me off here at the bank," like she was a grown woman. Matt looked at her, "I think I'd better go in with you," said Matt. "Yeah, me too," said Jim. "Oh, ok," said Lizzy, "but let me do the talking. They stopped the wagon in front of the bank, and walked inside, Lizzy walked up to the clerk's counter. The clerk asked with a smile, "can I help you, young lady," trying to sound older, Lizzy said, "yes, I need to set up two accounts here at your bank." "One in Matt Evens' name," pointing at her father, "and one in Jim Evens' name," pointing at her brother." Lizzy had learned from past dealings about what her gold should be worth. "How much would you like to deposit in each account?" asked the clerk. Lizzy emptied her pocket onto the counter, the clerks' eyes got big, as did Matt's and Jim's. "Five hundred dollars in each account and the rest in cash, or gold coins," said Lizzy with a smile. The clerk, surprised at her candor, weighed up the gold, then wrote out the deposit slip for each account and had Matt and Jim sign their names. The clerk then counted out two hundred and sixty-eight dollars in cash and coins. "Are you sure that's right, Mr.?" asked Lizzy. "Oh, yes, ma'am, "said the clerk. Lizzy smiled, "Ok, Mr., I'm going to trust you. Have a nice day." "You to mam," said the clerk, "come back to see us." "I will," said Lizzy. "Oh, and it's Ms. Evens," said Lizzy.

The three walked out of the bank and got onto the wagon. Jim and Matt were trying not to laugh. "Thank you, Lizzy," said Jim as he gave her a hug. "Yes, Lizzy, thank you," said Matt, "I'm so proud of you." They went to the mercantile store, and Lizzy bought mattresses for all the beds, pillows, blankets, sheets, and three rolls of oiled canvas to cover the main structure for the winter, as suggested by her father. From there, they went to the general store. Lizzy got flour, sugar, meal, coffee, salt, pepper, cooking oil, maple syrup, grape jelly, peanut butter, and lard. Fifty pounds of potatoes, salt pork, a curd ham, a slab of bacon, and two bags of candy, "ok, I'm done," said Lizzy, "let's go home." After everything was loaded, it was stacked up six feet high on the back of the wagon. Late that afternoon, they made it back to their homestead. Sara, Hanna, and Ezy came out to greet them and to see what they had brought back. "Wow," said Sara, "how were you able to buy all that?" Matt pointed at Lizzy, "little Ms. Evens over there," said Matt. They all jumped in and started unloading the wagon and carrying the things inside. After putting the mattresses on the beds and making them up, they put all the dry goods and meat in the small storage room and kitchen. It was like an early Christmas for the Evens family. Ezy and Hanna both screamed when they saw the syrup and jelly.

The next day, Matt and Jim rolled out the canvas over the main roof and tied it down. Then they started building the carol for the horses, and after that was done, they started cutting more trees for firewood. They had also saved all the cut-off pieces of logs from the build, and they split them for stove wood. In mid-November, everything was covered with snow, the wind blew most of the time, and they could not stay outside for more than a few minutes at a time. The cattle had moved up into the trees near the house for cover. There was nothing Matt or Jim could do for them now other than hope they served. Matt and Jim had stored some materials inside the main structure so they could keep working on the upstairs support beams through the winter. After the long, cold winter, things started to thaw out, and patches of grass were turning green again. Leaves began to unfold on the tree branches, and buds began to form for new blooms. Jim went out looking for his cows. He found nine and pushed them back close to the house. Ezy was also starting to blossom with a small baby bump that was now showing. Sara was thrilled with the thought of being a grandmother. Matt and Jim were back hard at work on the house. Sara, Ezy, Hanna, and sometimes Lizzy were working on a garden spot. Just a small area where they could raise a few vegetables to eat and store for next winter.

Jim and Hanna spent some of their spare time throwing their knives. Jim had taught Hanna how to handle and use her knife on the trail. Now they are just trying to stay in practice and have fun with them. Over the winter months, Jim had made two Bows and a few arrows; he and Hanna were also learning to use them. So far, Hanna seems to have the natural ability to use the bow best between the two. By mid-summer, the house was finished, and now the downstairs area of the main house was one big open room. With a large table and chairs to eat at, in one corner, Matt and Sara's old bedroom is all kitchen now, which also has a smaller table and chairs in it. Sara and Matt's new bedroom was upstairs now, and Sara needed material to make curtains for the few windows they had. Matt and Jim had started working on the foundations for Jim's and Ezy's cabin on their home steed, not far away. All the girls decided it was time for them to make a trip to town. Ezy hooked up the wagon.

They rode down to where Matt and Jim were working. "Where are y'all headed?" asked Matt. "To town," said Sara. "We need some things, and Lizzy says she has money." "Well, let us clean up, and we'll go with you," said Matt. "No, need," said Sara, "just keep working," "we will be back before supper time." "We made you some lunch," said Sara, as Hanna jumped off the wagon and carried a sack to Jim. Jim asked Hanna, "Do you have your knife?" "Yes, and my Bow," said Hanna. "Well, ok then," said Jim, "be safe," "we will," said Hanna as she climbed back on the wagon.

Ezy turned the wagon around, and the girls headed off to Oregon City. Jim looked at Matt. "Well, I guess it had to happen sooner or later," said Matt, "this is our home now." The two men went back to work as the girl drove on out of sight. Lizzy had Ezy pull up in front of the bank, "y'all come on in," said Lizzy. She wanted to show off a little in front of her family. They walked into the bank, Lizzy in the front. "Well, hello, Ms. Evens," said the Banker. Sara thought, how does this man know me. "Hello," said Lizzy, in her pretend grown-up voice, then Sara realized he was talking to Lizzy. "I have more gold to cash in," said Lizzy. "Ok," said the banker. "I can help you with that," "I see you served the winter ok," said the Banker, "let's see what you've got." Lizzy pulled out a small handful of gold nuggets and laid them on the counter. The Banker weighed them up. "How would you like this?" asked the banker, "Do you want to deposit any of it?" "Well, yes, if I can," said Lizzy. "Well, since I know who you are, I think we can do that," said the man. "Ok, give me two hundred in cash and deposit the rest in my father's account," said Lizzy. "Oh, and this is my mom, Sara, my sister, Hanna, and Jim's wife, Ezy, my sister-in-law. "Nice to meet you all," said the banker, with a smile. He counted out two hundred dollars. Lizzy gave Hanna one hundred dollars of it. The Banker said, "Here, sign your father's name here on this line for the deposit." "That brings his balance up to $ 837.52," said the banker. "Tell him and your brother I said hello," said the banker. "I will," said Lizzy. "If you don't mind me asking, Ms. Evens, how did you come by all this gold?" Lizzy smiled, "Well, my sister and I dug in every creek, river, and spring between here and North Kentucky on our way up here last summer." "But don't tell anybody," Whispered Lizzy. "Oh, no, ma'am, I want," said the banker. "I guess God knew we would need some money when we got here," said Lizzy, "I'll be back."

As the girls got outside, Sara asked Lizzy, "Just how much gold do you have?" "Oh, I gave Dad and Jim most of my first bag to put in the bank last year." "But Hanna and I, together we still have a lot more, don't we Hanna," said Lizzy. Hanna just nodded her head with a smile. "Well, then, let's go shopping," said Sara. They rode on down to the general store. As they got off the wagon, Lizzy handed her mom twenty dollars, then handed Ezy twenty dollars. "Y'all get what you want with that. I'll pay for the house supplies," said Lizzy. Sara and Ezy both hugged Lizzy, then they went inside the store. Hanna spotted what she wanted right off, hanging on the wall behind the counter. A 22 cal. Henry Lever Action Rifle, she bought it and a case of cartridges to go with it. Sara found some cotton materials to make curtains out of. Then she saw it, the most beautiful thing she had ever seen in her life, a new Singer Sewing Machine; she had to have it. She told the store clerk, "I want this, load it into my wagon," said Sara, she was so excited. She then started looking for materials to make dresses and baby clothes. It took every penny of her twenty dollars and more, but Hanna covered it. Ezy found some baby clothes and dippers, she got two baby blankets and some white baby socks, then she got herself a cotton dress. Lizzy ordered the staple goods, flour, sugar, meal, and coffee. She also got herself some boys' jeans, overalls, a couple of shirts, and some new boots. After everything was loaded into the wagon, the women headed back home.

Just before dark, the girls made it back home. Matt and Jim were there waiting. Sara had them unload the sawing machine and carry it up the stairs to her room. After everything was unloaded, Jim unhooked the wagon for them and fed the animals. Sara and Ezy started super. Lizzy walked over to her father and handed him the deposit slip from the bank. "You're welcome, pops," said Lizzy as she walked away smiling. Matt just shook his head. Jim came back in to look at Hanna's new rifle, and he promised to help her sight it tomorrow. It had been a wonderful day for the girls; they had so much fun just being out on their own. Matt and Jim would start stacking the logs for Jim's cabin tomorrow, and after that, the girls would start chinking the cracks. Hopefully, before winter, they would be through with it, just a one-room cabin for now, that they could add to it later.

After Hanna and Jim sighted in her gun, wild game was always on the menu for the Evens family. Hanna had taken over the forging for meat; she was always coming home with deer, rabbits, squirrels, ducks, turkeys, and even a wild hog. After Jim's cabin was finished, he and Matt started hauling rocks out of the river, from six to eight inches around. Jim wanted a rock fireplace in his cabin for heat to go along with their small wood-burning stove. After all, they would have a baby in their house this winter, and he wanted the cabin to be nice and cozy. Once Lizzy realized they were getting rocks from the river, she was happy to help. She knew what might be under those rocks at the bottom of that riverbed. Although the water was cold at first, her body adjusted to it as she moved along behind Jim and Matt, checking under the rocks they removed. While they loaded and unloaded the stones, she would set more out of the river for them to pick up. She was able to find a little gold, but most of it was small flat pieces, or flake gold, not like the nuggets she found along the way there. She knew there had to be bigger gold there somewhere if she could just find it. After a week of digging in the river, Jim had all the rocks he needed to build his fireplace, so Lizzy stopped looking. She had found close to ten ounces of flake gold while helping Jim, not a lot, but not bad either.

Lizzy studied the flow of the river as Jim and Matt loaded the rocks onto the wagon and took them to Jim's cabin before coming back for more. Just past where Matt and Jim had gotten the rocks, there was a sharp curve in the river. Lizzy watches the water current roll by her on the far side of the river, then crosses over to the other side of the river at the curve. It made a swirl at the curve, then straightened out, going down the middle for a while. That's it, thought Lizzy. She gathered her things and went to the house to find Hanna. Lizzy went to the kitchen door. "Hanna, come outside a minute," said Lizzy. Hanna wiped her hands off and followed Lizzy outside onto the porch. "What is it?" asked Hanna. "I know where the gold is," said Lizzy in a low voice. "What gold?" asked Hanna. "The gold in our river," said Lizzy, pointing to the river in front of the house. "But it's small pieces," said Lizzy, "we need some way to get it out of the sand and rocks." "Let's go ask Dad," said Hanna. "Ok," said Lizzy. The two girls walked to where Matt and Jim were starting the barn. "Dad," yelled Hanna, "can you come here a minute?" Matt walked over to the girls. "What are you two up to?" asked Matt. "We need your help," said Hanna. "Ok, what can I do?" asked Matt. Lizzy took Matt's hand. "Come with me," said Lizzy. She led him to the riverbank as Hanna followed, "You see that curve in the river down there?" asked Lizzy. "Yes, I see it," said Matt. "Do you see how the water current crosses over to the other side and hits that curve?" asked Lizzy. "Yes, I see that too," said Matt, "see how the water swirls their dad," "yes," said Matt. "That's where the gold is," said Lizzy. Matt took off his hat and scratched his head. "I think you might be right," said Matt. "Well, we need a way to separate it from the sand and rock in that hole," said Lizzy. She pulled a matchbox out of her pocket and opened it, "This is the kind of gold I found under the rocks here." Matt looked at the gold, small flakes mostly, and some pea-sized stones. "I see," said Matt. "Give me a couple of days to think about it," "I'll come up with something," said Matt.

"Ok, Pop's but keep it to yourself," said Lizzy, "Oh, I will," said Matt in a low voice with a smile.

Mid-August was when Matt and Jim had started building a barn between their homes for the livestock. Jim would work in the afternoons on the rock fireplace for his cabin. Hanna was helping him most of the time; the days seemed to pass by fast with everyone staying busy. Sara was making clothes for herself and the girls in her spare time. The memories of the hardships it took to get there were almost gone as they built their new lives in Oregon. Another winter would be coming soon, as they all worked to be ready for it. But Matt had a secret side project he was working on, he and Lizzy that is. Lizzy helped Matt as he made boards and slates out of leftover wood, "looks like a feed truffe to me," said Lizzy, except for those ridges in the bottom." Matt put four legs on the open top box, with the back leg higher than the front legs, "that's crooked," said Lizzy. "Yep," said Matt, with a laugh, "you'll see why later." September 17, 1851, just after breakfast, Sara helped Ezy deliver her and Matt's first grandbaby, a little boy. Jim and Ezy named him Thomas Matthew Evens. Lizzy, now eleven, and Hanna, now fifteen, happily took over baby petrol while Ezy recovered. Which didn't take long, Sara would tell them, "Y'all are going to wear the skin off that baby if you don't put him down. Jim would sit and hold him at night and just stare at him, with love in his eyes. Matt told his son Jim, "Enjoy him now while you can, because they grow up way too fast."

It was almost winter again, but the Evens family was ready; they had worked hard all summer preparing for it. Lizzy asked Matt one night after supper, "What about our project?" "It's ready," said Matt, "but the river is not." "Why," asked Lizzy, "well, the water's too cold for one thing, and the hole is too deep right now. "We need to wait until summer, when the water level is at its lowest," said Matt. "That makes sense," said Lizzy. Jim and Ezy had moved into their new cabin with their baby, and Hanna and Lizzy now had their own rooms. Matt and Jim had gotten a good start on the barn; most of the framework was up now, but there was no roof yet. They had all but run out of time as the first snow fell on the Evens ranch. Jim and Matt butchered the last steer, just before the snow, and now eight cows are all Jim has left. Jim hopes he can buy a young bull next spring from one of the bigger ranches near them. Jim had already talked to one of the main ranch owners, who had all the land on the other side of the river from them. That ranch had over fifteen thousand acres of land and several hundred, if not over a thousand, head of cattle on it. Pruit Ranch owner Mr. Pruit had told Jim he would sell him a young bull, but that his cows were not for sale. Pruit sold steers to be butchered for the markets in the area, but told Jim, "You never sell your cows." Mr. Pruit gave Jim the name of a man in Nevada who would bring him up a herd of mixed-breed cows that could take the cold winters. Mr. Pruit was known for being a hard man to deal with and didn't like many people, but for some reason, he liked Jim.

As the Evens settled in for the long winter months, there was a well-beaten path between Jim's cabin and the family house. Hanna, Sara, and Lizzy made daily trips to see the baby, as did Jim and Ezy to the main house for meals. To the North of Jim's home stead was a family that had traveled up with them on the wagon train. A man, his wife, and two young girls, five and seven years old, the last time Jim had seen them was in the spring as they came by going into town for supplies. They were foreigners who spoke very little English. The man's name was Josua; Jim didn't know the woman's or the girls' names. For some reason, Jim decided he should go check on them before the snow got too deep. Jim and Hanna saddled their horses and rode out through the snow, not sure where that family was building their homestead. Jim and Hanna stayed close to the river. Well past Jim's property line, they had seen no sign of anything other than a couple of elk. Jim and Hanna kept going along the river.

Jim could smell smoke, and then he saw the smoke above the trees. As they turned and moved away from the river, headed in the direction of the smoke, once they got closer, they saw the wagon. Jim and Hanna eased up close to the wagon. "Hello," yelled Jim, "anybody home?" Jim saw what looked like the beginning of a cabin, but there was no livestock around. The fire outside was only smoldering; no wood or coals were left. Jim eased up behind the wagon and opened the back flaps.

Jim choked and gagged at the smell coming from inside the wagon, the smell of urine and death. "Oh, my God," said Jim, as he held his nose. Then he heard whimpers coming from inside the wagon as one of the girls stuck her head out from under the blankets that were piled over her. Jim could tell the woman was dead; he could not see the man inside. The two girls were cuddled up together under the blankets by their mother. Tears filled Jim's eyes. "Come here, sweety," said Jim in a low tone. The little girls crawled out from under the blankets, first one and then the other. Jim took the smallest one out, pulled her clothes off, and threw them to the ground, then handed her to Hanna. "Rape her up inside your coat," said Jim, "Oh, God she smells," said Hanna as she gaged, "I know," said Jim. Jim took the other girl out and took her clothes off, then put her inside his coat. Jim took a kerosene lantern from the wagon, lit it, and then threw it back inside the wagon. "Come on," said Jim, "let's go home." The smell of the two girls was almost unbearable as Jim and Hanna pushed their horses through the snow. Jim and Hanna rode back up to the main house, "Mom, Dad!" yelled Jim. Matt opened the front door. "What is it, son?" asked Matt. "Get mom," said Jim in a sour tone. Sara came out as Jim unfolded his coat, "Oh, my Lord," said Sara, "Dad help Hanna down, please," said Jim as he choked. Jim took the horses and put them up under the shed, then went inside. Sara was heating water to bathe the girls; Lizzy went to get Ezy and the baby.

Hanna and Jim sit by the stove warming up, "Where did they come from?" asked Matt as he handed Jim a cup of coffee, then Hanna. "Josua's place," said Jim. "What were you doing out there?" asked Sara. "I don't know," said Jim, "something told me this morning to go check on them." "So, Hanna and I rode over there," "the woman is dead, has been far a while," "there was no sign of Josua or his horses." "The two girls were cuddled up under blankets beside their mother's body," said Jim. Jim sipped his coffee and just shook his head, "What kind of a man would leave his family?" said Jim, just like Ezy's dad did, how could a man do that?" "Well, we don't know what happened, son, probably never will," said Matt. Ezy, the baby, and Lizzy came in as Sara was putting the two girls in a tub of warm water to bathe; they were bone poor with their ribs showing through their skin. "Where did they come from?" asked Ezy. "Go ask Hanna," said Jim. "I can't talk about it anymore." Hanna looked up, "Ezy, you don't want to know," "Oh God, it was terrible," said Hanna. Sara and Hanna washed the girls off and shampooed their hair, then dried them off by the stove. Hanna started brushing out their hair, and Lizzy brought them some of her old clothes to wear. "I can take these up," said Sara, "they will fit just fine." Ezy fixed the girls some food to eat, and they ate so fast they were almost choking. "Stop that," said Ezy, as she pulled the food away from them. "Now you stop that, you eat slow and crew it up," said Ezy, or "you want eat," somehow the girls understood Ezy. The girls slowly ate as they looked up at Ezy's face. Ezy had tears in her eyes, and she wanted to cry, but she wouldn't let herself, not in front of those girls. She knew just how they felt and how scared they must have been. She had spent weeks alone before, but at least she was old enough to feed herself.

Through the winter months, Hanna and Lizzy worked with the girl; by spring, they were both speaking English and filling back out. They were now just part of the family; Ezy was their mom now, and

Jim their dad. Not knowing their real names, they called the oldest Missy and the youngest Sissy, which was Lizzy's idea. Sara just called them girls, because they were never apart; if you tried to separate them from each other, they would fight to get back together. Although they lived that winter in the big house with Matt and Sara, when Ezy was around, they stuck to her. Ezy had no problem keeping them in line and making them mind. Something about the tone of her voice, or the love in her eyes, let them know she was there for them. After the melt started in early spring, Jim and Hanna made a trip into town. They stopped at the land office first. Jim told the land officer about Josua's wife and the girls, "So just you took those girls in," said the man. "Yes, sir," said Jim, "and you plan on raising them as your own," the man asked. "Well, my family and I, yes, sir, if their father doesn't come back," said Jim. "I think the chances of that are slim and none," said the Landman. "Would you like to own that section of land?" "Sure," said Jim, "but how?" "Come back tomorrow, "and bring me ten dollars for the processing fee," said the man.

The next morning, Jim and Hanna rode back into town and went to the land office. The man had back-dated Josua's land grant to show four years and filled out a bill of sale from Josua to Jim. "Sign here, son," said the man. Jim signed the paper, and the man notarized it. Then said, "Here, sign this deed." Jim did, and the man stamped it. "My job is to make sure good people get the land in this area," "people that will help build something here." "Now you own that land too, son, show me I did the right thing," said the man." Jim handed the man ten dollars. "I want let you down, sir." "Thank you," said Jim. As Jim got outside, he asked Hanna if she had brought any gold. "I did," said Hanna. Jim and Hanna had talked the night before about buying some cattle from Nevada; Hanna was going to help pay for them. They rode on down the street to the bank; Hanna gave Jim a small bag of gold as they walked in. "Well, hello, Mr. Evens, said the man, and Miss Hanna. "I need to make a deposit," said Jim.

"Then wire some money to Nevada," said Jim. "Sure," said the banker, "let me weigh this up for you." "That's, $ 1,230.00 worth," said the banker. "Ok," said Jim, "I want to deposit $ 1,000.00 and then wire $500.00 to this account, laying a piece of paper down." "Sure thing," said the Banker. Jim and Hanna waited as the banker wired the money. "Ok, here you go," "here your deposit slip, your wire receipt, and here's your change," said the banker. Jim took the change and handed it to Hanna, and put the receipts in his pocket, "thank you, sir," said Jim.

Jim had put up his deposit on a hundred head of cattle; he would have to pay the balance on their delivery midsummer. Hanna would need to put up more gold than. "Well, do you need anything while we are here?" asked Jim. "Yep," said Hanna. They rode to the general store. Hanna bought two bags of hard candy; the store had gotten in two new Sharps rifles that she had ordered last fall. "Oh, my," said Jim, "what are those for?" "You and I to hunt Elk with," said Hanna. Jim picked one of them up, "Wow, now that's a rifle," "Thank you, Sis," said Jim. The family seemed to be growing faster than Hanna could keep meat for them to eat now that they had two more mouths to feed, and Ezy was showing again. "As bad as I hate to say it, we need another milk cow," said Hanna, "and more chickens too." "You're right," said Jim, let's go see what we can find." They rode off down to the livery station, and Jim told the man what they were looking for. He gave them a man's name and told them how to get to his place, South of town. They rode out of town, and they found the farm. An older man and woman came out. They bought a milk cow and a milk goat, then twelve chickens and a rooster. "We will take the goat and cow now," said Jim, "Hanna will come back for the chickens tomorrow in the wagon." "Sounds good said the man." Thank you, son," "Thank you," said Jim.

Chapter Four: Herd Arrival

Jim and his father Matt completed the barn mid-summer with a tack room and a feed room with a large loft above and a hen house. Stalls had been added on the ground floor for the horses, as well as a pen for the new milk cow and goat; their old milk cow didn't survive last winter. Mid-morning on June 5th. In 1852, a rider came to the main house looking for Jim. Hanna asked him what he needed. The man said Jim's cattle were at the edge of town waiting. Hanna ran to Jim's cabin, they both came running back, the man told Jim to meet him in town to Seattle up. Jim saddled his and Hanna's horses while Hanna went after some of her gold, then they rode off to town. The man was waiting at the bank. Jim and Hanna went inside to get the money, then came out and handed the balance to the man. "Ok, now, where do you want them?" asked the man. Jim said, "Just follow me." Jim and Hanna led the man back to their ranch, as the other men pushed the herd along behind them. They rode past Jim Cabin aways, then Jim stopped, "just let them go," said Jim, "we've got them from here. Jim shook hands with the man, then the man and his crew rode off. Jim had already bought a three-year-old bull from the Pruit Ranch last spring. Jim and Hanna went out to find him and the eight cows they already had. They pushed them back to the main herd and let them mix in. The bull went straight to work. "That didn't take long," said Hanna. "Nope," said Jim. They sat and watched the cattle for a while as they began to graze and spread out. "Well, sis," "looks like we're in the cattle business now," "we just need to keep them alive now," said Jim.

The groundwork had already started for a railroad spear to come into the edge of Oregon City, which was a big thing for the cattle ranchers in the area to be able to ship beef cattle out. Since the barn was finished now, Matt had started cleaning out from under the shed on the side of the main house. He had also taken down the coral attached to it; his plan was to close it in to make another bedroom for the two girls, Missy and Sissy. Sara and Hanna were moving the horse manure and piling it near their garden spot. Jim was setting foundation stones so he could add another room onto his cabin, since they had another baby on the way. So much had changed since the day they had located their home stead land. What once was just open and wild land now has houses, a barn, and corals on it, with horses, people, and cattle living there. It was now a home place, a place where a dream was starting to come true. Hanna, now sixteen, a young woman, had become the Rover; she loved the outdoors anyway and being on her horse. So, she had taken it upon herself to be the one to keep watch on the herd. She left the barn just after breakfast each morning on her horse and came back in just before dark each afternoon. She liked the seclusion and being away from the noise and commotion of Lizzy and the girls, alone out there; her soul was at peace.

Apart from the occasional wolf or badger that came close to the herd, the cattle calmly grazed along. Hanna would run the predator away from the herd, then she sat in the trees and waited for them to try to come back. That's when she would shoot them. The section of land Jim had bought was full of underground springs, which formed small creeks that ran to the river. That's where the cattle liked to drink best. Sometimes, some of the cattle would wander to the river to drink if they were close to it. Hanna's plan was to let the cattle graze off the bought section first, then push them over onto Jim's home stead. Then, once winter came, push them over to the main homestead near the house and barn area. That's when she figured most of the predators would come out looking for food. On her horse, she had everything she needed: guns, ammo, extra clothes, a bedroll, and her Bow and arrows as well. With her Bow, she would kill small animals like rabbits, squirrels, and birds. If she got hungry, she would build a fire and roast them.

Matt and Jim had started cutting and peeling more trees for both of their additions; they wanted to get them finished before the snow. Sara seemed to be sewing most of the time now, making clothes for her growing family. The township of Oregon City is also growing with plans for a church and a schoolhouse. With the anticipation of the railroad, the depot was already being built, and soon people from all over the country would be traveling to and through the city. Products from all over the world can be shipped by rail once the tracks have been laid. The estimated completion of the rail spur is in 1855, due to only having six good months of good weather to work in. The ground in the spring months is too wet from the melting snow, and the winter months are too cold, and the ground freezes. But the Evens have learned to cope with the elements and have adapted to the weather; it's not an easy life, but it's their life now.

Jim helped Matt finish the bedroom for the girls, and Matt helped Jim build his addition to his cabin. The family, all but Hanna, were headed to town to get supplies and hopefully pick up a couple of windows for their added rooms. Lizzy, now Sissy and Missy's big sister, cashed in more gold and bought the girls boots for the winter. While Sara got more materials, Ezy got supplies for her cabin, and Matt got supplies for the main house. Ezy cooked breakfast and lunch at her cabin for her, Jim, and the baby, but the whole family always ate supper at the main house. Jim picked up some leather chaps for Hanna and a long-insulated coat; he also got her some leather gloves. Hanna also told Jim she needed a pistol or a short shotgun, she could lay across her lap, something she could get out faster than her rifle. The Wolves were getting braver as it got colder. The other day, one grabbed the toe of her boot and dragged her off her horse; she had to kill it with her knife. Jim knew that meant that he would have to start helping her through the winter months. So, he could be close by if she needed his help. Once the temperature was down, the cows would be on their own, and by then, they would be closer to the main home stead. The cows that they thought were bred and were showing would be put in the large corral behind the barn and would gain feed through the winter. They are hoping the other cow would stay close by on the outside, still grubbing as long as they could. The snow would cover dry grass that could still be eaten by the cows under the snow for most of the winter. Since the cows don't move around as much in the winter, they become targets for the predators.

The family came back from town that afternoon, and Sara and Ezy started supper. Ezy's baby is trying to walk now and getting into everything. Lizzy is on baby patrol. Ezy is really showing now that the baby is due in October; it's now September. Lizzy just knows it's going to be a girl, that she can play with and dress up. Hanna came in from the barn; Jim gave her the thing he had got for her in town. "Thank you," said Hanna. "What about my gun?" asked Hanna. Jim pulls out a sawed-off double-barreled shotgun with a modified grip and a box of buckshot. With a smile, Jim said, "You'd better be holding on tight when you pull the trigger on that thing." "Oh, I will," said Hanna. "I'll put a leather strap on it and hang it from my saddle horn." "Well, I'm going to go out with you for the next few weeks," said Jim, "we will start separating the momma cows from the herd and bringing them into the lot." "Ok," said Hanna, "fine with me," Matt spoke up, "I'll get the lot ready and bring up some water to fill the water troughs." "I'll give you some money, Dad, so you can make a trip to town this week to get more grain, too," said Hanna. They sat down at the table as Sara and Ezy put food on it, Matt said grace, and they filled their plates.

The next morning, Jim and Hanna left the barn and rode out to the herd. They tried separating the momma cow from the main herd, but the cows kept going back as they tried to get the others. "Well, this is not working," said Jim, "let me go get dad and the wagon, we need to build a catch pen to put them in, then we can drive a few at a time to the lot," said Jim. "Ok, I'll be around here somewhere," said Hanna. Jim rode off back to the house. Jim went inside, "Dad, we are going to need your help," "ok," said Matt, "What do you need?" "We need the wagon, some tools, and rope," "we've got to build a catch pen to hold the cows as we separate them," said Jim. "Ok," said Matt, "let's go load everything up." They picked an area with small trees from three to four inches at the base and cut them down, removed the limbs, and used them to make rails between the remaining trees. It took the remainder of the day for Jim, Matt, and Hanna to build the catch pen. Jim told Hanna, "Well, I guess we will try it again tomorrow," "ok," said Hanna.

The next morning, Jim and Hanna brought one cow at a time to the catch pen until they had ten. That afternoon, they drove those ten to the lot behind the barn. Over the next two weeks, they moved forty-eight cows to the lot that they thought were bred. Almost half the herd was now penned up for the winter, so they pushed the remaining cows up closer to the lot. Then came the snow, and all they could do now was hunker down for the winter. Hanna helped Sara work with Lizzy and the sisters with their reading and writing. Math was not a problem for Lizzy, so she taught them their math, and the sisters seemed to learn fast. On October 27, 1852, Ezy gave birth to another baby boy with Jim's help. The next morning, Jim went to the main house to let everyone know, and they started putting on their boots and coats. Except Lizzy, she was mad, "another boy," said Lizzy, "what in the world is wrong with you, Jim Evens?" "Do you not know how to make a girl?" "Dang," said Lizzy, "you've got a pattern lying there in front of you." Matt and Sara laughed, "Come on, Lizzy," said Sara, "let's go see him," "dang stupid boy baby, I swear," said Lizzy as she pulled her boots on. They waded through the snow to Jim's cabin. Once Lizzy held the baby boy, her heart melted a little. "I guess he's ok," said Lizzy, at least he looks like his momma, thank the Lourd, they named him James Stewart Evens.

The Evens family served another winter, as did most of the cows, minus two; one was killed by wolves, and another one died of natural causes or the cold. After the melt started, Hanna pushed the main herd back to the North parcel Jim had bought. They would keep the momma cows close by on the South end. Jim and Hanna made a trip to town once the wagon trail cleared so Hanna could cash in more gold. It was the first time Hanna had been to town in over a year, and buildings were popping up everywhere. Hanna, with her chaps, hat, and long coat, looked more like a boy than a girl as they went into the bank. Hanna put her gold on the counter, the banker weighed it, twenty-three hundred Dollars said the banker. "Put two thousand into Jim's account and give me the rest," said Hanna. The banker counted out the three hundred. Hanna walked out of the bank while Jim waited for his receipt. Hanna mounted her horse. Jim and the banker were talking about the price of cattle when three strange men rode up to the bank. Two of them got off their horses and went inside; the third man stayed on his horse. He looked at Hanna.

"Go on, boy, get out of here," said the man, as he rested his hand on his pistol grip. "Yes, sir," said Hanna with a deep tone. She knew what was happening as she turned her horse to ride away; she also knew Jim was still inside the bank. The two men had covered their faces as they walked inside the bank. Jim saw them out of the corner of his eyes, and got ready, and outside Hanna grabbed her shotgun and laid it across her lap. One of the men inside yellowed, "this a hold up, give me the money," as the other man turned to Jim pointing his gun and told him to get on the floor. Hanna turned around on her horse and stopped with her shotgun pointed at the man holding the horses. He went for his gun. The men inside the bank heard a big BOOM, and a sound came from outside as Hanna pulled both triggers on her shogun. The horse nickered as it fell to the ground with the man on its back. The other two horses ran off. Jim pointed his gun at the man closest to him. "Don't try it," said Jim. The banker ducked behind the counter as the man at the counter turned to Jim and raised his gun. Jim shot him in the right shoulder, and the other man dropped his gun on the floor and yelled Don't shoot.

Jim walked over and kicked the other men's gun away, then put the barrel of his gun in the man's back who was still standing and pushed him out the door. Hanna swung around and covered him with her shotgun after reloading. The Sheriff came running up to the bank, as did other townspeople. "Jim," said the Sheriff in a relieved tone, "Sheriff Hill," said Jim, "there is one more wounded man inside. The Sheriff put cuffs on the man Jim had brought out, then sent his deputy inside after the other one. The banker, Mr. Carter, came running out, thanking Jim and Hanna for stopping the bandits. "You're welcome," said Jim. Jim looked at the man and the horse on the ground, both dead, "damn, sis," said Jim with a chuckle. Hanna smiled, "I didn't mean to pull both triggers," said Hanna, "but I did," "I was nervous." Jim got on his horse, "Let's go back home," said Jim. "We will come back after things settle down in a day or two. Hanna kicked her horse, and they rode out of town. Neither Jim nor Hanna told the family what had happened that day in town; it was nothing to brag about. The next day, Hanna went back to her cows and the solitude of the range. Jim went back to town a few days later, and the Sheriff saw him ride in. Jim went into the general store. The Sheriff followed him. As Jim ordered his supplies, the Sheriff walked up to him. "Morning, Jim," said the Sheriff. "Morning," said Jim. "Come by my office before you leave town, I have something for you," said the Sheriff. Jim finished his order and then walked across the street to the Sheriff's office. "Come in, Jim," said the sheriff. "Turns out those three bank robbers were wanted in Idaho," "they robed a bank there and killed the clerk," said the Sheriff. "The one you shot in the bank had a one-hundred-dollar bounty on his head, the other two fifty dollars each." The Sheriff laid an envelope on his desk, "You keep it," said Jim, "hire a guard for the bank." "They sure need one," said the Sheriff, "I'll get with Carter about that."

In late May and early June, the cows started dropping calves; by late June, they had thirty-eight calves in the herd with their mommas. Three more were born by cows they didn't think were bred, by July, they had forty-five calves. Thirteen bull calves were cut, and the rest were heifers. They moved both groups back together after branding the calves and cutting the males. The grass was tall, and it seemed that every wolf, bear, and badger in the world knew that they had new young calves there. As Hanna stayed with the herd, Jim would find a spot to set up with his Sharps rifle on high ground, keeping the predator away. Jim crossed the river to go see Mr. Pruit on his ranch. He wanted to find out what he did to protect his herd from the predators. Jim had thought about getting some kind of herd dog to stay with the herd all the time. But he wanted to see what Mr. Pruit thought. Jim rode up to the massive ranch house, and Mr. Pruit came outside onto the porch. "Hi, Jim," said Pruit, "what can I do for you?" "Well, sir," said Jim, "tell me how to handle all these predators I'm fighting." Pruit laughed, "Donkeys," said Pruit, "Donkeys," said Jim, "Yep," said Pruit, "I have about fifty of them." "They will fight off a wolf, or bear, now the wolverine, that's a harder problem, they live in the ground." "But the winter month is the only time they might kill a cow." "For your small herd, a couple of Donkeys would do, just turn them out with the cows, they will let you know if anything comes around." Jim thanked him, then rode off back to his herd across the river.

That night, he told his father Matt what Mr. Pruit had told him and asked him to see if he could find a couple of Donkeys to buy. A week later, Matt came out to the herd leading three gray Donkeys, and they turned them out with the cows. From that day on, if anything got close, the Donkeys would start braying. If it got too close, they would all three run it off or try to. Finally, things calmed down enough for Hanna to handle it alone again with the Donkeys. Jim spent more time at home helping his father cut firewood to get ready for another winter and working on the winter lot. Late fall, Matt, Sara, Lizzy, Missy, and Sissy went to town for winter supplies. Ezy stayed home with her two boys, as did Jim. While Matt ordered supplies,

Lizzy stocked up on candy, and Sara looked through the materials. The two girls, Missy and Sissy, followed Lizzy around the store like little ducks after their mom. She got them both some boots for the winter and coats; they were outgrowing everything. Out, in the back of the store where they kept the grain, Matt saw a cage with puppies in it; they were Huskies. He asked the store owner where they came from. The man said, "Oh, one of the settlers here brought them in. They said they were full blooded Huskies; they wanted me to try and sell them." There were two of them, both males, "they would make good watchdogs around your place," said the man. "I'll take them," said Matt, "just load them into my wagon with the grain."

As they got ready to go, the girls climbed into the back of the wagon. Sissy squealed as she saw one of the pups move. Lizzy looked, "Where did these dogs come from?" "I don't know," smiled Matt, "I don't either," said Lizzy, "but they're mine now," as she grabbed them up. "No," laughed Matt, "one of them is Hanna's, the other one is yours." "Thanks, pops, I've been needing me a dog, since my cat ran away," said Lizzy. Sara looked at Matt and smiled, "You're cleaning up after that thing, Lizzy," said Sara. That night, when Hanna came in, Lizzy brought her one of the puppies, "Here, this one is yours," said Lizzy. Hanna fell in love. "Oh, you sweet little thing," said Hanna. "Dad got them for us," said Lizzy. Hanna walked over and hugged her dad, "like I told Lizzy, y'all clean up after them," said Sara, "Yes, ma'am," said Hanna. "Momma, I need a sack with handles to put him in so I can hang it on my saddle horn," said Hanna. "Ok, I'll see what I can find after supper, now go wash that dog off of your hands." The next morning, Hanna put her pup in a canvas sack, then hung it on her saddle horn. "Ok, pup, let's go to work," said Hanna. The Donkeys had become a big help, letting Hanna know when trouble was around the herd. She had time to explore and look around the countryside without having to keep her eyes on the herd all the time.

While exploring the section that had belonged to Missy and Sissy's dad, Hanna came up on one of the small creeks. Looking for a spot deep enough to fill her Cantin with water, she rode up steam to where it came up out of the ground. To her delight, there was a deeper hole about three feet wide and a foot or so deep; someone had placed stones in and around it. "Perfect," said Hanna as she climbed down off her horse. She took her Cantin and sank it in the pool of water to let it fill up. When she pulled it out, and the water cleared back up, she saw something shining at the bottom of the hole. She reached her hand into the water and came out with the shiny object, it was some kind of ornate shield, crest plate, or necklace piece. She wasn't sure, something like an Indian Chief or Medicine Man would wear hanging from their neck, she thought. It was like three to four inches top to bottom and six to eight inches wide in a curved shape with carving or writing of some kind on it. It was beautiful, and she was sure it was made of solid Gold. She reached back into the hole and brought out a handful of small rocks. She started filling around some more, but found nothing else. She took the item and put it in her saddle bag, then marked the spot so she could find it again. That night, she said nothing to anyone, as she lay in bed, wondering how the thing got there. She thought, you don't lose something that big and not find it. Someone had to be wearing it when something happened to them.

The next morning, she took a shovel and a small pick with her. After checking the cows, she wandered back off to the small creek, then followed it until she found her marker. She took the shovel and raked the leaves back away from the hole. She got on her knees with the small pick and started digging around the outside of the hole. She felt something, slowly she moved the dirt away, and she could tell it was a bone. She cleaned it off a little at a time, then she saw something else, it was a bone, alright, an arm bone, and around it was a "C" shaped object. She eased it off the bone, then washed it off in the water; it too was made of Gold with the same marking or writing on it. Ok, that's it, thought Hanna, as shivers ran down her spine, that's a body, got to go. She covered it back up, took her things, and put the item into her saddle bag. "Come on, pup, let's get out of here," said Hanna. She rode back to the herd, killing a squirrel along the way. Once back at the herd, she built a fire in a spot she normally used. She cooked the squirrel over the fire while the pup played with the squirrel's skin. Hanna had the "C" shaped piece looking at it, where could this have come from? Hanna took her knife and cut pieces off the squirrel, then ate them. She gave the small bones to the pup.

All of a sudden, Hee-Haw, Hee-Haw, sounded off one of the Donkeys, "predator alert," yelled Hanna as she grabbed her pup and threw him into his sack, and she rode to the noise. A bear had gotten too close, the Donkeys had him surrounded, Hanna rode up and shot her shotgun into the air. The bear took off running with the Donkeys chasing it, "You better run, bear," yelled Hanna with a laugh. Hanna eased back to her spot, got off her horse, and walked back to the fire. She sat down, her squirrel was gone, she looked around, the Gold "C" shaped band was gone, she jumped up, startled. Jim stepped out from behind a tree laughing, "Jim Evens, I ought to cut you," said Hanna. Jim walked over to her, eating on her squirrel, then he pulled out the gold band. "So, where did you get this?" asked Jim. Hanna snatched it out of his hand. "I found it," said Hanna. "I figured that," said Jim, "where," "Oh, that's nothing," she walked to her saddle bag and pulled out the big piece. "Holly, sh-----it," said Jim, "what is that?" "I'm not sure," said Hanna, "but it's Gold," "damn right it's gold," said Jim. "You and Lizzy are the luckiest little shits I've ever seen," "show me," said Jim.

Hanna took Jim to the spot, "there's a body here," said Hanna, tapping the ground with her toe, "I was filling my Cantin and saw something shinning in the water, it was that big piece." "Today I started digging and found an arm bone, that's where the other piece came from." "Well, let's look some more," said Jim, Hanna got her tools, Hanna uncovered the bone, then followed it up to the shoulder bones. Then she uncovered the shoulders, the shoulder was right at the edge of the hole, they worked down the arm on the other side and found another "C" shaped band. They found the rib cage, the body was face down, they worked down the legs and found two more "C" shaped band, one on each leg. "Ok, that's it I'm done," said Hanna, "this thing gives me the he-bee gee-bees." "I found it, you cover it up," said Hanna, Jim laughed, he took the shove and covered the bones up.

That night when they got home, Jim talked Hanna into taking the pieces inside for Matt to look at. She put them in the pup's sack and then carried him in her arms inside. "Dad, Hanna has something to show you," said Jim. Hanna started taking the pieces out and laying them on the table. "Oh, my God," said Matt, as he picked up one of the pieces and looked at it. "Where," "what are they," "oh, my God," said Matt, "look at this," "they're beautiful." "Hurry, put them up," said Matt, as the other girls came into the room. Hanna stuffed them back into the bag. "We don't want little girls talking," said Matt, "go put them in your room." Hanna eased out of the main room to her bedroom and hid them in a safe place. Hanna came back and sat with Jim and Matt. "I wonder how much Gold that is," asked Jim. "Oh, two or three pounds," said Matt. "But they are not just gold," said Matt, "they are historical items, they are worth way more than just gold." "They are maybe Indian, or even Spanish, they may even have come from another country," said Matt, "it's not just gold." "How could Hanna find out?" asked Jim. "I don't know," said Matt, "let me think on it." Matt had always been a big history buff and loved to read about old battles and wars.

Chapter Five: Naming The Ranch

In March 1855, the first train pulled into the new train station in Oregon City, with only four cars. The engines, one passenger car, two freight cars, and the Cabos, but to the people there, it was a wonderful sight. The train brought mail, dry goods, and farm equipment from California. It was the beginning of a whole new way of life for the frontier town. Mr. Pruit from Pruit Ranch had sent his foreman to see Jim, who was putting together a shipment of beef cattle to ship to California. Where they would be processed and shipped overseas to market elsewhere, beef was in big demand in other parts of the world. Pruit wanted to buy Jim's steers so that he could add them to his herd to meet the order. Pruit was getting fifteen dollars a head for a thousand head order; his foreman and son, Charles, offered Jim twelve dollars a head for his steers. Currently, Jim has over one hundred head of steers in his herd. Jim shook the man's hand and said, "Deal." "Ok," said the foreman, "I'll bring a crew tomorrow and round them up and pay you for the final count." "Tell, Pruit, thank you," said Jim. "Oh, I will," said Charles.

After the count, Jim got $ 1,800.00 for one hundred and fifteen head of steers; he was so excited. He had started with ten heads of cattle, got ninety-eight heads from Navada, lost some to predators and the weather. Had calves, year after year, until he had over three hundred head of cattle. Now, after four years, he has just made enough money to pay for it all. Jim rode up to Hanna, who had been helping with the roundup. He had a big smile on his face. "What is it?" asked Hanna. Jim smiled at her. "We did it, Sis," said Jim, "we are a real Ranch now." "Did we make any money?" asked Hanna, "That's what I want to know." "Yes, some," said Jim, "we got $ 1,800.00, after I pay you some back, what's left will keep things going until we can make another sale in two years." "Oh, Jim, I love brother, but you don't know anything about running a business," "How much does a ranch foreman make in a year?" asked Hanna. "Oh, maybe a hundred dollars for top pay, and a rover, sixty to eighty dollars a year," said Jim. "Give me that money," said Hanna, "we'll settle this tonight at supper."

After supper that night, Hanna told her parents that she and Jim needed to talk with them about the ranch. So, Sara and Ezy cleared the table, then sat back down. "Ok, what's up?" asked Matt. "Well, we sold our steers today," said Jim. "We got a good price, and I thought that we should use the money to pay back Hanna, Lizzy, and your dad for what y'all have paid out." "Then use what's left to operate the ranch on until we can sell more steers. Everybody went on looking at each other, "but Hanna has another idea she thinks would be better." Hanna lays the bundle of money and a notebook on the table. "Well, Jim's way would be fine for Lizzy and me, but not what's best for the ranch." "Well, tell us what you think," said Matt. "Ok, here's what I think, from a business perspective," said Hanna, "we came here to build a Ranch and a new life, right?" "That's right," said Matt, "we've done that," said Nanna, "but how can we put a price on all the work that has been done here. Jim, you and Dad worked tirelessly on building the main house and the barn." "All the lots, and your cabin, what's that worth, Dad bought supplies, so did Lizzy." "Yes, I paid for the cows, and grain, and spent the last three years with them." "How much is that worth?" "That's a number we want ever know at this point, and one that shouldn't matter." "So, here's what I think we should do," said Hanna, "treat the Ranch as a business like any other ranch." "We are all investors in this operation in one way or another, and we all have jobs to do to keep this operation growing." "So, Dad, I think you should be the Ranch manager. Does everybody agree?" They all said Yes, "Ok, Jim, you should be Ranch Foreman." Everybody said yes. "I'm the Rover, Mom, and Ezy are the cooks. If or when Lizzy or the other kids take part in the operation of the Ranch, we will give them a title." "But for now, let's all get a little to make it fair.

Hanna said, "Dad, the Ranch manager pays $ 130.00 a year times three years is $ 390.00." Hanna counts out the money and slides it to him. "Jim, Foreman pays $ 100.00 per year times three years is $ 300.00," Hanna counts out his pay and gives it to him. "Top hand Rover, me makes $ 60.00 a year times three is $ 180.00, she takes out her money. "Head cook, "mom" makes $ 40.00 a year, times three is $ 120.00," Hanna slides her one hundred and twenty dollars. "Now, for the assistant cook Ezy, $ 30.00 a year, times three is $ 90.00, that's a total of $ 1,080.00." "Which leaves $ 720.00; this money needs to be put into a Ranch account at the bank." "Dad, you and Jim need to go to town tomorrow and set up that account with both your names on it." "All the Ranch supplies, food, and anything else we need to keep this ranch going should come out of that account. If the ranch needs more, Lizzy and I will loan it to the ranch." "Now, we need to talk about a Ranch name," said Hanna. "We have a name," said Jim, "Evens Ranch." "Ok," said Hanna, "that's fine," Matt spoke up, "Now, I've been doing some reading on the history of this area, those items that you and Jim found." "They're not native Indian, they are older than that." "The writing and marking on them are Aztec or maybe even Myon, they are old, they probably were worn by a King or Priest." "So, I think we should name the ranch something like 'King's Land Ranch." "But "The Evens Ranch," "is fine with me too," "well, I like that," said Hanna, "sounds impressive kind of," "Dad, you and Jim decide that we just need a legal name for the company."

Everybody was happy with the pay they received; it was all top pay for ranch work at the time, plus the ranch had a little money to operate on for a while. Matt asked Hanna, "How did you get to be so smart?" Hanna smiled, "I had the best teacher in the world," "my momma taught me everything I know," said Hanna, "well, about numbers and reading anyway." Hanna is now eighteen and will be nineteen soon, she is no longer a child. She is tough as nails and works as hard as any man; she loves this life. Her dog Patches, who stays with her everywhere she goes, is no longer a pup either, he is a big dog and would protect her with his life. At night, he lies in front of her bedroom door as she sleeps. During the day, he never leaves her side unless predators come around, then he takes off after them. Whatever she kills for their lunch, he picks up and brings back to her; they are a team. As for Lizzy's dog, he stays in the barn most of the time with the horses. The house gets a little loud at times with all the kids. He would rather stay outside and guard the main homestead, which is a good thing, with the railroad now operating and people of all kinds coming to Oregon City. Not all with good intentions, and now there's talk of another big land grant area South of Oregon City. With the Gold Rush in California playing out, a lot of the gold miners there will come north to grab up the free land.

The next day, Matt and Jim go to town to set up the ranch account, still unsure about the name of the ranch. As they walked into the bank, Matt looked at Jim, and at the same time, they both said, "Kings Land." They had taken the wagon so they could get supplies while in town. The streets were busy, as were the stores. The Sheriff came up to Jim in front of the general store, "Hi, Jim," said the Sheriff, "morning, Sheriff," said Jim. "Jim, I thought you should know, there's a man in town who came here from California on the train." "Talk is, he's looking for a girl who wheels a sawed-off shotgun, says she killed his brother." "Well, she did that," said Jim, "if his brother was one of the bank robbers." "Where's he at?" "Now, now, Jim, just calm down." "I'll keep an eye on him while he's here in town, just thought you should know," said the Sheriff. "Just tell Hanna to stay out of town for a few days," Jim said, looking at the Sheriff. "Well, you know, Sheriff, when a predator stalks our herd, we run them off or kill them," said Jim. "Where's he at?" asked Jim again in a demanding tone. The sheriff pointed to the Salon. "This is your lucky day, Sheriff; my dad and I are going to buy you a drink." "Come show me," said Jim. "What's going on?" asked Matt. "I'll explain later," said Jim. The three men walked over to the Salon and followed the Sheriff inside. Then walked up to the bar, "Barkeep, get my dad and the Sheriff a beer," said Jim, as he put down two coins. "What about you?" asked the barkeeper. "You got a soda pop?" asked Jim. "Nope," said the bartender. "Which one is he?" Jim asked the Sheriff. The Sheriff pointed to a man at the corner table.

Jim walked over to the man's table, "I hear you're looking for the girl who killed one of the bank robbers who came through here three years ago." "That's right," said the man, in a gruff tone, "why," asked Jim, "because he was my brother and she killed him and his horse," said the man in a mad tone. "Jim smiled, "Well, Sir, that's what happens when a fifteen-year-old girl gets pulled on by an outlaw around here, he dies." "She didn't do it because she wanted to; she didn't have any choice," said Jim. "That was three years ago. What took you so long?" "Will, I just got out of jail," said the man. "Looking to go back or die, are you?" said Jim, "Look, I'm sorry about your brother, "but he gave my sister no choice." "Now you have a choice, you can get on a horse or the train and ride out of town and don't ever come back." "Or you can pull on me, I'm her brother," "and my sister is worth ten of your brothers." "The man stood up from the table, he was wearing a fancy two-gun rig around his waist," "your choice," said Jim. Nice rig," said Jim, "but do you really think you're that fast?" The man pulled his coat back and put his hands on his guns. Jim drew his gun in the blink of an eye, looked at the man, and said Bang." "You want to try it again, Mr.," said Jim, as he put his gun back into his holster. "No, I'm leaving," said the man. "But I can't believe my brother pulled on a fifteen-year-old girl," "Well, if it makes you feel any better, he thought she was a boy," said Jim. "I'll leave on the afternoon train," said the man, I swear." "Well, the Sheriff will make sure you do," said Jim. The man walked out of the Salon. The Sheriff looked at Matt, "damn that boy of yours is fast with his gun," "so they say," said Matt. "Sheriff, you make sure that man leaves on the train," "Oh, I will," said the Sheriff.

Matt and Jim got their supplies from town and headed back to the ranch; Jim stopped every so often to make sure nobody was following them. Matt asked Jim, "Why haven't you told me about the Bank being robbed?" "It wasn't robbed," said Jim, "I was inside the bank when the robbers came in, Hanna was outside on her horse waiting, "their lookout man told Hanna to get." "She wasn't leaving with me in there with the other two." "So, she acted like she was leaving and got her shotgun ready." "When she came back up, he pulled on her; she was ready and shot first," said Jim. "When I heard her shoot, I shot one of the men inside, and the other one gave up." "Did she really kill the man's horse?" asked Matt. Jim laughed, "Well, when you pull both triggers on a sawed-off shotgun loaded with buckshot at close range, everything in front of it dies," said Jim. Matt and Jim both laughed out loud as they rode back to the ranch. Matt and Jim didn't say anything to Hanna or the family; Jim knew Hanna was always on the lookout anyway. Again, Jim and Hanna pushed the momma cow up to the winter lot behind the barn, winter was coming soon. Jim's oldest boy was three years old now, and the youngest was almost two years old. Lizzy told Ezy, "It's about time you had me a girl baby now." "Oh, lord," said Ezy, "we've got more kids running around here now than we can keep up with." "When are you going to find you a man?" asked Ezy. "I'm only fifteen, I don't need or want any man," said Lizzy, "will we know Hanna not going to find one. Always out there with those cows all the time," said Ezy.

Little did anyone know, other than Jim, that Mr. Pruit's son Carl had been crossing the river once a week to bring back the Evens' strays that had crossed the river onto their land. Then he would drive back any Pruit cows that had done the same. Carl and Hanna would spend time talking and having lunch together; they had become good friends. Carl was a good-looking young man with red hair, tall and slim, but they were just friends at that point. Carl was a year older than Hanna and had left the ranch that fall to go to school in California, but he said he would be back next summer. Just before the first snow, Hanna killed a big Bull Elk and dragged it up to the main house for Jim and Matt to dress out. That would last them through the winter, with the deer and pronghorn she had already killed. The long winter months went slowly by, as they looked forward to the spring and warmer weather. Patches and Hanna would go out in the mornings to check on the momma cows in the lot, but they spent the rest of the day inside the main house. Jim would clean out the stalls in the barn every morning and feed the stock. Sometimes he and Hanna would sit in the tack room by the wood-burning heater after their chores and talk. They had a lot in common: the same work ethic, the same determination, and they shared the same dream: to help their family build a future.

Jim looked at Hanna's boots, as she sat there with her socked feet by the heater. "Looks like you need some more boots," said Jim. "No, I just got these broken in good," said Hanna. Jim laughed, "They broke alright, the leather is breaking open on the sides." Hanna picked one of the boots up, "Maybe that's why my feet get wet," said Hanna. They both laughed, "Oh, well, I'll get more in the spring, you might have to loan me some money though, brother." "I'm just a poor old Rover," said Hanna. Jim chuckled, "Maybe Lizzy will loan you some." "How much Gold do you and Lizzy have anyway?" asked Jim. "Oh, enough for me to buy me some more boots, I'm sure," said Hanna with a smile. "You could always sell one of those Gold bracelets," said Jim. "No, that stuff needs to be in a museum somewhere," said Hanna. "I took paper and pencil and made a copy of the writing on them." "One day I'll mail the copies to a college or Museum somewhere and find out more about them," said Hanna. Jim slipped his boots back on, "Well, I'm going to play with my boys for a while, see you tonight at supper." "Ok," said Hanna, as she put her boots on, "come on, Patches."

Spring finally came, Hanna pushed the main herd back out to pasture, and new grass was popping up everywhere. Jim and Matt went into town for supplies. The long winter had depleted their stock of dry goods. They took Sara, Lizzy, and the girls along. Jim pulled up in front of the General Store on the wagon. The land clerk saw Jim pull up down the street; he sticks his head out of his office door. "Jim," ... yelled the Clerk. Jim turns to look, "over here," said the man, "come see me before you leave." Jim told Matt, "Y'all go ahead, let me see what he wants." "Ok, son," said Matt. Jim goes into the Land office, "I got something you might be interested in," said the Clerk. He folds out a map, "This section right here that connects to your father's Homestead is for sale," said the Clerk. "I rode out and looked at it the other day," "It's a nice place," said the Clerk. "It has a nice house and barn on it; they even dug a well there. It's not a cabin." "They are German, they know how to build a house," said the Clerk. "The man lost his wife last winter, so he and his son want to move to California to start their own business building houses there." "I don't know what he's asking, but you need to go see him," "his name is Mr. Urick, a nice man," said the Clerk, "I will," said Jim, "thanks." Jim walked to the general store and found his dad; he told Matt about the land for sale. "Take my horse," said Matt, "go see what he wants for it, I'll bring the wagon back to the ranch."

Jim took his father's horse and rode out to Urick's place; he rode up a long wagon trail off the main trail. The Urick's, unlike the Evens, had built their house away from the river up on a hill; it was like a picture in a book. A house with a white picket fence around it, the house was built out of cut boards, with wooden shingles on the roof. It had a porch that wrapped all the way around it, the house was painted white, with a red barn out beside it. It was the kind of house you would see in a big city, not in the small town of Oregon City. Jim rode up to the front of the house and tied his horse. A younger man, a little odder than Jim, came out of the barn. "Is this the Urick place?" asked Jim. "Yes, sir," said the young man. "I hear you want to sell this place, although I can't believe it," said Jim, "it's beautiful." The young man smiled, "I know, it seems out of place," said the man, "but my father and I are carpenters," "we tried farming, but it's just not what we're good at." "Come on up to the porch, I'll get my father," said the young man, with a strange accent. Jim looked as he waited. The grass inside the fence was cut, and everything was so neat and clean. The rails on the porch were hand-carved, and there were windows all around the house with lace curtains inside. He thought to himself, Ezy would love this place, but I'm sure it's more than I can afford. The young man returned with his father. Jim stuck out his hand, "Mr. Urick, my name is Jim Evens, we own the land next to you." The man took Jim's hand and shook it," Nice to meet you, son," said Mr. Urick. "Well, like I told your son, I heard in town you were thinking about selling out," said Jim. "We are," said the man, "so how much are you asking?" asked Jim. "Well, that depends," said the man, "are you married, son?" "Yes, sir, I am. I have two boys, one two years old and one almost four, and two girls I'm raising," said Jim. My father and mother own the place next door to you; we live on the other side of them in a small cabin now." "Well, go get your wife and sons and come back, and bring those two girls you saved," said Mr. Urick with a smile. "Oh, you know about that," said Jim. "Son, it's a small town," said Mr. Urick. "Go get your family and come back, and we will talk about a price then."

Jim got on his dad's horse and rode back to the main house; Matt and the girls were back from town. "Well, how much?" asked Matt. "I don't know yet," said Jim. "he wants me to bring Ezy and the boys back, and Missy and Sissy," said Jim. "Oh, ok," said Matt, "help me unload the wagon, then you can take it." After unloading the wagon, Jim loaded up Missy and Sissy, then went to his cabin to get Ezy and the boys. "Why does he want to see us?" asked Ezy. "I don't know, baby, but you've got to see this place; it's beautiful." After everyone was loaded up, Jim drove the wagon to Urick's place. As they came up the drive, Ezy saw the house. "Oh, my God," said Ezy, as they pulled up to the front. "I've seen this house before," said Ezy. "When asked Jim, in a dream, when I was alone in the woods before you found me." Tears came to her eyes, Jim got down, and helped the kids down, then helped Ezy down. Ezy stood there in awe, she thought there was only such a place as this in her dreams. Mr. Urick came out onto the porch with a big smile on his face. "Well, please, come on in and look around, Miss Evens," said Mr. Urick. As they walked to the door, Ezy made the kids take off their shoes as she did the same. Jim wiped his boot off on the mat, then they walked inside.

The walls were all painted or papered, stairs led up to more bedrooms, and the kitchen was huge with a big dining table. The main living room was open with windows looking out over the porch. Ezy took a deep breath; the furniture was hand-built and carved out of wood, with cloth covering the chairs. "It's wonderful," said Ezy. "Would you like to live here?" asked Mr. Urick. "Oh, yes," said Ezy, "I'd love it here." "Do you think you could keep it clean?" asked Urick. "Oh, yes, sir," said Ezy. "Well, you go look upstairs while I talk to Jim," Ezy and the kids climbed the stairs. "Well, son, I think she likes it," said Urick. "Yes, sir," said Jim, "I think so too." "Well, here's the deal," said Urick, "I know not many people around here have the money to pay what this place is worth." "It's not so much about the money as it is about somebody who will take care of the place. This was my wife's dream house; she's gone now," said Urick. "My son and I are not good at farming; we are builders, that's what we're good at. We built most of the buildings in this town," said Urick. "We want to move to California and help build the towns there." "There is a lot of building going on in California, since the gold was found." "I can't just give this place away to you, Son. "But I can make you a deal," "One thousand dollars cash and three hundred dollars a year for five years," said Mr. Urick. "Can you do that?" asked Potter. "I think so," said Jim. "Well, meet me at the bank tomorrow around ten a.m." Jim shook Potter's hand and told him Thank you. Ezy and the girls came back down the stairs. "You should go look," said Ezy. "I'll see it later," said Jim. They went back to the wagon, climbed in, and drove off back to the homestead. "Will, what did he say?" asked Ezy. "He said he wanted you and the kids to have that house, and so do I." "But I've got to figure out how to pay for it first." Ezy smiled. She thought what a dream come true that would be.

That night, Jim told Hanna that he would give her his cabin if she would loan him some money. "For what?" asked Hanna. "I don't need your cabin," Jim told her about the house and the added land that the Urick's had for sale. "I have the thousand dollars," said Jim. "How are you going to come up with three hundred dollars a year?" asked Hanna. "You don't make that much money." "I don't know," said Jim. "But I really want this place for Ezy and the kids." Hanna thought about it for a while, then looked at Jim. "Ok, here's what we can do if dad agrees," said Hanna. "I'll put up the money to buy the new place outright, no notes, no yearly payments." "We will have papers drawn up combining all the properties and livestock together as one, your land, dad's land, and the new place all as part of The King's Land Ranch." "The owners will be Dad, You, Me, and Lizzy," "a Corporation Under the King's Land Ranch name that includes all assets. Agreed," asked Hanna. Jim thought a minute, so the four of us would own part of everything," Yes, equal partners," said Hanna. "You talk to dad about it," "if he agrees, then you can get your new house." "Thank you, sis," said Jim, as he went looking for his dad. Jim told his father the plan and about the place and Hanna's Idea. Matt chuckled, "That Hanna, she's a smart young woman," "ok," said Matt.

The next morning, Jim, Hanna, Lizzy, and Matt took the wagon to town. They got to the bank about nine a.m., when it opened. Hanna put a small bag of gold on the counter. "I need to deposit twenty-five hundred into the King's Land Ranch account," said Hanna. "Sure thing," said the banker. "Wait said Lizzy, did you not buy the cows?" "Well, yes," said Hanna, "well, it's my turn then," said Lizzy as she put a bag on the counter. "Mr. Carter," said Lizzy, "weigh this gold for me." "Ok, that's $ 4,835.00," said the banker. "Now put $ 2,500.00 in the ranch account, just give me the change," said Lizzy. The banker counted out $ 2,335.00 to Lizzy. Hanna took her bag of gold back. Jim stepped up to the counter, "I need to get a $ 2,500.00 cashier's check made out to Mr. Urick out of the Ranch account," said Jim. The banker made out the check, then had Jim sign it. "You're not done yet," said Lizzy, as she put money on the counter. "Put this five hundred into my dad's account said Lizzy. She took out the $ 335.00 and handed the rest to her dad. "Hold this for me until we get home," said Lizzy. "Yes, ma'am," said Matt. The banker laughed, "y'all have a nice day, see you next time, Ms. Evens," said the Banker.

Jim stayed in front of the bank waiting for Mr. Urick while Matt, Hanna, and Lizzy went to the Land Office. Hanna told the land Clerk what they wanted to do by transferring all the properties into the name of King's Land Ranch. The land clerk, who was also the town Lawyer, started writing up the papers while they waited on Jim. Mr. Urick and his son came to the bank. They all went inside. Jim said,

"I was able to come up with all the money if that's ok." "Sure," said Mr. Urick. Jim handed him the check. Mr. Urick handed it to the banker, "I need to cash that, please." "I also need to close out my account," said Mr. Urick. He signed the title of the land over to Jim and handed it to him. "You can pick up your horse and buggy at the train station tomorrow after 2:00 p.m.," said Mr. Urick. "Me and my son are catching the 2 o'clock train to California," "my buggy," said Jim. Mr. Urick smiled, "Yes, son, all we are taking with us are our clothes and our tools; you bought the rest." Jim's eyes got big. "Good luck, Jim, enjoy the house," said Urick. I know your family will. Jim's hands were shaking as he shook Urick's son's hand. "Good luck to you, too, and thank you so much," said Jim. "God bless you," said Urick. "Oh, he does, every day," said Urick.

Jim went to the land office. He handed the clerk the deed. "Come back after lunch, I'll have these ready to sign," said the clerk. "Yes, sir, said Jim." The Evens went to the general store, and Hanna got herself some new boots. Lizzy picked up more candy, more jeans and shirts, and a small barrel of pickles. Jim got ammo, Matt got tobacco and coffee. They put their things into the wagon and went to the cafe to eat lunch. The Sheriff came in, Jim asked him to sit at their table with them, "How's it going, Sheriff?" asked Matt. "Will, it's going, there are more people to keep an eye on now than ever before." "Looks like it," said Jim, "I see you have a guard at the bank now." "Yep," said the Sheriff, "I need more deputies too, but the county is not going to pay for it, and the city is no help." "What are y'all doing in town today?" asked the Sheriff. "We just bought the Urick place," said Jim. "Really, I heard he was living, he helped build this town, a good man," said the Sheriff, "he sure is," said Jim. They all ate their lunch, and Matt paid for everyone's meal. "Thanks for lunch," said the Sheriff. "Anytime," said Matt. "Hey, Sheriff, Jim is going to be living on the edge of town now, don't you think he should be on the City Council?" "That's a great idea," said the Sheriff, "let me find out about that," "I'll let you know." They all walked back to the land office, "ok, everybody, sign by your name," said the Clerk. "Jim, you sign here and then you and Hanna sign here," "Matt, you sign here and you and Lizzy sign here." "The girls had to have an executor until they were twenty-one; they all signed, then he stamped the papers and gave them a copy. "That will be twenty-five dollars," said the Clerk. Hanna pulled out her money and paid him.

Jim was so excited; he couldn't wait to get home and tell Ezy as they loaded into the wagon and headed home. Once they got home, Jim took off running to his cabin to tell Ezy the news. "Well, I've got to go check my cows," said Hanna, "see y'all tonight." "Lizzy," said, "I'm so full I need a nap." Matt just laughed as he followed her inside the house. The next morning, Ezy started packing all their clothes and things into the wagon, getting ready to move to their new house that afternoon. Jim rode his horse into town to get the buggy. He tied his horse to the back of the buggy and drove it home. Jim put up his horse, then took the buggy to the cabin. The wagon was all loaded up. "Well, Ezy, you finally got your own horse," said Jim, pointing at the buggy. Ezy smiled. Jim drove the wagon, and Ezy drove the buggy with the two boys. They went to their new house. Ezy stopped in front of it and just stared; tears came to her eyes. She never thought she would ever have a house like this, not in a million years. Finally, she said, "Come on, boys, let's go see our new home," as Ezy looked on the inside, Jim went to the barn. Everything was there: feed, buckets, rope, tack. There was another horse in one of the stalls, a milk cow, three goats, and a pen full of chickens. Jim then went to the house, where there was a water well just off the back porch and an outhouse. A small garden spot, with vegetables still in it, a smoke house, "wow," thought Jim. He went inside. Ezy was standing in the kitchen holding a plate with tears in her eyes. "Look Jim," "China," said Ezy, "real China," then she opened a drawer, "Silver Jim, real Silver, Jim walked over and hugged her. "This place is a gift from God," said Ezy, "I know it is Ezy," "I know," said Jim as tears filled his eyes."

That night, as they lay in the softest bed they had ever felt, Ezy said, "You know, we had Missy and Sissy stay with your mom and dad because we had no room for them." "I know," said Jim. "We have room for them now," said Ezy. Jim kissed her lips. "We will go get them tomorrow," said Jim, "I promise," "thank you, Jim, "I love you so much," said Ezy. The next morning, they went after the girls. They asked Sara and Matt if they could take the girls to live with them." "Sure, honey," said Sara, "they've always been your girls." They made plans for everyone to come to their new house for supper that night, so they could see it. Jim rode out to find Hanna and tell her she was riding through the herd, counting cows, making sure none were missing when Jim rode up. He told her about the supper plans, as he turned to ride off, he said, "By the way, I heard in town yesterday that Carl would be home next week." Hanna smiled big, "So you might want to push a few of our cows across the river," said Jim with a laugh, then he rode off. That made Hanna's day; she was smiling and happy to know Carl was coming home.

That night, Ezy had fixed a huge meal for the family, and Jim had dressed a couple of chickens for her to cook. She had fried up both chickens, made mashed potatoes, gravy, biscuits, carrots from their garden, and some peas, also from her new garden. Jim said grace as all ten of them sat around the big table. It was a Thanksgiving meal in late May for the Evens family; they had plenty to be thankful for. After that night, the routine was the same as before, except that Sara only had to cook breakfast for Mitt, Lizzy, Hanna, and herself. Ezy cooked for Jim, herself, and the four kids. Midafternoon, Ezy loaded the kids into the buggy and then drove them to Matt's and Sara's house each afternoon so she could help with supper. After supper, Jim would lead them home in the dark; it wasn't that far, and Jim would carry a lantern. Summer always brought rainstorms in from time to time, but the rain didn't change things much. Hanna still rode through her cows, Patches was still right there with her, and predators still came around looking for something to eat. Hanna had built makeshift sheds in different areas where she and Patches could escape the rain and dry out a little at lunch. But then it was back to checking the herd. Hanna didn't mind the rain; it was the lightning that bothered her the most. Being in the middle of a herd of wet cows was not a safe place to be in a lightning storm. So, she and Patches would move away from the herd, but stay close enough to watch over them.

The next week, as Hanna was watching the herd, she saw a horse and rider coming her way, and she laid her shotgun across her lap. Once he got closer, she could see that it was Carl, and her heart skipped a beat for a second. Carl raised his arm up to let her know it was him; she hung her gun back on the saddle horn as he rode up. "Hello, stranger," said Hanna, "howdy ma'am," said Carl, trying to be funny. "What, no strays?" asked Hanna. "I didn't even look," said Carl. Hanna wanted to jump on him from her horse and take him to the ground. "So, are you just out riding or what?" asked Hanna. "No, just out hunting," said Carl. He rode up close beside her on his horse, "hunting for what?" asked Hanna, her heart beating faster. "Pretty girls," said Carl with a smile. "Have you had any luck?" asked Hanna. "Yep, just found one," said Carl as he leaned in and kissed Hanna's lips. Hanna threw her arms around him as they fell to the ground and started rolling in the grass. Carl kissed her again. Hanna was on fire, but then pushed him away. "I'm not one of those preppy college girls who can take advantage of," said Hanna. Carl smiled. "Lord, I hope not," "I like real girls, the kind that ride horses, and work cattle, do you know where any of them are?" Hanna pinned him to the ground and kissed him long and hard. "Oh, God, I missed you," said Hanna. As she lay her head on his chest, it was the first time she had been kissed by a boy and the first time she kissed one back. Her mind was still trying to process the feelings she was having in her body. “So, you missed me then,” said Carl. Hanna blushed, “Yes,” said Hanna in a low voice. But then she said in a stern voice, “Don’t you go thinking you're going to get me out of my britches, though.” Carl laughed as he stood up, then pulled her up from the ground, wrapping his arms around her, pulling her close, looking into her eyes. He leaned in and kissed her again, sliding his hands down and cupping her small butt, then pulling her even closer. “Are you sure?” asked Carl in a low tone. “No,” said Hanna, “but please don’t, not yet.” Carl smiled at her and slowly released his grip on her, then kissed her forehead. “Can I come see you tomorrow?” asked Carl. “Yes, please do,” said Hanna, and bring my cows.

The rest of the day was a blur for Hanna; that night, she relived Carl’s visit that day with anticipation of seeing him again. Jim and Matt were working on enlarging the pin behind the barn by extending it over onto the new land Jim’s house was on. Jim also wants to cut a road from Matt’s house to his new house through a wooded area, which would be closer. Just so that when the kids got older, they could ride or walk to their grandparents without taking the main trail. Lizzy has been offered a job at the new schoolhouse in town as an assistant. The teacher once she turns seventeen. With more people moving to the area, the school is already outgrowing the building. Plans to add to the existing building are already underway, and construction will begin soon. Missy and Sissy are taking turns riding the horse that was left on the farm, sometimes they ride together. Ezy plans to put the two girls in school once Lizzy starts teaching there in the fall.

The next day, as Hanna rode through the herd expecting Carl to show up at any time, she heard gunfire from across the river. At first, it seemed to be far off. As she moved away from the herd, so she could hear better, she could tell it was getting closer. She yelled, “Come on, Patches,” as she rode straight to the sound. She could tell it was just on the other side of the river and coming her way. She found cover and tied up her horse, pulled out her sharp rifle, and hid in the trees near the riverbank. Back at the house, Jim and Matt heard the shooting too. Jim yelled, "Hanna," as he ran for his horse, climbed on it, and rode down the river trail. Matt ran to the barn, saddled his horse, and took off a few minutes behind Jim. Meanwhile, Hanna waited, knowing that whoever they were, they were headed to the river. Jim came riding up to the patch of trees. He saw Hanna's white horse tied up, and he tied his horse, then yelled, "Hanna." "Over here," yelled Hanna. Jim ran into the trees with his sharp rifle. "Who is it?" asked Jim. "I don't know," said Hanna, "but they're coming this way fast." Jim and Hanna both got ready. The riders came over a hill across the river, "that's Carl in the lead," said Hanna. Behind him, about thirty yards, were four riders chasing him. He was turning around and shooting at them, and they were shooting back at him. "Take the two closest to him, I'll get the two in the back," said Jim. Hanna and Jim shot at the same time, two men fell, they shot again, the other two fell, and Carl made it to the river. He and his horse started across, "over here," yelled Hanna, Carl, fill from his horse into the river." "Go get him, Patches," said Hanna. The dog took off, grabbed Carl by the neck of his vest, and dragged him out of the river. Jim helped him up and grabbed the reins on Carl's horse, pulling them both to the trees to Hanna. "There's more coming," said Carl, out of breath, as he held his left arm. "Let me see," said Jim, as he tore Carl's sleeve open, "just a flesh wound," said Jim, "you're ok." "Who are they?" asked Jim. "I don't know," said Carl. "Rustler, I think," said Carl. There's about twelve of them, said Carl, "they were pushing about forty head up the river when I came across them." "They started shooting at me as soon as they saw me," said Carl, "then came after me." Matt made it to them, tied his horse, and came into the trees. "What up?" asked Matt. "Rustlers," said Jim. "They chased Carl to the river," he says there's more." Two more men rode up to where the other four had fallen, "Carl, do you know those men?" asked Jim. "Nope," said Carl. "Hanna, you take the one on the right. They both raised their guns and shot; the two men fell off their horses. "Damn," said Carl, "you Evens don't fool around, do you?" "Nope," said Hanna as she reloaded her gun. They heard more shooting in the distance, "sounds like my dad's crew found the rest of them," said Carl. The shooting stopped, they all stood up, "Hold on," said Matt, let's see who shows up. About that time, a group of men rode up to where the six rustlers lay, "That's my dad," said Carl, excited. They all walked out of the trees, leading their horses. Mr. Pruit rode up to the edge of the river on the other side, "See, you found my boy," said Pruit. "More like he found us," said Jim, "glad he did," said Pruit, "can he ride?" "Yep," said Jim, "send him home," said Pruit.

Carl turned to Hanna, and she smiled at him, "Will you meet me in town on Friday at the Café for lunch?" asked Carl. Hanna turned and looked at her father. "Oh, I'm sorry," said Carl. "Mr. Evens, can I take your daughter to lunch on Friday?" Matt nodded his head, "guess I'll see you Friday then," said Carl looking at Hanna. Hanna's face was red. "ok," said Hanna, "see you Friday." Carl got on his horse and rode back across the river, "Come on, Patches, we got work to do," said Hanna. "Oh, and thanks, Dad, Jim, for checking on me. We're good now," said Hanna with a big smile. As Jim and Matt rode back to the house, Jim said, "Dad," "I know, son," said Matt. The men went back to working on the lot like nothing had happened, just another day on the ranch. Hanna, on the other hand, was now full of anticipation, a date, a real date, this would be another first for her. Matt could tell Hanna and Carl were more than just friends now, just like he could see with Jim and Ezy. But he knew it wouldn't do any good to worry about it, Hanna was a smart girl. That Friday, Jim took Hanna's place with the cows, so she could go into town. Hanna wore jeans and a shirt, no chapes, no hat, her mother had braided her long hair and put a bow in it. She rode her horse into town with

Patches beside her. Carl was already there; she tied her horse to the hitching rail beside his. As she got to the door, she said, "Patches, stay." he lay down by the door as she walked inside. Carl saw her as she walked in. She was so pretty, he thought to himself. He stood up and pulled out her chair as she sat down. Carl sat across from her, staring at her, "What," asked Hanna, "do I have mud on my face?" Carl smiled, "No, you're just so pretty." "I can't help it," "Well, try," said Hanna, "you're making my face turn red."

They ordered the special "beef stew," they ate and talked, and they laughed a little. Carl was a gentleman the whole time; he made her feel special, and he was very attentive to her. They carried on talking for over an hour, for someone who spoke very little, most of the time Hanna talked and talked. Carl heard every word. They talked about themselves and their family, their likes and dislikes. Hanna asked Carl what college was like, and about the girls there. He said, "I don't talk to girls much," "we don't have girls at my school," "they have their own college." "I mean, I see girls around off campus, in town, but I don't know any of them." "I don't even know many guys there, other than my roommate, and he's strange, he's from New Hampshire or some place." "I haven't met any other Ranchers' sons there, mostly Bankers' and lawyers' sons, or businessmen's sons." "I'm just there to get a degree in business management and agriculture development, my father's idea, but his right." "If we don't do something to refurbish these lands, we will deplete the grasslands." "So, I'm trying to learn new ways to help my family and others with that." They ordered dessert, "Can I ask you something?" said Carl. "Sure," said Hanna. "How in the world did you learn to shoot a rifle like you did the other day?" asked Carl. "Jim," said Hanna, "on the way here from Kentucky," "I was kidnapped by Indians when I was thirteen, two other girls and me." "Oh, no," said Carl, "but Jim came and got us," said Hanna, "how?" asked Carl. "Well, my dad says Jim could track a flea across a bog's back when he was just a little boy," said Hanna. “What did he do when he found you?” asked Carl. “He killed the Indians, then more Indians came as we were running away on horseback,” said Hanna. “My big white horse was an Indian horse, the only one that didn’t run away.” “One of the other girls and I were on him, and Jim had one of the girls behind him on his horse.” “When the Indian got close, Jim got off his horse and made the girl ride on without him following me,” said Hanna. A tear formed in the corner of her eye, “How did Jim get away?” asked Carl. “He killed them all,” said Hanna. “He took one of the Indian’s knives and brought it to me. He told me to wear it and never take it off, as a reminder of what could have happened.” “Jim taught me how to use it, he taught me how to shoot a gun, and how to shoot a bow, so I could always protect myself,” said Hanna. “Did it bother you to kill those men the other day?” asked Carl. Hanna looked him dead in the eyes, with no smile, and no emotion, “they were predators,” said Hanna, “there’s only two ways to deal with a predator, run it off or kill it.”

Chapter Six: The Good Shepherd

Carl left on the first of August, going back to college, as Hanna and Jim were moving the herd closer to the main homestead. Their Hurd now numbered four hundred and ninety-two heads. Each year, they were dropping more and more calves on the ground, the predator in the area had been thinned out by the donkeys, and the help of Hanna and Patches. Hanna was sad to see Carl go back to school, but she understood his goal and told him that she would be waiting for him next summer. Lizzy and Matt had set up the slouch box they built last fall near the river's edge at the curve. The river was low now, but the hole in the curve was still three to four feet deep. Lizzy was in the hole with a bucket, dipping up sand, water, and rocks. Matt had a rope tied to the bucket handle. He pulled the bucket up on the bank and poured it into the slouch box, then slowly washed the sand out. They dug in that hole for two weeks until it was time for school to start. Lizzy had to start teaching at the school in town again, so the gold rush was over for now. Matt put all the gear up in the barn and hid a coffee can full of gold under a floorboard in the tack room. Missy and Sissy were attending school now, too, although Lizzy had no formal training to teach after years of being taught by Sara and helping to teach Missy and Sissy at home. She had the natural knack of working with kids, and at seventeen, she was no longer a bossy little girl. She had the ability to take children who spoke very little or no English and work with them until they did. Almost all the kids loved Lizzy; she had a tender heart and soul. Working with the kids made her happy, Sara and Matt could tell because she was always smiling.

Jim and Hanna had talked about hiring some help to work around the main house to help Matt with the day-to-day tasks. On the south ends of town, there was a group of small shacks and tents left over from the railroad crews after the track was finished. They had been taken over by people who had traveled there and missed out on the last of the land grants. They had spent everything they had to get there and had no means to travel anywhere else. Most of them had sold off their belongings to serve; for many of them, that was all they were doing: serving. Some worked in town at the Hotel and the café; some worked in the stock yard. But most did odd jobs for others when they could. Hanna went into the camp looking for a couple willing to work, for room and board. She talked to some of the people there, telling them what she was looking for. She talked to a German Lady whose husband worked in the stock yard for very little money, and she cleaned houses when she could. Hanna told her she would furnish them a cabin to live in on the ranch and pay them five dollars a month, two dollars and fifty cents each, plus furnish them food to eat. The ladies said she would tell her husband and let her know. The next morning, the couple was there at the main house with their belongings when Hanna came outside. She took them to the cabin and opened it up, "This is where you will stay, my brother Jim will bring you supplies." "He will tell you what needs to be done around here. Hanna got her horse and rode away.

Jim took the man to the barn and got him started cleaning up the barn, then took the woman inside the house to meet Sara. "Mom, this is the Lady Hanna hired to help you with the housework." "She and her husband are going to stay in my cabin; they will need some food supplies until I can go to town." "Ok," said Sara, "I'll take care of her." The lady smiled. Sara sat down at the table. "Now tell me about yourself," said Sara, "where are you from?" The lady told Sara how she and her husband traveled there with hopes of getting their own land to farm. But by the time they got here, the land was taken by others. How could they have moved to another part of Oregon, where there was still land, but they had no money left? They sold their horse and then the wagon to buy food, until her husband got a job working at the stock yard a couple of days a week, how she cleaned the banker's house one day a week, and cooked for the café on Friday nights. They had two young children, a boy and a girl, but lost their son on the way there. The girl is ten years old, and her son was way over fifteen when he died. After losing him, then getting here and there, with no land to get, they had lost hope. But now they were trying to recover from it all and make a new life. Sara put food in a wooden crate. "What's your name, dear?" asked Sara. "Reeha," said the lady. "Well, Reeha, take this food to your cabin, straighten it up, and make it a home for your family." "Come back tomorrow morning after you feed your family breakfast, and I will show you what to do." With tears in her eyes, Reeha gave Sara a huge hug and said, "Thank you."

Jim had found out the man's name was Paul-something he couldn't pronounce, and they still didn't know the little girl's name until Lizzy came home and told them it was Hidee. Lizzy had brought the little girl to the cabin from school when Paul came back to the cabin. Reeha had their supper cooked, and the cabin was clean and straightened up. As they sat there and ate, Paul said, "I think these are good people," "I think so too," said Reeha, "I believe God has blessed us." For the next few weeks after morning chores, Paul helped Matt and Jim cut firewood for the winter. Now there would be three houses to keep warm, plus the tack room in the barn. Reeha knew Hanna, but Paul had only seen her once, the day they came there. Hanna came in after dark and left before sunrise every day. Everyone in the family talked about her, but to them, she was elusive and never around. Until just before the first snow, when Hanna and Jim started bringing in the momma cows into the lot. Paul was working in the barn when he heard cows bawling. He walked outside and saw her and Patches pushing the cows into the lot. She was covered in leather from head to toe; all he could see were her eyes. She turned her head and nodded at him as she rode by him.

That night, as Paul, Reeha, and Hidee were eating supper, Paul said, "I saw her today." "Who?" asked Reeha. "The good shepherd, Hanna," said Paul, "she smiled at me with her eyes." "Why do you call her that?" asked Hidee. "She watches over the flock and cares for the people," said Paul. Working in the stock yard, Paul had heard all the stories about Hanna, and how she killed the bank robber, protected her herd from predators, and saved Carl Pruit from the rustlers. Everybody in town knew about Hanna and her brother Jim, and their exploits. Paul said, they say the big white horse she rides belonged to an Indian Chief who she killed with his own knife, and she still wears it on her side. The next morning, Lizzy came and picked up Hidee for school, then they went to Jim's house to get Missy and Sissy. Ezy was letting her use her buggy to haul the kids to and from school. After Jim and Hanna had all the cows moved up near the barn, Hanna rode to town. She took the wagon to get supplies and more grain for the cows and horses. Lizzy had told Hanna that some of the kids at her school had no winter boots or coats to wear, which was a month ago. Hanna had ordered boots of all sizes and coats for the kids, and they had just been delivered to the general store. Hanna loaded the two boxes on top of everything else she had bought and drove to the school. Hanna told Patches to stay with the wagon, as she carried the boxes in one at a time. "What is this?" asked Lizzy. "These are early Christmas gifts for the kids," said Hanna. She tore open one of the boxes and started handing out pairs of boots, then tore open the other one and passed out coats. The kids were so excited as they tried on boots and coats until they all found ones that fit them. Lizzy walked over and hugged her sister, "Thank you, Sis, you are so wonderful," said Lizzy with a tear in her eyes.

Hanna left the school and headed back to the ranch. Her heart was full of joy as she pulled up to Jim's house. She unloaded their supplies and carried them in. The two boys, Tim and Little Jim, were tied up on the floor, play-fighting as Hanna stepped over them, walking in. Hanna then went to the cabin and dropped off a box there, then took the rest to Matt and Sara. Just as she got everything unloaded from the wagon, it started to snow. Hanna looked up, stuck out her tongue, and caught a snowflake, "Hello, winter, I knew you would be back." Hanna unhooked the wagon and put the horse in the barn, then went into the tack room to warm up. She stoked the fire and added more wood, then pulled off her wet boots. Paul came into the tack room. "Do you need anything, Ms. Hanna?" asked Paul. "No, sir, I'm just fine," said Hanna." "Oh, but I did set a box of supplies by the cabin door." "You might want to go put them inside before they get covered in snow." "Yes, ma'am, Ms. Hanna, right away, thank you," said Paul. Hanna propped her feet up by the heater.

Matt came into the tack room to warm up. "It's getting colder," said Matt. "Here, I got you something," said Hanna as she reached into her pocket and pulled out a plug of tobacco. "Thanks, sweety, I needed that," said Matt, as he warmed his hands. "So, how is Paul and Reeha working out?" asked Hanna. "Great," said Matt, "Paul is a hard worker, and Sara is happy with Reeha. "Good," said Hanna. Over the next three weeks, the weather got bitterly colder, and they lost one of the older cows to the cold. Luckily, she was not carrying a calf. Hanna dragged her inside the barn with her horse, then hung her from the rafters. Jim, Matt, and Paul came in to help her skin the cow; she was one of the first cows they had gotten from Mr. Wagner, the trail boss. Matt cut out the back straps and carried them to the main house. Jim took an axe and cut off the ribs. Hanna cut out a roast from one hind leg and gave it to Paul to take to the cabin, then one out of the other hind leg for Jim to take home with him. "I'll cut up the rest and take it to town," said Hanna. Jim knew where she was going to take it, Jim said. "Paul, you help her, then load the meat up in the wagon and go with her," said Jim. "Yes, sir," said Paul with a smile. He also knew what she was going to do. After cutting the rest of the meat up Paul loaded it onto the wagon. Hanna hitches the horse up, and she and Paul head to town. As they get there, Hanna drives through the main street past the stores to the camp. "If there is anybody here that has ever helped you and Reeha in the past, you give it to them first," said Hanna. Paul took portions of the meat to his friends, then randomly passed out the rest until it was gone.

As Paul and Hanna drove the wagon back to the ranch, Paul had a big smile on his face. "Feels good, doesn't it?" said Hanna. "Yes, ma'am, it sure does," said Paul. "You and your family are special people," said Paul." "Well, we didn't always have plenty; we've been there too." As they pulled back up to the barn, Hanna told Paul, "Take that carcass down the trail to an open spot and burn it." "We don't need predators coming up looking for scrapes." "Yes, ma'am," said Paul. He loaded the scrapes into the wagon and carried them off. He built a big fire and burned everything until it was gone. That night at supper, Paul told Hidee, "I've got to help the good Shepherd today." "You did," said Hidee, "yes, a cow died, we kept the best parts, then took the rest to the people in the camp," said Paul. "They were so happy to have fresh beef to eat," "it made me see just how lucky we are to be here."

Paul didn't get to see or talk to Hanna much after that day. One morning, he saw her in the distance riding through the herd, then she was gone. Just before the holidays, the snow got so deep that the school was closed. Lizzy and the kids got to stay home for a while, but they didn't mind at all. Just before Christmas, Hanna found another dead cow from her herd. Hanna looked up at the heavens, "ok, Lord, I'll do this again," "but let me keep the rest of my cows, please." She drove the cow into the barn with her horse like before; they skinned the cow and cut it up. Hanna told Paul, "We need a sled, the snow is too deep for the wagon. Can you handle that?" "Yes, ma'am," said Paul. "Just let me know when it's ready," said Hanna. That afternoon, Paul went to the main house to tell Hanna the Slade was ready. This time, they only kept a little of the meat; they had plenty.

Hanna knew that almost everybody in town would be running low on meat by this time. So, she took a loan from the café, took the banker's wife a roast, took the owners of the general store a roast, to the Sheriff's wife a piece of loan, and the rest she took to the camp and passed it out. Paul said nothing the whole trip; he just smiled. Christmas morning, Paul opened his door to find a freshly killed Turkey.

Finally, spring came, the snow was melting, school had started back, and Hanna and Patches pushed the cows back out to pasture. Hanna loved this time of year, new grass, new leaves on the trees, and the sky turned from grey to blue. The river was filling up with water from the melting snow and ice. Before long, there would be new calves dropping, new Deer and Elk fawns to watch play in the fields. God's big plan unfolded each spring, and she got to see it up close. How great was that? Patches was glad too, as he ran through the herd barking and keeping the cows away from the river. Matt and Jim had gone to town to restock up on supplies for the Ranch. Jim was also looking to buy a couple of young horses for the girls, Missy and Sissy. He hoped it would make them stop fighting over the one extra horse he had. They both loved to ride, and he wanted to teach them to help work the cows when needed. Missy, the oldest of the two, was like Hanna; she could stay on a horse's back all day if they let her. But Jim also wanted them to know how to take care of their own horses as well.

Jim and Matt came back with the supplies and two horses tied to the wagon. That day when the girl got home from school, Jim had both horses saddled and waiting. He had ridden both horses; they were still green, but seemed to be solid horses. He turned the girl loose on them in the lot and sat back and watched as they rode. Later, Jim, Ezy, and the boys pulled up to the lot in the buggy. Jim told the girls, Ride your horses to your grandpas for supper. As he opened the gate, the race was on, and off they went down the trail to Mamaw Sara's house. After supper, he let them ride them back to his barn, then showed them how much to feed them and had them brush them down. From that day on, after school, they did their work, then saddled their horses and were gone. The only rules he gave them were not to cross the river or ride to town, and to be at Sara's house before dark. After a few weeks on Saturdays, Hanna started taking the girls with her to work the cows. After a while, she took her 22-rifle with her and taught them how to shoot. Later, she would teach them how to shoot a Bow and cook their own food over a fire.

Like Hanna, the girls loved to be outdoors except when it rained; Hanna would put them under one of the sheds. As time went on, Sissy lost interest in being a cowgirl, but not Missy; she was always eager to go with Hanna when she could. The calves were dropping now, so the extra set of eyes was a big help to Hanna. When school let out for the summer, Hanna took Missy to town and outfitted her and her horse. Missy got new boots, chaps, a hat, a long raincoat, a bedroll, saddle bags, and a knife. Her horse got a breast collar, tiedown rig, rope, gun saddle holster, and new shoes. Missy's horse was a buckskin mare with lots of spunk; she was making a great cow pony. For the rest of the summer, Missy worked with Hanna every day, from Hanna she learned to talk to the cows as she rode through them. To give Patches commands, and what to look for, what foot track was from what animal, and what animal was dangerous. Where the property lines were, and which cows to be castrated when they had calves, Missy was learning to be a Rover, and she loved it. After a while, Hanna had given Missy her 22-Rifle to put on her horse, following the rules and instructions. She would put Missy on one side of the herd, and she stayed on the other side. The herd had grown to over five hundred head, which was a lot, more than one person could watch.

One day, Jim came out to check on them. He found Hanna, "How many calves?" asked Jim. "As of today, one hundred and three," said Hanna. "Wow," said Jim, "that's great, that bull's doing his thing." "Yep, it's not over yet," said Hanna. "Where's Missy?" asked Jim.

Hanna pointed; she was way on the other side of the herd. "How is she doing?" asked Jim. "Learning fast," said Hanna, "she's got a good horse, and she's got a good head on her, she'll be fine." "I'm going to look at another plot of land next to this one," said Jim, "I'll see you tonight." Jim rode off around the edge of the herd. The donkeys brayed as he passed by. He stopped and spoke to Missy, then rode on. The next day, as they watched the cows, Hanna heard a donkey bray on Missy's side of the herd. She looked and saw a rider headed to Missy; Hanna took off through the cows, making her way over to Missy. As she got closer, she could tell it was Carl, his home, she thought to herself. As she got close to them, Hanna said, "Missy, don't let his good looks and charm fool you; he's a stranger." Hanna rode up beside him and wrapped her arms around him and gave him a kiss. "Aunt, Hanna," said Missy in a shocked tone. Hanna and Carl laughed. "This is Carl," said Hanna, "Carl Pruit, I told you about him." Missy nodded, "This is the kind of guy you want to stay away from, always going off and leaving you," said Hanna. "Now, Hanna," said Carl, "who's your help?" "This is Missy, my niece, I told you about Missy and Sissy," said Hanna.

Hanna told Missy, "You failed that test. Don't ever let a stranger ride up on you and not be prepared to fight. "I didn't," said Missy, as she opened her coat, revealing the 22 in one hand and her knife in the other. Carl laughed, "just like her aunt, I'd say." Hanna smiled, "I take it back, good job." "Come on, Carl, I need to talk to you," said Hanna as they worked their way through the herd to the other side, then disappeared. Missy smiled and shook her head. She was only thirteen, but not a dumb thirteen-year-old. Carl and Hanna were locked together in a passionate kissing spree when they heard two shots from Missy's 22. Then the donkeys sounded their alarms, "Oh, no, yelled Hanna, "Patches, get to her," said Hanna as she grabbed her saddle horn and slung herself up on her horse's back and took off running through the herd. Carl got on his horse and followed behind Hanna, "What is it?" yelled Carl. "Bear," said Hanna, as she kept pushing her way through the cows. Hanna saw Missy coming around the back of the herd, then she saw her break out away from the herd into the open range. Good girl, thought Hanna, Missy starched her buckskin horse out into a full gallop, moving away from the herd. Hanna heard Patches get there as he ran in and knocked the bear sideways, stopping the bear's pursuit of Missy. Patch worked the bear, running in and out, keeping it occupied until Hanna got there. Hanna and Carl broke out of the herd. Hanna pulled out her Sharps rifle and leveled off on the big Grizzly Bear. "Don't shoot yelled Missy as she rode back up. "Why?" asked Hanna. "She's got cubs," said Missy, still breathing hard. Hanna pointed her rifle into the air and shot. The bear took off running back to her cubs, whom she had put up in a tree.

Hanna looked at Missy, "Well, now we need to move the herd," said Hanna. "I know," said Missy, "I'm sorry, but her cubs are so small, they want to serve without her." "Ok, let's push the herd South," said Hanna, "if that bear follows the herd, we will have to kill her." "Yes, ma'am," said Missy. Carl helped as they pushed the herd out of that area to a new spot. Normally, bear cubs, which are small, only get berries and fish from the river and their mother's milk; there is plenty for them to eat right now. Missy just got too close to the cubs without knowing it. Mother bears are very protective of their young. After moving the cows, they stopped to rest. Carl told Missy, "That's one fast little horse you've got there. Do you want to sell her?" "Nope," said Missy. Hanna smiled. Missy had just passed another test, Hanna had taught her that if a bear got after her, to lead it away from the herd and outrun it in the open range. After shooting two times into the air, they had signals for different predators, once for wolves, twice for bears, three times for Badgers, and four times if one of them was hurt and needed help.

Back at the home stead, Sissy and Hidee had become friends. Sissy would ride her horse to Hidee's cabin, and they would ride together around the Ranch. Or go back to Sissy's house and play for a while with the boys around the farm. Jim had found another plot of land for sale connected to theirs, and he was hoping to sell the steers this summer so the ranch could afford to buy it. That night at supper, Hanna asked Jim, "What about that land you were going to look at a couple of days ago?" Jim said, "I was going to talk to you about that. I told Dad about it." "It's a nice little valley with a natural pond on it, about forty acres, fed by a string." "There's a three-room cabin on it with a small barn and lot. I'd like for you to see it." "It's about an hour's ride from where the cows are now, but we would need to sell our steers to be able to afford it," said Jim. "Well, come by the herd tomorrow, and we will ride over there," said Hanna. "Missy can't stay with the herd," "alone," said Sara, Hanna smiled, "she'll be ok, want you, Missy," Missy nodded, "I'll leave Patches with her," said Hanna, "she can handle it." The next day, Mid-Morning, Jim rode up to the herd. Hanna was telling Missy what to watch for while she was gone. "Although Missy already knew what to do, Hanna told her anyway, "Patches, you stay with Missy," said Hanna.

Jim and Hanna rode away from the herd and headed North along the river. After a while, they turned east and rode up over a ridge. As they come over to the other side, it opens into a valley. "Oh, my God," says Hanna, "it's beautiful," the large lake set in the middle of the open valley with hills around it. The grass was waist high and dark green, the cabin set close to the lake with blue sparkling water. She could see the small creek running into the lake on one end and then coming out at the other end like a crooked snake. Hanna looked at Jim, "I've got to have it," said Hanna, "I'll build my house here one day, right over there on that hill." "Well, we need money first," said Jim. "I have money," said Hanna. "I want it, just like you wanted your place." "Ok," well, let's try to sell some steers, and let the ranch pay for it this time," said Jim. "You will need your money to build a house on it later." Hanna was so excited; it was the most beautiful place she had ever seen in her life. Jim and Hanna rode back to the herd. Missy was watching the cows. “Well,” said Jim, “you can start separating the steers whenever you're ready.” “I’ll go put up a deposit on the land,” “sounds good,” said Hanna.

“What now?” asked Missy. “Oh, we’re going to buy more land,” said Hanna, “we need to sell the steers to pay for it.” “So tomorrow we’ll start rounding them up and moving them away from the herd,” said Hanna. “Sound like fun,” said Missy, “it’s not that bad, we’ll just get everything with a goober,” laughed Hanna, “oh, Aunt Hanna,” said Missy. “No, not really, just the two-year-old and older, we will leave the yearling and calves.” The next morning, Jim sent Sissy to help them. Hanna, Missy, and Sissy started moving the steers up to the catch pin. In the afternoons, they pushed them onto the main house lot. Jim went to see Mr. Pruit to find out if he was moving a load of cattle this year. “No, not this year,” said Pruit. “I’ve got a load going next year though.” Jim frowned and dropped his head. “How many do you have?” asked Pruit. “Around a hundred and thirty head of two- and three-year-olds,” said Jim. “If you kept them another year, you would get more for them,” said Pruit. “Yeah, I know, but I need to sell them now,” said Jim. “Sorry, I can’t help you, Jim, but if you keep them, we can do something next year,” said Pruit. “Yes, sir,” said Jim. “Thank you.” Jim went home and told his father what Pruitt had said. “Well, son, that’s not your fault,” said Matt. “But Hanna wants that land badly, Dad,” said Jim, “I'd better go tell Hanna.” Jim found the girls at the catch pin; Hanna could tell by the look on Jim's face that something was wrong.

“What’s up?” asked Hanna. “Well, I talked to Pruit, he’s not selling anything until next year,” said Jim. “He’s right,” said Hanna, “I just told Missing that these steers were too thin, and they needed another year.” “That’s no problem,” said Hanna, “I’ll loan the ranch the money for the land and next year when we sell the steers the ranch can pay me back." "It's like money in the bank to me," said Hanna, "ok, Sis, if you say so," said Jim. "We will go to the bank in the morning," "ok," said Hanna. "Girls, turn them back out, let's push them back to the herd," said Hanna, "tell Momma we'll be late for supper." "Ok," said Jim, "I will." Jim watched as the three girls moved the steers out away from the lot, with Hanna in the middle. Jim thought back on the shy girl who left Kentucky and how much she has changed to become the woman he sees today. What an amazing transformation it was.

The next morning, Hanna sent Missy and Sissy to the herd while she went to town with Jim. They got the deal done and the deed recorded. Hanna went by the general store and picked up two big bags of candy and three soda pops. She also got two bags of jerky for her and Missy, and more ammo for her guns. Hanna left Jim in town and rode back to the herd, and the girls, she gave them both a pop and a bag of candy. Then, Hanna toasted Missy with a bag of jerky to put in her saddle bag. Hanna pulled a piece of jerky from her bag and gave it to Patches. "Y'all want to see something beautiful?" asked Hanna. "Sure," said Sissy. "Let's take a ride," said Hanna. They rode to the river, then turned east and went over the ridge, "wow," said Sissy, "oh, my God," said Missy, "welcome to Hanna's Valley," said Hanna. "Is this what you and Dad were talking about?" asked Missy. "Yep," said Hanna. "Look at that lake," said Sissy, "look at the green grass," said Missy, "you should raise horses here." "That's not a bad idea," said Hanna. "I'm serious," said Missy, "plenty of grass and good water." "Don't put any cows on this," said Missy, "save it for horses." "How much land do we have now?" asked Missy. "Three thousand two hundred arches," said Hanna. "That's a lot," said Sissy, "yep, that's a Ranch," said Hanna, "The King's Land Ranch." The girls rode back to the herd. Hanna was still thinking about what Missy had said. She was right, it would make a great place to raise horses.

The next Friday, Hanna got Jim to take her place with Missy watching the herd while she spent the day with Carl. Hanna met Carl in town again for lunch, and she told him about the Valley they had bought and that she would one day have a house there. She also told him about Missy's idea that she should raise horses there. Carl told her that he would like to see this place, which she was so excited about. So, after lunch, they rode out to see Hanna's Valley, then rode down to the cabin. They opened the door to look inside. not much there: just an old table and a few candles. In one room, there was still an old bed frame and mattress, no lining, no pillows. There was a wood-burning stove in one corner of the main room. A fireplace in the middle of the back wall that was open on both sides, the bedroom, and the main room. The other room was smaller but was empty, "What do you think?" asked Hanna with a smile. "I like it," said Carl, "it would make a good base camp in the winter." "I don't see any signs that the roof leaks; it needs a good dusting out," said Carl.

Carl walked over to Hanna and put his arms around her, then leaned in for a kiss. They stood in the main room kissing. Hanna melted into his arms, then put her arms around his neck. She kissed him back. Carl slid his hand inside the top of her jeans. She pulled back. Carl kissed her harder. Grabbed her butt and pulled her tight against him, she let out a slight moan. Carl picked her up and carried her to the old bed, still kissing her. He laid her on the bed, never breaking their kiss, and he slid his hand inside her jeans again, this time touching her. Hanna let out a moan. Carl unsnapped her jeans and worked them down to her knees, then touched her again. "Carl, no," said Hanna in a soft tone. Carl rolled over on top of her. Hanna let out a loud gasp. There was no stopping him now, and she didn't want him to stop.

Afterward, they lay and talked; Carl had one more semester of school left, then he would be home for good. After a while, they left the cabin and rode back down along the river. Hanna wasn't sure how she should feel. In a way, she was ashamed of what she had let happen, but she loved him even more. As they reached the crossing spot in the river, Carl leaned over and gave her a kiss. "See you in a few days," said Carl, as Hanna rode on to her house. She started to cry. So many emotions were running through her mind and body, she didn't understand. Should she be happy, should she be sad, she just couldn't get a hold of her feelings. That night, she relived every second of that day. The next morning, without much sleep, she started her normal routine. The mornings were getting colder as she and Missy rode out to the herd. She didn't talk much that day. At lunch, Missy asked Hanna, "Are you ok?" "Yes, I'm fine," said Hanna. "Ok," said Missy, "you just seem down or sad." Hanna wanted to cry, but she fought back the tears.

Three days later, Carl came back pushing four stray cows that had crossed the river; they pushed them back into the herd. As Missy went back to her side of the herd, Hanna took Carl to one of the shelters. There was no hesitation, no resistance, just wild passion. Once they finished, Carl kissed her and left. This time, when it was over, Hanna was smiling; she couldn't stop smiling. The next week Carl came back again, afterwards he told Hanna, "I'm leaving tomorrow to go back to school." "But when I come back, I'll be finished with school," he reached into his pocket and pulled out a gold band. "I want you to wear this for now, but when I come back, I'll bring you a better one," said Carl. He slipped it onto her finger. Tears filled Hanna's eyes. "I love you, Carl," "I love you too," said Carl. "Don't cry," said Carl, "I'll be back before you know it." Carl got on his horse and rode away. Hanna wiped her face and stared at the tiny ring. It meant more to her than all the diamonds in the world.

As the air got colder, Hanna and Missy started moving the momma cows to the lot with Jim's help. Felt like winter was coming early this year, luckily, with the help of Paul, the firewood had already been cut. They would wait if they could before they brought the rest of the herd to the Ranch. Hanna had already put two new beds in the Valley cabin, cooking supplies, and food. She and Missy had cleaned it out, hung curtains Sara had made, and stocked up on firewood just in case. Hanna missed Carl, but tried not to think about him too much. It had only been a few weeks since he left. Paul kept the barn clean, and the horse stock fed, while Reeha helped Sara with everything in the house now. Lizzy was still taking the kids to school and then bringing them home. Lizzy was the first to notice the ring on Hanna's finger at supper one night. "What is that?" asked Lizzy. Hanna smiled. Carl gave it to me. "Who is Carl, and why don't I know about him?" Missy giggled. Sara was in shock. "Hanna, do you have a boyfriend?" Jim spoke up, "he's Carl Pruit, the youngest son of Mr. Pruit, owner of the Pruit ranch." "How did you meet him?" asked Sara. "He brings our strays back across the river and rounds up his," said Hanna. "He is in college in California, this is his last year, he told me he wanted me to wear it, and when he comes back, he's bringing me a better one." "Hanna, are you getting married?" asked Ezy. "I don't know," said Hanna with a smile. "Matt, did you know about this?" asked Sara. "I knew they were talking and meeting for lunch in town, "Carl asked for my permission the day Jim and Hanna saved him from the rustlers." "Rustlers," said Sara, "what Rustler?" "There are too many secrets in this family," "not secrets," said Jim, "we're not hiding anything," "we just don't talk about every little thing that happens." "And we didn't know about the ring," said Jim. "Nope, me either," said Matt.

Chapter Seven: The Big Secret

In mid-October, Hanna, Missy, and Jim moved the rest of the herd up to the pasture near the lot. Hanna had been sick in the morning lately and was glad to get them close to home. After a few more days, Hanna realized her jeans were getting tighter, and then she thought about her monthly cycle. Oh, no, she thought, no, this can't be happening, no, it's just because I've been sick and not feeling good. She put it out of her mind. Each morning, she checked the herd, then warmed up in the tack room, then went to the house. Just before Christmas, as if God had planned it, she found another dead cow; they dressed it, and she and Paul carried the meat to the camp. By now, Hanna had no doubts; she was with child, she told no one, her small belly was pooching out, and her breasts were getting larger. But she hid it all under her clothes. How in the world was she going to explain this to her mom? Hanna sat down one night and wrote Carl a long letter; she thought he deserved to know. She had Lizzy mail it to him. After a couple of weeks with no reply, Hanna wrote to him again. Still no reply, Hanna was convinced that bad weather or delays in the mail were the cause. After all, Carl loves her as she loves him, and he would respond to her if he knew.

Hanna continued to hide her condition from everyone; she seemed to always be hungry and looking for a snack as time went by. Spring finally came, and the snow was melting. They moved the momma cows out of the lot and put all the steers in it instead to be sold. Hanna told Jim that tomorrow she and Missy would push the herd to her valley land. For the spring, and that she and Missy would stay there in the cabin until they push them to Josuha's old place. Since it was so far from the homestead, "I know Ezy will not like Missy not going to school this spring, but I need her with me," said Hanna. Jim could tell something was wrong. "What is it, Hanna? What's wrong?" asked Jim. "You know you can talk to me, Sis." A tear fell from her eye,

“I’m with child, Jim, I’m pregnant,” “don’t tell momma, please, I’m so sorry,” said Hanna. Jim reached over and hugged her. “How long?” asked Jim. “Since last August,” said Hanna. “You're due in another month or so,” said Jim, “Oh, my God, Hanna.” “Ok, take Missy,” “awe oh,” “my Lord,” “awe does Carl know,” asked Jim. “I wrote him a letter,” said Hanna but I don’t know if he got it.” “Take it easy,” said Jim. “I’m fine,” said Hanna, “I can do my job with Missy and Patches there to help me.” “Ok,” said Jim, “as soon as I get these steers sold, I’ll come check on you and bring more supplies.” “Oh, lord.” Jim hugged her again, “Please, please, stay safe,” said Jim.

The next morning, Hanna, Missy, and Patches pushed the herd to the valley. It took all day, but they made it there. They built fires in the fireplace and the stove. The nights were still cold, and Hanna cooked them something to eat. After supper, Hanna pulled off her coat, chaps, and boots and sat by the fireplace. “Aunt Hanna,” said Missy, “is that you? 'Aunt Hanna, your belly is huge.” Hanna laughed, “Yes, I’m pregnant,” “I’m going to have a baby.” “How,” “when,” “oh my God,” “wait, is that Carl’s baby?” asked Missy. “No, this is my baby,” replied Hanna in a gruff tone, “but yes, Carl the father,” said Hanna, “I knew it,” said Missy, “I knew you two were fooling around.” “Well, it looks like I’m the fool,” said Hanna, “want be long, and you will know more than you ever wanted to know about just fooling around with a boy.” “I don’t know anything about delving, no baby,” said Missy, “you will, it’s not hard, you’ve watched cows.” “I figure it’s about the same thing,” said Hanna, “what if it gets hung up like a calf,” said Missy, “Oh, Lord Missy,” “please don’t make me laugh,” “I’ll pea on myself,” said Hanna. “Well, do I need the calving ropes?” asked Missy. “Oh, stop Missy, just be quiet,” “Oh, please,” said Hanna, laughing.

The next morning, Missy cooked breakfast. After they ate, they went out to the lot and saddled up their horses. The valley was the perfect pasture; the bowl-shaped area kept the cows bunched up together. The cows didn't move around much; there was so much grass that they could stand in one place and eat for an hour. The donkeys brayed as a herd of Elk came into the valley and ate alongside the cows, then a few pronghorns moved in close to the lake. It was a beautiful sight, the clear blue sky overhead, and the lush green grass on the ground. Hanna thought, Yep, this is where I'll raise my child, she had never gotten a reply from Carl. For whatever reason, she had decided not to make plans about whether Carl would be in the picture or not. If he didn't get her letters, then he'll be in for a big surprise when he gets home. For the next two weeks, the girl had some good, easy days just watching the cows. Every day, the air was getting warmer as all the ice and snow melted away. It was getting harder for Hanna to stay in the saddle all day. The more she moved around, the harder it was; she knew she wouldn't be able to keep up this pace much longer.

The first week of April, Jim came riding up to the cabin, and Hanna saw him ride in. She went to the cabin to talk to him; she climbed off her horse slowly, Hanna told Jim. "Come inside, I got coffee on the stove," they said as they went into the cabin, and Hanna sat at the table. Jim poured them both a cup, then sat down. "Sis, it's getting close, isn't it?" said Jim. "Yap, I think so," said Hanna. Jim slid an envelope over to her, there's your money," said Jim. "How did we do?" asked Hanna, we did well," said Jim, "we have the money to keep us going until we can sell again." Hanna let out a moan as the baby kicked. "You need to stay off that horse until after the baby comes," said Jim. "I know," said Hanna, "I wish I had Sissy here to help Missy. "Jim shook his head, "You need Sissy and mom both," said Jim, "you know mom is going to be hurt and mad if you don't let her help you with this." Hanna started to cry, "Oh, Lord," said Hanna as the baby kicked again. "She's going to be mad anyway," said Jim, "go get her then," said Hanna, "just her and Sissy, nobody else." "Ok, I'll be back before dark," said Jim, "I'll send Missy up here to put up the supplies I brought." Jim rode to Missy and told her he was going after Sara and Sissy. "Thank God," said Missy. "Go to the cabin and put up the supplies I brought before Hanna tries to do it herself," said Jim, "I'll be back soon." Missy went to the cabin, as Jim rode off back to the home stead.

Late that afternoon, Jim came back with Sara in the buggy with Sissy following on her horse. Jim had told Sara on the way what was going on. At first, she was mad. Mainly because they hadn't told her, then she started to cry, then Jim said. "Momma, you know Hanna has always been the one who never asked for help with anything." "If she fell, she wouldn't let anyone help her up," "she got that from you," said Jim. "I know," said Sara, "I pushed her to be independent and take care of herself." "But this is it," said Sara, "there will be no more secrets in this family, you hear me, Son." "Yes, ma'am," said Jim. As they pulled up to the Cabin, Jim told Sissy, "Go find your sister, she's out there with the cows." Sissy rode off, as Jim took Sara inside the Cabin, Hanna was lying in her bed. Sara walked over to the bed. Hanna was crying, "I'm sorry, Momma," said Hanna. Sara hugged her, "It's going to be ok, I'm here now." "Get those clothes off, so I can check you out," said Sara as she left the room. "Jim, go home and take care of your family. I've got this," said Sara. Jim took the buggy and headed back home. On his way out, he went by the girls and told them to come get him if anything happened. Sara went back to Hanna. She felt around Hanna's belly, then below, "This baby is coming soon," said Sara. "All we can do now is wait," said Sara with a smile. She didn't ask Hanna how or why; none of that mattered at this point. All that mattered was Hanna and the grandbaby she was carrying.

Missy and Sissy came to the barn at the cabin and put up their horses, then came inside the cabin. Missy went to prep food for supper,

Sissy went to see her aunt Hanna, and Missy had told her what was going on. “Hi, Aunt Hanna,” said Sissy, “you need anything?” “No, sweety, I'm fine,” said Hanna, “thanks for coming to help Missy.” “We're going to need some bucket of water,” said Sara to Sissy. “Just put them in the kitchen by the stove,” said Sara. Sissy went out for water. Once Missy had supper ready, she set the table, then went to Hanna’s door. “Supper is ready,” said Missy in a low voice, “are you getting up or should I bring it to you?” “No, I’m getting up,” said Hanna. The four women sat around the table, Sara said grace, and they started eating. Missy was a good cook; Sara and Hanna had taught her well. The girls sat and talked as they ate about everything but Hanna’s condition. After supper, Hanna sat in her chair by the fireplace while the girls cleaned up. Hanna was surrounded by love now; her mom and her nieces were there to take care of her.

The next morning, Hanna stayed at the cabin with Sara while Missy and Sissy took care of the stock. Patches didn’t want to leave the cabin as the girl kept calling him; he sensed something was about to happen. Hanna reached down and rubbed his head, “I’m ok, boy, just go with Missy,” said Hanna. Patches looked at her. He went outside but wouldn’t leave the cabin to go out with the girls. After the girls rode off, Patches lay on the outside of the door; somehow, he knew. Mid-morning, Hanna’s water broke, Sara got her back into her bed, then went back to the kitchen and put water on the stove. Sara never got excited; she calmly prepped Hanna by removing everything but her gown. Then, I went back to check on the water. Just before noon, the labor pains started. As Hanna let out a loud moan, Patches stood up, and as she let out another moan, he barked. Sara was ready; she knew what was coming. She tried to keep Hanna calm as Hanna let out a scream. Patches took off running out into the valley, finding Sissy and circling her, then ran to Missy, crazy dog thought Sissy. As he got to Missy and circled her, Missy thought of the baby. She took off on her horse, running to Sissy, “Come on,” yelled Missy as she rode on to the cabin. They ran into the house in time to hear the baby cry, as they went into Hanna's room, Sara said in a calm voice. "Get me some more dry cloths, girls, Sara swaddled the baby in cloth and laid it on Hanna's chest." When the girls came back into the room, Hanna was crying, looking at her baby. "What is it?" asked Missy. Sara smiled, "It's a little girl," "a beautiful little girl," said Sara. Hanna pulled the cloth from the baby's head so the girls could see her face. She had bright, red hair and blueish green eyes. "Oh, how sweet," said Sissy. Sara kept cleaning up Hanna, then she had Hanna lift her behind so she could pull out the folded sheet she had put under her bottom. "Bring me a bucket," said Sara. She placed the sheet into the bucket along with all the cloth rags. "You, girls, go start me a fire outside," said Sara, "you can hold the baby later." Hanna got her baby to start sucking her breast, and Sara put a blanket over them both. "Get some rest, sweety," "I'll take care of this," said Sara as she picked up the bucket and took it outside. "Y'all go back to your cows now, girls, you don't want to smell this burning," said Sara. Hanna named the baby Sara Anna, after her and her mom.

Three days later, Hanna was up and around, and taking care of her baby on her own. Sara told Sissy that morning, "Go tell Jim, Hanna, and her baby are fine and that he can come get us." Sissy rode off back to the Ranch and got Jim. They came back midday with the buggy. Jim loaded Hanna and her baby into the buggy, then Sara, and then Jim got in the buggy. Hanna told the girls, "Y'all stay alert, I'll be back in a few days." "Missy, if you run low on meat, shoot a pronghorn. I'll bring back supplies." "Patches, you stay with Missy and don't come looking for you, hear?" Patches dropped his head and whined. Jim drove them away, as the girls went back to the cows, Patches went out with the girls. As Jim pulled up to the main house, Matt came outside. Jim had told his dad about Hanna and why he had to come get Sara and Sissy before he took Sara to Hanna. Matt went to the buggy and helped Hanna and the baby out, then walked them inside the house. Matt took the baby from Hanna's arms and went to his chair; he sat there talking to his granddaughter with tears in his eyes. That tough old man melted away to a blob of mush holding that baby girl in his arms. That night, Ezy, Jim, and the boys came down for supper, holding that sweet baby girl, who was making Ezy want another baby of her own. Lizzy was just happy somebody finally figured out how to have a baby girl. That night, Matt heard something scratching at the door. He opened it. Patches came walking in, he went to Hanna and the baby, "I told you not to come, boy," said Hanna in a stern tone. Patches sniffed the baby, wagging his tail. Hanna rubbed his head. "I need you to go help Missy," said Hanna. Patches walked to the door, Matt let him out, and the next morning, he was gone. While she was there, Hanna got Sara to make her a shoulder bag so that she could put the baby in it like she had toted Patches when he was a puppy. Except for this one, which had leg holes and padding, so Hanna could keep her arms and hands free to ride her horse. On the third day there, Jim went to town and picked up supplies for Hanna and her cabin. The next morning, Hanna and her baby loaded back up into the wagon, and Jim carried her home to her cabin. Sara begged Hanna to stay or just leave the baby there with her. But Hanna said, "I love you, mamma, but my place is with the cows, and Anna's place is with me; we will be fine, and we'll come back soon."

They pulled up to the cabin in the valley around noon, unloaded the wagon, and Jim headed back home. That night, when the girls came in, Hanna had supper ready and was waiting. Patches came over to Hanna, sniffed the baby, looked at Hanna, and sniffed some more. Then licked the baby's face and lay down at Hanna's feet. Hanna had told Jim on the way that she would move the herd North in three weeks, and for him to look for some horses to buy. The girls took turns holding little Anna and playing with her. On the first of July, Hanna put Anna in the sack Sara had made, then got on her horse. She and the girls move the cows North to Missy and Sissy's old homestead land. Once they had them there, Hanna told Sissy that she could go back home now and go back to school. Sissy smiled. She hated to leave baby Anna, but she was ready to get back home. She hugged Hanna and Missy, then kissed little Anna and rode off down the river road. While the cows were there, Hanna and Missy rode back to the cabin each night to eat and sleep. Missy asked Hanna, "When is Carl coming home?" "I'm not sure," said Hanna, "sometime in August, next month I think." "Are you mad at him?" asked Missy. "No, honey, not mad," said Hanna. "I'm not sure if he got my letters or not." "Either way, when he gets home, we will talk, and he can meet his daughter." "If he wants us, he will have to man up and take care of us." "If he doesn't, well, I might just kill him," said Hanna with a smile. Missy laughed.

Hanna had thought about all the reasons why she hadn't heard from Carl, but none of them really made her feel content. Mid-August, Hanna talked Jim into going to the Pruitt Ranch to see if Carl had made it back home yet. Mr. Pruit told Jim that he and his wife had gone to California to Jim's graduation ceremony, and then to Nevada for Carl's Wedding. They had paid for him and his new bride to take a trip overseas for their honeymoon. They should be back here at the ranch by the first of September, no later. "Why do you need him for something?" asked Mr. Pruit. "No," said Jim, "I just haven't seen him around this summer." As Jim was leaving the Ranch, Carl's older brother Charles rode up to Jim. Charles took his hat off and dropped his head. "Hi, Jim," "Hey, Charles, "How are you?" asked Jim. "Well, Jim, I'm just sick in my heart," said Charles, "I took some of your strays across the river to Hanna this morning and brought back ours." "Well, thank you," said Jim. "You're welcome," said Charles. "Jim, is that Carl's baby Hanna has with her?" Jim dropped his head. "Look, Jim, I'm not trying to pry, "but is that what you came to see my father about?" asked Charles. "Well, no, I didn't tell your father," Jim said. Hanna wanted me to come see if Carl was back home."

"Hanna wrote him a few times to tell him about the baby, but got no replies, and she hasn't seen him yet." "That little bastard," said Charles, "I'm going to beat his ass." Charles was mad, "that spoiled little S.O.B.," "Jim, I'm so sorry, but Carl got married to a girl from Nevada," said Charles. "I know," said Jim, "your father told me, Carl gave Hanna a ring before he left last fall and told her he would bring her a better one this summer." "Then she found out she was with child," "she tried to let him know," said Jim. "Well, he was at a different facility this last year than before for his final year of classes," said Charles. "I guess it is possible that he didn't receive her letters, but I still want to choke him." "Well, just do me a favor," said Jim, "don't say anything to anybody, let Hanna handle it her way." "When Carl gets back, I'd rather you be the one to do the stray whops if you don't mind," said Jim, "I really don't want him around her anymore." "I understand," said Charles, "I'll take care of it, thanks, Jim."

Jim left Charles and crossed the river, then he rode to the herd to find Hanna. "Well," asked Hanna, half expecting bad news from Jim, "is he dead?" "Not yet," said Jim, "but he did get married to a girl from Nevada," "they are on their honeymoon overseas." Hanna opened the sack and looked at her baby girl, "Well, Anna, looks like it's just you and me, kid." Hanna looked at Jim with a tear in her eyes, "Well, that's good," "good for him," "thanks, Jim," said Hanna. "Missy," yelled Hanna, "move them up a little bit." "Ok," said Missy. Missy yelled, "Patches, push them up, boy, come on!" Jim didn't know what else to say as he watched the girls move the cows. Jim wanted to be mad, he wanted to avenge his sister's honor, he wanted to, but all he felt was sadness. Jim knew now the best thing that he could do for his sister was to help Hanna with her dream of raising horses. Paul, Jim's ranch hand, had told him about a family that lived at the camp in town. He said the man was a good carpenter and he had two teenage boys who were hard workers too. That the wife was a good cook on the campfire and the stove. So, Jim went into town after leaving Hanna to find the couple and see if he could hire them to work at Hanna's Valley. Jim found them and made them an offer to move their tents to the Valley and build rail fences and a new horse barn on Hanna's place. Then, later, to help build Hanna a house there, he and Hanna would furnish the materials and supplies. They agreed, and Jim told them how to get to Matt's Home Stead the next day.

The next day, mid-morning, the Pryor's showed up at Matt's Home Stead. Jim went out to greet them. "Follow me," said Jim, as he got on his horse. The Pryor's had everything they owned packed into one wagon. Jim led them down the river trail until he got to Josuha's old place, then had them stop and wait for him. Jim rode into the hills to find Hanna. As he saw the herd, Hanna was coming his way. "What's up?" asked Hanna. "I've got some people I want you to meet," said Jim. "Why?" asked Hanna. "Well, I found some horses," said Jim, "but you need a place to put them." "Are the horses coming now?" asked Hanna. "No," said Jim, but they are next spring." "Just come meet these folks, the man is a builder, he has two sons, and his wife cooks." "Oh, ok," said Hanna. Hanna and Jim rode off down to the river. "Mr. Pryor, this is my sister Hanna, the one I told you about," said Jim. "This is who you will be working for," "nice to meet you," said Mr. Pryor, "this is my wife Grace, my two sons, Arron and James." "Nice to meet you," said Hanna, "just set up your camp on the East side of the barn," said Hanna, "I'll get with you in the morning on what to do." Hanna turned and rode off back to the herd. Jim led the Pryor out to the valley. The Pryor couldn't believe how beautiful it was there. Jim showed them the spot where they could set up camp on the other side of the barn, away from the cabin.

The next morning, Hanna got with Mr. Pryor, "John," she showed him how and where she wanted the fences, the corals, and then the barn. She also showed him the spot where her house would be set, but told him that it would come last. Then she took him out to the spot where they could cut the small trees for the fence rails and posts. Hanna warned him about the bears in the area and told him to let her know when they needed wild meat, that she would decide what was taken for food there. Then she left to go to the herd. Missy was already there with the herd when Hanna got there. Missy had gone to the main Home Stead the night before to visit the family and spend the night there. Jim had asked Missy how Hanna was doing, "ok," said Missy, "but she doesn't talk much anymore." As the weeks went by and the nights started to cool off, Hanna went out to sit by the fire with the Pryor family. Hanna missed the campfires they had on their trip to Oregon, and the ones she had in the winter while watching the cows. It was still too warm to have one in the fireplace yet, so she sat with them and stared into the flames. Clearing her mind and cares away, Grace walked over to her and sat down beside her. "May I hold your baby?" asked Grace. Hanna looked at her and smiled, then handed her the baby. Grace sat there talking to Anna. "I would love to watch after your baby for you if you would like sometimes," said Grace. Hanna smiled, then said, "Maybe, we'll see when she stops nursing and can eat soft foods, maybe." "Ok," said Grace.

The Pryor's had been cutting, peeling, and stacking poles and posts to dry for weeks now. Soon they would start digging post holes and setting posts for the fences. Missy and Hanna move the cows onto Jim's homestead; the main homestead was closer now than the valley cabin. So, Hanna and Missy start going to the main house for supper and to sleep there at night. This made Sara very happy, and now she gets to see her new granddaughter, Anna. The next morning, Hanna leaves Anna with Sara while she and Missy ride into town; they both need new boots before winter." Hanna stops by the bank and cashes in some gold; she has cash money put away but never spends it. She slowly tried to cash in her gold a little at a time. They left the bank and rode on to the general store. Hanna saw in the display case two small twenty-five caliber six-shooter pistols with

Ivory handles and a belt with two holsters. The barrels were only about six inches long, perfect for her and Missy, she thought. Hanna taps on the case, the store clerk comes over to her, "yes, Ms. Hanna," "I want those guns," said Hanna, the clerk got them out, Hanna looks them over, "now give me two boxes of bullets." Hanna pulls the belt off the holster, "Here, you can keep that," said Hanna. Hanna loads both Pistols, then puts them back into their holsters. "Here," said Hanna to Missy, "put that on your belt with your knife." Hanna paid for everything, then they left the store.

The two girls rode out of town in a gallop, headed back to get Anna, with Patches running along with them. The store clerk stood on the boardwalk and watched them ride away. A young man from town was standing there, "Who in the world were those two girls?" he asked. "That was two of the Evans girls," said the clerk. "Man, they looked wild," said the young man. The store clerk chuckled, "You don't want to mess with those two," said the clerk, "not those two." Hanna got Missy the gun because she was having to leave her alone with the cattle more and more these days. Now she needed to teach her how to use it, just in case she had to one day. The next day, Charles came across the river with straws again and found Hanna and Missy eating lunch. Charles got off his horse and sat by Hanna, "Can I hold my niece?" asked Charles. Hanna gave him a hard look; he held his hands up. "I talked to Jim," said Charles, "he made me swear not to tell anyone, and I want." "I just want to hold her," Hanna said as she picked Anna up from the blanket where she lay sleeping. Then handed her to Charles, little Anna opens her eyes, "hi, sweety," says Charles, "oh, look at those eyes, you're so beautiful baby girl." "Oh, my, you sweet little thing," says Charles, "Jim told me he would prefer me to bring the strays from now on." "That's fine," said Hanna. "Look, Hanna," said Charles, "I don't know what my brother Carl told you, but it was probably a lie." "He has always been a liar; he lied his way in and out of so much trouble growing up." "Well, I'll put it this way, you're probably better off without him," said Charles. "But if you or this little angel ever need anything, you let me know." Hanna smiled and took the baby back from him. "We're just fine," said Hanna.

The next few days, it rained, so Hanna left Anna with Sara at home, while she and Missy slowly moved the cows closer to the main homestead. Paul was still taking care of the stock at home, and now he, Jim, and Matt were stocking up on firewood for the winter. Reeha was keeping house for Sara, giving her more time with the grandchildren and time to sew. After the rain, Hanna rode to the valley to check on the Pryor family and the cabin. They had one section of fence up and the poles standing for the new barn; they had cut firewood and stacked it by the cabin for her. Hanna told them to make a list of supplies they needed for the winter so she could get them. Hanna took the list and returned to the herd. It was late September, and it wouldn't be long now until the snow started. That night, she gave Jim the list and told him to have Paul deliver the things to the Pryor family. The next week, Hanna and Missy started bringing in the momma cows to the lot at the barn. Then they pushed the rest of the herd up closer to the lot. The next week, Hanna told Jim, Let's go hunting, they left the next morning with the two Sharps rifles, going after Elk. Hanna knew a spot just past the Valley where the Elk moved to just before it snowed. They tied their horse and walked a while, then sat by some rocks and waited. The Cow Elk and yearlings were already there. Mid-morning, the big Bull Elk started coming into the meadow looking for the Cow Elk. They both picked a three- or four-year-old with a small rack. When they were both ready, they shot at the same time. The two big animals dropped to the ground, and they returned to their horses and rode down after them. They dragged the two elk out of the meadow, then field dressed one of them and quartered it, then packed half the meat on each horse. They tied two ropes to the antlers of the other elk, then got on their horses, wrapped the rope around their saddle horns, and dragged it back to the valley for the Pryors. Hanna told the two boys to hang the elk up in the old barn for their dad. She told John to make sure they burned any scraps off the elk. Hanna went to the tents and told Grace to move their things into the cabin for the winter. "Oh, thank you," said Grace, "thank you so much, that will be wonderful." "You're welcome, but do it now," said Hanna, "snow is coming."

Hanna and Jim got on their horses and rode off, as the boys and their father, John, were skinning the elk. Hanna and Jim made it to the barn at Matt's right before dark, and light snow had just started to fall. "Paul," yelled Jim, "yes, sir," said Paul, coming out of one of the stalls, "unpack these horses and feed them," said Jim. "You can put mine up," said Hanna, as she and Jim walked into the tack room to warm up. Missy came walking into the tack room to, "y'all move over, it's cold out there," said Missy. Hanna and Missy spent the winter there. Missy went back to Jim's and Ezy's house and went back to school until the weather shut it down. Hanna and little Anna stayed with Matt, Sara, and Lizzy. Hanna went out every morning to check the cows. Reeha's daughter, Hidee, spent a lot of time there helping her mom and playing with Anna. Charles Pruit came to visit little Anna. He and Hanna sat and talked about horses. Which ones had the best bloodlines and could stand the cold weather? It seems Charles has a love for horses, too. The Pruitts raised horses for working their cattle, but not for sale, but Charles's father had developed a sound bloodline of his own over the years of a hearty stock. Hanna wanted to do the same, but she wanted horses with a little more size to them, like her white horse. The Pruit horses were short and stocky, great for working cows. But she wanted something with longer legs and a body that could carry a heavier load faster.

Charles Pruit started coming to the Kings Land Ranch once a week through the winter, supposedly to see Anna, but spent most of his time talking with Hanna, in the house or in the tack room. Charles never spoke about Carl, and Hanna never asked. Charles was two years older than Carl. He was the middle son; his older brother Chanler Pruit was five years older than him. Chanler ran the day-to-day operations of the ranch, with Mr. Pruit, "James Chanler Pruit," calling the shots. Everyone called him J.C. Pruit or Mr. Pruit; his wife's name was Marria, and the boy's mother's name was Marria. J.C. and Maria had settled there almost thirty years ago as a young couple when Chanler was just a baby. J.C. Pruit was one of the men who traveled with Lewis and Clark as a young man and helped map out the Western States. After the expedition, he returned to Oregon with the authority from the President of the U.S. to claim all the land between the river and the coastline from Oregon City to the Washington State boundary and South of Oregon City to where the Clackamas River runs into the Ocean for his self. He met his wife, Marria, on his return trip, and took her as his wife; she was of Mexican descent. They built one of the largest Ranches in Oregon, and they had their own shipping port on the coast at one time. Pruit was also the main backer for the Railroad station in town and a stockholder in the railroad company. Chanler uses Charles as a foreman on round-ups and branding operations and as a fill-in where needed. They have over thirty-five employees who work for the ranch in one way or another. To Chanler, his youngest brother Carl was a nuisance more than anything else and couldn't be trusted to do the simplest task alone. But to Mr. Pruit, he is the one who, with his education, will help bring the ranch into modern times. Carl's new wife, "Mary," is from Nevada, where her father owns one of the biggest ranches there. A business associate and longtime friend of J.C. Pruit, Carl's and Mary's engagement was arranged when they were babies, with the agreement that Carl would get a college education before the wedding and then work to help both Ranches. In Charles's mind, Carl should have never encouraged Hanna into any type of relationship at all, knowing he was bound to marry someone else. Charles had made up his mind to watch over little Anna and to make Hanna an honest woman if she would have him. He didn't care how long it took to win her over, the child was a Pruit, and he wanted her to have the Pruit name.

Missy had cabin fever bad and had to get out of the house, so she saddled her horse and rode to the main house. Missy found Hanna with the cows. "What are you doing out here?" asked Hanna. "I can't stand it anymore," said Missy, "I had to get out." "I'm going to check on the Pryor's," said Hanna. "You want to go?" "Yes, please," said Missy. "Anything but being couped up inside with those two boys." Hanna just laughed, "Ok, let's go tell Jim where we are going," said Hanna. The two girls rode off down the river trail through the snow to the valley where the Pryor family were staying. The younger son came out and took their horses to the barn. Hanna and Missy unwrapped and went inside the cabin. Hanna and Missy sat down by the fireplace. "What are you girls doing out in this weather?" asked John. "We thought we'd better come check on y'all," said Hanna. "We're fine," said John, "other than Arron. He had a little accident sharpening the axe the other day and cut his hand." "Where is he," asked Hanna, "he's in the bed, it's a bad cut," said Grace. Hanna got up and went to the back bedroom; she smelt the infection when she opened the door. "Oh, my God," said Hanna, "Missy, come here, open that window." Hanna felt Arron's forehead, "dumb, stupid people," thought Hanna, "he's burning up." "Help me get him up," said Hanna. "What are we doing?" asked Missy. "Trying to save his life," said Hanna. "James opened that door," yelled Hanna. James opened the front door. Hanna and Missy took Arron outside and laid him in the snow. Hanna ripped his night shirt off, exposing his naked body, "pack snow around him," said Hanna to Missy. "Cover him up with it," Hanna unwrapped the cut hand. "Oh, my God," said Missy. His hand was swollen and reddish blue. Hanna packed the hand in the snow, then felt his forehead again. Hanna pulled his hand out of the snow, "Turn your head," said Hanna. Missy covered her eyes as Hanna took her knife and cut the wound open. Then squeezed the infection and blood out of it onto the snow. Then she felt his head again, "ok, let's get him up," said Hanna, "James, get me a blanket, not the one he was on." James met them at the door with a blanket, "wrap him up," said Hanna. They laid him down in front of the fireplace, "Is he going to be ok?" asked John. Grace was crying. "Maybe," said Hanna. Arron started coming back around. "Missy, go to the barn and get that jar of salve we use on the horse's cuts," "Hi, Ms. Hanna," said Arron, "What are you doing here?" "Trying to save your life," said Hanna. "Am I dead?" asked Arron, looking around the room. "Almost," said Hanna.

Hanna put the wound paste on the cut and then wrapped it in clean cloths. His fever had been coming down some. "John, keep him here by the fire tonight." "Missy, you stay with him, make him drink water. If his fever comes back, through his butt back into the snow." "I'm going to get the Slade to haul him out of here," said Hanna. Hanna jumped on her horse and rode through the snow back to the homestead barn. "Paul," yelled Hanna. She heard Yes, ma'am, come from the tack room. Paul opened the door. "I need your Slade," said Hanna, "hook it up to one of the draft horses." "Yes, ma'am," said Paul. Hanna warmed up by the heater while Paul hooked up the Slade. "It's ready," yelled Paul. Hanna took the lead rope and wrapped it around her saddle horn, and led the draft horse pulling the Slade behind it. Hanna made it back to the cabin just before dark. Arron was more alert now, but his hand was hurting. "Ok, James, help us load him onto the Slade." They wrapped more blankets around him, then through a canvas over him and tied it down. Hanna looked at John, "If he survives, I'll bring him home in a few days," "If not, I'll bring him back away." Hanna took off leading the draft horse, and Missy followed her on her horse. The moon lit up the trail just enough to see it. Missy rode ahead once they got close; she opened the barn doors. When Hanna got there, she rode right on into the barn with the horses and the Slade. Paul closed the doors, as Hanna and Missy untied the canvas cover, then Paul helped them get him into the tack room. "What happened to him?" asked Paul. "He cut his hand open, sharpening an axe three days ago. Infection has set in, and he had a bad fever," said Hanna. "We are going to need more firewood and water," "Missy, we need rags, go get Momma and some rags, see if she has some antiseptics." Hanna put water on the heater to warm it up. Arron asked Hanna, "What happened?" "That cut you have gotten infected, and the infection got into your bloodstream, you're very sick," said Hanna.

Missy brought Sara to the tack room with supplies. Sara unwrapped the hand. She took a warm, wet rag and wiped away the salve. "Good job, Hanna," said Sara. Arron was moaning the whole time Sara worked on his hand. "Y'all hold him down," said Sara, "this is going to hurt." She took a knife and cut the wound open even more, exposing all the original cut." Arron was screaming by now, and she then cleaned it out with antiseptic on a clean rag. Sara then took a needle and thread and sewed the cut up in the palm of his hand. She wrapped the cut up with a clean cloth, "Only time will tell now," said Sara. "Somebody needs to stay with him tonight. If the fever comes back, let me know," said Sara. "I will," said Missy, "y'all get some sleep," "ok," said Hanna. The next morning, Missy walks to the house and gets breakfast for her and Arron. "Is he still alive?" asked Hanna. "Yep, he's sleeping now. He cried and moaned all night. Men are such babies," said Missy. Hanna and Sara laughed, "Well, here's y'all some food, make him eat," said Sara. "Ok, I will," said Missy," Thanks, she walked back to the barn. Paul was there. "Is he ok?" asked Paul. "Yes, I think so," said Missy. "Well, that's good. I thought he was a goner."

A week later, Arron was up and around helping Paul around the barn some. Sara came every morning to dress to cut. It was healing up fine, no redness, and the pain was gone, just a little soreness. But Sara wanted to wait a few more days before removing the stitches. Hanna had ridden out to the valley a few days ago to let his parents know he was ok and would be home soon. Missy came every afternoon and visited Arron in the tack room. They had become friends; they were the same age, seventeen years old. The only thing was, Missy was seventeen going on twenty, but Arron was seventeen going on fifteen, he was a momma boy. His brother James, who is fifteen, was more grown-up acting than Arron. A week later, Arron went home to his parents and Missy, and Hanna pushed the cows out of the lot. The snow was melting, and it was time to start moving the cows up the river. The Pryor's were moving out of the cabin and back into their tents for the summer. Grace was cleaning the inside of the cabin, getting it back to the way it was. The men were back working on the fences and the new barn in the valley. Hanna and Missy pushed the cows to Joseph's old place and left them there. Hanna wanted to let the Pryor's get the fences built before moving the cows onto her land. But she and Missy moved back into the cabin, to their surprise, it was clean just like they had left it. But there was no food left, Grace told Hanna y'all will eat with us now, I'll cook.

By mid-April, the fencing was finished, and the men were working on the new barn. The plans were that once the new barn was built, the Pryor's could turn the old barn into a house for them to live in while Hanna's new house was being built. It would take two or three years to complete her Ranch house. Hanna and Missy pushed the cows on over to Hanna Valley, with the gates closed on fencing, the cows could eat around them, but not go inside. Letting the grass inside the pastures grow for her horses to eat later. Now that they are set back up at the cabin, Missy and Hanna make one more trip back to the home stead, to get baby Anna. Hanna gives Jim a list of food supplies they would need for the summer, along with a list of building supplies for the barn. Missy and Hanna hugged everyone and told them goodbye for a while, then took off back to the valley. When they got back to the cabin, Grace had supper ready. Two days later, Paul showed up with the food supplies, Hidee was with him, and they had Sissy's horse tied to the wagon. "What's this?" asked Hanna. "Hidee wants a summer job," said Paul. "I was hoping she could help you." "I was hoping you could teach her how to work the cows." Hanna looked at Missy. She said, "I don't care. Get your things. Put them in the cabin on the table for now." They unloaded their supplies and put them away, then carried the other supplies to Grace. She had the boys unload them and put them away. Paul headed back to the ranch. "Ok, Hidee, get on that horse and follow me," said Hanna. As soon as they started moving, Hidee started, "How do you work, cow? I mean, is it hard? What are we trying to do?" in unaccents. Missy and Hanna said, "Shut up, Hidee," as they split up.

Chapter Eight: Horses

Paul and Jim showed up with the building supplies for the barn, and Hanna went in to talk to them. She left Hidee to watch her side. Once she got to the wagons, she could still hear Hidee talking. "What's that noise," asked Jim, "that's Hidee," said Hanna, "what's she doing," asked Jim, "talking," "that's all she does," said Hanna, "to who," asked Jim, "to the cows I guess," said Hanna, "I don't know." After unloading the wagons, Jim told Hanna her horses would be here in two weeks. "Well, the brood mares will," said Jim, "you never told me what kind of stud horse you want." "I know," said Hanna, "I'm working on that," "ok," said Jim, "just let me know what I can do." Paul and Jim left with the wagons, Hanna got Anna from Grace, and took her along with her. From across the field, Hanna hears Missy yell, "Shut up, Hidee." Hanna laughs, and little Anna tries to laugh too. "Funny girls, and they," said Hanna, as she rides back out to them.

Charles comes riding up the next morning, Hanna rode up to him, "Man, this place has changed," said Charles. "Y'all have been busy," said Hanna. "Yep," said Hanna. "I've got mares coming in two weeks," said Hanna. "How many?" asked Charles. "Twenty head," said Hanna. "That's a good start," said Charles. "Well, I've been doing some checking," said Charles, "I found an English thoroughbred stallion you might be interested in." "I might," said Hanna, "tell me about him." "Well, he comes from a good bloodline, I have all that written down," said Charles, "but he's been injured." "What's wrong with him?" asked Hanna. "Nothing that would keep him from breeding mares," said Charles, "he's six years old; he was a jumping horse, he tore a tendon in a hind leg." "The owner had his vet reattach it, and he's heeled up now, but." "But what," asked Hanna, "but he can't jump anymore, the leg heeled up with a twist at the ankle, and he has a slight limp," said Charles. Hanna thought about it for a minute, "So he's crippled," said Hanna, "yep," said Charles, "but he can walk, he just can't jump or be ridden." "He's in San Francisco, California," said Charles. "What are they asking for him?" asked Hanna. "Two hundred dollars," said Charles, "for a crippled horse," said Hanna in a shocked tone. Charles dropped his head, smiling, "With his bloodline, I think he would be worth it," said Charles. "I have train tickets for you and me to go see him next week," said Charles. Hanna's eyes got big. She looked down at Anna, then back up at Charles, "I can't just," "how could I," "I'd have to talk to Jim," "Anna, what," Hanna stammered. "It's just two days," said Charles with a smile, "you traveled three thousand miles by wagon, this is just a few hundred miles by train." "You could have your stallion here when the mares arrive," said Charles. Hanna looked up at Charles. He stared into her eyes with a grin. "Ok, but this is a business trip," said Hanna. "Oh, yes, ma'am," said Charles.

The next Monday, Hanna and Charles loaded onto the train; Hanna was wearing a dress for the first time since she had gotten to Oregon. Sara was keeping little Anna, and Jim was going to check on Missy and the Pryor's. Hanna had money with her and her knife and pistol on, covered by a waist wrap. She was also wearing shoes, something else she hadn't worn in a while. This was also the first time she had ever been on a train, as the whistles blew, and the train started to roll. Hanna had a lump in her throat, but no matter how uncomfortable or scared she was, she would never let it show. Charles smiled at her as the train built up speed. Soon, she relaxed as she and Charles talked about the horse they were going to see. Within a few hours, they would be in a place that would take a week to get to on horseback. Once they arrived in San Francisco, California, at the train station, Hanna was in awe of the size and magnitude of the city. As they stepped off the train, Charles took her arm and led her inside the train station. They waited for the baggage handler to bring them their bags. Once they had them, they walked out onto the cobblestone street. Charles hired a buggy to take them to their hotel. He had already reserved them both a room there. At the hotel, a bellhop took their bags and led them to their rooms. Put your things away, and we will ride out to see the horse," said Charles, "I'm just next door."

Hanna walked into her room. There was a large bed, a chair, a large tub, a bassinet with a pitcher of water, and a closet of sorts with a strange-looking seat with a lid. A brass pipe ran up the wall to a box that had a chain hanging from it. Hanna had no idea what it was used for. She raised the lid on the strange seat and stood there looking at it. The bowl-shaped seat under the lid had water in it. Hanna let the lid back down. Then she went to the bathroom and wet a rag to wash her face. Hanna heard a knock at the door. "It's me, Charles. Are you ready to go?" Hanna walked to the door and opened it. Charles was standing there, "You ready?" asked Charles. "Yes," said Hanna, "but I need to stop by the outhouse on the way." Charles smiled and stepped inside the room. "Here, let me show you," said Charles, as he walked to the closet. He raised the lid, "You set here," "then when you're finished," Charles reached up and pulled the chain; it made a swishing sound, and the water swirled around, then disappeared. Charles picked up a little box of thin paper and handed it to her, "These are to wipe with." "I'll be in the hall, take your time," said Charles. Hanna heard the door close; she pulled up her dress, pulled down her underwear, and sat down. When she finished, she pulled the chain and watched everything disappear. "I've got to have one of these things in my new house, thought Hanna. She washed her hands and went into the hall. Charles showed her how to lock her door with the key, and they went out onto the street.

Charles hired another buggy to take them out past the edge of town to a large barn and stable. Charles asked for the owner, and a very distinguished-looking man came out. "My name is Charles Pruit, and this is Ms. Hanna Evens," said Charles, "I wired you about the six-year-old stallion with the bad leg." "Oh, yes," said the man, "follow me." he led them to the stables. "Here he is," said the man.

He was beautiful standing there, so proud and regal with a bark brown shiny coat, long black stockings on all four legs, black mane and tail. "Oh, my," said Hanna, "he would have been a champion if not for that bad leg," said the man. "Can I go inside?" asked Hanna. "Sure," said the man, "he's a lamb easy to handle. Hanna walked inside the gate, the horse lowered his head for her to touch, she rubbed his face, then walked around him. "His name is a mile long," said the man, "but we just call him Chester because of his chestnut color." Hanna was trying not to act too excited, but she loved him; she could see in her mind the Colts he might throw. "How much were you asking?" asked Hanna. "Two hundred dollars," said the man. "If you will deliver him to the train station in the morning, I'll give you One Hundred and Fifty," said Hanna, "One Seventy-Five and you've got a deal young Ladie," said the man. Hanna turned and shook hands with the man then counted out the money, "let's go get you a Bill of Sale," said the man. Hanna was so happy; the horse was perfect for what she wanted to do. Hanna and Charles rode in the buggy back to their hotel. "Now, where can I go to buy one of those Toilet apparatuses for my new house?" asked Hanna. Charles laughed, "Well, I'm not sure. Let's ask somebody," said Charles. They went inside the hotel, Charles asked the Clerk if he knew who sold the toilets like the ones in the hotel, the Clerk suggested that they try the Hardware store around the block. They left the Hotel and walked down the sidewalk for one block, then turned left. They found the store, and went inside, they had everything in there, beds, chairs, coaches, porcelain-coated wood-burning stoves from two burner holes to eight, wood heaters, and yes, Toilets.

Hanna asked for the store manager, and an elderly man came out to see her. "How can I help you?" asked the man. Hanna introduced herself. She told him she was building a house in Oregon on her ranch and would need some of everything he had there. "Not now, but possibly by next summer," said Hanna. The man told Hanna that if she wanted to pick out some things and put down a fifty percent deposit, he would store the items until next spring and ship them on the final payment. So, Hanna picked out the things she wanted, and the man wrote them all down. Then took Hanna into his office, as the man wrote out an invoice for the items. Hanna looked around his office. There were paintings hanging on his walls. Some of the wagon trains crossing the plains, railroad workers laying tracks, a ship in the harbor, but there in one corner were pictures of native Indians. The one painting that caught her eye was of a Native man wearing a large headdress and gold bands around his arms and ankles. He was also wearing a gold plate on his chest that hung from a gold chain around his neck. Hanna's heart stopped; the gold pieces had the same strange markings as the pieces that she had found on the ranch. "Who is this man asked Hanna. "That is King Uka-man-dao," said the man. The Aztec King who ruled this area many years ago. He fled with his family and a few guards when the Conquistadors from Spain attacked and destroyed his city here. Nobody knows where they went, or what happened to him; he just disappeared.

Hanna stared at the painting, "Would you sell that painting asked Hanna." "I guess so," said the man, "but why would you want it?" "I can tell you're not of Spanish descent." "No, but I am interested in the local history of this area," said Hanna. Plus, my sister is a schoolteacher in Oregon City, it would be fun to research his story. "That it would," said the man. He gave her some printed flyers of his merchandise that she could look over and order from for anything else she might need. Hanna paid the deposit for her things, the man said, "Here," as he removed the painting from his wall, "you can have this. I'll have it wrapped up for you." Hanna and Charles left the store and walked back to the hotel. As they walked along, Hanna took Charles' hand in hers. She looked up at him, "Thank you for this," said Hanna. Once back at the hotel, it was time for supper. They went back to their rooms for a while, then met back downstairs in the lobby. They went to the restaurant in the hotel and got a table.

Charles ordered an array of foods he knew Hanna had probably never tried before. Sea foods, Italian dishes, Chinese dishes, breads, and desserts. They spent the evening talking as Hanna tried all the dishes. She really liked the Italian and Chinese dishes most; a few of the seafood items were ok, but the desserts were wonderful.

Near the end of the evening, after a wonderful day, Charles told Hanna, "I need to tell you something." "I've fallen in love with you and little Anna, and I want to marry you." Hanna started to say something, but Charles stopped her. "Before you answer," said Charles, "I want you to know." "I know you have your own plans and dreams, and I don't want to change any of that." "I want to help you make those dreams come true and give that little girl her family name." Tears filled Hanna's eyes, "I know you care for Anna and me," said Hanna, "you have been a great friend to us both." "But after what Carl did to me, my heart has crusted over," said Hanna, "I don't know how to fix it." "I understand that," said Charles, "but that little girl needs a father, and I will spend the rest of my life helping you fix your heart." "I don't care how long it takes," Charles pulls out a box, then opens it exposing a ring, "we will do things right this time," said Charles, "Marry Me Hanna." "We can do it here, in the morning, before we leave," Hanna looked Charles in the eyes, she could see his love for her in them. "Yes," said Hanna, "I will be your wife, and yes, you can be my child's father, "but just don't ask me to change who I am."

That night Hanna went to sleep in her room, and Charles stayed in his. The next morning, they got married before loading her new horse onto the train. They got married in a small Chapel; they kissed for the first time. Hanna was unsure before the ceremony, but once they kissed, it felt right. They went to the train station, paid for the passage for her horse, and boarded the train. As they traveled back to Oregon, Hanna looked at Charles, "What will you do now?" asked Hanna. Charles looked at her, "I mean, will you keep working for your father?" "No," said Charles, "my father doesn't need me; he has my brothers and plenty of hired hands." "I'm going to be wherever you are," said Charles, "I have plenty of money put back." Hanna loops her arm around his and lays her head on his shoulder as the train rolls along the tracks. That afternoon, they pulled into the station in Oregon City, Hanna unloaded her horse while Charles got their bags. "What now?" asked Charles, "We don't have time to make it to the valley before dark, leading this horse." "No, we don't," said Hanna, "why don't we take the horse to Jim's place and put him up there for the night?" "Then we can come back and stay in town tonight," said Hanna. "Ok, let me go get the buggy from the livery," said Charles.

They rode in the buggy to Jim's, leading the stallion behind them. Jim came out to see the horse, as did Ezy and the boys. Jim took the horse and put him in his barn. "y'all are welcome to stay here tonight," said Ezy. "No, I think we will stay in town tonight," said Hanna, holding out her hand to show off the big diamond ring. "Oh, my God," said Ezy as she hugged Hanna. Jim shook Charlese's hand. Then hugged Hanna, "I think you did the right thing, Sis," said Jim. "Me too," said Hanna. "Don't tell mom or dad yet," said Hanna, "we want to do that ourselves," "ok," said Jim. Hanna didn't know it, but Charles and Jim had a long talk before their trip. Charles confessed his love for Hanna and her baby girl to Jim, and his plans to marry her if she would, Jim gave him his blessing. Hanna and Charles rode back to town, got a room at the hotel, and then ate supper there. That night, they crawled into bed together as newlyweds; the next morning, they left town as husband and wife. They stopped by Jim's and got the new horse, then went to Matt and Sara's house to show her dad. Then, they announced their marriage to them. Sara cried and hugged Hanna, then hugged Charles. Matt shook Charles's hand, Hanna went inside, got little Anna, and brought her out to Charles. "Here, Charles, take your daughter," said Hanna, as big tears filled Charles's eyes. "I'm driving," said Hanna. Hanna reached into the back of the buggy,

"Oh, yeah, Dad, I got you something," as she handed him the wrapped-up painting, then smiled. "We will talk about that later," Hanna, Charles, and Anna got into the buggy and drove off. Matt tore the paper off the painting, "Oh, my God," said Matt.

The next morning, Hanna left Anna with Grace while she and Charles went to tell his parents about their wedding. Carl and his new wife were in Nevada with her family. Mr. Pruit knew Hanna and Jim very well, but Hanna had never met Marria, Charles's mother. The Pruitts had a large Ranch house with many other outbuildings around it. Charles pulled the buggy up to the front steps. He walked Hanna up to the big front door and opened it. As they walked inside, Charles yelled, "Mom!" "Dad!" They heard, "In here, Charles," said Mr. Pruit. Charles led Hanna into his dad's office. Mr. Pruit was setting behind a large wooden desk, his mom was setting on a coach, "Mom, I want you to meet Hanna, "Hanna Evens," from the Kings Land Ranch," "she's now, "Hanna Pruit" "we got married yesterday," Marria's mouth flow open, Mr. Pruit stood up with a big smile on his face. "Congratulations, Son, that's great. He walked over to Hanna and gave her a big, huge, "I'm so happy for you two." "Marria," "this is the girl that shot and killed the bank robber and his horse," Mr. Pruit laughed. "That was what three, four years ago," Hanna nodded, "Oh, and she and her brother Jim saved Carl from the rustlers," said Mr. Pruit. Maria got up and walked over to Hanna and gave her a huge hug, then she hugged her son, Charles. Marria still seemed unsure about how she felt. "Sit down," said Mr. Pruit, "so did you get that stallion you were telling me about?" "Hanna did," said Charles. "That's great," said Pruit. "So, Hanna, what type of mare do you have?" "I have twenty Quoter Horse mares coming next week," said Hanna. "Oh, yes," said Pruit, "that's going to be a good mix." "It will take a while to see a return on them, but that's great," said Pruit, "so Charles, what are your plans now?" "Well, Dad, Hanna has built corrals and lots for her horses, also a new barn in the valley," "she has plans to build a new house there also," said Charles. "I think I'm going to help with that," "I'll put a crew together and get started right away." "Well, son, I know you'll do a good job, and you know horses," said Pruit, "Hanna, I wish you both the best," "keep him busy." "I will," said Hanna, "I'll ride over and see you soon," "I want to see that stud horse." "You're Welcome Anytime," said Hanna.

Charles and Hanna rode back across the river and went to the valley. Charles said, "Show me where you want that house." They rode up to the top of the hill, "right here," said Hanna, "looking over the valley," "ok," said Charles. They went back down the hill, Hanna introduced Charles to the Pryors, then told John. "Tomorrow, go ahead and move everything to the new barn and start converting the old barn into your house." "Missy, take Hidee back home in the morning. I will be here from now on to help you," said Hanna. "Oh, thank you, thank you," said Missy. "We've got horses coming next week, so we need to be ready for them." The next morning, Charles rode to town to look for help to start the foundation work on Hanna's new house. He hired a few men from the camp, then he bought an old wagon and a mule for them to use to get back a fourth from town. The next morning, he would start laying out the foundations while the men haul rocks to the site.

Lizzy, by being in town most days, had heard about a property for sale. She told Jim that she would give him the money if he would buy it for her. Turns out Mr. Urick, the man Jim bought his house and land from, had a younger brother who owed the section between his brother and the town. Mr. Urick, after getting set up in California, had sent words to his brother to bring his family, a wife, and two young girls, to California. Where he and his son were at now to help them build buildings and houses there, he told him to sell his place in Oregon, that there was more money to be made there than he could ever make in Oregon City. Mr. Urick had already bought his brother a house for him and his family in California and told him to come quickly. Jim told Lizzy, "Let the ranch buy the land and house for you." "I want this place, Jim," said Lizzy, "and I have the money." Jim told her he would meet her at the bank the next morning. Lizzy got the cash, then she and Jim went to the land office. The deal had already been made; all Jim had to do was give the man the money and sign the deed. When Jim saw the price, he asked Lizzy, "Are you sure?" The price was way more than what he had paid for his place. "Yes," said Lizzy, "just do it," "ok," said Jim, "if you're sure," "I am," said Lizzy, "I've never been surer in my life." "Well, the ranch doesn't have that much money," said Jim, "let's draw up loan papers so the ranch can pay you back your money." "Just get me that place, Jim," "pay the man, and sign the deed," said Lizzy. Jim did. Jim told the lawyer to write up the loan papers and put the deed in the King's Land Ranches' name. "Ok, let's go see this place you had to have," said Jim.

They didn't have to go far, the property was just on the edge of town, and extending over to the property that Jim's house was on, as they pulled into the driveway of a house that was almost the same as Jim's house, only smaller. They unlocked the house and went inside, as it was with Jim's house, it was fully furnished. The rooms were arranged a little differently, and upstairs was only one large bedroom. "Wow," said Jim, "this is nice, Lizzy." "Now let me show you the best part," said Lizzy. They went back outside and got back into the buggy. They rode back down the driveway to the end, and Lizzy had Jim turn left. As they reached the edge of the main street of town, Lizzy had Jim turn left again. They followed a well-used road a little way from town. Up ahead, Jim started to see structures of some kind. "Turn left up here," said Lizzy, as they turned in. Jim could not believe his eyes; there was a fully operational Sawmill. The sawmill was running as steam rose up from one of the buildings where a steam engine powered the large saw that cut the trees into lumber. There were stacks and stacks of lumber under an open shed. An older man came out to the buggy. "Jim, this is Mr. Wright, who runs this sawmill." "Mr. Wright, this is my brother Jim Evens, who runs our ranch, Kings

Land." "Mr. Wright, I've ordered a new sign. I need you to take down the old one. The new sign will say 'Kings Land Lumber Company. '"Yes, ma'am," said Mr. Wright. "We are almost out of timber, Miss, my logging crews are cutting the last of the big trees on this section," said Mr. Wright. "That's why I brought Jim," said Lizzy, "he can show you where to cut next." "Jim, can you meet with Mr. Wright tomorrow and show him which timber to cut next?" asked Lizzy. Jim looked at Lizzy, then shook his head. "Yes, ma'am," said Jim, "I can do that." "Good," said Lizzy, "well, that's all I needed today, you men work out the details." Lizzy had Jim take her back to Matt's and Sara's. Jim said, "Lizzy, you have always surprised me in many ways," but this, "this is amazing," said Jim.

The next day, with Sissy's help, Lizzy moved into her new house at the edge of town. Lizzy told Missy that she could stay with her if she wanted to, "What?" "Live here on the edge of town in walking distances of everything," said Missy, "are you crazy?" "Yes, please." "Ok, then, let's go get your things," said Lizzy. The girls rode to Jim's house. Sissy went inside to talk to Ezy and Jim, "Mom, Dad," "Aunt Lizzy wants me to move in with her at her new house." Ezy looked at Jim, "Well, Sissy, you're old enough to decide where you want to live, but you need to finish school." "Yes, sir, I will," said Sissy, "we will miss having you around, but it's up to you, you're always welcome back here," said Jim. Ezy gave her a huge, "behave yourself and mind Lizzy," said Ezy. "I will, Momma, said Sissy. Jim hugged her too, she got her things, and left with Lizzy. Ezy started to cry, "Now both my girls are gone," Jim hugged her, "but you did a great job with them," said Jim, "they will be fine." Ezy's and Jim's two boys were growing fast, too; soon, they would be old enough to start school. Lizzy continued to teach school in Oregon but was fast becoming known for her business skills. Lizzy may not have helped much in the building of the cattle ranch, but with her Sawmill now included, the financial side of the operation was growing faster than ever. Fast enough that Jim was now looking for more land to acquire North of Hanna's valley. Turns out that there was more money to be made in lumber production than there was in cattle, since they had their own timber to cut. Jim hired a crew of men to clean up the land that Lizzy had bought by burning the limbs from the downed trees and cutting the tree tops up for firewood. Then he had plans to plant oats, wheat, and corn on its next spring. Matt, their father, was to be a big part of that operation, once the land was ready to plant.

Charles was working on the house's foundations, Hanna had got her mares, but only twelve of them she thought were old enough to breed; the others were two- and three-year-old fillies. She was going to hold them back; she wanted good, strong colts to build her herd out of. Missy was taking care of the cattle; they were all in the valley now, almost six hundred head. Arron's younger brother James turned out to be the only cowboy in the Pryor family. Missy was teaching him the ropes, while Arron helped his father convert the old barn into a house. Anna spent most of her time with Hanna and Charles; she was walking now. With winter coming in a few months, the rush was on to get the Pryor house completed and the foundation set for the new house before the first snow. Jim had the Kings Land Ranch pay Hanna back for the Stud Horse and told her to turn in tickets to Matt for the materials and labor to build her new house in the Valley. Jim purchased another twelve hundred acres for the ranch north of Hanna's Valley. It was mostly timber land, but it did have a few good meadows on it for grazing. After Hanna was sure the horses were bred, and Charles had finished the foundations, Hanna, Charles, Missy, and James moved the cows and the donkeys north onto the new land. Hanna knew there was a risk of moving onto new land this late in the summer when the bears were fattening up for the winter. But she had a plan. Once the cattle were settled, she went out in four directions and shot Elk and Mule Deer. Then, she ripped them open and left them for the bear to find, hoping that by giving them something else to feed on, they would leave her cows alone. The plan worked for the most part, other than the occasional wolf, they had very few problems.

Jim had the timber crew cutting trees off the land behind his house; they wanted to get enough trees stockpiled to keep the Mill going through the winter. This year, for the first time, the main stockholders of the company "Kings Land Ranch" that Hanna had set up would not only get their annual salary, but they would also get dividends from the profits of the Ranch and Sawmill. Matt, Jim, Hanna, and Lizzy were the four stockholders in the Corporation. Lizzy was now also the Lumber company's operations manager, a fancy name for the bookkeeper. Lizzy and Hanna were wealthy young girls when they got to Oregon. With their backing, the family business has grown into the now corporation of "Kings Land Ranch and Timber." Charles and Hanna were living a happy life in their little piece of heaven with Anna, who grew more and more attached to Charles each day. Missy was the new Hanna made over; she drifted among the cattle covered in leather. Everything she needed was strapped to her horse, like Hanna, she loved the seclusion of being out with the cows. Patches now stayed with Missy most of the time, he went where she went, he ate what she ate, and he slept where she slept. Hanna had taught Missy that a good rover becomes part of the herd; it makes them feel safe and stay calm knowing you're there to protect them. Over time, you learn about the cows in the herd, and they learn about you. Missy took the knowledge she got from Hanna and used it to connect with the herd. She would stop by some of the older cows, reach down and scratch their back or head, then ease on. Most of the time, if an older cow was in trouble or scared, they would find Missy, or if she yelled, it was like a Donkey braying, they all turned and looked at her. Six hundred cows and one bull were a lot to keep track of, but Missy looked at every cow or calf every day. There are three kinds of cows in a herd: the "Herd-stirs", the ones that stay grouped together; the "Loners", the ones that stay away from the herd; and the “Wanderers”, the ones that wander off without notice. The last two are the ones Missy has James watching; they are the ones that will get the rest of the herd in trouble if predators come around. But next spring Jim will sell off the steers about one hundred and forty head, which will help until the calves start dropping again, then it's right back to more to watch.

In August, Charles’s father is having a birthday party for his wife, Marria; it’s always been a big event. They have a big cookout, and people from all over come, mostly to show their appreciation to Mr. Pruit, not to see his wife. But they bring gifts and tell her how beautiful she is, and she eats that up. Pruit had sent word to Charles that he wanted Him and Hanna to come to the party and to bring Jim and his wife. Jim said no, but Ezy thought it would be fun; besides, they never went anywhere, so Jim decided to go. Hanna takes Ezy to town and buys her a new dress for the party. Hanna gets one too. Charles is not sure that this is a good idea, seeing how Carl and his new wife will be there too, and he knows how his little brother can be. But, on the day of the party, Jim, Ezy, Charles, and Hanna load up into Ezy’s Buggy, Anna stays with Grace, and the boys stay with Sara. They ride into town and then cross the river bridge that leads to the Pruit Ranch. As they pull up to the house, there are hundreds of people there. All the ranch hands, cooking and prepping things, businessmen and their wives, politicians and their families, and ranchers from neighboring Ranches. All the men were drinking and talking politics, while the ladies branched off into groups. Charles and Hanna walked up to Marria. “Happy Birthday, Mom,” said Charles. Hanna bent down as she and Marria touched cheeks. Jim stuck out his hand and said Happy Birthday, Mom. " Ezy cursed, not knowing what else to do. They walked on as a line had formed behind them. Charles walked over to his dad and shook his hand. Jim did the same, come here, Hanna, " he said as he hugged her. It was all for show. Chanler walked up to Charles and shook his hand, “Have you seen Carl?”

asked Chanler. “No,” said Charles, “I was hoping not to,” “he’s over there,” said Chanler, “drunk as always.”

“Y’all get you a plate,” said Chanler, so they moved over to the food tables, as Chanler followed. They all filled their plates, there was steak, of course, seafood, pasta, and Mexican food. Charles leads them to a bench away from the crowd. There was only room for two to sit, so Charles and Jim stood up while the ladies sat down. Jim and Charles were standing there eating and talking to Chanler when Carl came staggering up with a drink in his hand. “Hey, Charles,” said Carl, “how have you been, brother?” “I’ve been great,” said Charles. Carl looked, and Ezy and Hanna were sitting there in their beautiful gowns. Carl didn’t recognize Hanna in her dress with her hair up. “Well, who are these two beautiful ladies?” asked Carl. Charles stepped up in front of him, “Hey, brother, I heard you married that Evens girl that has that bastard baby, where’s she at?” Jim went for his gun, then remembered Ezy had made him leave it in the buggy. Charles said, “Here, Jim,” “Hold my plate, please.” Jim took Charles' plate, as Charles reared back and hit Carl in the jaw, knocking him smoothly out. They stood there and watched as Carl fell to the ground. Charles looked at Chanler, who was standing by them. “Tell Mom and Dad thanks, the food was great,” said Charles, “as he reached down and took Hanna’s hand, “come on dear, we need to get back to our baby girl.” Jim reached down and took Ezy’s hand, and they followed Charles and Hanna to the buggy. As they crossed the bridge into town, Ezy asked, “what was that all about,” “oh, nothing,” said Charles in a claim voice, “my brother just drinks too much, then runs his mouth.” At Jim’s house, Charles and Hanna get into their two-person buggy and ride back to the Valley. Hanna was smiling, Charles had defended her honor, and she saw the kind of man Carl had turned out to be, not a good man like his brother, Charles.

Two days later, Mr. Pruit came riding up on horseback to the cabin. Charles was up on the hill with his crew, setting posts for the porch. Hanna and Anna were in the barn. "Can I help you, sir?" asked John Pryor. "Well, I was looking for Hanna," said Pruit. "I wanted to apologize for something that happened at my wife's Birthday Party." "She's in the barn, sir," said John as he pointed. "Thank you," said Pruit. Mr. Pruit walked up to the barn and went inside. Anna was playing in the dirt in the alleyway, and Hanna was cleaning out a stall. Mr. Pruit cleared his throat, Hanna stood up, and turned with her pistol in her hand. "Oh, Mr. Pruit, I'm sorry," "habit, I guess," said Hanna as she put her pistol away. Pruit looked at Hanna, then looked at Anna. "Well, I wanted to come by and apologize for the other night," said Pruit, "what Carl said was not appropriate." "Oh, it was correct," said Hanna, "just not called for." Pruit dropped his head. "Hanna, is that my granddaughter there?" Hanna wiped the sweat from her brow with her arm. "Yes, sir," "her name is Anna," said Hanna, "she may have come from Carl," "but that's not her father, Charles Pruit is her father," "you may know him, he's a good man." "Like his father, I think," "a way better man than Carl Pruit," said Hanna as she scooped up more horse manure. "Well, I think that's best," said Pruit, "Charles will do you right; there's no need for anyone else to know the truth." "Can I meet her?" asked Pruit. Hanna walked over to Anna and picked her up from the ground. "Anna, this is your pawpaw Pruit, Charles' daddy," Hanna handed her to him. Mr. Pruit's eyes filled with tears as he looked at the little girl. "She's so beautiful," said Pruit. "I always wanted a little girl, but never had one," "just boys," "she is a gift from heaven." "I promise you this, Hanna," said Pruit, "she will be accepted and known as yours and Charles' daughter and my granddaughter." "Thank you for letting me know her."

The next week, Lizzy's sawmill started delivering the beams and floor joists for Hanna's new house, with the framing lumber to follow. Charles and his crew were ready to start framing up the house floor and the porch. Missy and James had the cattle under control, and John and Arron were almost finished with the barn conversion. Then they would move up the hill to help Charles with framing up the house. Hanna spent most of her time with the horses and working around the barn, with plenty of help now, she had more free time. In the afternoons, she and Anna would take long rides exploring the property and looking for more places to graze the cattle on the new land. She wanted to keep the cattle off the original homesteads so she could give that grass time to recover. One afternoon, while riding along the North border of the new ranchland, Hanna came upon a small valley. In the valley was a small herd of cattle, maybe forty head; there were three men with the cattle. Hanna watched the herd for a while from cover in the trees, she couldn't make out a brand. So, she left and rode back to her valley. Once she got back, she told Charles what she had seen and asked him to go get Jim and Chanler to come to her place. She told Charles she felt that the herd may be stolen, that she couldn't make out the brands, but that they weren't all the same. Charles came back to the cabin after dark and said Jim, Chanler, and some of Pruit's men would be there the next morning.

The next morning, the men were there at daylight. Hanna left Anna with Grace while she took the men out to where she spotted the herd. When they got there, the herd was still there, only bigger; it looked to be sixty or more heads now. There were still three men with the herd, "Jim asked, "how do y'all want to play this?" "Well, we need to see who they are and if the cows belong to them," said Chanler. Charles spoke up, "Jim, if you will cover me with your rifle, I'll ride down there and see who they are," "not without me you want," said Hanna. Charles looked at Jim, "Ok," said Jim, "Hanna, you see those rocks there about halfway down." "You and Charles go set up there with your raffles. Once you're there, I'll ease down into the valley on foot and check the brands." "If they are Pruit or Kings Land brands in the herd, I'll wave my arms," "if not, I'll ease back out." "Ok," said Hanna, Jim started taking his saddle off his horse, "what are you doing?" asked Charles. "Well, if I'm carrying my saddle, maybe they want to shoot me on sight, they will think I lost my horse." "Come on, Charles," said Hanna. They tied their horses and eased down to the rocks, once they were set, Jim said. "Ok, Chanler, if they start shooting at me, y'all come running," "we will," said Chanler." Jim eases down the hill, then walks out into the valley. He moves over close to the herd, trying not to be seen. He looked at the brands on the first few cows, "Bar-P Brand," he eased up There were more Pruit Brands, then he saw an "H" brand, he didn't know that one.

Jim looks in the direction of Hanna and waves his arms, then starts walking to the closest man on horseback. "What is he doing asked Charles. "Just get ready," said Hanna. The man saw Jim and started moving his way. Jim stopped and put down his saddle as the man rode up to him. "Morning," said Jim, "I was out Elk hunting, and a damn bear came into my camp last night and scared my horse off." "I've been following his tracks all morning, then I saw these cows, and thought there might be a farm nearby." "No, farm," said the man in a cold tone. "Oh, ok," said Jim, "well, what's the name of your outfit? Maybe I can buy a horse." "I don't think so," said the man, "well, who's the boss," asked Jim, "I am," said the man. "Well, if you're the boss, maybe you can tell me why all these cows have different brands on them." The man smiled, "That's none of your business," "You're right," said Jim, "I think I'll just shoot you and take your horse." "You can try," said the man as he pulled his coat open. Then he went for his gun. Jim drew first, shooting the man. Then Jim grabbed the man's horse. The other two men came riding through the herd. Hanna fired from the rocks, the second man fell, the third man turned and rode away from the herd and into the trees. Chanler and his crew came down the hill. "Well, Chanler looks like most of these are your cows," said Jim, "except for those 'H' brands cattle, I don't know that brand." "That's the Hamilton Ranch, they are a long way from home, they are from Idaho," said Chanler.

"Well, I'm going to go get my horse and go after the man that got away, maybe I can ask him how they got here," said Jim. Chanler and his men started pushing the cattle out of the valley.

Jim got on the outlaw's horse and rode him up the hill to his horse. Hanna and Charles were there waiting. Jim saddled his horse back up and gave Hanna the reins to the other horse, "Here, take this one with you, he might be a good horse." "So, where are you going?" asked Hanna. "You let one get away, Sis," said Jim with a smile. "I'm going to go find him," said Jim. "Why?" asked Charles. "Well, do you see a camp here?" asked Jim. "No," said Charles, "me either," said Jim, "they were just holding this herd here, building it up." "There are more men somewhere at a main camp, I'm going to find them," said Jim. If I don't, they are just going to come back, or still from somebody else, "we're going to," said Hanna. "Well, stay behind me," said Jim. They rode off in the direction the third man had gone into the woods. Jim found broken limbs where the man had gone through the trees; they followed as Jim looked for signs. Jim stopped and held up his hand. "What is it?" whispered Hanna. "I smell smoke," said Jim. He got off his horse and tied it to a tree, Hanna and Charles did the same. They eased through the trees until they came to an opening. There in the clearing was a camp, with a wagon, some tents, and about five other men. One older man was cursing and throwing things as the third man was telling him what had happened with the cows. Jim heard the man say, "it took us two weeks to gather that herd," "y'all mount up, let's go get them back." Jim motioned for Hanna and Charles to move; they went back to their horses. "Let's go," said Jim. They rode back out into the valley and raced across it, following the cattle trail. On the other side, Jim stopped, "Charles, you ride ahead and tell Chanler that they are coming." "Tell him to get the cattle across the river, then hunker down and be ready," said Jim. Charles took off after his brother as Jim and Hanna followed for a while, then turned off and went up into some rocks.

Jim and Hanna pulled out their Sharps rifles and set up on the rocks. "What's the plan?" asked Hanna. "Well," said Jim, "an old man once told me, when you're outnumbered, just keep killing them until they stop coming." In a few minutes, they heard the horses coming. "You take the right side, I'll take the left," said Jim, "just work your way to the middle." There must have been more men in the tents, because when they came into sight, there were more than a dozen men riding hard. "Get ready, I'll tell you when," said Jim, as the riders got closer. Jim said, "Now Hanna." They started firing, two men fell, the others spread out looking for cover, two more fell. The ones that had made it to cover started shooting back. Charles had made it to Chanler. He left two men with the cows on the other side of the river while he, Charles, and the others went back to help Jim and Hanna. Jim picked off another one, Hanna caught one moving to another spot, and picked him off. The rustlers had figured out where Jim and Hanna were hiding and just kept firing into the rocks. "We've got to move," said Jim, "they have us pinned down here." Jim looked at Hanna, "Sis, I love you," as he jumped up and swung up onto his horse and rode out from behind the rocks into the clearing. As the rustlers stood up to get a shot at Jim, Hanna picked them off, one, two, then three. Chanler and his men rode into the clearing and opened fire on the last few outlaws. Two of the rustlers made it to their horses and were trying to get away, Chanlers' men chased them down and shot them. Everything got quiet. Jim rode back to Hanna, "Don't you ever do that to me again," said Hanna in a scared and angry voice. Chanler came riding up to Jim and Hanna, "You Evens are a crazy bunch," said Chanler, "what about all these horses," asked Chanler, "string them together and let Hanna have them," "let your men have their guns and money," said Jim. "Sounds fair to me," said Chanler. Charles came up, got off his horse, and hugged Hanna. "You, ok?" "I was worried," said Charles. "I'm fine," said Hanna as she gave Charles a kiss.

Chapter Nine: New Discoveries

After another long, hard winter, Charles and his crew were back working on Hanna's new ranch house. The house was completed on the outside, and it looked like they would finish the inside before fall. The Kings Land Ranch had lost a couple more of the older cows to the weather, but all in all, it wasn't that bad. Missy, James, Jim, and Hanna had moved the steers to the lot at Matt's barn to be fattened and then sold. Lizzy was busier than ever with her sawmill shipping lumber all over the country by train. She had orders back logged for months so she bought and installed another big saw and a planning machine. Kings Land Ranch and Timber Company were well off now, making more money than they ever dreamed. Mr. Pruit made trips to the valley at least once a week to see Anna, she was trying to talk some now. Pruit loved to hear her say "pawpaw" when he picked her up Charles and Hanna had not taken her to see Maria. She knew about her, well, she knew what Pruit had told her. He told her that after Carl had gone back to school and Charles was tending out the strays, he and Hanna started spending time together and Hanna got pregnant by Charles. That's why they went off to California to get married, after the baby was born. Maria still doesn't think Hanna is good enough for Charles, and that she trapped him for his money. But Mr. Pruit knows the truth and thinks that Charles is the one who doesn't deserve her or that little girl. But he's so happy she is part of his family, and wishes he had a son like Jim.

Ever since Hanna brought back the painting from California of the Aztec King, Matt has been doing research in his spare time. Trying to find out the story behind the King and the items Jim and Hanna found. So far, he has learned that the King and his family, a wife and four children, fled what's now known as San Francisco, California, with five guards. Along with them, they took a chest of gold and precious stones. The conquistadors destroyed the city and took all the other valuables they could find. The king was assumed to have a gold mine somewhere near the city that was well hidden. The conquistadors searched for years, looking for the mine, but there is no written record of it ever being found. The King and his family were taken along the Clackamas River up into Oregon, according to symbols found in rocks along the way. But nobody knows where they stopped or how far they got; some think they made it to Canada or to the Washington State area. But Matt, Jim, and Hanna know how far the king made it. They just didn't know about the others with him. Matt kept digging for information on the Aztecs and their beliefs.

Matt told Jim that he should go with Hanna and that they should go back to where they found the skeleton and look for some more signs. He told him to look for an old stone structure of some kind, where the King may have started building a new Village or something. He told Jim the story about the box of Gold and Stones. Jim said he would tell Hanna the next time he went to the valley. Hanna's house was almost finished, and her things from California had come in. She had the toilets in her bathrooms, all three of them. Hanna, Charles, and Anna would be moving in soon, but Missy wants to stay in the cabin for now. Jim rode out to the valley to see Hanna; he told her about what their father had found out about the King. Hanna laughed, "A box of Gold," "wouldn't that be something," said Hanna. "Well, it's going to be next spring before I can help do any exploring," said Hanna as she pulled open her coat. "Hanna," said Jim, "another baby," "yap," said Hanna, "when," asked Jim, "November," said Hanna. Jim hugged his sister, "That's great," said Jim. "We're going to have a big cookout next month," said Hanna, "when the house is finished, so I can show it off to everyone." "Tell everyone back home, I'll let you know when," said Hanna. "Sounds good," said Jim.

Jim decided on his way back home to go by the spot where they had found the skeleton. Once there, he started circling the area around the springs. Jim was a good tracker, but trying to find signs hundreds of years old was something new for him. He worked his way out around the area, looking for piles of stones. It was getting late, so he marked the spot where he stopped looking so, he could start there later. As Jim was leaving, he saw something sticking out of a big tree above his head. He rode over to it and stood up in his saddle. It was a long spearhead made of some type of metal. It was embedded in the tree. Jim took his knife and dug around it. There was no handle; there was only about three inches sticking out from the bark. It looked like the tree had grown around it over the years. Jim figured it was closer to the ground at one time, but as the tree grew up and out, it went up with the tree. Could this be something from when the King was there, thought Jim, maybe he is close to their old village.

The next morning, Jim took his father, Matt, and a crosscut saw and an axe to the tree; the two men cut the tree down. Jim wanted the spearhead if that's what it was; he was hoping that was a clue to the location where they were staying. Jim took the axe and chopped around the spot where the blade was embedded. After a few hours of cutting and chopping, they got the spearhead out of the tree. It was about eight inches long by two inches wide at the widest point, with sharp, tapered edges back to a narrow shank. It was metal, alright, but what kind, wondered Jim and Matt. It was the blackest grey color, all but about two inches at the tip, it was a shiny silver color. They could tell that the metal had been hammered out somehow and sharpened. "I believe it's silver," said Matt, I think the tip is what was embedded first by throwing it and sticking it into the tree. Then, over time, the rest tarnished, and the tree grew around it, embedding it there. Matt knew from his research that the local Indians used rock spear tips, not metal. "This would have been smelted, poured into a mold, and then hammered out, something the American Indians knew nothing about," said Matt. "Maybe it was a Spanish Conquistador's spear tip," said Jim. "Could be," said Matt. "Let's look around and see what else we can find," said Jim. They walked the area over, looking for something, anything that looked to be that old.

Jim walked up to the top of the ridge, "Up here, Dad," yelled Jim. Matt went to where Jim was. "What is it, son?" asked Matt. "I don't know," said Jim. "It's something, maybe," he brushed the leaves back and uncovered what looked to be a pile of rocks. They uncovered an area of about six feet wide and four feet high. Jim stood back and looked at it. "Just an old pile of rocks," said Matt. "I don't think so," said Jim. "Look at how these rocks in the middle are stacked," Jim moved some more brush and leaves. Jim took a stick and drew a line around one area, "Look, see how these rocks are stacked in an unformed pattern," said Jim. He took his hands and wiped the dirt and moss off the rocks. "It's an opening," said Jim. "What are you talking about?" said Matt. "These rocks didn't come from here. These are river rocks," said Jim. "See how smooth they are compared to these over here, only running water makes rock smooth like that." "I see it now," said Matt, "you're right, they are in like a half circle," said Matt. "Good eye, son," "What does it mean?" asked Matt. "It means somebody put that rock there to hide something," said Jim. "Like a chest of gold," said Matt, "let's not get carried away, but something's behind those rocks," said Jim. "It's getting late," said Jim, "let's hang a flag up close by and throw some leaves back over it." "We need some more tools, like hammers, picks, prybars, and such." The two men left after covering the rocks and went back to Matt's house, where they put the tools into the wagon to haul out there the next morning.

Neither Jim nor Matt got much sleep that night because of thinking about what could be behind the rock wall they had found. The next morning, the two men headed back to the wall; Matt was driving the wagon. They knew they couldn't get the wagon all the way into the wall, so they parked it as close as they could. Then they carried the tools on Jim's horse; everything was just as they had left it the afternoon before. They brushed the leaves away again and started chipping at the rock joints. There was no mortar holding the rocks in place. But somehow whoever stacked the rocks did it in a way that locks the rocks together. Matt said, "I read about this kind of structure, there is a key stone somewhere in it, we just have to find it." "There is a single stone that locks it all in place," said Matt. They cleaned all the dirt, moss, and roots away from the smooth stones. They looked at each stone one at a time; they were all the same size and shape. Then Jim said, "Here." There was one stone near the top that had been chiseled and shaped to fit. "That's it," said Matt. Jim took a bar and started working around the edge of the stone until it moved just a little. "Get another bar, Dad," said Jim. Matt took another bar and put it on the other side. They wiggled the stone until it came out and fell to the ground. Jim tried to look inside the hole, but there was just darkness on the other side. They put a bar in the hole crossways. Then, Jim tied a rope to it, got on his horse, wrapped the rope around his saddle horn, and backed the horse up. The rocks started to fall. Matt yelled, "Yahoo, as the top half of the wall fell to the ground. Jim tied his horse back up, then went to his dad, "Well, now we've got to move these rocks," said Jim. They started moving and stacking the rocks to one side until they were able to get back to the opening. The hole behind the rocks looked to be about ten feet deep by six feet wide by eight feet tall. They started pulling down the rest of the stones and throwing them to the side. Jim said, "I'm going to be pissed if there is nothing in here."

Jim crawled up inside the hole, "Dad, there is nothing in here," said Jim, "just some old writings and carvings on the wall. "Bullshit," said Matt. Jim crawled back out of the hole and stood up, I need more light," said Jim. "There is no way somebody went to all this trouble to build this wall for nothing," said Matt. He took a green limb and wrapped a bandana around it, then took a match and lit it. Matt then crawled up into the hole. He looked all around him and up above him, "There's got to be something here," said Matt. Then he saw it, "Jim over here." Jim crawled inside with his dad. "There, son." Matt pointed to a stone in one of the side walls. It had strange writing carved in it and a line going down to the ground. "What does it mean?" asked Jim. "I don't know, but it mines something," said Matt. "Here, hold this torch," said Matt. He ran his finger down the line to the ground, then grabbed a handful of sand. Matt turned and looked at Jim. They both said it at the same time, "It's buried," "Let me get a shovel," said Jim. He crawled out of the cave, came back with a shovel, and started digging. He dug about two feet deep, but there was nothing. "damn," said Jim, "they sure went to a lot of trouble to hide whatever it is." Jim kept digging as the hole got deeper, wider, and longer. Finally, after digging almost three feet deep, Jim hit something with his shovel. The two men lay on their bellies and started digging by hand. It was a rectangular box; they uncovered the lid. It was made of wood but had ornate carvings on it, and as they dug along beside it, their anticipation was building. After a while, they reached the bottom of the box. They were both breathing hard. Jim got his fingers under it and tried to lift one side. It didn't move, then they noticed that on each long side, there were two slots made in the wood to put poles in. Jim dug the hole longer on one end so he could get down into the hole with the box. He put the two prey bars into the slots on one end and lifted, and the box broke loose from the ground. Jim had his father go cut two green poles that would fit into the slots and be five feet long each. Matt came back and handed Jim the poles. Jim slid them in place, and Matt dug out a spot on his end where he could stand and help lift the box. Together they lifted the box out of the hole and set it to the side.

The two men were exalted; they sat on the edge of the hole, looking at the box. It was beautiful. With ornate carving all over it and writings, the box had gold straps nailed to it, gold hinges, and a gold latch. It was heavy, over two hundred pounds at least, 18" x 36" x 24" tall. Jim looked at Matt, "You ready to take it outside, Dad?" "We can try," said Matt. They lifted the box and slowly moved to the opening. Once outside, they set it down. "What now?" asked Matt.

"I don't know," said Jim, "should we open it?" "I don't know how much more excitement I can take right now," said Matt. "How are we going to get it down this hill to the wagon?" "Will, let's build a traverse," said Jim, "I'll cut two long poles, put them in my strips with a couple of cross pieces, we will set the box on the poles and tie it down." "You can lead the horse while I watch the box," said Jim. "Sounds like a plan," said Matt. They got the traverse rigged up with the box on it and started down the hill. Once they had made it to the wagon, they put their tool into the wagon, lifted the box, and set it on the back of the wagon. "Well, Dad, I think now's the time," "it better not be full of rock," said Matt. Jim opens the latch, but the lids are stuck. Jim takes a bar and gently breaks the seal on the box, and raises the lid. Jim and Matt just stood there looking; they said nothing, they just stared inside the box for a few minutes. "Oh, my God," said Matt. Jim was speechless; there were some rocks in the box. Some gold rocks, some silver rocks, but mostly raw gemstones, blue, green, red, and diamonds, large diamonds uncut raw as big as hen eggs. Jim slowly closes the lid and latches it back. Jim looks at his dad, "We did it, Dad." "We found the King's treasure." "Never in my life," said Matt. "Let's go home," said Jim. Matt nodded, Jim put a canvas over the box, then got on his horse. Matt drove the wagon.

They rode off back to Matt's house. Jim was thinking, how is this possible? This doesn't happen by chance. Hanna and Lizzy find all the gold on their way to Oregon. Hanna finds the King's body, then a picture of the King, the spear tip in the tree, and now this. Jim looked up to heaven, "Why us, Lord?" "Thank you, thank you, thank you, but why, Lord!" Matt pulls up to his porch steps. "We need to get mom to send Reeha home early," said Jim, "the fewer people who know about this, the better off we'll be." Matt went inside the house. After a little while, Reeha came out and walked to the cabin. Jim uncovered the box, and he and his father carried it into the house. They set the box on the floor by the table, "y'all better not be making a mess in there," said Sara as she came out of the kitchen. "What is that?" asked Sara. Matt hugged her and smiled, "We did it," said Matt. "Did what?" asked Sara. "Remember me telling you about the King and the research I have been doing about him," said Matt. "Yes, vaguely," said Sara, "I didn't pay a lot of attention to you and your wild goose chase." "Well, there's the goose, woman," said Matt pointing at the box, "Jim told his mom, "Open it." Sara bent down and unlatched the box then opened it; she stood there looking at it. Sara looked at Jim, then looked at Matt, "how," "where," "oh, my God is that real," Jim laughed. "Yep, it's real, it's the Kings' treasure, and now it's ours," said Jim.

"We need bags," said Jim, "sugar sacks, meal bags, coffee bags, anything you can find to put this stuff in." Sara went to the kitchen and came back with some empty bags. Jim and Matt started going through the box, picking out the gold first. They separated the nuggets by size and put them into three separate bags. Then they picked out the colored stone and separated them by color, saving the diamonds for last. After removing the diamonds, there was more gold at the bottom of the box, and Torques, stones, red, and blue. After bagging everything up, they had five bags of gold, three bags of diamonds, a bag of each color of Gemstones, a bag of red Torques, and a bag of blue Torques, thirteen bags in all. Plus, gold bracelets, rings, and chains that filled another bag, "How much is all that worth?" asked Sara. "I don't know," said Matt, "more than our family will ever need," said Jim. "Historically, with the painting and the gold item that came off the body, plus the story, and the treasure box, Millions."

They put all the bags in the box, but the bags of gold would be the easiest to sell without suspicion. "Now, where should we put the box?" asked Jim. "Under the floor in Missy and Sissy's old room," said Matt. "We can remove some of the floorboards and dig a hole in the ground, bury the box, then put the floorboards back. "Ok," said Jim, "let's get started. They carried the box to the doorway of the girls' room. By supper time, they had the box buried and the floor back down. The next day, Jim rode to Lizzy's house with a bag of gold. He went inside and told her the story of how Hanna found the body and how he and Matt found the treasure. He gave her a bag of gold and said, "This is your part of the gold." "I don't know when or how we will sell the other." "Thank you, Jim," said Lizzy, "I have money, but I was about out of gold." Jim left Lizzy's and went back to Matt's. He got two bags of gold and headed to Hanna's. She had been the one who invested the most in the cattle and now the horses. Jim and Matt thought it only fair that she should get the most gold. Jim rode up to her barn, knowing she would probably be there, and he was right, she and Anna were inside. Jim told Hanna the story about how he and Matt found the chest. Hanna said, "damn, I hate I missed that adventure." Jim gave her the two bags of gold. "Oh, my God," said Hanna, "thank you, Jim." "Us Evens' sure have been blessed, haven't we?" "We sure have," said Jim. "Ok, tell everyone next weekend I'm having my Bar-B-Q. I expect everyone to be here," said Hanna. "We will," said Jim. When Jim got back to Matt's, he gave Matt the bag with the biggest nuggets, and he took the other one. "Ok, Dad, the rest is up to you. Let me know what you find out." "Sure thing, son."

The next Saturday, Hanna had her big cookout. She butchered a young steer. Sara and Reeha came out that morning to help Hanna and Grace cook. Paul, John, and Charles were cooking the steer over an open fire, with Arron, James, and Missy watching. Sara fell in love with Hanna's toilets. Hanna told her she would order one for her house. Matt, Jim, Ezy, and the boys got there mid-morning, and Paul and his boys had set up long tables the day before by the fire pit. Hanna had invited Mr. Pruit and Marria, although she didn't expect Marria to come; Charles had invited Chanler and his wife, Gail, an Indian woman Marria didn't approve of either. He also invited some of Chanler's ranch hands, whom he knew. Surprisingly, just before noon, Pruit and Marria showed up in one buggy, Chanler and his wife in another buggy, followed by five of their ranch hands. Mr. Pruitt pulled up to the new house while Chanler and his bunch went to the barn area. Hanna pulled off her apron and went to the door to meet Mr. & Miss Pruitt. Hanna opened the door as they walked up the steps. Marria walked in first, Hanna gave her a hug, as if she didn't know Marria disliked her, then she hugged Mr. Pruit. "Welcome," said Hanna, "make yourself at home." "Oh, my," said Marria, "are you expecting?" "Yes, ma'am," said Hanna, "in November." "Y'all come on back, I want you to meet my mom," "Mom, this is Marria, Charles' mother, and his father, J.C. Pruit." "This is Grace, she works for me, and Reeha, she works for my mother, Sara." "We are just about through cooking," said Hanna. "You two look around," said Hanna. They went through the house, "your son Charles built this house for Hanna," said Mr. Pruitt. "How much did it cost him?" asked Maria. "Nothing," said Pruit, their ranch paid for everything, they have their own sawmill, and Hanna has her own money." "She doesn't need Charles' or ours," said Pruit, "not everybody you meet is looking to get to our money, dear."

As the Pruitt's were walking out, they asked Hanna, "Where is my granddaughter?" "With her father somewhere," said Hanna. "I'll find her," said Pruit. He and Marria walked out and down the steps, then down to the barn area, where everything was gathered up. Charles was surprised to see his mom walking up. "Hi, Mom," said Charles as he gave her a hug. Mr. Pruit had spotted Anna, "There, my baby girl," "Pawpaw, said Anna as she ran to him. "Who's that?" asked Anna, looking at Marria. "That's your grandmother," "What's her name?" asked Anna. "You can call me Marria," said Marria. "Come on," said Anna as she grabbed Maria's hand. Anna started pulling her to the barn. Marria looked back at Pruit. "Just go with her," said Pruit. "I have baby horses' moan," said Anna. She led Marria inside the barn. Mr. Pruit just laughed, "You ride horses," asked Anna. "I used to," said Marria, "but not anymore." "Why?" asked Anna, "I ride every day." "My mom got a baby in her belly," said Anna. "I saw that," said Marria. "It's a kid, not a horse," said Anna. Maria's heart was melting, and as much as she tried not to, she just couldn't help but fall in love with Anna. "Moan, Mari, said Anna, "I'm hungry." Anna pulled Maria back out to the fire pit, "Dad," yelled Anna, "cut me and Mari a little piece of that meat." Charles smiled. He shaved off a little piece of meat and handed it to Anna. She put it in her mouth. "Good," said Anna, "well give Mari a piece," "oh, ok, said Charles, he shaved a piece for Marria and handed it to her with a smile. Marria put it in her mouth, "in case you're wondering mom," said Charles, "Anna is the boss of this outfit," Marria smiled.

The rest of the food came out, and everyone started to fill their plates to eat. Anna ran between her pawpaw and Marria, making them taste everything. By the end of the evening, Marria was broken like a wild horse; she was talking baby talk, hugging Anna, and even hugged Chanler's wife before they left. Charles and Chanler said, "It's a miracle, but Sara said, "No, it's just grandbaby love, the strongest love there is." The rest of the guests stayed around until late that afternoon, the ladies all helped clean up, then Chanler and his wife left the valley along with the ranch hands. Lizzy and Sissy spent the night at Hanna's while Jim, Matt, Sara, Ezy, and the boys went home, along with John, Reeha, and Hidee. It had been a good day, and one Marria Pruit wouldn't forget, she realized now that no matter how she felt about her two sons' lives, they would go on with or without her blessing. The next week, Hanna had Missy, James, and Charles bring the herd back to the valley for the winter. The bowl-shaped valley is more sheltered from the cold winter winds than the main homestead, especially since more trees have been removed from there. Hanna is too far along with her pregnancy to be riding her horse now. Charles wants her to take it easy and be more careful, something that's very hard for Hanna to do.

On November 14, 1860, Hanna gave birth to her second child, another little girl, they named her Cristina Louise Pruit. She looked a lot like Sara, her grandmother, Grace, and Missy helped deliver the baby. Charles was a proud father, and he doted over the new baby and Hanna when Anna let him. That baby was her, she thought, just like every newborn colt or calf on the place. For the next few days, there was a constant trail of visitors to Hanna's home coming to see the new baby. Even Mr. and Mrs. Pruit, Marria, sat and rocked the baby as Anna stood guard over them. Charles was doing Hanna's chores with the help of Arron, while Grace took care of the house and Anna. Mr. Pruit slipped out of the house and went to the barn to look at the horses and talk to Charles. "Congratulations, Son," said Pruit to Charles, "that's a beauty, child." "Yes, sir, she is," said Charles with a smile. "I'm proud of you, son," said Pruit, "your mom is too, although she'll never say it." "I know, Dad," said Charles. "But that's ok, we're happy," said Charles, "that's all that matters to me.

After a few days, Hanna was up and around. She left the baby with Grace while she and Anna worked in the barn. Well, while Hanna works and Anna plays with Patches, he's never far away when Anna is outside now. Patches don't go out with Missy since Anna got big enough to play around the barn, but he will still help with moving the cows. But the rest of the time, he's watching over Anna; he follows her around, wherever she goes. If she gets too close to a stall with a horse in it, he stands between her and the stall. "Move Patch," says Anna, but he's not moving. If she keeps trying to get to the horse, Patches will bark, alerting Hanna. "Anna, get away from those horses," "you know the rules," Hanna would walk by and rub Patches' head. Hanna was content; her life was full of love and joy. She was doing what she loved to do, but it seemed like yesterday, she and Jim were throwing knives, shooting arrows, and hunting game. Now, she had her own family, and Jim had his; their mother and father's dreams had come true. But their journey was not over yet, not by a long way, as the whole family grew and so did the problems and the challenges. Hanna raised her voice, "Anna, what did I say?" "Yes, Momma," said Anna.

Chapter Ten: War

Matt had been in contact with a Museum Curator about the artifacts the family had found. They were more than interested in obtaining them to display them in their museum. However, they were also interested in the skeleton remains of the King, so Jim and Matt went back to the site to recover the bones. Matt had Lizzy have her men build a box to put the items in, including the skeleton, the gold bands, the chest plate, and the painting. The treasure chest was not included, nor was it mentioned to the Curator. The Museum was sending a man to Oregon City by train to view the items and make an offer to obtain them. Matt was to meet the man, Mr. Eles, at the train station on March 27th. 1861. Jim told Hanna about the man coming, and she said she would be there with Jim and Matt. The pieces were placed in the casket-shaped box, with the skeleton party arranged. They placed the bands back on the arm bones and leg bones. Then, I placed the breast plate on the rib cage, put the lid on it, and propped the painting agents in the box.

March 27th. Matt met the train in Oregon City and waited for the passengers to unload. He spotted a man in a suit and hat wearing wire-rimmed glasses toting a briefcase. He knew that was probably his man, "Mr. Eles," yelled Matt. The man turned and smiled, "Mr. Evens, I presume," said the man. "Yes, Sir," said Matt as he reached his hand. "This way, sir," said Matt as he took him to his buggy. They drove out to Matt and Sara's house, and Matt took him inside, where Jim and Hanna were waiting impatiently. "Mr. Eles, this is my son Jim and my daughter Hanna; they are the ones who found the body, and Hanna acquired the painting in California. The man looked at the painting, then Matt showed him his notes on his investigation of the King. Then the man wanted to see the artifacts. Jim removed the lid from the box, and the man took a deep breath. "Oh, my," said the man, as he looked at the skeleton, then back at the painting. "What an amazing find," said the man, "and you found him on your land," said the man, "yes," said Hanna. "Amazing," said the man, "how, where?" Hanna told the man the story of how, while filling her canteen with water, she found the chest plate, then she and Jim found the skeleton.

"He was not buried there; the bones were only a few inches deep. He died there," said Hanna. Fallen leaves and brush over the years had covered him up, "Yes, yes, I see," said the man. "I can see where a rodent has nibbled on the bones at one time." "What can you tell us about the marking on the gold?" asked Matt. "Aztec," said the man, "definitely," "we're not sure how he died," said Jim, "but we did find this nearby." Jim pulled the spear tip out of his back pocket and handed it to the man. The man's eyes got even bigger. He looked the spear over closely. "Do you know what this is?" asked the man. "A spear head," said Jim, "no, no, not just a spear head," said the man, "a Spanish Spear Head." "Conquistador," said the man. Hanna told the man the story the store owner told her about how the King fled from his city because of the Conquistadors. "So, how much is it all worth?" asked Jim, getting to the point. The man said, "You cannot put a price on this, it's priceless. "It's worth is beyond monetary." "The gold, yes, you could sell, but the history, the story of this man, oh, unconceivable worth." By now, the man was shaking, "I know you expect to get something for your troubles," said the man. "Mr. Evens, if you would be so kind as to take me to town, where I can wire my office, I will make you an offer." "Sure," said Matt, and Matt got into the buggy; Jim and Hanna followed on horseback.

Matt took the man to the telegraph office and waited outside with Jim and Hanna. After about thirty minutes, the man came back outside. "Well," asked Matt, "the Museum is willing to offer you a finder's fee of fifty thousand dollars, plus you will get credit for the discovery of the artifacts." Matt looked at Jim, Jim looked at Hanna, "That's ten times the value of the gold pieces," said the man. Hanna and Jim said, "ok, let's go to the bank." The man got into the buggy, and Matt drove him to the bank. They all went inside. “Hello, Matt, Jim, Miss Pruit,” said the banker. “This man needs to get some money wired to us,” said Matt. “Sure thing,” said the banker. Jim, Matt, and Hanna sat down while the man got with the banker. After about an hour, the man brought Matt the cashier's check for fifty thousand dollars. Matt handed it to Jim. “Ok, let’s go get your box,” said Matt, so you can get it ready to put on the train. “Jim, you and Hanna take care of money deposits,” said Matt. “We will,” said Jim. Jim had the banker put forty thousand dollars into the Ranch account, Jim put three thousand into Matt’s account, three thousand into his account, and gave Hanna four thousand dollars cash. They still had the Gemstones and the Diamonds, they would split up later, but there was no need for any of that now.

That same year, seven of the Southern States, in January 1861, seceded from the United States over the election in 1860 of President Lincoln. On April 12, 1861, the War broke out between the states, over decades of tension over Slavery expanding into the Western States. Political reasons mostly, over the export of Cotton, Sugar Cane, and other goods out of New Orleans, but Lincoln needed a cause to declare War on those states other than the money. After all, not being able to tax the goods leaving the richest states in the country was not acceptable and had to be stopped. But to get his party’s support behind him, he had to declare Slavery as the reason for the War. Even though at that time there were just as many slaves in the Northern States as in the South, not only Blacks, but also Chinese. Thankfully, but for the few men from Idaho, Oregon, and Washington States who decided to fight for the Union Army, the War had very little effect on those States. Most of the fighting was done on the Eastern Seaboard, but eventually spread out into the middle of the Southern States along the Mississippi and Missouri Rivers, and then into New Orleans.

Local newspapers reported on the events of the War regularly, but other than reading about it in the papers, the Evens and their neighbors were mostly isolated from it, until the fall of 1861, when the Union Army was paying top dollars for horses broken and ready to ride. A group of men claiming to have a contract with the Union Army to supply them with horses. Came to Oregon and visited all the Ranches around the area. They were told by most of the Ranchers that they had no horses to sell. Their horses were needed to run their cattle operations, which were their livelihood. At first, the men thanked them and moved on to the next ranch. There was one supposed enlisted man in uniform with the ten other men. After a week, the men had left Oregon City and had not been seen again for a while. Then, suddenly, horses started going missing, horses tied outside businesses, the salon, and from the livery station just disappeared. After three days, reports from some of the ranchers that horses had been stolen from them also. On the fourth day, Chanler Pruit came to Jim's house. They had lost twenty-five horses overnight. Jim rode out to Hanna's valley. He told her about the horses being stolen and to be on guard. Hanna moved all her horses inside the barn, and the carols, they stood guard over them day and night.

The Sheriff wired the Union authorities asking if they had men in the area to purchase horses, they wired back no, not anyone that for West. The Sheriff notified the Ranchers that the government was not buying horses in their area. Chanler came back to Jim, asking him if he would help them find out where the horses were being taken. Jim said he would help, but first, he needed to go tell Hanna what was going on. He told Chanler that he would meet him at his ranch in the morning. Jim saddled his horse and rode out to the valley. When he got there, John and Missy were standing guard at the barn. Missy told Jim that Charles and James had been shot last night when rustlers came into the barn and took eight of Hanna's brood mares. They headed South. "Where's Hanna?" asked Jim. "Where do you think?" "She's gone after them," said Missy. "Charles and James are ok," "James has a flesh wound, but Charles was shot through the right shoulder." "Damn," said Jim, "Missy, go to the Pruit Ranch and tell Chanler that I'm headed North along the river, that I will leave flags for him to follow," said Jim. "John, turn the horses out all but the stud horse, take everybody to the main house, and guard Charles and the kids." "I'll go after Hanna," said Jim, "Missy, when you leave the Pruitt, go by the homestead and tell Mom and Dad to go to my house and stay with Ezy and the kids.

Messy left in a gallop, as did Jim. As Jim got to the river, he started looking for tracks; he found fresh horse tracks over older ones. He got off his horse to get a closer look. The fresh track was Hanna's big white horse. Jim got back on his horse and followed them. Just before dark, he reached the end of the Evens' property. He kept going, he stopped, and got off his horse. Jim followed the tracks on foot, leading his horse. Jim had been tying flags along the way. The tracks turned Northeast across an open area, after about four or five miles it turns back Nouth. All at once, as the group of tracks keeps going north, Hanna's tracks turn east into the trees. Jim hung a flag on the tall grass, then he followed Hanna's tracks into the trees just as it got daylight. He saw her big white horse tied to a tree. Jim ties his horse and eases up close to Hanna's horse. "That's close enough, Mr.," said Hanna. Jim raised his arms, "Don't shoot, Sis," said Jim, as he turned around. Hanna crawls out from under a pile of brush and leaves she had put over her bedroll. She picks up her bedroll and then shakes it off. She then rolls it up. "What took you so long?" asked Hanna. "Well, no one sent me word," said Jim, "I came by your place to tell you I was going after them for the Pruit's." "Why the Pruitt's?" asked Hanna. "Because they lost twenty-five head to the same night," said Jim. "Well, they're not far from here," said Hanna, "they stopped just before dark, I stopped here and walked through the woods." "They have a carol built just over that ridge with fifty or sixty horses in it," said Anna. "But there are only five men there, didn't they say there were about ten men in town?"

"Yep, that's what I heard," said Jim, "maybe this bunch is wanting on the others to get here with more horses." "That's what I figured," said Hanna, "I was going to wait until they all showed up." "I knew you would be along sooner or later," said Hanna. "That's good," said Jim. "Chanler should be getting here soon." "I left them some markers to follow," said Jim.

"Leisen," said Jim, "I hear horses coming." Jim grabs his rifle and eases out to the edge of the trees. Hanna hears Jim whistle; it was Chanler and five of his hands. Jim leads them into the woods. "Hi, sister in-law," said Chanler, "what are you doing here? They hit us last night, they took eight of my mares, and shot Charles and one of my ranch hands," said Hanna. "Oh, Charles is ok, the bullet went through his right shoulder," said Hanna. "She was already here when I got here," said Jim, "Hanna said they are just over that ridge with about sixty horses, but there's only five men I saw." "They must be waiting on the others," said Jim, "I think we should go through the woods and spread out along the ridge with our rifles and weight." "Sounds good," said Chanler. They all tie their horses and get their rifles. Hanna leads the way as they walk through the woods using the trees as cover. Once they get to the ridge, Hanna takes three men with her to the left, and Jim takes Chanler and the other two with him to the right. They wait the rest of the day watching, as the men below sit around a fire talking. Mid-afternoon, they see two men jump up and go to the carol gate, then more men and horses start coming into the clearing. The two men open the gate as the others push the horses into the carol. Looks like another fifty to sixty head of horses, "well, there they are," said Jim, "what now?" "You want to take them in, or leave them here?" asked Jim. Chanler thought about it for a minute. "Horse stealing is a hanging offense. Those two that seem to be in charge need to hang." "Ok," said Jim, "I'll shoot them two in the legs, go tell the other when they hear my second shot to shoot the rest of them." Chanler lives, then comes back, "ok," said Chanler.

Jim aims with his sharp rifle, then shoots the first man, then the second. The others opened fire, and the horse thieves tried to run, but they didn't get away before they were cut down.

Jim, Chanler, and the rest make their way down the hill. Jim pulls his pistol when they get closer. The two men Jim shot, and two more were still alive, the Pruit men took the rustlers' guns and tied their arms behind their backs. Jim sat down at the fire; he looked over at one of the older men holding his leg. "So, you thought you would just come here and take horses and sell them to the Army." "I have a contract," said the man in a painful voice, "not to still horse you don't," said Jim. "We checked, and the Army said that they have not been buying horses for them." "Not that it would matter," said Jim, "buying and stilling is not the same thing around here." "How did you find us?" asked the man. Jim laughed, "You see that woman over there." "Some of your men hit her place the other night, shot a teenage boy, and her husband," said Jim, "she tracked you down." "She just followed the tracks of her horses." "Now you're looking at attempted murder and horse thieving," said Jim. "Look, I've got $ 2,000.00 in my saddle bag," said the man, "just let me go." "You know, out here, we Ranchers have our own style of Justus." "Oh, we go by the law now." "Hanna," said Jim, "cut your mares out, and take them home," "oh' and get his saddle bags on your way." "I'll stay here and help Chanler, and his men herd the rest of the horses to town." "He can cut out his, and the Sheriff can find out who owns the rest." Once Hanna was gone, Chanler's men let the horses out of the carol. They hung the dead bodies of the rustler's upside down by their feet, from the cross rail over the carol. "Where's that contract you have?" asked Jim. The man pulled it out of his pocket. Jim took it, then took the burnt end of a stick and wrote "Rustlers" on the back of it. Jim put it on one of the man's buttons, then they hanged him and the other three rustlers by the neck. The Pruit men drove the horses to Oregon City and put them in the train yard carol. Chanler took the horses that belonged to the Pruit ranch back home. Jim told the Sheriff to find out who the other horses belonged to and let the people know that they were there. "Where are the rustlers?" asked the Sheriff. "In the next county where the horses were found," said Jim. "I take it they won't be coming back here for trial," said the Sheriff, "nope," said Jim. "They shot Charles and one of the Pryor boys when they hit Hanna's place the other night," said Jim. "That was a mistake," said the Sheriff, "yelp," said Jim, "attempted murder and horse rustling, the trial didn't last long." "They were caught red-handed, but Charles and the boy will heal up." "Good," said the Sheriff. Jim went home and let his father know that the coast was clear for now. Matt and Sara went back home.

About two months later, a group of about six men came to town, asking about horses for sale. The Sheriff laughed, then informed them that there were no horses for sale in his county. The man stated, "But I have a contract to buy horses for the Army." The Sheriff laughed again, then said, "So did the last ten men that came through here." "They tried to take the horses after being told that there were none for sale," "I sure hope you don't plan to try the same thing." "Those men made it to the next county, but we got our horses back, and those men are no longer with us." "So, I suggest you go somewhere else to buy your horses." "Oh, but keep that piece of paper with you." "It came in handy last time, the Ranchers wrote on the back of it, "Horse Theft." They pinned it to that buyer's shirt before they hung him." The Sheriff watched as the men rode out of town; that was the last time anyone came to Oregon City to buy horses for the Army. From what the papers read, the War raged on, but not in Oregon or any of the other States nearby.

Everyone was preparing for the winter there; Lizzy had a new project going on in town. She had men building a new building on Main Street for a dress shop, Sissy wanted to sell women's dresses and apparel. She would order things from the large city in the East and have them shipped by rail, with Lizzy's backing, of course. Lizzy's sawmill operations and Jim's cattle business have made the Evens family very wealthy. Hanna's horse operation will start selling stock soon, it only seems natural that one of them would start a retail business in town. Matt sits on his porch and thinks back to the day they all left Kentucky, and how much things have changed over the past few years. They lived from hand to mouth in that small two-room shack, saving money to make a trip that seemed to be across the world. Was it worth it, almost losing a daughter to the Indians, his son having to become a man overnight? Then he thinks of Ezy, the girl Jim found and married, and their two sons, Sissy and Missy, the other unexpected additions to their family. Then Hanna, the quite shy girl, became the toughest one of them all with her two girls and husband Charles. Plus, Lizzy, the outspoken young girl, became a successful businesswoman. Yes, despite it all, it was worth it and more. Without opportunity, no one can succeed. Matt and Sara gave their children that chance, and they ran with it.

The next spring, Hanna had ten colts old enough to break to ride and then train to work cows, plus several younger ones that would be ready next year. She had colts from newborns up to three-year-olds; it was time for Charles to do his part. Hanna had been working with each colt as they grew, teaching them to lead and making them easy to handle. Charles would start working with the older ones. Now that his shoulder had healed, it was time for him to go back to work, and he was ready. Jim and Hanna had bought more land for the King's Land Ranch with some of the money they got from the artifacts they sold. Another twenty-eight hundred arches North along the Clackamas River. Jim and Hanna decided that the herd was just too big to keep in one group anymore, over six hundred head of cows and heifers, plus five bulls. Plus, over a hundred steers Missy and James had left in the valley at Hanna's for Jim to move to the homestead. Jim ran an ad in the local paper, "Cow Hands Needed."

The only qualifications were that they be able to ride a horse and shoot a gun. Hanna had the spare horses and tack from the rustlers; all she needed was men or boys to put on them, or girls. After a few weeks, Jim had hired six hands, two young boys just out of school, three older men, and one woman named Kate. There were others with more experience, some who were ex-Pruit hands, and some whom Jim just didn't feel good about. Jim was most impressed with the woman named Kate. She was thirty-two years old; she and her older brother had come up from Nevada with a herd going to Pruit's Ranch. Her brother was the trail boss. Chanler hired him to stay on with the ranch to take Charles' place. But Pruit ranch wouldn't hire the woman, so she had been working for the blacksmith and the livery station. Jim thought she would fit in fine with Hanna and Missy, and she did; she had never been married, but like Hanna, she had a close bond with her brother. Hanna put one of the older men with James, and he paired up the two younger boys with one of the other two older men. Hanna put Kate with Missy and made Missy range boss over them all, with Kate as her right hand.

For a while, Missy kept all the hands and the cows together so that she could see which ones had the knack. Hanna also stayed close by keeping an eye on them. Once Hanna and Missy were comfortable with them, Missy took Kate and one of the two-man teams with her to move the steers to the homestead for Jim. Kate was a natural; she had done this before. The men followed her lead as they drove the steers along. Hanna had John and Arron get started building a bunk house South of the valley near the river, along the river road away from Hanna's valley. For now, Kate would stay with Missy in the cabin, while the men camped near the cows. Jim had also hired an older Mexican man with a chuck wagon to cook for the hands; his name is Mantel. After moving the steers to the home stead, Hanna and Missy went to see the new land. They took Kate with them. Hanna had told Kate her main job was to keep Missy safe. Missy looked at

Hanna. "I know you can take care of yourself," said Hanna, "but it doesn't hurt to have backup." "I've always had Jim backing me up," said Hanna, no matter what. They found a good spot to put half the herd for a while to graze. On the way back, Hanna gives Missy her shotgun, "Here hang this on your saddle horn." "Hold on tight if you pull the trigger," said Hanna, "it will jump out of your hand.

The next morning, Missy took Kate, James, his man, and another two-man team to cut out about two hundred head and two bulls, then they drove them to the new pasture. Once the cows were there, Missy left the young boy with James and his men and sent the older man back to where the other cows were. That way, she would have three men at each spot. She sent Mantel to set up a camp in between the two herds so he could cook for both teams, breakfast and supper. Missy had trained James, so she felt better about having him there in the new area, with the unknown predators and new hands. She and Kate would keep a close eye on the three new men at the old spot. Now that Sissy has her dress shop open in town, with all the latest fashion from back east. As well as perfumes and cosmetics for the ladies of Oregon City. Lizzy has expanded the Sawmill again and added a planning mill to finish out the lumber. She is still getting all her timber off the Ranch land, and Jim manages that operation for her. Matt is still in charge of reconditioning the land after the trees have been cut, by replanting it with young trees or planting grass seeds. He planted wheat and corn on the section that came with the sawmill for the past two years, and it has yielded a good crop each year.

With the help of the Sheriff, the Mayor, and Mr. Pruit, Jim was elected to a seat on the city council of Oregon City. The town was growing fast, and they had a lot to do to keep up with the growing pains. The Evens had become a huge part of the community and employed a lot of people in their operations there. So, it only made sense that they had a say in what happened in the town. Mr. Pruit went out to see Charles and Hanna, and Maria came with him to see the girls. Pruit wanted to look at the three-year-old colts Charles had been working with. Five of the colts are marked up and colored just like the stud horse, which is what Hanna wanted. Three of them are mares, and two were stud colts that have now been cut; the others are good-looking horses, either dun or red colored, but not chestnut like the stud. Anna came down to the barn looking for her pawpaw with Patches following her. She walked up to Pruit and took his hand. "Well, hello, baby girl," said Pruit. "These sure are some nice-looking horses you have here." "I know," said Anna, "Dads, getting them ready for me to ride." "I wish he would hurry up." "Well, it takes time to make a good horse out of a colt," said Pruit, "which one are you going to ride?" "All of them," said Anna. Pruit laughed, "I have to try them out to make sure they're ok," said Anna in a grown-up tone. Anna may look like her mama, but she acts and sounds just like her aunt Lizzy did at that age. Sassy does not even start to describe this child, but also fearless; she's not scared of anything. Charles rides up to the fence on one of the colts he's training, gets off, and speaks to his dad. "Is that one ready for me to try?" asked Anna. Charles smiled at his dad and shook his head. "Come on," said Charles. Anna started to crawl through the fence, and Patches grabbed her britches leg. "It's ok, Patches, I got her," said Charles. Patches let her go; Charles picked her up and put her in the saddle. Then led the horse around the lot a couple of times, then stopped at the rail where his dad was. "Ok, this one's tired, let me get another one," said Charles. He takes her off the horse and hands her over the fence to Pruit. "Take Pap-Paw to the house," said Charles, "I'll be up there in a minute, it's lunch time. Anna takes Pruit's hand and walks him up to the horse. Hanna had made sandwiches for everyone and had cake. Charles came in and washed up, then poured coffee for himself and his dad. Hanna and Maria were drinking tea. Anna said, "Where's my coffee?" "Oh, sorry, ma'am. " Charles pours just a little coffee into a cup, then adds a lot of milk and honey. "Here you go, ma'am," said Charles. Anna smiles, then sips her coffee.

“So, how are the Colts doing asked Pruit. “They're all ready to ride,” said Charles. “They need some training working with the cows.” “I’ll bring up a few heifers next week to work them with,” said Charles. Maria holds the new baby as she eats her sandwich and sips her tea, and it seems she realizes she can’t deny the bond between grandparents and their grandbabies. “Well, thank y’all for coming, but I’ve got to get back to work,” said Charles, as he hugged his mom and shook his dad’s hand. “Stay as long as you want, and come back anytime,” said Charles, as he walked out the door. Anna crawled up into Pruit’s lap and helped him eat his cake. Hanna smiled. Knowing that not long ago, Maria did not see her as being worthy of Charles and the Pruit name. Once the Pruitts had left, Hanna put the baby in her sack and took Anna’s hand as they walked to the barn to clean stalls. The Pryor’s, John and Arron, were finishing the bunk house for the hands; it would be ready by the time the crew moved the cows South of the valley. Hanna had plans to have the Pryor’s build a couple of small line cabins on the new property after they finished the bunk house. So, when the cows were there in the spring, the men would not have to sleep on the ground; after all, Hanna knew exactly what that was like. She lived that life for a long time, mostly by herself, but she did have Patches.

Jim sold their steers and put the money in the bank, but beef prices were down. The war had devastated the economy, and the Southern States were in shambles. Plantations and farms were burnt to the ground, and Cities were destroyed. There was no one to buy beef in most of the country, beef was being shipped over sea or traded for other goods. The Northern Government had spent most of its money fighting the South. The effects of the war were finally reaching the Northwestern States, because the War had cost much more than lives. Hundreds of Thousands of slaves had been freed, but free to do what? They still had no rights. No right to own property, even if they could afford it, which none of them could at the time. If they left their owners' farms, they had no place to live, and there were no jobs. Yes, they were free to survive without anything, most discovered it was worse being free than being a slave. The most asked question after being told that they were free was, "Where do I go?" They were told, "You're Free." You can go anywhere, you can do anything. With no place to live, no money, no food, no means of travel, and no education, Freedom was a hardship, not a saving. Some were able to stay with their ex-owners and work for Pennies, some were allowed to work the land as sharecroppers. Many wandered around looking for jobs that just weren't there to be had.

May 21st. In 1865, the War ended, and the soldiers who managed to survive the war came home. In the Southern States, most had nothing to come home to but a few surviving family members. It would take years to rebuild the South, if not decades, and it would never be the same. But in the Northern States, they return home victorious but with little to be proud of, other than stopping slavery as it was known. This created new problems for the Union as to what to do with them, but the biggest change that came because of the war was the creation of thousands of trained killers from both sides. On Paper, the war was over, but in reality, the real war had just started, and it would last for decades. This war was not just between the states; this war was between towns, businesses, individuals, farms, ranchers, and anyone who didn't like your ways or who wanted what you had. This was the war of survival of the fittest, or the fastest. Agreements were settled in the streets and barrooms, not in the courtrooms or in Washington, DC. Banks and the Railroads were no longer safe from outlaws. Since the War, the rule of law has been ignored. Often, the Army was sent in to keep peace, which in the Southern States only caused more chaos and more killings.

Chapter Eleven: The After Math

With no jobs available and no way to support their families, some of the ex-soldiers from the Northern and Southern States turn to robbing Banks, Trains, and businesses across the country. With their way of life destroyed by the war, they were trained in covert operations and killing. Any place that held large amounts of cash or gold was no longer safe from these groups of men. Cattle rustling had also increased across the Western States, along with horses and other livestock. Everybody wears a gun now, or has one in their purse or pocket while in town. In June 1866, Hanna, Missy, and Kate, who was driving the wagon, went into Oregon City for supplies. Hanna had left the girls with Grace. Since the addition of the bunk house plus her house, the Pryor's' and Missy's cabin, she was having to get supplies more often. Kate pulled up in front of the general store with the wagon, and Hanna went in and ordered her supplies. The Sheriff walked over to the wagon where Hanna was standing, "Hanna," said the Sheriff, "Morning, Sheriff Hill," said Hanna, "Is Jim with you?" asked the Sheriff. "No, he's at his place or in the log woods," said Hanna. "Why, what's up?" asked Hanna. "Oh, probably nothing," said the Sheriff, "but a group of men rode into town yesterday afternoon." "They've been held up in the salon since they got into town. I just have a bad feeling," said the Sheriff.

A man walked up to the Sheriff and whispered into his ear, then walked away. "What was that?" asked Hanna. "He said he overheard one of the men say, we'll do it at noon, while everybody is eating lunch." "Do what?" asked Hanna. "I don't know," said the Sheriff. Hanna looked at Missy, "Go find Jim, bring him back." "I'll be on the roof of the dress shop across from the bank." "Give Kate your shotgun. Kate, you go to the South side of the bank and hide. Missy, when you get back, go inside the dress shop with Sissy." Hanna pulled her sharp rifle out and headed behind the buildings. Missy rides out after Jim, Kate hides the shotgun, and walks to the bank. The Sheriff goes after his deputy; they mount up and ride like they're leaving town slowly. They go to Lizzy's place, loop around her house, and hide their horses. Then they eased inside the bank, the Sheriff told the guard to hide in the back room and watch the back door, as they thought the bank was going to be robbed.

The Sheriff and his Deputy hid behind the counter, Hanna was on top of the Dress shop with her rifle, watching the front door of the bank. Jim and Missy came into town. Missy stopped at the Dress Shop and went inside, and Jim rode to the Salon. Tied his horse and went inside and ordered a beer, then stood at the bar. The bartender knew Jim didn't drink beer, but he also knew something was up with the strangers in town. So, he served Jim a beer, like it was normal business at straight up 12:00 noon, the six men stood up and walked out of the Salon. Jim eased over by the door and watched them get on their horses; the men rode down the street to the bank. Jim walked out of the salon and down the sidewalk. Five of the men went inside the bank. While one man held the other horses, one of the men inside threw two saddlebags at the bank clerk. "Give me your money," said the robber. The clerk ducked down behind the counter as the Sheriff and the Deputy stood up. Hanna took out the man with the horses, Kate stepped out and shot into the air, running off the horses. Jim waited at the other side of the bank, the three men near the door made a run for it, as the three men came out Hanna shot the one in the head, Jim shot the second one, and Kate shot the third one. The other two dropped their guns and gave up The Sheriff cuffed them and took them to jail. Everybody met up in front of the bank, Jim, Hanna, Kate, and Missy, the clerk came out with the guard. "Well, looks like the Even's saved the bank again," said the banker. "Well, we have a lot of money in this bank," said Jim. "Yes, you do," said the banker.

Hanna, Missy, and Kate went back to the store to get their wagon, "just another exciting day in town," said Hanna as they drove back to the Valley. As they rode past Jim's place, Thomas, Jim's oldest son, rode up to them on his horse. "Hi, Aunt Hanna," said Thomas. "Hi, Thomas, how are you?" asked Hanna. "Good," said Thomas, "when can I come and work for you and Uncle Charles? I'm fifteen now, I can ride, shoot, rope." "I know you can," said Hanna, "let me talk to your dad." "He's not the problem," said Thomas, "it's mom." "I'll get Jim to talk to her, she should let you work this summer helping Charles," said Hanna. "Let me talk to Jim first," "Yes, ma'am," said Thomas, "Thank you!" Jim's other son, Stew, was thirteen now, and he seemed to be more interested in the Sawmill and Timber operations. Not Thomas, he loved horses; he had three of them. The one he was on that day was a young horse he had broken and trained himself. He has a knack for horses, his grandfather Matt says it's a gift. But of course, his mom Ezy still sees him as her little boy and wants to protect him, she thinks he is too young to be breaking horses. Jim tries to tell her that Thomas is a young man now, as he was when he left Kentucky driving a covered wagon.

The next week, early one morning, Jim and Thomas rode to the Valley. Hanna saw them coming. "Well," said Jim, "it took some doing, but here he is. Send him home before school starts." Hanna smiled, "I will, tell Ezy I'll watch after him, not to worry too much." "His vocabulary may change a little," said Hanna, "but he'll learn something." Jim smiled, "I know he will, love you, Sis," said Jim as he rode off. "Well, welcome to the world of wild horses and crazy cows, Thomas," said Hanna. "Put your things in the house, then go find Charles, he'll tell you what to do. Thomas fit right in with Charles and started working with the cows on the broken horses with Charles' help. Anna, now eight, is also riding her horse, the first colt born on the Ranch. Hanna spent a lot of time working with this mare when she was a filly and feels safe with Anna riding her. Hanna's youngest girl, Christy, is only four years old and rides with her mom; she's not as fearless as Anna. Jim and Hanna have decided to buy more land East of what they have now. The government is offering to sell it and other sections to raise money. The section they want connects to theirs and would add five thousand arches to what they have now. Most of it is covered in timber; they both agree that having their money invested in land and timber would be much safer than the bank having it after the latest attempted bank robbery. After all, Jim's sons are almost grown now, and well, one day they will want a spot on the ranch.

After the land had been purchased, Jim took his youngest son, Stew, with him to survey the new land. They packed down two horses with supplies to take along with them. The trip Jim figured it would take at least two weeks or more, by the time they marked out the boundaries. The two left the next morning, and they went to the Valley first, so Jim could let Hanna know he would be gone. Jim gave Hanna a copy of the survey map and showed her where they would start marking. Just in case something happened, and they didn't make it back when he thought they would. Hanna offered to let somebody go with them, but Jim said he thought that he and Stew needed this time alone together. Hanna watched as the two crossed the valley and disappeared into the trees. She wished she could have gone with them, but with the two girls, she knew she couldn't. Thomas had become a real horse handler and could work wonders with the young horses. Charles was happy to have him there to help; like the cow herd, the horse herd was growing fast, too. Hanna had plans to sell off some of the older stock, like the outlaw horses, as she called them. Almost all the range hands were now riding King's Land Stock, which they raised and trained, and their old horses would be sold off, too. But the big white Indian horse, Hanna said, would never leave. That horse had saved her life more times than she could count.

Jim and Stew made it to the Southeast boundary of the current property line just before dark. They set up camp for the night and warmed up some leftovers they had brought along with them. They sat by the small fire and ate while they listened to the sounds of the night. This was something new for Stew, and something Jim felt his youngest son really needed to experience. Stew's head was on a swivel; every noise got his attention. Jim smiled as he watched his son. A pack of wolves in the distance started their vocal calls. Stew jumped as an owl searched nearby. To put him at ease, Jim started talking about the new land and his plans for expanding the ranch. How one day, if they wanted, they could pick a spot to build a house somewhere on the ranch. Stew, who would be turning fifteen soon, had been working with his father and grandfather in the summers, marking timber and cleaning up the timber cuts. Stew told his dad that he thought that they should build a narrow rail line from the Sawmill to the areas where the timber would be cut. Maybe they could even have a portable Sawmill that could also move from location to location. Jim was surprised. Jim knew by the way he was talking that Stew had put a lot of thought into this. Jim said, "Son, that's a good idea." Stew smiled, "I hadn't thought about that," said Jim. "But we are buying land farther away from the Mill," "it's miles from this end of the property back to the mile." "That's something to think about," said Jim, "let's get some sleep." They rolled up in their bedrolls. Stew didn't notice the sounds as much as he lay there thinking about his idea.

The next morning, they packed up, drank coffee, ate a cold biscuit, and headed out to find the Southwest corner of their new land. Mid-morning, they located it; Jim drove a steel rod into the ground and marked a tree near the rod. Then they moved along the South boundary heading East, marking trees along the way by the plot maps they had. The further they went the more Stew idea made sense, the trees were huge there. Four- and five-foot diameter trees all through the virgin timber land, sixty and eighty feet tall. It was a timber, gold mine, but moving them to the Sawmill would take forever with mules and horses. It took them three days to mark the

Northern boundary, then they turned southward, marking the eastern line. The trees were the same, huge in size, all along the way, "look," said Stew. Up ahead, they could see a clearing. As they got closer, they also saw something they never expected to see. Teepees, about twenty of them, in an open meadow. Jim stopped. "Dad," said Stew in a soft voice, "who are they?" "I don't know," said Jim in a whisper. They sat there in the trees and watched as the Indians moved around. They saw a group of small children near a small creek of running water, playing. They saw women at their teepees cooking over small fires, and men working in a garden spot along the creek. There were corn stocks six feet high, loaded with corn and other crops, too.

"What do we do?" asked Stew in a whisper. Jim's last encounter with Indians was on the trail from Kentucky. That seemed like a lifetime ago. He took out his plot map and looked it over. "Yep, they were on his land, alright, but this was different; these were families, men, women, and children. Jim looked at his map again. There was no way around them, other than going miles out of their way. Jim thought, damn, I wish Hanna were here, then he saw one of the women hang a shiny metal pot over a fire. That's not normal, thought Jim. He looked at Stew, "Stay close to me, Son," said Jim. "Take your hat off," "Why?" asked Stew. "I want them to see that you're a boy, not a man," said Jim, "just do it." They eased slowly into the opening, Jim moved in the direction of the biggest teepee, they didn't notice them until they passed one of the women. She ran into the big teepee, and an older man came out. Jim held up his hand and said, "Hello." To his surprise, the man replied, "Hello, welcome." Jim breathed a sigh of relief. He stopped and got off his horse. The man walked up to greet him, "My name is Jim Evens." "This is my son, Stewart." The man nodded, "They call me 'Spotted Elk," said the man, "Come, welcome, come." Jim told Stew to get down, as others saw them, they started coming up to the teepee, and they were all smiling. Soon Jim realized they thought that they were traders, looking to trade goods, maybe because of their pack horses.

Jim told the older man that they were just traveling through marking trees and boundaries. The man didn't understand about marking trees or the word boundaries, but did the passing through. Spotted Elk said, "You eat, come." Jim and Stew followed him inside the big teepee. Inside, they had food laid out on an Elk skin. They started setting around the skin on the ground, they had roasted ears of corn, some kind of beans, a flat bread, and meat Jim guest was Deer or Elk. The old man took a piece of each food and held it up over his head as an offering to their God. Then he put it on a special plate to the side, and then waved his arms. As they all started eating, it was a welcome treat for Jim and Stew, who had only had cold food for days. The corn was so sweet, and the meat just melted in their mouths, the beans had a nutty, buttery taste, but the bread had a potatory, bland taste. But it was mainly used to hold the other food; there were no plates or other utensils used. After they ate, Jim sat and talked with Spotted Elk, trying to find a way to tell him that they owned the land they were on. But he didn't think the man understood; he did find out that the tribe was a Yakima Indian tribe. Oddly, their skin was not as dark as that of the Plains Indians, like the Sioux and the Cheyenne, and their faces had European features like those of white men. Their hair was long and black, and they dressed like other Indians. That had been there many, many years, according to the old man, they had moved there from a place near the mountains. After finding this place on a hunting trip for Elk, Jim decided not to push the ownership of the land thing for now. He thanked the Chief Spotted Elk for his hospitality and told him that he would come back soon with gifts for him and his people.

Jim and Stew left the Village and kept heading North along the East boundary, marking it as they went. The small meadow with the creek running through it would be a great place for a house one day or a workstation for the timber crews. But Jim just can't see making these people leave at this point, if they had been threatening to torture them, it might be different. But they were peaceful and kind to him, and Stew, Jim's father, Matt, had always told him to fight the fight you have to, but don't start one if there's no need to. Jim could see no need at this point, and Stew was amazed at the fact that they got to see real, live Indians up close. His father reminded him that not all tribes are like that and that some are very dangerous. After nine days they made it to the end of the Eastern boundary and headed back West along the South End. The trees had gotten somewhat smaller going South, and there were more evergreen trees than hardwood trees. The ground was rockier than it was where the huge trees were growing. It took four more days to get back to the old boundary of the ranch. The next day, they made it back to their house. Jim sent Paul to tell Hanna that they had made it back home ok. All Jim wanted to do was soak in a hot tub of water, after two weeks of riding, he sent Stew to tell Ezy at Lizzy's house.

Stew told his mom all about the Indians and their Village, also about the food they ate there, as he drove his mother back home. Ezy had stayed with Lizzy and Sissy while the men were gone, she was glad to get back to her house. She went upstairs to find Jim in a tub of water, soaking. She started taking her clothes off, walked over, and stepped into the tub with him. "Well, hello, dear," said Jim. Ezy smiled as she sat on Jim's lap. "You need a shave," said Ezy. She leaned in and kissed his lips, then rubbed her chick against his scruffy face. "Stew said the young girls just wore leather patches over their tops and bottoms," "Is that true?" asked Ezy. "Yep, that's true," said Jim with a smile. After their bath, they both got dressed and went downstairs. Jim went to Stew's room, and he was sound asleep. Jim went back to the kitchen and poured a cup of coffee, then sat at the table with Ezy. Jim told Ezy about finding the Indian Village, and how it was on their land, but didn't think it was a problem yet. He told her about the huge trees and Stew's idea about how to get the trees out, not just from there but also from other places. The next day, Jim sent Paul out to let Hanna and Lizzy know that he wanted to have a stockholder meeting to discuss what he had found. He wanted to meet them at Matt's house on Friday afternoon and talk about the big trees, the Indians, and the idea Stew had about the timber.

Friday after lunch, Hanna and Missy showed up at Matt's, then Lizzy and Sissy, shortly after Jim rode up. They all sat down around the big table at Matt's house, Jim started by saying, "I want to thank you all for all the hard work you do first and foremost." "Now, I took Stew with me to mark out the boundaries of the new property we bought," "it took two weeks like I figured it would," said Matt. "For the cattle business side of things, the new land is not going to help us as far as the grazing side of things, the land is eighty-five to ninety percent timber." "But on the Lumber Mill and Timber side," "it's amazing, on the North end there's hardwood trees four and five-foot diameter trees, eight to ninety feet tall." "There is one spot on the East boundary that opens into a meadow about fifty or sixty arches, with a small creek running through it." "But it's miles from any of our other pastureland through a big forest, and also, there is a tribe of Yakima Indians living there." "What," said Matt and Hanna at the same time, "now, wait," said Jim, "it's about thirty-eight to forty Indians, men, women, and children living in teepees," said Jim. "I'm sure the Government didn't know, but they sold us land that these Indians live on." "Or didn't care," said Matt, "that's possible to," said Jim. "According to their chief, they have been there for three generations," said Jim. "I tried to explain to them that we now own the land, "but they don't understand that concept." "What are we going to do?" asked Lizzy. "Well," said Jim, "that's why I'm telling you. They are peaceful people; they welcomed us and fed us." "They have a big garden with corn and other vegetables; their meat source is deer, elk, and other wild animals." "I saw no need to start a fight with them over that small amount of land now." "But it's something we need to think about later when we go after the timber."

"Speaking of that," said Jim, "my fourteen-year-old son told me about an idea he has on building a narrow rail line into our timber lands for removing the timber faster and easier." "He must take after his aunt Hanna," said Hanna. They all laughed. "I'm just putting this out there," said Jim. "He also mentioned a portable sawmill," "I know he takes after me now," said Hanna, they laughed again. "Look, I just wanted to give y'all these things to think about," "nothing to be done now," said Jim. "But I'd like to take Hanna, Lizzy, and maybe her timber guy, and Dad, you too, to see the trees, on the North end, then maybe go by to the Village and meet the Indians." "That sounds great," said Hanna. "Jim, you can take the Logging Crew Foreman, but I think I'll stay here," said Lizzy. "Ok," said Jim, "that's fine." "Dad, what about you?" "Sure, I'll go," said Matt, Let's take Stew with us. I want to hear more about his ideas." "Good," said Jim, "we will all meet up at Hanna's next Wednesday morning." "Me, Hanna, Dad, Stew, Phil, and maybe Ezy, I'd like for her to see it too," said Jim. "Yep, I'd like to take Missy too," said Hanna, "she needs to know our boundaries." "Ok, then," said Jim, it's all horseback there, no trails for wagons or buggies." "I'll pack the supplies," said Jim. "Hanna, I might need a couple of horses," "Thanks, no problem," said Hanna.

The next day, Jim and Matt took the wagon into town for supplies to take with them on their trip. The Indian tribe had made a big impression on Jim; they didn't need anything. They had been living off the land their way for years. But Jim had noticed a few modern things that they had treaded over the years, a metal pot, and other items. Jim got rice, flour, salt, sugar, cornmeal, and lard to take to the Indians along with cotton materials and blankets. Then he got supplies for his family to have on the trip. Jim was excited about the trip; this would be a grand adventure. On Wednesday morning, everyone met at Hanna's barn. Jim, Matt, and Ezy came to Hanna's in the wagon, pulling Jim's horse and two pack-horses behind them. Stew and Phil followed on their horses. Ezy got off the wagon, ran over, and hugged Hanna. "Jim was hoping you would go," said Hanna. "I've got nothing better to do, my kids think they are grown now," said Ezy. Hanna laughed, "They are grown," said Hanna. Anna was standing by her mom with a sad look on her face, "What's wrong with you, honey?" "I want to go too," said Anna. "Anna," said Hanna in a stern voice. Ezy leaned down and whispered in Anna's ear, "Go tell Uncle Jim." Anna eased over to Jim, "Uncle Jim, can I go?" asked Anna. "Sure, baby, what did your mamma say?" asked Jim. "She said no, that I couldn't ride well enough yet," said Anna. "Stew," yelled Jim, "make room for Anna on your horse." Hanna turned and looked at Jim with a hard look. "It's time, Sis," said Jim. Hanna yelled to Anna, "Go get your coat and a blanket." "Stew, don't you let her out of your sight." "I want Aunt Hanna," said Stew, "he went with her to get her things from the house." Hanna saddled a horse for Ezy and one for Matt, and tied on the bedrolls. Jim went over to help her. "Jim Evens," "you better hope nothing happens to my child," Jim laughed, "it won't," said Jim, "she's just like you were Hanna." "I know," said Hanna, "that's what scares me the most."

Jim had studied the maps and figured out that the creek running through the Indian Village was the same one that ran through Hanna's valley and fed her lake. Once everyone was ready, Hanna gave Charles a kiss, Jim told Charles, "The Indian Village is about eight miles up this creek, the timber is not far from there," "we should be back in three or four days." "Ok," said Charles, "take care of my girls," "we will," said Jim. Jim had put Anna with Stew because he was a talker too; he figured they would keep each other occupied on the trip. The group headed out with Jim and Hanna in the lead, then Ezy, Matt, then Stew with Anna, then Phil, with Missy watching the back. The eight-person group rode up the side of the creek to the wood line, then crossed over onto the other side. Jim was leading one pack horse, and Hanna had the other one, as they went into the trees. As they rode Northeast along the creek bank, it started to open some after about two miles. The creek was six to eight feet wide in most places, about a foot and a half deep, with a rock bottom. Jim told

Hanna, "Good thing Lizzy didn't come, she would be stopping to pan for Gold in this creek." Hanna laughed. In the back Stew had to stop to let Anna go pee, Missy went with her, then put her back on Stew's horse. In a few minutes, they caught up with the others. The further they went, the more it opened alongside the creek. After about five miles, they stopped to let everyone stretch their legs. After about thirty minutes everyone mounted back up and they moved on. After a couple more miles, Missy noticed Anna was falling asleep, Stew had his arm behind his back holding her on. Missy rode up to them, took her lead rope, and tied Anna to Stew. "Thank you," said Stew as they rode on. Mid-afternoon, they could see the teepees up ahead. "Wow," said Hanna, as the clearing opened into the Village. Stew shook Anna, "We're here," said Stew. Anna was in awe as she looked around and watched as they got closer, "Why is this rope around me?" asked Anna. The Indians started coming out to meet them. Jim held up his hand, as if to say hello, and the young kids circled them as they rode on into the village.

Ezy had tears in her eyes, she didn't know why, she just did, the Indians all seemed so happy to see them. Jim got off his horse and shook hands with the Chief Spotted Elk. " Come, come, " said the Chiff. The younger men shook hands with Stew and Missy, "We brought you some things," said Jim, to the Chiff. Jim started untying the things on the pack horse, first the blankets, then the cotton cloth. He untied the flour, meal, sugar, salt, and rice. The Indians took it all inside the big teepee. Jim untied a large cast-iron Dutch Oven and the other things. Missy helped Anna down. Three little Indian girls around her age ran up to her, and they took her inside the big teepee, with Stew following them. After all the introductions, everybody moved inside the big teepee and sat around the big area of skins on the ground. The women were scurrying around bringing food in for them. It was cold leftovers, but still good. The Evens crew had not eaten all day, and most of the Indians spoke some English, not a lot, but they understood most of what the Evens said. A little toddler crawled over to Ezy, she picked her up and put her in her lap, then fed her small bites of food. It was like a big family reunion with people you didn't see often enough. Jim told the Chiff that they came to see the big trees North of their village and would stay two nights, then go.

Ezy couldn't help but notice their attire, as Stew had told her, the grown women wore leather dresses, the men leather pants. But the teenagers and down wore just patches over their private parts; every time they moved much, they exposed themselves, boys and girls. She watched Stew as he watched the young girls, she wanted to scold him and tell him not to look. But they were just there in front of him to see, there was nothing she could do. Hanna was talking with the women and telling them that in the morning, she would show them how to make biscuits and gravy with the flour. Missy was being surrounded by teenage girls and boys; she, too, had noticed the skimpy clothing they wore. Her face was red as she tried not to look. Finally, Jim stood up, "Thank you for the food," said Jim, "and your hospitality, but we need to go set up our camp for tonight." Jim waved to his group to follow him; they led their horses over to the edge of the trees away from the village. They set up a camp and built a fire, then laid out their bedrolls. "Anna was the first one to bring it up, "Momma them people need them some clothes," Ezy squealed out laughing, "oh, Lord," she said. Everybody started laughing, Anna put her hands on her hips, "it's not funny," "I know baby," said Ezy, then she squealed again. Missy took Anna and gave her a hug, "baby we're not laughing at you, we're laughing at those kids for not wearing clothes," said Missy. "Oh," said Anna, "your Uncle Jim brought them cotton material and blankets, they can make clothes out of," said Missy. "Thank you, Uncle Jim," said Anna. "You're welcome, honey," said Jim. There were still some sneakers after Jim changed the subject to talking about the trees.

The next morning, they woke up to another Ezy squeal. Seems she woke up at daylight needing to pee, she crawled out of Her's and

Jim's bedroll and headed to the bush. On the way back, she spotted one of the teenage Indian girls curled up beside Stew with one of the new blankets covering them both. Everybody rose up to see what was wrong. Ezy was standing by the fire, pointing at Stew. "Stew Evens," yelled Ezy, Stew opened his eyes, then looked beside him and saw her, "Mom, I didn't touch her," yelled Stew "as he went to stammering." Ezy yanked the blanket off them to reveal Stew rolled up in his bedroll and her on the ground beside him. Ezy breathed a sigh of relief, "Oh, thank God," said Ezy. Everybody started to laugh again. Ezy was beside herself. Hanna walked over and took the Indian girl's hand, come on, sweety, let me teach you how to make biscuits. As they walked off, Hanna couldn't help it, she yelled, "Stew likes Biscuits." Ezy picked up a rock and threw it at Hanna. Everybody had tears in their eyes, except Anna, who didn't know what was going on.

After a lot of laughter and coffee, they all went down to the big teepee where Hanna and the Indian women and girls had made biscuits, pancakes, and bacon for everyone. They all sat in the big teepee as the Chief lifted each item above his head, then put it on a plate to the side. Then everyone started eating. The young Indian girl they found sleeping by Stew sat by him on the skins with Anna on his other side. Ezy couldn't eat because of trying to watch the two of them, Stew and the girl. Finally, Ezy couldn't take it anymore. "Stew, bring your biscuit and come help me saddle my horse," said Ezy. Stew looked at her with sad puppy dog eyes. "Yes, Ma'am." "Pour Stew," said Hanna with a giggle, "bless his heart." "I'd better go try to save him," said Jim, as he got up. After breakfast, they left their camp and rode off through the trees, headed North. After about two miles, they started seeing the big oaks. Phil jumped off his horse and started measuring the trees, three- and four-foot Diameter, "come on Phil," said Jim, "those aren't the big ones." They rode on another mile or so, Jim stopped, "Oh, my God," they heard Phil say. Stew helped Phil measure the massive trees, nobody but Jim and Stew could believe what they were seeing. They moved further North, they rode into a Hickory Nut Grove, the ground was covered with nuts, they all started picking them up and putting them in their pockets and saddle bags. As they moved on, they found Black Wall Nut trees and Burch trees, along with some massive Spruce trees.

Mid-day, Jim said, "ok, let's start back, we've seen enough to know what's here now. They mounted up and headed back South. They got back to their camp about an hour before dark. Stew, Anna, and Missy were at the back of the line as they rode into camp. The Indian girl was sitting on Stew's bedroll, "Oh, know," said Jim. Hanna giggled, "Honey, just stay calm," said Jim to Ezy. Missy saw her first. "Boy, you're in trouble," said Missy to Stew, but I didn't do anything," said Stew. They all got off their horses and tied them. Ezy walked over to the girl, "Chiff says Come eat," said the girl. "Stewart," yelled Ezy, "get over here," "tell this girl you don't like her and to leave you alone," said Ezy. Stew just stood there, "now," said Ezy, "tell her." "I can't, Mamma," said Stew. Jim woke up. "What is it?" Stew looked at his dad. "I can't, Dad." "You can't what," asked Jim, "I told him to tell this girl that he didn't like her and to stay away from him," said Ezy. "Dad, you told me not to ever be mean to a girl, or to lie to a girl or woman," said Stew. "Mom will just have to whoop me," said Stew, "I'm not going to hurt her feelings." Suddenly, it wasn't funny anymore; it was no longer a joke about two kids' infatuation. It was about the Honor of a young man's word and his standing up for what he had been taught. Jim took Ezy's hand and led her away from the others. "Let's go eat," said Hanna. The rest of them walked to the teepee. Jim set holding Ezy as she cried; she realized she had been giving Stewart such a hard time over this girl, but he had done nothing wrong. She was the wrong one, she had assumed the worst of Steward. Jim knew he had instilled honor in both his sons. He had not worried about Stew's honor once on this or the last trip. "Ezy, do you remember when you crawled into my bedroll on our trip to Oregon, just a few days after we met?" "Yes," said Ezy. "What happened that night?" asked Jim. "Nothing," said Ezy. "That's right, because I made the same promise to my dad that Stew made to me."

After a while, Jim and Ezy went to the teepee to eat with the others. The Indian girl came and sat by Stew again. Ezy got Anna to move over. She sat beside her son, leaned over, and kissed his cheek. "I love you, son, I'm sorry," said Ezy. Stew put his arm around his mom and kissed her back. They ate and visited with the Indians; Ezy found out which one of the women there was the girl's mother. She sat with her and talked. Ezy asked her about their clothing. The woman told her, "Children grow fast, we don't have time to keep making clothes." "When they grow, we make clothes." Her simple answer made sense in a way; it wasn't about fashion. Everything they do is about survival. She also told Ezy that girls her daughter's age are taught to pick a mate by lying with them. If the young man tries to have her, he is not right for her, she fights him off and finds another. A true mate will wait until after the ceremony; only then can she give herself to him. As they left the teepee and said their goodbyes, Ezy had a new respect for these people and their ways. Stew told the young Indian girl that he would come back next summer to see her. She said she would be waiting for him. That night, she lay with him again, but she was gone before daylight, so she did not upset Ezy. The next morning, they all headed back to Hanna's Valley. Late that afternoon, they made it to the barn. They all had stories to tell about this trip. Phil would tell of the massive trees, Anna would tell of the Indian Village and the kids there, Matt would tell of how his son taught his son what he taught his son, Hanna would tell with great joy how Ezy reacted to the dress codes of the Indians. Missy and Jim will simply remember the trip, the time together, and the possibilities for the future. Stew will remember the Indian girl and his grandfather's interest in his ideas about moving the timber. All in all, it was a great trip. After everyone told Lizzy about what they had seen, she asked, "So what are we going to do about the Indians?" "Nothing," said Jim and Hanna.

Chapter Twelve: Growing Pains

One of the young cowboys Jim had hired to help Hanna with the cows was now sweet on Missy, his name was Tye. She knew it, as everyone else on the ranch did, the problem was that James, John Pryor's son, was the problem. James and Missy had worked together every day long before the new hands were hired. They faced all kinds of troubles with predators together, as well as the weather. Missy had trained James and trusted his judgment when it came to the herd, but she had never really thought of him as anything other than a friend and co-worker. James was younger than Missy, not by much, and he seemed to be more mature than his older brother Arron. Nothing surprised Missy more than when she realized that James was jealous of Tye over her. James was the crew boss and the person Missy counted on the most, other than Kate. James had heard the talk around the camp and the bunk house about Missy and Kate. Men will be men; James tried to ignore most of it as just talk. But with Tye, he knew his admiration was more than just talk, and he let what he said bother him more than what the other men said. They had just moved part of the herd to a new location with Missy and Kate's help.

They were all standing around talking after the move. Tye was standing beside Missy as she explained her plans. When she finished talking, Tye leaned over and said something to her under his breath. Missy blushed, and her face turned red. James couldn't hear what Tye had said, but after hearing the older man coach Tye on what to say to her. He knew it wasn't appropriate, but James knew he should wait until they were alone to confront Tye, but he couldn't. He also knew that the best thing to do would be to just let Missy handle it, but he didn't. James lowered his head and charged Tye like a bull, hitting him in the gut and knocking him to the ground. James crawled on top of Tye and hit him in the face over and over. Missy was in shock, Kate was smiling, she knew how James felt about Missy, "Stop, stop, yelled Missy. The other men pulled James off Tye. James stood over Tye, then said, "I've listened to your talk for months and said nothing." "No, more," said James, "This woman is your boss, you will show her respect, or I'll beat you too." No one said a word, all heads were down, finally James reached down and pulled Tye up to his feet. "Now you men get out there with them cows," said James. James walked off to his horse, then mounted him, and rode off alone. Missy looked at Kate, "What just happened?" asked Missy. Kate laughed, "Just two young bulls fighting over a Heifer," said Kate. "What?" said Missy. "What did Tye say to you anyway?" asked Kate. "He just said, you sure look pretty today." "But I didn't know anyone heard him," said Missy, "James didn't have to hear sweety, the look on your face said it all." "But James, we're just friends," said Missy. "Yep, keep telling yourself that," said Kate as she got on her horse. Missy mounted up and followed Kate to where the rest of the herd was located. James was there, but he stayed out with the cows. Missy started to go out and talk to him. But she really didn't know what to say to him or even where to start. Days went by, and nothing was said, but the talk around the bunk house about Missy had stopped.

Back at the main home stead, Heidi had finished school and was now working for Sissy in the dress shop in town. A few of the young men in town were stopping by the store and just looking around. Heidi thought they were just curious about the things they sold there. She asked Sissy, "Why are those young men coming in here all the time, Sissy smiled. "Well, I'm sure it's not to buy a dress or one of our hats," said Sissy. Heidi, still clueless, asked, "Then why?" Sissy laughed, "You're silly girl," "they didn't come in here before you went to work here," said Sissy. "Oh," said Heidi with a smile, "well, maybe we should get some men's clothes then." "Or, maybe you should try to sell them something for their girlfriend, wife, or sisters," said Sissy. "Oh, yeah, I didn't think of that," said Heidi. Sissy just shook her head. There was one young man who came by the store, who wasn't there to see Heidi. His name was Dave, he was the banker's grandson and had gone to school with Sissy. He had been back East to College and now worked at the bank with his grandfather. He would come by and take Sissy to lunch at the café, or sometimes just go for coffee or tea in the mornings.

Stew, Jim's youngest son, wanted to go see the Indian girl he had met, but he didn't want to go alone, and he surely didn't want to ask his mom, Ezy. So, he went to his grandfather's house and talked to Matt about the narrow rail idea. "Maybe we should go out and pick a route from the sawmill to the next cut," said Stew. "Then we could pick a spot between Aunt Hanna's place and the Indian Village to build a bridge across the creek." "We could do that," said Matt, "maybe even visit the Indian Village." Matt smiled. Stew knew he had been caught, "Can we, Grandpa?" asked Stew. "Let me think about it," said Matt, "and talk to your dad." A few days later, Matt told Stew that they would leave in two days. It was early spring, so Matt had told Stew to bring his winter gear along for the trip. At the last minute, Jim decided to go on the trip too; his father, Matt, was only in his fifties, but still, Matt didn't feel right letting just Matt and Stew go alone. They left out that morning with one pack horse; they started at the Sawmill. Jim had drawn a straight line from the Sawmill to the big timber on his map. They would mark that line, then adjust as needed. There was still some snow in places, but most of it was gone now. After three days, they had made it to the creek below the Indian Village, just a couple of miles downstream from it. That night, they camped there by the creek; the next morning, they rode on into the big timber. Jim told Matt and Stew, "This is for enough;" they had also been measuring the distance from the Mill to the big timber. Jim said, "We will stay at the Village tonight." Stew smiled at Matt, then they rode back to the Village.

The young Indian girl saw the men coming and ran as fast as she could to meet them, but now she was wearing a cotton dress her mother had made for her. With a blanket over her shoulders, Stew, Stew, yelled the girl as she ran. He jumped off his horse and caught her as she leaped into his arms. Matt laughed as Jim shook his head, "Ezy is going to kill me," said Jim. Stew led his horse while carrying the girl back to the Village. When they got to the Village, Spotted Elk didn't come out to meet them. Jim thought that was odd, "Where is the Chief?" asked Jim. The girl pointed to a smaller teepee near the large one. Jim walked down and opened the flap; inside, an older woman was with Spotted Elk. He was lying on a bed of skins with his head wrapped up with cloth, "Come, come, welcome," said the Chief. "What happened?" asked Jim, "Angry men came, said we must leave, said the land belongs to them," "I say no, Yakim's land." "Hit me with the butt of a gun," said, would be back, "Yakims to be gone from land." "I say no again," "hit me again," "I have no warriors, we simple people, grow crops, hunt." "You have Warriors now," said Jim, "how many men?" "One old man, three young men," said Spotted Elk. Jim left the teepee and went outside. He told Matt and Stew what was going on. "Who's going after Hanna?" asked Jim. "I'll go," said Stew, "I know the way, I can't be there before midnight." "If I ride hard before dark," "go son, tell her to bring anybody she can spare." Stew jumped on his horse and rode off in a gallop along the creek. Jim looked at the girl's sad eye, "he'll be back tomorrow," said Jim. She smiled. "Dad, let's unload our gear and get out our guns," said Jim.

Jim and Matt stood guard that night. The next morning, right after daylight, they heard horses coming from the Southwest along the creek. Hanna was in the lead, with Stew, Kate, Missy, James, and Charles behind her; they rode into the Village. Jim had coffee going on a fire, they got off and got coffee, "where the Chief," asked Hanna, "in that teepee," said Jim, pointing to it. "What's the plan?" asked Hanna. "We're gonna go find those men and make sure they know where our property line is," said Jim. "Just in case, Missy, you and Stew stay here and guard the Village with Dad," "if anybody shows up before we get back," "well, there's only four of them," "their predators, you know what to do." "Yes, sir," said Stew and Missy, ... Jim, Hanna, Kate, Charles, and James all mounted up and headed up the creek to the Northeast following Jim, who had already found a track from two days ago leading back up the creek. They followed the creek as it twisted and turned through the trees. After about six miles, it started to open. Then, after a couple more miles, they came out into an open field. Up ahead, they saw the beginnings of a cabin, a big Army tent, and a wagon. They eased up closer, and they saw the men working on the cabin; one of them ran for his rifle. James raised his rifle as did Charles, "We just came to talk," said Jim. The old man stepped out from behind the cabin. "What do you want?" asked the old man. "I just have a question for you," said Jim. "Ask it then," said the old man in a mean tone. "Can you read a land map?" asked Jim. "Well, hell yeah," said the man. Hanna and Kate were easing around behind the other men, circling all of them just in case. "Then why were you on my land beating up an old Indian man?" asked Jim. "That's my land," yelled the old man in an angry tone. "No, sir, it's not," said Jim. "I bought this here plot, and they said I could run stock or use any government land connected to it." "That's right," said Jim, "problem is, I bought that land from the government three years ago, over five thousand acres, and I have the deed to prove it."

The man dropped his head. "My plot map shows that to be government land," said the man. "Well, you need a new plot," said Jim. Jim turned in his saddle, "You see those tall oak trees back there, that's where my land stops," said Jim, "You were eight miles over on my land when you found those Indians." "Well, why are those Indians even there?" asked the old man. "Because they've been there for four generations, and I let them stay," said Jim. "Well, Indians killed my wife on the trip up here," said the old man, in a mad tone, "not those Indians," said Jim, "they're all the same," said the old man, "nope, you're wrong again," said Jim. "Indians stole my sister, setting right there on that horse," pointing at Hanna, "and two other girls when we were on our way here," said Jim, "I killed them all." "But they weren't those Indians," "you must think you're pretty tough," said the old man, "you don't want to find out," said Jim. "I killed eight Indians when I was sixteen years old to get my sister back. I killed two bandits on that same trail." "Since I've been here, I've killed two bank robbers, five horse thieves, and over ten rustlers." "If you don't think I will kill you and your boys over an old Indian man, try me." Hanna spoke up, "Sir, you've got a nice place here, good water, good grass, it would be a shame to lose it and your life over a mistake." "Don't make another one," said Hanna. The old man and his boys put their guns down. "Everything west of those trees to the Clackamas River belongs to me, my family, and the Kings Land Ranch." "From the Washington State line to Oregon City," "I'll tell you once," "stay off our land," said Jim. He turned his horse and started back down the creek bank. Slowly, the rest fell in behind him as they rode out of sight. "For a minute, their brother, I thought you were going to kill that old man," said Hanna. "I wanted to," said Jim, "but those boys shouldn't have to pay for his stupidity," "that might be a fight for another time," said Hanna, "I know," said Jim.

Back at the Village, Jim told Spotted Elk he shouldn't have trouble with those white men anymore, but if he did, to let him know. He told one of the younger men how to find Hanna's place if they needed help. They all sat around inside the big teepee and ate with the Indians. Jim gave the Indians their leftover supplies, which they had brought. The Indian girl's name was something they couldn't pronounce, so she was given a new English name, "Patina", which was the only thing that sounded close to her Indian name, "Pati-a-nipa". Stew and Patina seemed to be so in love, but time would tell, they were still young, life changes every day. The next morning, as they got ready to go, Stew asked his dad, "Can I have that pack horse?" "For what?" asked Jim. "I want to give it to Patina's father," said

Stew. "Why would you do that, son?" "They can use it to plow with, haul water, Carrie Deer and Elk, and come get help if they need to," said Stew. Jim looked at his son, "Why not, son?" said Jim, "But you owe me a pack horse," "Yes, Sir," said Stew. He took the horse over to Patina's family teepee and put the lead rope into her father's hand, "a gift for you and your family," said Stew, then he walked away. As they headed back to Hanna's Valley, Missy felt like she had missed the fun a little. But she was glad it worked out without bloodshed, and Stew got to see his Indian girlfriend. Patina, or as Hanna nick-named her, "Squatting Heifer," Jim almost fell off his horse when Hanna said that. Missy told Stew, "You know you just made Patina's father the richest man in the tribe." "How?" asked Stew. "A horse is a sign of wealth to the Indians," said Missy, "he has the only one there."

School had started back up last fall, for Thomas and Stew, but in the afternoons, while Thomas was training his horses and a pack horse for Stew to give to their father. Stew was at Matt's house; he and Matt were making drawings and sketches of the rail system. Lizzy had a similar rail system in her Mill that carried the logs to the saw, on small rail carts. Matt and Stew's rail system would be the same, but the rail carts would be pulled by a steam engine of sorts with wheels, not cables and chains like in the Mill. Matt had been in contact with a company in California that built Steam Engines for the railroad. They needed about one third, the size of those about four feet wide, to pull three to five carts, forty feet long. The company was drawing up plans to build one of that size, which would pull the massive trees. Once they had the drawings ready, Matt and Stew would take a trip to California to see them. But now it is spring again, and school will be letting out soon for the summer.

Jim had told Ezy about the trip to the Indian Village and the men who tried to make the Indians leave. She was relieved to hear that the

Indian girl was now wearing a dress, then Jim told her about Stew giving her father a horse. Ezy flipped out again, saying, "Now he's gone and bought her." Jim laughed, "No, it's just for them to haul things and plow with." Ezy had been very emotional over the past few months and seemed to be eating more than normal. She knew she had missed a couple of cycles but thought nothing of it. Besides, she was getting older, and it had been fifteen years since her last child was born, she figured it was just something older women go through. Jim, Ezy, Thomas, and Stew went to Matt's and Sara's for supper one night. Sara had noticed how much more Ezy had been eating lately, and that night she noticed her belly. As they sat there eating, Sara couldn't help it; she asked, "Ezy, are you pregnant?" "No, just fat," said Ezy. Jim looked at his mom. "Are you sure?" asked Sara. "No, I can't be, I'm too old," said Ezy with a laugh. Sara wasn't convinced. "Have you had any morning sickness?" asked Sara. Ezy started to say no, then remembered a couple of times, and the missed cycles. "Oh, my God," said Ezy, "no, I can't be, Jim Evens," said Ezy, like it was his fault. Then she started to cry, she realized she had all the symptoms, mood swings, appetite, and belly, she looked up with tears in her eyes. "I think I'm pregnant, Jim," said Ezy. Jim hugged her with a smile. "I'm sorry," said Ezy as she cried. Jim was happy, surprised, but happy, "Don't be sorry, honey," said Jim, "I think it's great.

As summer weather started, and the cows started dropping calves, Hanna was faced with another problem. A good one, but still a problem just the same. The more cows you have, the more calves you get each spring. They must be vaccinated and branded before winter. This year, Hanna had divided the herd into three groups and had her cow hands spread thin, in three locations. It looked like she had no choice but to hire more help, which was getting harder to find. With the Sawmill, the timber crews, and the ranch hands, the King's Land Ranch had over thirty employees now. Charles had sold fifteen horses to a ranch in Montana and had to get Jim and his two boys to help him take them to the train yard. Because Hanna had no hands to spare, Jim ran an ad in the local paper as before, not only for ranch hands, but Matt and Stew would need help laying the short rail line soon. Lizzy had ordered twenty miles of rails, and her mill was already cutting the ties for the track. Not only that, but the steers would have to be brought in soon to the lot at Matt's place.

After a few weeks, Jim was able to hire four ranch hands, and Hanna put them to work for James. This freed Missy and Kate back up so that they could check on all the groups. But to cut out the stents and bring them up, Hanna and Charles would have to help them out. Knowing Grace could not handle watching Cristina and Anna, both Charles and Hanna let Anna come along on her horse. Now, she's ten years old and riding almost every day, and they feel she needs to see what is done on a cattle ranch. Hanna, Charles, Missy, Kate, and Anna leave early one morning, going North of the Valley. Charles is leading the pack horse, they travel to the farthest group first, where James has the new crew. He had about thirty heads of steer in his group. Hanna made Anna stay to the side and watch as they cut them out of the herd. Then they pushed them South to the lot in the Valley. Once they had them penned, they headed back North to the next group. They got there right before dark, one of the older ranch hands, Clif, was over this group. Hanna told Clif that they would start cutting out the steer the next morning, "Yes, ma'am," said Clif. Hanna and her crew left and went to the Chuck Wagon to camp there for the night. Manuel was cooking supper for the hands, beans with rice and corn bread, and the coffee pots were steaming. Charles and Kate poured themselves a cup, then Charles poured Anna a cup of coffee, milk, and honey. Missy got herself and Hanna a cup. Then they filled their plates, and they ate when they finished. Missy washed their dishes so the men would have them. Charles laid out their bedrolls away from the wagon and the fire, he put Anna's bedroll between him and Hanna. All the men came in to eat after dark. Tye smiled at

Missy but said nothing. James got his plate and sat by Missy and Kate. Once the men had eaten and talked a while, they started going back to their herds. After all the men were gone, Mangal had noticed Anna didn't eat much other than her corn bread. So, he warmed up two pancakes and some bacon left over from breakfast and carried them over to Anna. "Look what I found, sweety," Anna's eyes lit up, "that's mine," said Missy, "nope," said Anna as she grabbed the plate. Anna picked a piece of bacon and handed it to Missy, "I will share through," said Anna. She slathered the pancakes and syrup in seconds and ate the other piece of bacon. "Come on, cowgirl, let's go to bed," said Hanna. They walked over to their bedrolls, Hanna tucked Anna in, then kissed her head. "Night, Momma," said Anna, as she closed her eyes and was gone.

The next morning, they woke up to the smell of coffee and a real need to pee; the four girls headed for the bushes. Charles went to the other side of the wagon, then got coffee for himself and Anna. Mangal handed him two biscuits, one with bacon inside and one with syrup inside. The girl came to the fire, Charles handed Anna her coffee and the biscuit with syrup. The women got coffee and a bacon biscuit, and they sat by the fire as Charles picked up the bedrolls and put them on the horses. "Y'all ready?" asked Charles. "As we will ever be," said Missy as she got up, "let's go get those steers so that the crew can come eat breakfast," said Jim. As they got to the herd and started cutting the steers out, Anna watched for a while, then Hanna heard her, Yall, Yall, Yall, she looked around. Anna was in the middle of the herd, cutting out a steer. Kate rode in to help her, and they pushed it out. Then went back for another one. Hanna wanted to be mad, but she also wanted to cry, seeing her little girl working those cows like a pro. Hanna turned and looked at Charles, he was smiling, from ear to ear, get him, Anna yelled, Missy, as she pushed one out. Kate was smiling too, staying right with Anna, coaching her all the way. After cutting out forty heads, they pushed them to the lot in the valley.

"One more group," said Hanna, "let's go get them." They rode to the last group. They started cutting them out, the men couldn't believe what they were seeing, little Anna was working those steers. Y'all, y'all, she yelled as she pushed them out of the herd. Missy was laughing as she watched. Kate was backing her up They took out thirty-five steers and pushed them to the lot. That night, they stayed in the Valley in their own beds. Anna took a bath and went to bed with no supper. She was too tired to eat. The next morning, after breakfast, they started pushing the hundred and twenty-five head to the main homestead. As they hit the river road, Charles and Hanna were in the lead, and Missy, Kate, and Anna were bringing up the rear. They could hear Anna in the back, "move on, cow," Y'all, y'all, "get back in there." Charles started to giggle, Hanna shook her head, and as they got to the lot, Missy and Kate moved one on each side. Matt opened the gate. Anna was in the back, Y'all, y'all, get in their cow." She said as she pushed the last one into the lot, Matt closed the gate. "Where did y'all find that cowgirl?" asked Matt. "We have to grow them ourselves," said Charles with a laugh. Matt smiled. "Well, lunch is ready," said Matt, "y'all come eat, they all tied their horses, except for Anna, she just turned her loose. Missy picked up the reins and tied the horse. Kate said, "She's not there yet," "Nope," said Missy.

School has let out now, and Thomas has gone back to the Valley to work for Charles. Stew and Matt are leaving next week to go to California to see the drawing of a Steam Engine. Their mother, Ezy, is getting bigger by the day and is keeping Jim busy fixing up a nursery. She also had Jim order her and install a Toilet like Hanna has in her bathrooms. Lizzy went to see her sister-in-law Ezy to ask if she needed anything, as they talked. Ezy asked Lizzy when she was going to find her a man, "who says I don't have one," said Lizzy with a smile. Ezy sat up in her chair, "Who is he?" asked Ezy. "You don't know him," said Lizzy, "well, tell me about him." "He's smart, good looking, he just moved back here from California," "that's about it," said Lizzy. “No, you can’t just stop there,” said Ezy, “well, his father, Mr. Kimball, runs the Land Office in town.” “The Lawyer Mr. Kimball,” said Ezy, “yes, Eric is a Lawyer too, he worked in San Francisco for a while after college.” “But his father asked him to come back home and help him with his Law practice here in Oregon City.” “Now known as 'Kimball & Kimball Ink,” said Lizzy. “When do we get to meet him?” asked Ezy. “Soon, maybe?” “I don’t know, we’ve only been seeing each other since January,” said Lizzy. “Well, look at you,” said Ezy, “successful businesswoman, now with a nice house and a new Bo,” “I’m so happy for you.” “And you,” said Lizzy, “a rancher's wife with two grown boys, a nice house, and another baby on the way.” Ezy smiled, “Yep, I’ll never forget the look on your face when Jim rode up to camp with me on his horse,” said Ezy. “We thought he had gone out deer hunting,” said Lizzy, “then he comes back with a girl,” they both laugh.

Matt, Stew, and Sara boarded the train to California. Jim suggested that his mother go on the trip since the only time she had ever traveled was on the wagon train. Jim made sure that they had plenty of money to spend on this trip and had told Stewart to make sure that Sara had a good time there. As the train started to move, it reminded Sara of the day they left their home in North Kentucky with Jim driving the wagon. Again, she was nervous and excited at the same time. She reached over and took Matt’s hand. He was also nervous but was trying not to show it. He turned his head and smiled at her. In the scheme of things, he knew this was not nearly as dangerous as the last trip they had made together. The train whistle sounded, as they picked up speed, Stew was smiling from ear to ear, he loved it. In just a few hours, they were pulling into the station on the other end of their trip. Aunt Hanna had coached Stew on what to do when they got there, and he rented a buggy to take them to their hotel. Once inside, their luggage was carried to their rooms and placed inside them. Stew told his grandparents to rest in their room and that he would come get them for supper. Matt decided to take a nap while Sara was unpacking their things.

After about an hour, they heard a knock at the door, then heard Papaw say, It's Stewart, time to eat. They went to the door, then followed Stew downstairs to the hotel lobby. They went into the side room with tables and chairs. The restaurant was nice with white linen on the tables. A waiter came over, set them at a corner table, and handed the menu. Sara was in shock at the prices, but was told not to look at them by Stewart. Matt said, "I know what I want." "A big steak with all the trimmings," Stew laughed. "Me too," said Stew. Sara was more selective; she wanted something that she couldn't get at home. She ordered seafood, as they were waiting for their food, Matt and Sara heard a familiar voice as a man walked up to their table. "Well, Matt Evens," said the man. Matt turned in his seat, then stood up. "Tom Wagner," said Matt. "I can't believe my eyes," said Matt, as he shook Tom's hand. "Here, have a set with us," said Matt. "Oh, ok, but I can't stay long, said Tom as he sat down. Tom reached over and took Sara's hand. "Hello, Sara," said Tom, "and who is this young man? He looks a lot like Jim." "Yep," said Matt, that's Jim's youngest son, Stewart, "so what are y'all doing here?" asked Tom. "How are things in Oregon City?" "They're great," said Matt. "We're here to look at buying a steam engine for our timber operation," said Matt. "Timber," said Tom, "I thought you were going to build a cattle ranch." "We did," said Matt, "then Lizzy, our youngest girl, bought a Sawmill in Oregon City," "thing just grew from there." "Sounds like things are going great," "what about that other girl, the one that got taken by the Indians?" asked Tom. "She is good, she built a big ranch house on part of our land," "she married one of the Pruit boys, Charles, and they have two girls now."

"What about you?" asked Sara. "Oh, well, I came here after the wagon train, did a little gold mining, and found some gold." "Started buying up some land in town," "sold some, bought some more," "I'm doing ok," said Tom with a grin. "Matter of fact, I own this place here," said Tom. "Oh my, that's great," said Sara. Tom looked at Stewart, "Has your grandfather ever told you about the outlaws who they to kill me on the trail?" asked Tom. "No, sir," said Stewart. "Well, if not for your dad, Jim, I wouldn't be here today," said Tom. "You see, Jim was one of the night watchmen on the trail," "what was he, sixteen, seventeen?" asked Tom. "Seventeen by then," said Matt, "well, six men rode into camp, asked one of the other guards where I was at, Jim overheard them talking." "He ran to my wagon where I was sleeping, and he made me get out of my wagon." "He handed me his rifle; he had his pistol on, and we hid behind one of the other wagons." "The men rode up to my wagon and emptied their rifles through my wagon, thinking I was still in there." "I would have been, if not for Jim," "while they were reloading, we stepped out, I said, you missed." "One of them went for his pistol, before I could even raise the rifle, Jim drew his pistol and shot that man." "I shot the other one, two more rode in, and Jim shot them both." "The other two high-tailed it out of there," "yep," said Tom, "ole Jim saved my skin that night." The waiter came out with their food, "Well, I've got to get," said Tom. "Good to see y'all, tell ole Jim I said Hello, y'all enjoy your stay," Tom shook Matt's hand, then shook Stewart's hand and walked off.

As Matt, Sara, and Stew ate their meal, Stew said, "I never heard that story." "Nope," said Matt, "Jim never talked about that." After they finished eating, Stewart tried to pay their bill, but he was told that it had been paid in full. The next day, they went to the Engine factory and looked at the drawings and the specifications. They told them they could have it built in three months; Matt placed the order for the Engine. Then Stew took his grandparents out to see the sights around town. Late that afternoon, they came back to the Hotel. They had been trying all the local food stands around town all day, so they were not hungry. They got ready for bed; their train was leaving early the next morning, going back to Oregon City. Once back in Oregon City, they stopped by Jim's house to show him the drawings. "Well, looks like you two better get busy building tracks," said Jim, "yep, said Matt. Sara had enjoyed the trip for the most part, but was glad to be back home. Jim had hied four men that would start next week clearing the ride away for the train tracks threw the forest.

Matt and Stew put a crew together to start laying track behind the clearing crew. They were setting the ties by hand and dragging the rails in place with mules. A slow process, but the only one they had until the Engine got there. They had plans for once the Engine arrived, then they would use it to haul the rails and ties from the staging yard down the tracks to where they needed them. Jim rode out to Hanna's Valley to see how things were going for her and the cattle. Thomas and Anna were out in the lot riding two new three-year-olds that had been broken this spring. They had four calves in the lot with them. Anna was holding them in the corner with the horse she was on. Charles was backing her up on the other horse. Charles saw his father and rode up to the rails. "Hi, son," said Jim, "hey, dad," said Thomas, "Anna's sure working that horse," said Jim. "Yep, she's a natural," said Thomas, "she can ride the skin off of anything around here." Jim laughed, "I believe it," "so where's Hanna, asked Jim. "She rode out to check on Missy," said Thomas. "She'll be back," "I think she is planning on rounding up the calves soon and bringing them into brand." "She told me to get two more houses ready for the roundup," said Thomas. "So, Anna and I are getting these two readies," "where's Charles, asked Jim. "he's in the bathroom with the Colts," said Thomas. Jim turned and rode to the barn; Charles was working with a colt on leading. "Hey, Charles," said Jim. "Hello there," said Charles. "Looks like you got your hands full," said Jim. "Yep, this one is more than a little wild," said Charles, "but she'll come around."

Hanna rode up to the barn and got off her horse. "Hi, Jim," said Hanna. "Hey, sis," said Jim. "What brings you out?" asked Hanna. "Oh, just checking in on you," said Jim. "I saw Anna working that young horse, she looks good," said Jim. "Yeah," said Hanna, "she's as wild and crazy as that colt Charles has there." Jim laughed, "When are you going to brand calves?" asked Jim. "Next week," said Hanna. "You need some help," said Jim. "I always need help," said Hanna. "I'll come help and bring Paul," said Jim. "What about Stewart?" asked Hanna. "Oh, he and Dad are building a railroad," said Jim. Hanna laughed, "I bet Dad's enjoying that," "I knew you, and he was thinking about it," said Hanna. "Yep, I think it's the best way to get those big trees out," said Jim. "I've been thinking about that too," said Hanna, "I think we should protect those Hickory trees, cutting the oaks around them, to open that area up." "But not the Hickory, let them grow and spread, those nuts are wonderful, there may be a market for them one day," said Hanna. "I think you're right," said Jim. Ezy has been using them in cookies and cakes; they are good.

The next week, Jim and Paul came to help with the roundup. Charles, Hanna, Jim, Thomas, and Anna went out to the herds with Missy, James, and Kate. Paul stayed at the catch pen building fires for the branding irons. The rest went out to get the calves, and they came back before noon with about one hundred eighty calves. They pushed them into the catch pen, in the branding lot, Paul was heating the irons. While Hanna, Charles, Jim, and Missy divided up into two groups to brand and vaccinate the calves and cut the steer calves. James, Kate, Thomas, and Anna roped the calves, one at a time, and dragged them to one of the teams. After working on them, they turned the calves loose as the wranglers dragged up another café. Anna, stay right with the older cowboys and cowgirls and never miss a café. This went on all the rest of the day and until dark, they stopped at dark and cleaned up to eat. The next morning, they went right back at it until all the calves had been done. They kept the calves there in the lot a few days to make sure they would be ok. Then they returned them to the herds, another big task completed for the year.

Missy and James decided it was time to talk. James confessed his love for Missy. He told her that if she didn't feel the same way, he would understand and would ask Hanna to move him, or he would be quiet. Missy bagged him not to quiet and told him she needed him to help her with the cows. But that was not what he wanted her to say; she told him that she did care about him, but just not in that way. That they had been friends for so long, and she didn't want to lose that friendship. James smiled, although his heart had been broken, and just said OK. At the end of the week, James went to Charles and Hanna and told them he was leaving, that he would stay until the cows were moved back to the Valley. They asked him why, and he told them that he was in love with Missy, but she didn't feel the same. He told them what had happened with Tye and about the other men talking. James said I just can't take it anymore; Charles asked him if he was sure Missy wouldn't change her mind. James smiled and said I don't think so and told them about their talk. Hanna thanked him for agreeing to stay until the cows were moved. Charle asked, what will you do, James said he wasn't sure yet, that he may find a job in town. Hanna told him to let her talk to Jim and see if he needed anyone on the timber side of the ranch.

Hanna told Charles that she had seen the signs and knew James had feelings for Missy and had thought maybe Missy had feelings for him, too. She knew one day it would be an issue, but not in this way; she had thought maybe they would get married. The next day, Hanna rode to the Homestead with her youngest girl, Christina, to see Sara. She left Christina with her grandmother and went to find Jim. Sara had told her she thought they were working out behind Jim's homestead on the rails. Hanna rode to the backside of Jim's old place and found the ride away and rails, she thought, they really are building a railroad. It was her first time seeing it, and she followed the tracks North away, then saw them up ahead. She rode up beside Jim, "This is something else," said Hanna. "Yep," said Jim, "The old man is still a hard worker." "What are you going to do when you get to the Valley?" asked Hanna. "We will turn Northeast before then and cross your creek about two miles West of the Indian Village," said Jim. That is something," said Hanna, "I need to talk to you about something." "Sure," said Jim, "let's go somewhere quieter." "They ride back to Sara's and sit on the porch, "What's up?" asked Jim. "Well, I'm about to lose my best cow hand," said Hanna, "who," asked Jim, James," said Hanna. "Why," asked Jim, "well turns out he's in love with Missy," said Hanna, "I figured that," said Jim. "What's the problem?" asked Jim. "She doesn't feel the same way," said Hanna. "Well, damn," said Jim. "Yes, she does. I saw the way she looks at him." "He said he would stay until after the cows are moved this fall," said Hanna. "Well, tell him once he helps you get the cows settled to come see me, I'll find him something to do," said Jim. "Stew will be going back to school soon, James can help Dad with the Railroad," "ok," said Hanna.

Chapter Thirteen: Love Finds a Way

James helps Hanna and Missy get the Cows moved to the land South of the Valley near the bunk house. James tells his mom, Dad, and brother Arron that he will buy and come see them next spring. Then he goes to Hanna's house and tells Anna and Christina, but Hanna gives him a hug, and Charles shook his hand. James mounts his horse and rides off to the river road. He passes by the bunkhouse but doesn't stop. He rides up to the barn at Matt's place. He takes his horse inside the barn, and Paul tells James that they have set him up with a bed in the tack room. He also told him that Reeha would be cooking for him, and he would eat at their cabin each morning and night. "Thank you," said James. "You're welcome, son," said Paul. "I'll come get you in the morning to eat." "Then I'll show you where Matt and his crew are working on the railroad." "Put your things away and come to the cabin to eat supper," said Paul. "No, thank you," said James. "I don't feel much like eating tonight." "Ok, then," said Paul, "I'll see you in the morning." James took off his gun belt and hung it on the bedpost, kicked off his boots. He lay on the bed thinking about Missy and the Valley, he missed it already. The next morning, Paul came and got him and took him to the cabin for breakfast. As Paul, Reeha, and James sat at the table eating, Heidi came out of her bedroom wearing nothing but her nightgown. She looked up and screamed as she saw James, then ran back to her room. Paul and James laughed, "Momma," yelled Heidi, "ok, we better go," said Paul. The two men got up and left the cabin, then walked to the barn.

Missy didn't know that James had left, no one had told her, not even James. The next morning, Missy and Kate rode to the bunk house to tell the men what to do. After drinking coffee with them, Hanna said, "James, you take your crew North to look for strays." There was no reply. "James," "where's James?" asked Missy. The men looked around and shrugged their shoulders. "James," yelled Missy, "I haven't seen him since yesterday when we moved the cows," said one of the older men. "Well, Damn," said Missy, "he must be sick," she lined out the other hands. Then Missy and Kate rode back to the valley, and Hanna was in the barn with Christina and Anna. "Hanna," yelled Missy, "have you seen James?" "Not since yesterday afternoon," said Hanna. "He's not here anymore, he came to tell us goodbye on his way out," said Hanna. Kate dropped her head. "Why," "where did he go," asked Missy in a mad tone, "well, honey, he's quiet, but I got Jim to give him a job helping my dad." Sissy's eyes filled with tears, "I can't believe he just up and quit me like that," said Missy. "Well, he told me that you and he had talked about it," "and you knew he was going to leave," said Hanna. "I didn't think he was serious," said Missy, then she started to bawl, "Why would he do this to me?" said Missy. "Come on, Kate," said Missy as she got back on her horse, "we've got work to do."

Missy and Kate rode off. "Momma, why was Aunt Missy crying?" asked Anna. "Oh, she lost a friend, I think," said Hanna. Anna went back to play with Christina, Thomas was gone now, school had started back, and all the older horses were trained now. It was time to get ready for winter now, snow would be coming soon.

Paul and James rode out to where Matt and his crew were working. James tied his horse, and Paul went back to the barn. "Morning, James," said Matt. "Morning, sir," said James. "Just call me Matt," said Matt. "What do you need me to do asked James," Today, I want you to watch the crew, learn what they're doing and how they are doing it." "This is new to all of us, son, including me," said Matt, "if you see a faster or better way to do something, just tell me, we'll talk about it." James watched as the men moved the rails in place, placed a spreader bar across them to keep them in line, then spiked them down. These were small rails compared to a normal train track, but they did the same thing, just with smaller loads. Another crew was up ahead bedding the ties and lining them up, and ahead of them was a clearing crew, cutting trees and clearing brush. James was amazed by the process and the results and wanted to know more.

At lunch, he and Matt sat and talked. James had seen the big trees on the North end but wondered how they would be hauled on the rails. Matt told him that the carts for moving the trees were being built now. Unlike the flatbed cart, they were moving the rails and ties on it now. The log carts would be chained to the logs, the big tree would be cut, then the limbs removed, and they would drag the logs to a loading spot. Mules will roll the log between the rails. A Gin pole will be added to the front of the Engine, with a cable around one end of the log. The log will be lifted and a cart rolled under that end and chained to the log, then the other end lifted and another cart under that end. Then you have a log on wheels, which the Engine will pull down the tracks to the Sawmill. "That's great," said James, "yep," said Matt, "my grandson Stewart came up with that idea."

Back at the Valley, Missy was still mad and taking it out on everyone around her. When Tye heard that James was gone now, he saw it as a chance to move up and take his place. But he knew that now would not be a good time to make his move. Kate asked Missy, "Why are you so pissed off at everybody?" "I don't know, I just am," said Missy. "I still can't believe James is gone. I hate men; they're stupid," said Missy. Kate laughed, "Well, I'm not going to argue with that," "but why is it James' fault?" "It's not my fault," said Missy, "I didn't do anything to him, we were friends, I count on him." "Ok," said Kate, "pretend you really liked a boy, maybe even though you loved him, and you worked around other girls who thought he was cute too." "Oh, they talked about his cute butt, his lips, his eyes, and what they do to him if they had a chance," said Kate, "what would you do?" "I'd beat their butts and tell them not to be talking about him that way," said Missy. "Yep," said Kate, "and what did James do, honey?" Missy started to cry, "I just always wanted him to stay with me," said Missy. "We were good together, we liked the same things, I could trust him, he understood me," said Missy. "Honey, I think they call that love," said Kate, "but what do I know, I'm just an old cow hand."

That night when James came to supper, Heidi was still dressed up from work. She sat across from James and stared at him. Every time he reached for something, she handed it to him, smiling. Heidi had always liked James, even back when she spent the summer with Hanna and Missy. Heidi didn't know the full story as to why he had left the Valley, but she was glad he was there now. After a few days, Heidi went up to the tack room and cleaned it up for James while he was still at work. She had left a little note on his pillow, "sweet dreams, Heidi." James just smiled, but it did feel good to have someone thinking of him, he wished Missy would have. If he only knew, just how much Missy was thinking of him now, when he was there with her, she had taken him for granted. James had stopped watching and was now helping the crew lay the tracks. The first snow came, but the railroad crew kept working, knowing that before long they would have to stop for the winter. Matt was impressed with James; he was a hard worker and smart, a fast learner.

Lizzy and her lawyer friend "Eric" had been spending more and more time together. Taking buggy rides in the afternoons and having picnics along the river. But now, with the snow, they had been meeting at the restaurant in town for lunch almost every day. Lizzy finally took him to her mother and dad's house for supper one night, to meet the family. They announced that they would be getting married next June. Lizzy was wearing a diamond engagement ring. Ezy was thrilled for her, as was Sara, and promised to help with the wedding. Ezy was due at any time to have her baby, and Jim was staying close to home now. Sissy and her new friend Dave were also spending time together a couple of times, and she and Lizzy had double-dated with Eric and Dave. Heidi told Sissy about James staying at the homestead and working for Matt now. Sissy told her to stay away from him. "Why?"

asked Heidi. "Because I don't know what happened, but I do know James liked Missy a lot," said Sissy, "and you don't want Missy mad at you, that's for sure." That night after supper, Heidi slipped James a note as he was leaving. When James got to the tack room, he read it. "I'll see you in a little while," signed Heidi, James through the note in the heater. About that time, he heard a knock on the door. Dang, he thought that was fast. He opened the door, and it was Missy standing there. "Can we talk?" asked Missy. "Sure," said James, "come on in." Missy sat down at the table, and James sat on the other side with his head down, thinking he was about to get chewed out. "Missy started to speak, but then started to cry, "How could you leave me, James?" asked Missy. James looked up at her, "You know why," said James, "I love you, Missy. I know you don't want to hear that, but it's true, and I can't help it." "When it was just you and me, I didn't care if you felt the same, but once the other men came and I saw how they looked at you every day and heard the things they said." "I had no claim on you, or any right to be jealous, but I was, I couldn't take it anymore," said James.

They heard a light knock at the door, oh, shit thought James, Heidi, come in," said James. Heidi opened the door. She saw Missy setting there, "hi, Missy," "hello Heidi," said Missy, Offaly late for you to be out," James grabbed a shirt and handed it to Heidi, "tell your mom it's missing two buttons," said James. "Ok," said Heidi, "I'll see you at breakfast." Heidi left as fast as she could. "So, laundry service too," said Missy. "Well, her mom offered to fix it," said James. "Missy smiled. She knew it was time to stake her claim on James. She stood up, walked to the door, and opened it. Then walked back over to James and pulled him up from his chair. She wrapped her arms around him and kissed him. It was the first kiss for them both, "Ezy, thought me and my sister that it was wrong to sleep with a boy before we were married," said Missy. She started unbuttoning his shirt as she stepped out of her boots. James unbuttoned her shirt as she pulled down his pants, then wiggled out of hers. "But we are meant to be together," said Missy, "the ring will have come later." They fell to the bed, they rolled around on the bed kissing, "I do love you James," said Missy, as he rolled over on top of her." Afterwords they lay in each other's arms, and talked, then made love again. The next morning, they made love for the third time, "your mine," said Missy, "no, body else's, you understand," "Yes, mam, said James. James got dressed for work, saddled his horse, then rode off to the rails line, a light snow was falling. Missy stood in the doorway of the barn, wrapped in only a blanket, waiting for Heidi to come by on her way to work. When she did, Missy gave her a big smile and a wave. "Have a nice day," yelled Missy. Missy then got dressed and rode back to the Valley, knowing that James would be coming back to the Valley soon.

On November 8th. Ezy gave birth to a little girl, Jim was overwhelmed with joy, as was Lizzy, who thought Jim didn't know how to make a girl. They named her Elizabeth Diann, what a beautiful thing she is, said Sara. Two weeks later, James asked Jim if he could marry Missy. "It's about time," said Jim. "Go get her and bring her home." "We'll have the wedding here tomorrow," James, rode to the Valley, he told Hanna and Charles, then went and told his mom, dad, and brother. James went to the cabin and told Missy, "I need you to come with me." "Where are we going?" asked Missy. "Your father told me to bring you home," James dropped down to one knee and pulled out a ring. "Marry Me Missy," said James. She said, "Yes," "Kate, get the things you're both going with me," said James. "Missy and I are getting married tomorrow at her father's house. "What about a dress?" asked Missy. "Your sister owns a dress shop," said James. "Come on, let's go," "Your father is waiting." Real parents are a grey area on the King's Land Ranch. Jim found and saved Missy and Sissy when they were very young, and he raised them as his own.

The next day, James and Missy were married, and a big party was held directly after the wedding for them. The Pruitts were invited, as well as the rest of the Evens family and their guest. It was a first for the Evens family, a winter wedding. Jim and Ezy sent them to California for their honeymoon, while they were gone, Hanna laid off Tye from the ranch. Heidi was at the wedding with her parents, but didn't say much. Anna and Christina were Missy's flower girls, Hanna was her maid of honor, and Jim gave her away. Kate and Sissy were her bridesmaids, Arron, Thomas, and Stewart were the groomsmen. The next morning, James and Missy Pryor boarded the train for California.

Stewart, now seventeen, had only been to see Patina once that summer, but after the wedding, he seemed to miss her more than ever. Hanna had a cow die and had sent a message to Jim that she had some meat if anyone needed it. Stew asked his dad if he could take some of the meat to the Indians before the hard snow. Jim said yes, but to take Thomas with him just in case, and be back in two days. The next day, the two boys packed their horses down with supplies, along with their guns. Jim had taught both his sons how to shoot a gun. Neither one was as good as Jim, but Thomas was close, a fast draw, but Stewart was best with a rifle. They headed out and rode to the Valley and Aunt Hanna's place; they loaded up the beef, then headed up the creek bank in the direction of the Indian Village. The weather was cold, but the snow was lit and only about a foot deep on the ground. Late that afternoon, they made it to the Indian Village with the beef. Chief Spotted Elk was glad to see them. Patina was nowhere around; they unloaded the beef and gave it to the tribe. Stew went to Patina's family teepee. She was there with her mother and father, and she was sick. Bad sick, she had a high fever, Stewart remembered what Hanna had done with Arron, he scooped her up and carried her outside, she was burning up. Her mother was trying to stop him. Thomas didn't know what to think. Stew was screaming at Patina's mother to let her go. Stew pulled all her clothes off and then buried her in the snow. Patina was unconscious. Stew patted her face. "Walk up now," said Stew. "Wake up, sweetie, it's Stew. "Finally, after about twenty minutes, she opened her eyes. "Stew," she said in a weak voice. "I was praying for you to come," "you came," Stew picked up her naked body and carried her back inside the teepee. Stew covered her with skins and blankets and told Thomas to get more wood for the fire. "Water," said Stew, "get me some water." Patina's father went out and got water. Stew made her drink water, then he poured the rest into a pot and put it on the fire. "Snow," "get me snow," said Stew. The girl's father got snow, and Stew placed small amounts of snow in her mouth. The mother was crying, she was scared for her daughter's life, but her father knew Stew was trying to help her and would not harm her. Patina looked up at Stew, "You came for me," said Patina. "Yes, I came for you," he kissed her forehead. The fever was down, and the water had started to boil on the fire, filling the teepee with steam.

Stew took snow and rubbed it over her face and forehead. "When's the last time she ate?" asked Stew. Her father said, "One, two days." "Thomas, go cut me a chunk of that beef off, please." Thomas went and found the meat in the big teepee where the women were cutting it up. He grabbed a chunk and took it to Stew. "More water," said Stew. The father went for more water. Stew took a smaller pot, cut the meat into small bite-sized pieces, and put it in the pot, adding a little water. "Salt," said Stew, "get me some salt, beans, corn, potatoes." The father took off again. When the water started to boil in the meat, stew added a little more, then a few beans, a small chunk of potatoes, and a few kernels of dried corn. Then he added salt. "I've got to get out of here," said Thomas, "it's hot in here. "Go," said Stew, "I've got this now, Patina was staring at him as he stirred the things in the pot. The girl's mom had already left the teepee, sweat was pouring off Patina, her father, and Stew. Stew waited until the potatoes were soft and would mash, then he took the pot off the fire and added cold water to cool it down. Stew took the skins and blanket off her, exposing her naked body. Stew helped her set up, then he covered her with one blanket. Stew told her father to open the flap on the teepee.

Steam was still coming off the big pot, and Stew poured the rest of the water into it. It had been three hours since Stew had gotten there, but Patina was setting up and alert, she was eating the food as Stew fed her. The teepee had cooled down some, as had Patina's fever, so her father closed the flap back.

The next morning, Stewart told Patina's father that he was taking her with him. "She needs medicine and rest," said Stewart, "I will bring her back next spring." Stew bundled her up and put her on his horse, then climbed on behind her. They rode off along the creek. Midday, they made their way back to Hanna's, and Stew carried her to the house. "What's wrong?" asked Hanna. "I think she has pneumonia," said Stew. "When I got there, she was burning up with fever," "she was unconscious," Stew told Hanna what he had done, and that when she came too, she had a bad chafe, and trouble breathing. "I didn't know what else to do," said Stew. "Take her to the barn and put her in the tack room," said Hanna. "I'll bring blankets and food," said Hanna, "if the fever leaves, I'll bring her into the house." "I can't take a chance on making my family sick," said Hanna. "I understand," said Stew. He took her to the tack room and put her by the heater." Hanna came to the barn with a cup," asked Stew. "Hot tea," said Hanna, "with some whiskey and honey." "I'll take care of her. You go let your folks know you're back." "Ok," said Stew, he hugged Hanna and said, "thank you," "you're welcome," "now go home." Stew and Thomas rode the rest of the way home; after putting up their horses, they went inside the house. "Where have y'all been?" asked Ezy. "They had to do something for me," said Jim.

Jim and Stew went into the front room, "Patina is at Aunt Hanna's," said Stew. "Why?" asked Jim. "She's really sick, Dad, pneumonia, I think." "Aunt Hanna said she would take care of her," said Stew. "Does she need a doctor?" asked Jim. "Probably," said Stew, "but she is so weak I didn't want to make it worse by bringing her further. “Aunt Hanna gave her some antibiotics,” said Stew. “That’s good,” said Jim. “I’ll go get the doctor and take him out there,” said Jim. “Ezy, I’ve got to go check on things, the boys will be here,” said Jim, “it may be after dark when I get back.” “Ok,” said Ezy. Jim went and hooked up the buggy, then went after the doctor in town. Once they got to Hanna’s place, they took the doctor to the barn. “That's an Indian girl,” said the doctor. “Yep,” said Hanna, “a sick one.” “I don’t know about this,” said the doctor. “You don’t know what,” asked Hanna, “her blood is red, and everything else she has is just like mine.” The doctor knew he had no choice but to try and help her, he examined her, “yes, she has a bad case of pneumonia,” said the doctor, he took two bottles out of his bag. “Give her this one in the morning and at night to help get the fluids out of her lungs, give this one for the couch and the fever.” “Make stay inside,” the doctor picked up his bag, “that’s all I can do for her,” said the doctor. Everyone could tell the doctor didn’t want to be there or help an Indian. Jim carried him back to town, and put him out, “thanks Doc,” said Jim, the doctor didn’t reply, Jim knew that was something he would deal with latter. Hanna moved Patina to the house and put her upstairs into a bed.

The next week, school had let out for the holidays, Stew asked his father if he could go to Hanna’s for a few days. “You'll be back here the day before Thanksgiving,” said Jim. Stew rode out to Aunt Hanna’s. Patina was a lot better. She hugged Stew, “Thank you for saving me,” she said. “My life belongs to you now,” said Patina. She was able to get up and move around. The couch was gone, but she was still a little weak, she had lost weight. “She needs exercise,” said Hanna, “take her for a walk to the barn and back.” Stew puts his coat on, Hanna loans Patina one of hers, and they walk outside. The glair from the snow blinded her for a second, she had been inside for so long. They walk to the barn, Stew shows her the horses, “Hanna, say she will show me how to ride,” “when I get better,” said Patina. “She is a good teacher,” said Stew, as they walked back to the house. Stew takes her back to her room and sits with her until she goes to sleep. Then he goes downstairs to talk to Aunt Hanna, "So what are you going to do with her?" asked Hanna. Stew shakes his head, "I'm not sure," "Momma is going to have a fit," said Stew. "Yes, she is," said Hanna with a laugh. "Look, you do what your heart tells you to," said Hanna. "Do you love her?" asked Hanna. "I think so," said Stew, "I mean, when I'm not with her, I want to be, when I am with her, I feel good, and I'm happy." "I like being around her, talking to her, I like the way she looks at me." "Sometimes I just feel like I want to scream when she's not with me," said Stew. "Sounds like love to me," said Hanna with a smile, "you still have another year of school." "If I was you, I would take her home next spring and let her stay with her family." "You help finish the railroad, finish school, and go see her when you can." "I think by the end of the summer you will know what's best for you and her," said Hanna.

That winter, with his father's help, Stew found plenty of reasons to go to the Valley to see Patina. Jim understood that when you make the decision to try to save someone's life, you do. You have a vested interest in that person; if it's someone you already care for, it only makes those feelings stronger. Jim knew Stew had fillings for the Indian girl before, by helping her those fillings had grown, he expected no less from his son. Early spring, Patina was completely well, Hanna and Anna had taught her to ride a horse. She even went with them to move part of the herd out into the Valley; she didn't look Indian anymore. Jeans, shirt, boots, and a hat, when Stew came to take her home, he didn't recognize her. "I don't want her to go," said Stew to Hanna, "I don't either," said Hanna, "but it's for the best." A tear came to Stew's eyes. "It's not forever," said Hanna, "I'm going to give her that horse she's been riding," "we will see how long it takes her to come back." "Ok," said Stew. Patina hugs everyone and tells them buy." Hanna says, "That's your horse now. Take care of him." Patina hugs Hanna again. "I will," said Patina. "I'm here if you need me," said Hanna.

Stew and Patina rode off to the creek, then followed it out of sight. Hanna had tears in her eyes. After two and a half months of having her there, it was hard to watch her leave. But she knew that she would be back soon, that she had no doubt about. When Stew and Patina rode into the Indian Village, no one recognized her. They got off their horses, and the Chief welcomed them. Patina's father was working in the crop field. She walked out to him, "Father," said Patina. He turned and saw her, he grabbed her up and hugged her, he kissed her face all over. Then looked up to the heavens, saying, "Thank you, thank you." He walked with her back to the main teepee. On the way back, they stopped at their teepee, "Mother," said Patina. Her mother came out, Patina took off her hat, her mother screamed and started to cry, as she grabbed her, Stew had tears in his eyes. Then everyone came around to see her and welcomed her back. Patina's mother looked at Stewart, then walked over and hugged him. They went inside the big teepee. Stewart spent the night with Patina and her mother and father in their teepee. The next morning, before Stewart left, he told Patina's father that he would come back for her in the fall. The father said, "Then we will have a ceremony," "Yes, we will have a ceremony," said Stewart. Patina grabbed Stewart and kissed his lips for the first time. They walked hand in hand to Stewart's horse, then kissed again, "I love you," said Stewart, "I love Stew," said Patina. He mounted his horse and rode away; it was the hardest thing he had ever had to do.

The next day, Stewart went back to his place with Matt on the rail line. James had gone back to the valley after the Honeymoon. Thomas had also gone back to the Valley to help Charles with the horses. He had a choice to make, whether to go to college or just work for the ranch, he had already finished school. Stewart had one more year of school left. He knew what he was going to do: marry Patina, build a house, and work for the Sawmill, moving timber. James and Missy were living in the cabin in the valley, and they were still letting Kate stay there, too. Anna was still riding horses and helping with the cow if needed, when she wasn't studying. Grace and Hanna were teaching her and Christina at home; the school was just too far away. Stewart told his grandfather Matt, that he was going to marry the Indian girl this fall. Stew waited for his response. "Well, Son," said Matt, "a man needs a good woman to keep his head on straight." "You going to build her a house?" asked Matt. "Yes, sir," said Stew. "Good," said Matt, "I can help you with that, but let's finish this railroad first."

Heidi had taken Sissy's advice and was trying to sell things to the young men coming in to see her. Missy overheard one of the men tell Heidi that he would buy a pair of undergarments if she would model them for him. Heidi giggled, then said Buy two pairs, and I will, Missy jumped up from her seat and ran up front. "No, you will not," yelled Missy, "get out of here," Missy told the man, "Get out." Heidi tried to act innocently, "What," asked Heidi, "you know what, I heard what you said to that man." "But we were just joking around," said Heidi, "I wouldn't have done it." Missy was so mad that Heidi left the front crying. That afternoon, Heidi went home and told her parents that Sissy had scolded her for no good reason and that she wasn't working there anymore. Her parent torn between their daughter's word and the word of Sissy, calming Heidi did something they knew their daughter would never do. The Potters packed up and moved out of the cabin and left the ranch. Paul didn't want to leave, but his wife and daughter felt their honor had been questioned. Since the kids were grown and had their own houses, Sara and Matt haven't needed their help for a while now. But out of the kindness of their hearts, they had just let them keep staying there.

The next day, Matt told Stewart that he knew of a cabin that was empty now. Then he told him about the Potter family leaving the ranch and what Heidi had supposedly done. "So, I guess you can use it until we can get you a house built somewhere," said Matt. "That's great," said Stew, "that's if it's ok with your dad," said Matt, "it's his cabin." Stewart worked hard pushing the crews; he wanted to reach the creek crossing below the Indian Village so he could visit Petina. The rail crew caught up with the clearing crew after four weeks and had to stop. Matt told Jim to bring the cutting crew in to where they were at, that he had the carts, and they could test the rail system with trees there. Jim said that was a good idea while they were waiting for the clearing crew to move on. It took them a couple of days to get a system going on lifting and loading the log carts, but once they did, everything was working fine. They had enough carts to haul five logs at a time; the round trip took two hours from that point, five trips a day, thirty logs. That was three times as many as they could drag in a day with the mule teams, the narrow rail was a success. Stewart had done it, well, almost; they still had a way to go to get to where the big timber was. But the system did work, and that's the important thing for the timber operation.

Lizzy now has her eyes set on buying up some of the empty lots in town, the area near the railroad where the makeshift building had been left by the railroad. Although people who had no place to go had been living in them for a while, now the railroad has torn them down and is offering to sell the lots. If Lizzy can acquire them, she wants to build a warehouse where bundles of lumber can be stored until they are shipped by rail. With all the expansions at the Mill, she is running out of room, and with the new rail system able to bring the large trees she needs to keep what room she has open to store the logs. Lizzy meets with the railroad, and now only buys the lots in that location, but also buys all the other empty lots along the railroad in town. The only thing she doesn't own now on that side is the Train Station, the rail yard, and the stock yards. Thanks to the Pruitt's and the Evens, there is no shortage of jobs to be found in Oregon City. Although Lizzy no longer teaches at the school, she plans to donate part of the land for a new school building, since they've had to add on to the old building many times. Lizzy has formed a committee of prominent people in the area to govern the town's school and has been able to obtain the money for the building through government grants. Also, the money to furnish it with a desk, chairs, chalkboards, and the study books needed.

Matt and Stewart have now made it to the creek below the Indian Village and are building a bridge for the rails. The others ride the Engine Car back to the Mill each night, except for Matt and Stew, who camp at the work site. Patina rides her horse to the camp each night, and cooks for them, then sleeps by Stew. Matt really likes Patina; she calls him Papa; he will just sit and listen to them talk. She never complains or asks any questions; she's just content to be with Stew. Near the end of May, they will finish the bridge and install the rails over the creek. Lizzy is getting married in a few days. So, Matt shuts down the rail crew for a few days, so he and Stew can attend her wedding, "let's take Patina with us," said Matt. "Ok, why?" asked Stew. "She's family now and needs to see how we do marriages," "ok," said Stew, "but momma's going to flip." "Well, your dad found your momma abandoned in a wagon and saved her," "you saved Patina, no difference," said Matt. "Let's go home. "She can stay at my house, and Sara will fix her up with clothes." The three rode to the Vellage to tell Patina folks, then rode off to the Vally so she could see Hanna. "Hi, dad," said Hanna, "Patina how are you doing," Hanna hugged her. "Where are y'all going," asked Hanna, "home to get ready for your sister Lizzy's wedding." Hanna looked at Stew, "are you taking Patina," Stew smiled, "yes," "you're a brave young man," said Hanna, "good for you," "I'll see y'all there," said Hanna.

They rode on to the river road that led to Matt's house. Once they got there, they stopped at Jim's cabin. "Come on, Patina," said Matt, "I want to show you something." They got off the horses. Matt opened the cabin door and went inside. Patina looked around. "What is this place?" asked Patina. "This is where old Stew was born," said Matt. Patina smiled, "Would you like to live here?" asked Matt. "With Stew," asked Patina. Matt nodded, "Yes, with Stew." "Ok," said Matt, "I see what I can do." They rode on up to the barn. Matt put up his and Patina's horses, "go on home, Stew," said Matt, "I'll take care of her," "will see you tomorrow at the wedding." Stew gave Patina a kiss and rode off. Matt took Patina into his house, "Sara," said Matt. "Somebody I want you to meet," Sara came out of the kitchen, "this is Patina," said Matt, "the Indian girl everybody has been talking about." "So nice to finally meet you," said Sara. "I thought she might need to see how one of our weddings is done," said Matt. She and Stew are getting married next spring, "oh, how wonderful," said Sara. "Well, let me get my food off the stove so we can run to Sissy's store for a dress," said Sara. "We will get you one for Lizzy's wedding and order you one for your Wedding." "You, go get the buggy, Matt," "Yes, ma'am," said Matt. Sara sets her pots off the stove and takes off her apron. Matt pulls up to the front porch with the buggy, and they get in and ride off to town.

Patina had never seen a town before, or Vellage as she called it, with rock and wood teepees. She was in awe of it all. They parked in front of the dress shop and went inside. "Hi, Grandma, Papaw," said Sissy, "who is this?" "This is Patina." "Hi, Patina." "Oh, my God, she's beautiful. Oh, look at that hair." "So, what do we need?" asked Missy, "something for the wedding tomorrow, top to bottom." "Great," said Sissy. She started grabbing dresses. "Come with me," said Missy. Patina and Sara followed her to the back room. She tried on one, "No, that's not it," said Sissy, "tie this one," No," "here this one," "that's it," said Sara. It was a beautiful white dress with yellow flowers on it, and a matching bow for her hair. It had a yellow lace around the neckline, and at the bottom of the dress, they found some white shoes and yellow socks to match. With her brown skin, brown eyes, and long black hair, she was beautiful. Then they got white underpants, bra, and slip, "perfect," said Sissy, they stood her in front of the mirror, "is that me," asked Patina. "yes, that's you honey," said Sara, "Stew like," asked Patina, "yes, Stew will like," said Sissy. Patina changed back into her jeans and shirt. Sissy folded and placed everything into a bag. "We also need to order Patina a wedding dress for herself, she's marrying Stew next spring," said Sara. "Well, congratulations," said Sissy, "See you tomorrow," "Come back later and we will find you a wedding dress to order." Sara and Patina got back in the buggy, and Matt drove them home. After supper, Sara helped Patina get a bath, then put her in bed. Sara and Matt sat at the table, "she'll make us some beautiful great grand babies," said Sara, "yes, she will," said Matt.

The next morning, after breakfast, Sara brushed out Patina's hair, trimmed the ends, and put the bow in her hair. She let her stay in just her slip. Patina didn't like the bra, not that she really needed it, her breasts were so small. About an hour before leaving Hanna, Anna, and Christina showed up at Sara's house. Patina had just put on her dress before they came in. "Oh, mamma, Patina looks like a real girl," said Anna, Sara, and Hanna laughed. "She is a real girl," said Hanna, "a real young lady." "You're beautiful, Patina," said Hanna. "Stew likes," asked Patina. "Yes, honey, Stew will like," Patina smiled. They all left and headed to the church in town. Stew was pacing outside, waiting for them to get there; you would have thought it was his wedding day. When Matt's buggy pulled up, Stew could not believe his eyes. He helped his grandmother down, then helped Patina down. Stewart just stood there and stared at Patina, "Stew like," asked Patina in a low voice, "Stew love," said Stewart. Patina smiled. Charles, Missy, and James rode up on their horses. Matt took Sara's arm, Charles took Hanna's arm, Stewart took Patina's arm, James took Missy's arm, and Anna took Christina's arm, and they all marched into the church. When Ezy saw Stewart and Patina file in behind the rest, she couldn't believe her eyes. The last time she saw Patina, she was only wearing patches. This beautiful young woman, who was with her son, could not be that same Indian girl, but she was. Jim just smiled. Sissy walked up and hugged them both, then Stewart and Patina sat in the row behind his mother and father. Thomas came in at the last minute and sat by Stew, as they started playing the wedding marsh. Lizzy was beautiful in her white gown; Eric was wearing a tuxedo, as was Matt, as he walked his youngest child, Lizzy, down the aisle. Sara was already crying before the ceremony started. Patina just stared at Stew. She had never seen anything like this, beautiful people and music, some people smiling, some crying, but the feeling of love filled the air. She could feel it in her heart and see it on Stewart's face what a wonderful thing it was.

Afterward at the reception, Ezy walked up to Stewart and Patina, "You both look so beautiful together," said Ezy, "I guess your wedding will be next." "Yes, ma'am," said Stewart, "next spring sometime after the rail is finished." "Will you finish school?" asked Ezy. "Yes, ma'am," said Stewart, "then I'll work for the Sawmill." Ezy hugged Stewart and then Patina, "God bless you both," said Ezy. Ezy looked at Patina, "Hanna tells me we were both saved by Evens' boys," "we are very lucky girls," said Ezy. Patina just smiled at her, then Ezy walked away. Stewart knew then that everything would be ok with his mom. Hanna walked up to them and hugged them both. "Thank you, Aunt Hanna," said Stewart. "Oh, I didn't do anything," said Hanna. "I love you both." "If you ever need anything, I'm always here," said Stewart with a smile. "I know," Jim eased over to them, "I hear y'all might be interested in a cabin," said Jim, "It's your son, whatever you need." Stewart hugged his dad, "It's a beautiful day," said Jim, "a beautiful day." Jim walked over to Lizzy and Eric, Matt and Sara walked up to Stewart and Patina, "Well, kids, y'all ready to go?" asked Matt. "We've got to go back to work tomorrow." "Y'all can stay with us tonight, we'll leave out in the morning," said Matt. "Sounds good," said Stew.

Chapter Fourteen: Good Nabors

Matt and Stewart completed the rail line to the North end of the properties with their crews, only three weeks after school was out and Stewart's graduation. Stewart left the work camp to ride to the Indian Village to find Patina. He was ready to get his girl and take her home, but first, he had to follow her father's wishes. Matt was going back to his house, but on his way, he stopped by Hanna Valley to see Hanna and the girls. Matt told Hanna that Steward and Patina were having their Ceremony at the Village in two days. He wanted her and her family to come, along with Missy, James, and Thomas, to show support for Stewart's choice. Hanna asked about the Church Marriage, Matt said he wanted them to have it the next day at the church in town. That he and Jim would set that up, once he got back home, Hanna said she would send John and Arron out to build a coral at the creek crossing tomorrow. The next day, she would take horses there for everyone living near town, so Matt could take them there on the train cart, then they could ride horses from there. I don't want Mom, Ezy, Lizzy, and Sissy to have to ride ten miles from town on horseback; this way, they would only have to ride two miles. Matt said, "That's a great idea, leave a horse for Jim and me too.

Matt made it home that afternoon. He told Sara about the Ceremony, then went to Jim's. They rode into town and made arrangements at the church. They stop by the Mill to tell Lizzy, for her, Eric, and Sissy to come, that he would haul them all on the train. Then he asked her to have benches built and mounted on the flat car for about eight people. That they would leave the Mill yard that morning around 8:00 a.m., he told them the wedding in town would be the next day. Lizzy agreed, then Matt took Jim back home so he could tell Ezy. Jim told her the plans. Ezy said, "I hope he knows what he's doing," "probably no more than we did when we got married," said Jim. "That turned out good," "I think this will go well." Ezy hugged him, "I know," said Ezy, "it's just hard for me to let him go, he is my baby boy." The next day, while John and Arron built a carol at the creek crossing near the rails, Lizzy had her men add benches to the flat car. Sara was baking bread, cakes, and pies for the Indian Ceremony. Charles put a beef roast on the fire pit. Hanna and the girls also cooked a couple of pies and a Hickory nut cake.

The second day, Charles put the racks on one of the pack horses and loaded the roast and the sweets the girls had made. Then he saddled his horse, Hanna's horse, Anna's horse, and eight more. Hanna wanted to go a day early to help get Patina ready. Charles helped Anna onto her horse, then put Christina on behind Anna, then he and Hanna mounted up. Charles led four of the spear horses, and Hanna led the other four, as Anna followed behind them. Midday, they reached the coral, they put the eight spear horses in it, and left them there. Then they rode the rest of the way into the Village. Patina saw them coming and ran to meet them. She was happy to see Hanna and the girls. Charles took the horses and unsaddled them, then unloaded the pack horse. Stewart came out of the big teepee with the Chief. He shook Charles' hand, then hugged Hanna. Anna and Christina were gone; they had taken off with the young Indian girls. There was an atmosphere of celebration in the air, everybody was happy. Patina was excited as she took Hanna to her teepee to see her ceremonial dress. It was beautiful, bleached out Elk skin, with breads sawed on it, matching moccasin boots that came almost to her knees. Stewart sat and talked with Charles while the girls were looking at the dress. The Indians were planning a big celebration tonight for Stwart and Patina, although the others would not be there until the morning. Thomas, James, and Missy did make it there just before dark, just as the celebration was starting.

Inside the big teepee, they had all kinds of food laid out, corn, beans, potatoes, flat bread, deer meat, Elk, and the beef Charles had cooked. Outside, they had a big bonfire going, and the Indian girls were dancing around it, dressed up as animals. Anna and Christina were dancing with them, they didn't understand the words they were chanting, but they didn't care. At one point, they pulled Stewart into the circle with them and danced around him. Then the young men did the same, as they danced and yelled, then pulled Patina into their circle and danced around her. Once that was over, they went inside to eat. The Indians had some kind of sour drink that the grown-ups drank. A liquor made from sugar beets, like wine, Hanna and Missy seem to like it. Charles and James wouldn't try it; everyone ate their food and then went back outside. After a while, Charles and James had to help Hanna and Missy into their bedrolls. Charles put Anna and Christina in a bedroll together, while he and James sat by a fire.

The next morning, Charles and James rode to the corral at the train tracks and got the horses ready for the others that were coming from town. It wasn't long until they heard the train whistle, the small train stopped just past the coral. Matt and Jim started helping each other off the flat car. Sara, Lizzy, and Sissy were in awe of the train track through the woods. They loved it and thought it was fun. Jim got everyone on their horses, and they rode to the Indian Village. Hanna and Missy were still in their bedrolls, Anna and Christina were off with the Indian kids. Charles carried two cups of coffee to Hanna and Missy. They sat by the fire and sipped the coffee. Lizzy came over to them. "What's wrong with you two?" "Don't drink the punch," said Hanna.

After a little while, the Ceremony started. Stewart was brought out dressed as an Indian and stood by the Chief. Then Patina was brought out in her outfit and stood on the other side of the Chief. He raised their arms up to heaven and said some words, then two men stood face to face. They took Patina's right arm and put it behind her back, then took Stewart's right arm and put it behind Patina's back, and tied them together. They took Stewart's left arm and put it behind his back, and then Patina's left arm and put it behind Stewart's back, and tied them to gather. They were now chest to chest, bound together, a rope stretched out, Stewart and Patina at one end and the chief at the other end. The Chief said, "You must be able to navigate through life bound together as one." "This won't be easy," "you must always work together to reach your destination in life." "Now come to me," Stewart looked the situation over, then smiled at Patina. "Do you trust me?" asked Stewart. "Yes," said Patina. "Then do as I say." "Stand on top of my feet," Stewart was barefoot. "It will hurt your feet," said Patina. "Yes, but only for a little while," said Stewart. Patina stands on his feet one at a time. Stewart side steps along the rope until they reach the Chief, the other Indian cheer, "You have passed the test," said the Chief. "You have shown that you can find a way together to reach your destination. The two men untie Patina and Stewart, then turn them facing the Chief. They have them hold their arms out, and they lay the rope over them. The Chief said, "God, let the rope that bound them together now set them free to live and love together forever. The Indians cheer and yell as they dance around Patina and Stewart. Ezy makes her way to them and hugs Patina, then Stewart, as does Patina's mom, then the two mom's hug. "That was beautiful," said Hanna, "yes, it was," said Charles, "now we get to do it again tomorrow," said Hanna. The Indian's led Patina and Stewart to a new teepee and pushed inside and closed the flap. "Wait," said Ezy, "they can't do that yet." Jim smiled, "Ezy, honey, they are as married today as they will be tomorrow," said Jim.

Everyone sat around talking and snacking for about an hour or so, and then the flap flew open, and Patina and Stewart came out dressed. Patina had on her jeans, shirt, and hat, as did Stewart. Patina had a small bag in her hand. She walked over to her mom and hugged her, then went to her dad and gave him a kiss. Stewart brought his and Patina's horses around. They mounted their horses. "Thank you all for coming," said Stewart, I'm taking my wife home now. "All aboard," said Matt, "last train to Oregon City." Charles hugged

Hanna, “Let’s take our stock home now.” “Mount up, Anna,” said Hanna. They all left the Indian village and went to the coral. Once the train left, Hanna, Charles, Missy, and James led the other horses back to the valley with Anna and Christina following. The next day, Stewart and Patina were married again in the church in town, to satisfy his mom, Ezy. It was not as glamorous as Lizzy’s wedding, but they didn’t want it to be; besides, she only did it once. Stewart and Patina fixed up the little cabin the way they wanted it with a little Indian and white man decor.

One week later, Stew went back to work, Patina spent a lot of time with Sara learning to cook and sew, and she helped Sara cook supper each night. Stew would go to the Sawmill, Lizzy had him working on plains to lay more tracks from the sawmill to the warehouse she was building near the main Railroad tracks. Although the work won’t start until next spring, he is laying out the route and what materials he would need. Lizzy has ordered another steam engine just like the one they already have. The Lumber business was booming, and Lizzy had Jim looking for more timber land to buy. They had planted most of the land from which they cut timber. But it takes years to grow trees big enough to get lumber out of. At the rate they are going, they could be out of timber to cut in five years. Jim had talked to some of the landowners in the area, and one man told him that he would not sell his land but that he would sell the trees on it. That opened a whole new side operation for their timber business that they had not thought of. After crunching numbers, Lizzy and Jim came up with what they thought would be a fair price. It would be based on board feet of lumber that they should get out of trees of a certain size. Eric helps them write up a standard contract to purchase and remove the timber from someone else’s land. The profits would be less for contract-cut trees than cutting their own trees, but would help supplement their operation longer. Once the word got out that the “Kings Land Limber Co.” would remove sections of trees and pay the landowner for the trees they cut. Landowners from all over the area were coming to them and offering to sell their timber.

In the spring of 1870, Thomas had enrolled in college, after being pushed by his father and his Aunt Hanna to become a veterinarian. With his love for horses and cattle, it only seems natural that he should pursue that profession. So, with their support and encouragement, Hanna and Jim agreed to share the cost; they both saw it as an investment for the Ranch. Stewart had started laying the rail system from the Sawmill to the warehouse building in town. Patina was four to five months pregnant and had a small baby bump showing. But she still helped Sara every day, and she and Stewart were so happy together. Ezy's baby girl and Stewards' little sister would be only two years old when Patina and Stew had their baby. Their baby will have an aunt just a little older than it when it's born. Anna was now thirteen years old and a full-blown cowgirl. She helped Charles most of the time working the young horses, but would herd cattle if needed. Missy had lost a baby this past winter; it was a little boy, and she blamed herself. But the doctor said, it was nothing she did wrong, stillborn just happens sometimes. She and James are trying to get past it and stay busy with the cows. Calves were dropping every day; it seemed like this would be another productive summer for the ranch. Mr. Pruit, who normally came to visit every couple of weeks, had not been to the Valley all spring. Hanna told Charles that he needed to go check on his mom and dad and make sure they were ok. Charles said that he would ride over there in a couple of days to check on them. The next day, Hanna rode out to see Missy and James and checked on the herd. As she passed by one of the catch pens, which they used to separate steers, she saw cows in it. She wondered why there were cows there now. She rode up to them; the cows were Pruit Cows, about fifty of them. Hanna rode on to find Missy. As she rode up to one of the herds, she saw James first. "Why do we have Pruit cows pinned up?" asked Hanna. "Well, we thought that they would have come to get them by now," said James.

"We've never had that many at one time," Missy said, If they don't come after them today, we will drive them back across the river," said James.

Hanna rode on to the next group of cows. She found Missy there. "How long have the Pruit cows been here?" asked Hanna. "Over a week," said Missy, "we cut them out yesterday," "we are going to push them back across this afternoon on the way in." "That's odd," said Hanna, "they never leave them that long." "I know," said Missy, "there's another group by the river on our side." "But they are just staying to their selves," said Missy, "show me," said Hanna. They rode West to the river, sure enough, there were about eighty cows, some with calves in a group alone grazing along the river. "Something's not right," said Hanna, "I've got to go get Charles, and go see what's wrong over there." Hanna rode off back to the valley. She rode up to the barn and got off her horse. "Charles, we've got to go; something's wrong over at the Pruit Ranch." "What?" asked Charles. "I don't know," said Hanna, as she got her sharp rifle. "But we've got fifty cows pinned up, and there are eighty more along the river that nobody's come for in over a week." Charles grabs his guns, "Grase," yelled Hanna, "watch the girls," "yes, ma'am," said Grace.

Hanna and Charles rode to the river, then crossed over to the other side, and headed to the Pruitt ranch house. They saw a horse grazing with the cows, with no rider. They eased up closer to the ground. One of the Pruit ranch hands had been shot in the back. Looked like he had been there a couple of days. They eased through the herd, and they saw another horse without a rider near the trees. They rode over, and there was a man propped up against a tree, who looked like his leg was hurt. Charles got off his horse, walked over to the man, who was passed out, and gave him some water. "What happened asked Charles. "Bandits, I guess," said the man, "about twenty of them, they came through the herd shooting everybody." "They got me in the leg, the bones broke," "I played dead, until they left, then crawled to this tree." "What were they after?" asked Charles. "I don't know, they rode in the direction of the ranch house," said the man. "I heard more shooting, that was two days ago," "it's been quite since then." "We will get you some help," said Charles, "but first we've got to see what's going on at the ranch house." Hanna and Charles got on their horses and rode slowly in the direction of the house.

They stopped about a hundred yards from the house. They saw a man sitting in a chair on the front porch holding a gun, but he hadn't seen them yet. Hanna said, "Let me find a spot with cover, and I'll keep my Sharps Rifle on him in case he tries to shoot you." "Ok," said Charles, "I'll ride up like I'm just coming to visit, and see if I can find out what's going on." "Ok," said Hanna, "but if he makes a move, you ride like hell and go get Jim, I'll go after Missy and the crew." "We'll meet up at the bunk house," said Hanna, "then we will make a plan," "Ok," said Charles. Hanna gets off her horse and leads him to a small hill. Charles starts riding to the house. As he rode up to the porch, the man stood up. "Hello," said Charles, "you must be new here. I don't know you." "What do you want?" asked the man. "Oh, nothing, I just came to visit my father and Mother for a while. Are they home?" "They're tied up right now," said the man with a smile. "What's your name?" asked the man. "I'm Charles Pruit. I live across the river." "Tom," yelled the man, "we've got another Pruitt out here." An older man came out the door onto the porch. "So, your Charles Pruit," "yes, sir," said Charles, "well, you might be able to help me," said the man, "if I can," said Charles. "Good, that's good," said the man, "well, I figure you're wondering what's going on here." "Well, I'll tell you, your brother Carl and I had a business deal back in Nevada. I hired him to treat my land to make my grass grow faster." "He did, the grass shot up fast, but it killed my whole herd."

"See, it looks like to me Carl owes me some money, and of course I'd like to get it, so I came to talk to your dad about his son's mess up and see if he would make things right." "But so far, he has been reluctant to give me the $ 50,000.00 his son has cost me, saying he doesn't have that kind of money." "Now we got into his safe, but there was only about five thousand dollars in it, that leaves me short about forty-five thousand, and I'm sure you understand that's not enough to make up for my whole herd." "So, we're holding this ranch until your little brother does the right thing. If he doesn't have it, I understand." "He can just pay me out of his inheritance once I kill his mom, dad, and brother." "Of course I'll have to do something about you too," the other man guarding the porch raised his gun at Charles, "suddenly his head blew up as Hanna pulled the trigger, Charles spun his horse around and rode off as fast as he could, the older man ducked for cover. As Charles rode out of sight of the house, Hanna got on her horse and rode back to the valley. The other men came out of the house and the bunkhouse when they heard the shot. "Who was that?" asked one of the men. "That was Charles Pruit, I think he is going to be a problem," said the old man, "Y'all spread out and get ready."

Charles rides to Jim's house, "Jim, I need your help, men are holding my mom, dad, and Chanler hostage at the ranch," said Charles. "What," said Jim, "the man claims Carl owes him $ 50,000.00 for dead cows or something," "he's holding them until Carl gives him the money." "If he doesn't pay him, he is going to kill Mom, Dad, and Chanler." "That explains something," said Jim. "What?" asked Charles. "Stewart said that there are two armed men guarding the main gate in town." "What do you need from me?" asked Jim. "Help us get my family away from them," "Ok," said Jim, I'll go get Stewart and take care of the gate." "Where do you want to meet?" asked Jim, "at the bunk house, Hanna's getting the crew together." Jim rode to town and found Stewart, "Stew, I need you to go home and get your rifle and ammo and meet me at Hanna's bunkhouse." "Ok," said Stew, "he didn't ask why, he knew better, he could see the look in his father's eyes. Jim rode up to the main gate. "Open those gates, boys," said Jim.

They didn't move. Look, said Jim, "you can do it, or I'll do it for you." One of the men put his hand on his pistol. "ok," said Jim, as he drew and shot them both, then rode up and swung the gates open. Jim rode to the sheriff's office and told him to guard the gate in case some of them came that way to get out. Jim ran his horse all the way to the bunkhouse. Hanna and her crew were there; everybody had rifles. Charles spoke up, "Some bad men are holding my family hostage at the Pruitt ranch." "We don't know what kind of shape my family members are in." "Stewart said that there are two men guarding the main gate," said Charles, "not anymore," said Jim. "The sheriff is there now," "ok," said Charles, "we didn't see any of the ranch hands. We hope they have them locked up somewhere." "But we know a few are already dead," "if you don't want to go and face these men," "I understand." "But my family is in trouble," "if you're going, let's ride," said Charles.

"We are going to come up on the house from the back side. I know the layout of the house." "If Jim goes with me, we will sneak inside and find my family and try to bring them out." "I need James and four men to surround the bunk house. "I need Missy, Kate, Hanna, and Stewart to set up around the house with rifles, about fifty yards out. "I need the rest of you to watch the barn. "If Jim and I get my family out and to safety, and some of you can get the ranch hand out." "We will take the outlaws out, don't let any of them escape," "ok, let go get them," said Charles. They all mounted up and rode across the river. As they got in sight of the house, the sun was starting to set. There was a group of cows between them and the ranch house, they used them for cover. They stopped and got off their horses. Jim pulled out his Sharps rifle and handed it to Stew, "Here, son, use my rifle, it has a light trigger, but it will hit what you aim at." Everybody starts to spread out. Jim and Charles wait until everyone is in place, then they start easing through the herd. There was a man at the back door. Jim takes out his knife and crawls through the grass. When he gets close, he jumps up and throws his knife, stabbing the man in the heart. The man falls to the ground, Jim waves for Charles, he crawls up close, then runs to Jim.

They go into the back door, and they hear talking in front of the house. As they go through the kitchen, Jim picks up two more knives. They peek out into the hallway. There are two men in the hallway, one at each bedroom doorway. Jim steps into the hall, throwing the knives one, then the other. The two men fall. They go to the first door and open it, inside is Mr. and Ms. Pruit, "get them," said Jim. Mr. Pruit was hurt, Charles and his mom helped him up and out the back door. Jim goes to the other room, inside is Chanler and his wife, Chanler is also hurt and bleeding. Jim gets them to the back door, and Charles meets him there. "Get them away from the house," said Jim. He turns and heads back down the hallway. It nearly barks outside now. Jim stands in the hallway. The older man tells the other two men with him, "If Carl's not here by noon tomorrow with my money, we will kill those four and go find that other son, Charles." "Somebody is going to pay me my money around here," "I doubt that," said Jim. The two men went for their guns. Jim shot them both, then held his gun on the older man. "Take your gun off," said Jim. The man unbuckled his gun and dropped it. Jim heard a board creak on the stairs. He turned and shot. The man rolled down the stairs. "Any more up there?" asked Jim. The man shook his head no. "Why don't I believe you?" asked Jim. "How many do you have outside?" asked Jim. "More than you can take," said the man. "Oh, I don't know about that," said Jim, just as shooting started outside at the bunk house. Then more shooting at the barn, "you did have a few out there, didn't you?" said Jim. "I was just trying to get my money back," said the man, "well, you should have been more careful about who you did business with." "Are you going to tell that man in the other room to come out now?" "Come on out, Jake," said the man. The man stepped into the room. "Drop your gun," said Jim, "now outside on the porch, both of you."

Once out on the porch, Jim yelled, "Charles, bring your dad to the front porch." Charles came around the house with Chanler and J.C. Pruit, who had both been beaten badly. Hanna kept Maria and Chandler's wife around back; she knew this would be something they didn't need to see. The ranch hands who had survived came to the front, too. Jim walked over to Mr. Pruit, and Charles was helping him stand. Jim hugged him and placed his pistol in J.C.'s hand, then stepped aside. J.C. shot both men three times each and kept pulling the trigger. Jim took the gun from his hand. Stew steps up from behind Jim and tries to hand him the Sharps rifle, "You keep it, son, it's yours now, shoots good, doesn't it?" "Yes, sir, never misses," said Stew. "Now, Son, ride to my house and get my buggy, tell the Sheriff on the way out he can come in, it's over now." Jim looked at Charles, "Are they all dead?" "Yes, sir," said Charles, "ok, then, somebody get J.C.'s buggy, he and Maria are coming home with me, you to Chanler, bring your wife." "Y'all can stay with me until we get this mess cleaned up. The hands brought J.C.'s buggy up to the house, Jim helped J.C. get into the buggy, then Maria. The Sheriff came up, "What do we have here, Jim?" asked the Sheriff. "A lot of dead bodies," said Jim. "They were holding J.C. and Chanler, a hashtag for money supposedly owed to them by Carl." "Looks like they worked the old man over," said the Sheriff, "yeah, Chanler too." "I'm taking them to my house. I'll bring them to your office in a couple of days to make a statement." "Sounds good," said the Sheriff, "get what you need off the bodies, I'll have my men bury them tomorrow by the gate." "Why by the gate," asked the Sheriff, "you'll see," said Jim.

Stewart came back with Jim's buggy, they loaded Chanler and his wife in it, "Hanna, I may need some help tomorrow cleaning this up," said Jim, "Sure thing," said Hanna. Jim drove J.C.'s Buggy, and Stewart drove Jim's to Jim's house. No one on the Evens Ranch side of things was badly hurt, luckily, but Stewart had a rough couple of days. After things were cleaned up and the bodies were buried near the gate, Jim put up a sign that read. "Twenty-Five Men Tried to Take This Ranch," "They did get to stay." After J.C. and Chanler got checked out by the doctor and healed up at Jim's house, they went back home, and everything had been cleaned up. Hanna had John and Arron fill in all the bullet holes and repair the broken furniture. The place looked like it was new again; some repainting had to be done after removing blood splatter from the walls, and some windows had to be replaced. Jim went to see Stewart, who was almost finished with the rail in town. Jim sat him down and told him, "Son, I'm sorry I had to ask you to do what we did the other day." "I know how it makes you feel sick in your stomach." "It took me a while to get over killing the Indians that took your Aunt Hanna," "but I did, over time I realized how to look at it." "I told your Aunt Hanna, and she told Missy, now I'll tell you," "a predator is a predator, whether it's a man, a wolf, a bear, or a wolverine." "If they are harming our stock, or your family, or our friends, there are only two ways to handle it: run them off or kill them." "Son, these men weren't going to run, they made their choice, we did what we had to do, we didn't want to kill them, but they chose to be killed."

Mr. and Mrs. Pruit ran an ad in the local paper that said: "Thanks to our great friends, the Evens family and our son Charles, we were saved from some very bad men and their gang. We were beaten and humiliated beyond reason, but thanks to the Evens' bravery and their kindness, we are back home now. We would also like to thank the brave men and women who work for the King's Land Ranch; they are wonderful people. Mr. Pruit took a page from the outlaw's book and placed guards at a new gate he installed near his home, as well as the front and back doors of the house. Another grave sight was made for the ranch hands who were killed by the outlaws who had no family near the ranch. Two of the men's bodies were sent back East to their families, and five more were buried there on the ranch. The man that Hanna and Charles found alive was sent to California, and the bone in his leg was shattered and beyond repair. They had to remove the lower part of his leg. He has a new job now, sitting on Pruitt's front porch with a shotgun on his lap.

As they always do, the full story finally came out about Carl and his business dealings in Nevada. Carl Pruitt married into one of the richest families in Nevada through an arranged agreement between Maria Pruitt (Carl's Mother) and her lifelong friend, Rosa Lancaster. They had grown up together in a small village South of the Mexico and Arizona border, as dirt-poor little girls. They wanted so badly to be sisters and pretended they were most of the time. They were always together, Rosa's father was never home, an outlaw of sorts, and Maria's father had been killed in a gun fight. The two girls made a pact that one day they would be family. As they grew older, they always said they would marry brothers. Then they would have the same last names and be sisters, as young ladies, both seventeen, they worked in the local Cantina. Both pretty, with the same features, they were often thought to be real sisters, as they claimed. One day, two young gringos came into the Cantina for drinks after a long, hard ride. The girls served them drinks and food. These men were rouged-looking young men with Caliste hands and sun-beaten skin. The girl asked them their names. J.C. Pruit, my brother Bart, said, "J.C., you are brothers," asked Maria. "Sure, we are, can't you tell?" said J.C. with a laugh. But J.C. had red hair, and Bart had black hair. "We are sisters, said Maria, "me and Rosa," "well I'll be damned," said J.C., "and that's something." As the two men kept drinking, the two girls kept asking questions.

"Bart was the quite type and didn't say much, but J.C. just kept taking, "so why are you here," asked Maria, "just passing through," said J.C., "where are you going," asked Maria. J.C. looked at Bart, "where are we going," asked J.C., "North," said Bart. "Oh, yeah, North," said J.C., pointing South; they were both drunk. The girls had decided that these two gringos were their tickets out of their small town. They took the men to a room and put them to bed, then lifted the men alone. The next morning, they came back and woke the men up, still dressed from the night before, and they staggered out of the room. The girls led them right back into the Catina, where they served them breakfast and more to drink. Med morning, they led the two men, still drunk, to the church, and they were married. A Marriage decree was written, and the girls had them sign their names. Bart and J.C. could not read Mexican, and the girls could not read English. It was years before the girls realized that Bart and J.C. were not real brothers. That night the girls took them back to the room and seduced them into bed. Once Bart and J.C. sobered up and realized that they had married the two girls. They both bought another horse apiece for their wives to ride; the two girls had no idea what they had just gotten themselves into. They traveled together to the Northern border of Mexico, each night camping on the ground. Rosa asked Bart where they were headed. He showed her on a map the Northwest corner of Nevada, "right there," said Bart with a smile. "Do you have a house there?" asked Rosa. "Nope," said Bart, "just ten thousand acres of wide-open grassland." Rosa started to cry, "We have no house," said Rosa, "not yet," said Bart, "We will build one, a great big beautiful one." The two young men, Bart and J.C., after serving with Lewis and Clark's expedition, were given ten thousand acres each for their service. Bart picked his spot in the Northwest corner of Nevada, J.C. picked his spot in the Northwest corner of Oregon, near the Ocean.

The girls were in shock when they found out that they were going to have to build their own houses in a place with no other people. Even worse, they would not be together anymore, they would be hundreds of miles apart. This was not part of their plan; this was not what they had wanted. They talked about going back home with each other. But to what, the same thing they were trying so hard to get away from, little did they know at the time that one day they would have more than they could ever dream. It took them three days to get into

Arizona, then three weeks to get to Nevada, then four more weeks to get to Bart land in Northern Nevada. Bart and J.C. wasted no time in getting started on a building, a cabin near a small lake on Bart's property. By now it was fall, and winter would be coming soon. The two men worked from sunup to sundown every day, cutting, piling, and stacking logs, while the women cooked and packed grass and mud in the cracks of the logs. Once the logs were stacked and the roof was on, the men hauled in rocks on a sled to the cabin and built a large fireplace. Just as the last rock was placed, it started to snow. J.C. and Bart built a big fire in the fireplace. The cabin had three rooms: one main room with the fireplace and a lean-to off each side to sleep in. One for each couple, Pruitt's, would be spending the winter with Bart and Rosa. Once the cabin was warm, Bart and J.C. took the rifles and went after meat. Late that afternoon, they came back with an Elk and a brown deer. They skinned them outside in the snow, then brought the carcass into the cabin and hung them from the rafters in one corner. They had packed dry goods in with them when they came; all they needed was meat. Now they had that.

The two women huddled by the fireplace while the men-built furniture for the cabin. Spring came, and the snow was melting off the cabin roof. Bart and J.C. got the horses ready to go. "Where are we going now asked Rosa. "Oregon," said J.C., "where is Oregon?" asked Maria. "North," said Bart and J.C. at the same time. They nailed the door shut on Bart's cabin and mounted their horses; the women were not happy about leaving a cabin with a roof. They had decided that these two men were just crazy and could not stay still. After two days, they crossed over into Oregon. The snow was melting fast, and the tall green grass was pushing through. It took them five more days to cross the Clackamas River, after another day of riding. Maria asked, "How much father?" J.C. stopped, "We're here," said J.C., "See that ridge over there," "That's where we will build our Ranch." They rode up to the ridge; from the top, they could see in all directions for miles and miles. This time the men had to go out and drag the logs in, they built the same cabin that they had built before at Barts place. They used river rocks to build the fireplace. After six weeks, the cabin was finished. Maria and Rosa learn through overhearing the men talk that they were not real brothers, just as Maria and Rosa were not sisters, just great friends who bonded through their working together. Maria had married John Cloud Pruit, and Rosa had married Bartholomew Lancaster; they were still not sisters at all. The two women made another pact that one day, one of Maria's children would marry one of Rosa's children to bind the two families together.

Bart and Rosa left the Pruitt's after their cabin was completed; the two men had fulfilled their promise to one another to help build cabins on both their lands. They were now free to go their own way and chase their own dreams. Maria and Rosa both had a baby in the fall; they each had a son, Chanler Pruitt and Marcus Lancaster. After a couple more years, Maria was pregnant again, praying for a girl; she had Charles Pruitt. The two women's dreams were dashed again. The next year, Rosa had a child, another son, Bart, and named him John Ross Lancaster after his friend. It seemed the stars would never align for the two girls from the small Mexican town. Although the men they married bought and sold cattle and horses and more land, creating two of the largest Ranches in the Western United States. The two Mexican girls had everything they could have ever wanted, except for a family connection. When lo and behold, Rosa gave birth to a baby girl, they named Mary Anne Lancaster, in the spring, and Maria gave birth to another son that fall, named Carl Lewis Pruitt. The following spring, Maria made J.C. take her to Rosa's and Bart's home in Nevada with their baby boy, Carl. The two childhood friends were so happy, although the men, Bart and J.C., knew nothing about their wives' plans. They enjoyed seeing each other again after they both had become successful Ranchers. The two men sat and talked for hours about old times and the adventures they had; Marcus, Bart's oldest son, was now running the day-to-day operation of the ranch as Chanler was doing the same for Pruitt's ranch. The Pruitt's stayed a week, then went back home. Those two babies were now cursed and bonded together. Their lives would be controlled from this day forth; they were pampered and schooled on the finer things, and both were taught to speak English and Spanish. The last stipulation of the agreement was for Carl to have a college degree before they wed.

After their wedding, all Carl had to do was enjoy life with his new bride, as he spent the first year with her family. He received an allowance from his family, and Mary received one from her parents, more money than most people made working. All they were expected to do was to produce an heir and a grandchild. But it's hard to make love when you fight all the time, both spoiled Brates were doomed to fall. Carl took up drinking and gambling to the point that they were broke, and Mary was going to her mother for more money. Remarkably, Carl started to win. In just a few weeks, Carl replaced all the money he had lost and then some. Mary begged him to stop while he was ahead; she agreed to do anything he asked if he would only stop. So, he did stop gambling, but not the drinking, after his and Mary's trip to Oregon City for his mother's birthday, and being knocked out by his brother Charles. He swore never to go back to Oregon. Returning to Nevada, he started helping around the Lancaster Ranch, a welcome surprise to everyone. Carl, using his education, developed a process for the feudalization of the pasture land, which increased grass growth by two folles. It produced thicker, taller, and greener grass with more protein per stalk. His process was only used on a forty-acre hay field that Bart allowed him to use; the grass was then cut, dried, and bundled up for winter feeding. The results were amazing; the cattle could eat less and get more protein in the winter.

After that winter with Bart's endorsement, other Ranchers were waiting for Carl to do the same for them. A rancher approached Carl in town, telling him that he had a hundred-acre plot he wanted to make into a hay field. Carl, who wanted to make a name for himself, and with his confidence in his process, agreed to treat the man's land with the warning that the treated grass was for dried hay only, not for cattle or horses to eat green due to the chemicals involved. Carl's calculations were based on forty arches of grassland, not one hundred arches. He assumed that to be two and a half times the amount he used on Bart's forty-acre lot. Without any other calculations, he treated the field, and within a few weeks, the grass was seeded out and ready to cut. The rancher had the grass cut in the field; the grass would need to lie in the field for a week, turning it over every other day. To allow the adsorbed Chemicals from the ground to evaporate from the grass. However, the gate to the field was left open, and in two days, when the men came back to rake the cut grass in the field, it was full of dead cows. Hundreds of them were everywhere, despite Carl's warning to the Rancher; he was blamed by the rancher for the death of his herd. Estimated to be worth $ 50,000.00, Bart stood up for Carl, saying that the rancher took the same chance that he did when letting Carl treat his field. And alleged that it was not Carl's fault that the gate was left open, the other ranchers in the area agreed with Bart. But the rancher who had lost his herd was devastated. After twenty years of building up his herd, it was wiped out in two days. He demanded that Carl pay for his lost herd, but Carl didn't have the money, the man made all kinds of threats.

Bart told Carl, You will have to kill that man one day, but Carl was not a killer; he was not raised that way. His mother or his brothers had always protected him, he never had to stand up for himself, he just didn't know how. So, he ran, Rosa put him and Mary on a train with some money, and sent them to the East Coast. The old rancher had stewed over his loss to the point it drove him crazy. He hired a group of gunmen and went to the Lancaster Ranch to take Carl. Thinking that Lancaster or Pruitt would pay to get Carl back, but

Carl was gone, they held everyone at gunpoint and searched the ranch. They beat Bart trying to make him tell them where Carl had gone, but he didn't know, no one knew but Rosa. They finally left. The old man knew that Carl's father had a big ranch in Oregon, so he headed to Oregon, thinking Carl might have gone home to hide. Bart had his son send J.C. a telegram warning him about the men, but he didn't get it until after it was over. The old man and his men found the ranch and took it over, rounding up the ranch hands and locking them up. They shoot the ones that tried to run, the rest we already know. The Evens, sensing their Nabors were in trouble, went to their rescue. Rosa sent Maria a letter after everything was over, telling her where Carl and Mary had settled. They are planning a trip to see them next spring.

Chapter Fifteen: The Gun Fight

The town of Oregon City has grown by three times its size over the years. For the past three years, after the Pruit Ranch ordeal, everything has been quiet. Anna was sixteen now, and wearing a gun, like her mom, she knows how to use it as well. Some say she is as fast as her uncle Jim was when he was young. Patina and Stew have a little girl named Winona Evens (Winona means First Born Daughter). The couple is very happy together. Missy and James have a little boy also named James Even Potter; they call him Jimmy. The Pruitt's and the Evens are closer than ever now, spending a lot of time together. Plus, Matt, Jim, Charles, Chanler, and Thomas meet every third Saturday in town for lunch to discuss cattle prices and which market they should try to sell to. By combining their steers together as they have done for years, they can compete for better prices, being two of the largest producers in the area. Chanler wants to rebuild the old shipping port on the Pruit ranch, he believes the railroad is charging too much to ship beef now. But he and his accountant are still crunching numbers to see if they could save money there. The lumber company business is still booming and may also be able to save by shipping on steamships from the port.

One afternoon, a well-dressed man got off the train in Oregon City. He walked to the hotel, got a room, and then proceeded to the land office. He inquired into the property that the Sawmill was on and who owned the property. Then asked to see all the bill of sales and the deeds to the property, the Land office told him that he could view the documents there, but could not take them out. The man asked, "Who or what is this King's Land Ranch Corporation?" "Well, let me get you someone to talk to about that." As the man reviewed the papers, Eric walked in. "I understand you have some questions," said Eric. "Yes," said the man. "And you are?" "I am the owner's Lawyer," said Eric. "Oh, great," said the man, "I would like to purchase this property," said the man, "well, I'm not sure you could," said Eric, "you see it's not for sale." "Oh, poppy cock," said the man, "everything is for sale." "I don't think so," said Eric, "but I can ask my clients," "Please do so," said the man, "I want to move on this right away." The man left. Eric laughed, that man's something else, he thought. That night, Eric told Lizzy about the strange man who wanted to buy the Sawmill. "No," said Lizzy, "that's what you tell him."

The next morning, the man returns to Eric's office, where Eric informs him that the owner said no, the Mill is not for sale. The man stormed out of the office, then walked over to the Sawmills office, where he demanded to speak to the owner. Lizzy came out and confronted the man. The man states, "I will not be engorged, Ma'am, I intend to own this Mill," he said, as he writes a number on a piece of paper. Lizzy looks at the piece of paper, then smiles. Trying to be professional, she replies, "Sir, as you have already been told, this property is not for sale." She turns and walks back to her office, laughing at the man's offer. The man finally leaves and walks to the telegraph office, where he sends a message. Two days later, he meets two more men at the train station wearing suits. They leave the station and go to the Land Office. They spent the next two days reviewing the deeds and paperwork for all the King's Land Properties. On the second day, Eric asked the men what they were looking for. One of the men stood up and introduced his self as Mr. Wainright of Wainright and Hohman, a Law firm from San Francisco. Then he introduced the other man in the suit as his associate, Mr. Hohman. Eric introduced his self as Eric Kimbell of Kimbell and Kimbell.

"I represent the Evens family," said Eric, "maybe I can help you find what you're looking for." "Well, Mr. Kimbell, our client, Mr. Guttery, owns a large lumber operation in San Francisco, the largest in the State." "Seems your client's operation here is hurting him, by undercutting his prices and costing him money and sales." "From what we've found here, the Sawmill is a small part of a larger Ranch operation all under one Corporation," said Mr. Wainright. "Let me be honest with you, Mr. Guttery wants to buy your client's Sawmill and shut it down, but because it's part of a larger corporation." "We've explained to him that it's not an independent operation or property, and the only way he could buy it would be to buy the corporation, Kings Land, outright in its entirety." "Which would not be feasible," "we recommend to him that he try to make a business arrangement with your clients to stop their operation or sale exclusively to him." "These are the only legal avenue we see currently for Mr. Guttery," said Mr. Wainright, "well, I know personnel that my clients have acquired timber rights that will keep them operating for ten years and beyond." "Perhaps your client would be interested in selling out his operation to my clients," said Eric with a smile." Mr. Guttery replied, 'We're through here, let's go, gentlemen."

A couple of weeks later, at a family supper, Eric told Matt and Jim about the strange man who tried to buy the Sawmill. A Mr. Guttery from San Francesco who owned a Sawmill there and claimed Lizzy was taking his customers from him. Eric thought it was quite funny and then told them how he shut him down. Matt and Jim did not find the humor in it and asked why they were not told at the time, "Well," Lizzy said, "No, it's not for sale," replied Eric. "Well, that may be true, but anytime an outsider wants to dig through our property deeds and business papers, we need to know about it," said Jim. "I assumed Lizzy had told you," "nope," said Jim. Eric got quiet, and Lizzy came into the room. "So, we had someone wanting to buy the Mill," said Jim. Lizzy looked at Eric, "You didn't tell them, "Asked Lizzy. "Just now," said Eric, "I thought you did." "I'm not their lawyer, you are," "they pay you, not me," said Lizzy, "I'm your wife." "Damn stupid men, I swear," said Lizzy as she stormed out of the room. "So why did he want the Mill," asked Jim, "to shut it down, to get rid of his competition?" "But once his lawyers told him the way the corporation is set up, to get the

Mill, he would have to buy the anticorporation ranch and all, "he gave up and left," said Eric. After Lizzy and Eric left, Jim told Matt, "We may need a new lawyer." Things were all going well for a month or so, then for the first time, the Mill had a fire. There was not much damage done, it seems some sawdust piled near one of the saws, smoldered through the day, but then blazed up that night. The night watchman caught it in time to notify the Mill manager, and they put it out. The Evens' added another night watchman at the Mill, to watch for fires, and just in case the last fire was not an accident. Three weeks later, two men were seen trying to put dynamite in the fireboxes of the steam engines. The two men got away and were never seen again. Once the dynamite was removed and the whole Mill was searched, it started back up. Eric is convinced that Mr. Guttery had something to do with it, but they had no proof. Matt decided to send Tom Wagner a telegram in San Francisco telling him what was going on. He asked him to check out Mr. Guttery and report back. Sheriff Hill was also told. Two days later, Tom sent a message back stating that Mr. Guttery had lost a large contract three months ago to supply lumber for a new building going up in San Francisco. Because Lizzy was able to feel the order right away, at a competitive price. Guttery's Mill is the only Mill in San Francisco and the largest in California, but it has a backlog of orders with all the building going on in the state. His greed would not allow him to let the other Mills help him feel his orders, and he expected his clients to wait for him. Before the railroad put the spear in Oregon City, and Lizzy started shipping her lumber by rail to California, his clients had no choice. Now they do, and Lizzy has also taken most of the contract to supply dress lumber to the Furniture Factories in California, making Mr. Guttery angry.

Seems Mr. Guttery never had to deal with a real competitor until the Kings Land Lumber Company came to be. Tom said he would not put anything past Mr. Guttery, that ten years ago, another Company had plans to buy a Big Lumber Mill in San Francisco. But before the

Mill was completed, their Steam Engine exploded one night before it was ever fired up. The Company could not recover from the loss of the Engine, causing the land to be sold to an investment company. Who built a warehouse there on the site where Mr. Guttery now stores cross ties cut for one of the railroad companies? Matt shared the message from Tom with Jim and the others. Jim wanted to go to California and take revenge. But still, they had no proof that Guttery was involved; Jim went to Mr. Pruit to see if he had any contacts in California. J.C. told Jim that he and the Governor of Oregon (La Fayette Grover) were close friends, and that Grover of Oregon was friends with the Governor of California (Newton Booth). Pruit had campaigned for Grover to become the Governor of Oregon. "I can go with you to Salem," said Pruit, "I'll get us train tickets." "You can state your suspicion to him, and he can have the California Governor check him out." "Sounds good," said Jim, "I'll put more guards at the sawmill while I'm gone.

The next day, Jim and Pruit boarded the train to Salem to see the Governor. Jim told Pruit, "I think I'm going to have to kill this Guttery man." "Anything you need?" said Pruit. They met with Grover; Jim told him the story and why he suspected Guttery was trying to shut his mill down. The governor was taken with Jim, and being with Pruit didn't hurt. Grover told him that he would contact Booth right away. Grover said, "You do whatever you need to do to protect your family and your business." "Oh, I will," said Jim. Pruit had told Grover about how the Evens family, mainly Jim, had saved his family, and by that, he knew Jim was not one to back down from a fight. Jim and Pruit came back home the next day to Oregon City. The next week, unknown to Jim, Governor Booth launched a full investigation into Guttery and his business activities in San Francisco. Jim had brought Steward and Thomas, who had returned from college, to help guard the mill. He had put Hanna and her crew on standby in case of trouble; everyone was on pins and needles, expecting the worst.

Grover sent a message to Pruit stating that Booth had shut the Guttery operation down until the investigation was over. He believed that Guttery knew Jim had instigated the investigation and would try to retaliate since he had not been arrested yet. Tom sent Matt a message stating that over a dozen men and horses were loaded onto a train in San Francisco that morning. That they looked like hired guns and were headed to Oregon City, Matt went to find Jim. When Matt got to Jim at the Mill, Pruit was there already. Jim told his father to take Sara, Patina, and Stew's baby, Sissy, Lizzy, Ezy, and his little girl to Hanna's, "tell Hanna to come running with everybody," said Jim. Jim asked Pruit to go tell Sheriff Hill, then get who he could from his ranch. "I don't want anybody in town hurt," said Jim, "tell the Sheriff to have everybody close up shop and stay off the streets." Jim had them shut down the Mill and told the workers to leave and go home. A few refused to go home, stating they would stay and fight for their Mill.

At 4:00 P.M., the train pulled into the station right on time, but no men and no horses got off the train. Only the mail was unloaded, and two ladies with luggage, the Sheriff was watching the train station, something was wrong, thought the Sheriff. He then rode to the Mill. Hanna, Missy, Charles, and James had come, so had Kate. Jim was telling them to spread out around town. The Sheriff said they were not on the train, "they're coming, they must have gotten off South of town," said Jim. "Get ready, everybody," Anna had been left at home with Grace and the others. After a while, Anna slipped out of the back door of the house. She went to the barn and saddled her horse, strapped her gun and knife on, and grabbed the bow & arrows Patina had given her. She slowly rode away from the barn, then broke into a gallop, running through town along the river road. She looped in behind Lizzy's house and hid there, watching and waiting. After a while, four men rode into town and stopped at the saloon, which was the only thing still open in town. "They're here," said Jim, "Hanna was on Sissy's roof, Missy and Kate were in the stables, Stewart was on the Bank roof, everybody was watching and waiting. The rest were at the Mill. Finally, a shot rang out from the roof of the Salon tongue, the Bank Roof where Stew was at. Stew returned fire, and the man fell off the salon's roof. Six men came riding up to the Mill, firing at Jim and his crew there. Hanna shot one of them from the top of the dress shop. Jim shoots two, and Charles shoots one of the men, after he had already been shot with an Arrow. "That bang girl," said Charles. The other two men rode off. "What is it?" asked Jim. "Anna's here somewhere," said Charles. "We told her not to come," "where's she at?" asked Jim, "who knows, said Charles, but you see that Arrow in the man I just shot," Jim smiled, "well, we might need her before this is over."

Out of the four that went into the salon, only three came out and eased down the boardwalk to the Mill. As they got in front of the stables, Missy and Kate jumped out and shot two of the men. Hanna shot at one from the roof but missed. He started to run away but was hit with two arrows. "That little shit," said Hanna, "I'm going to skin her hide." Hanna crawls down off the roof to go find Anna. No one knew how many men were left hiding. Jim wanted to smoke them out somehow and get this thing over with. Jim walked out from the Mill, then onto the main street. A shot rang out as a bullet hit the ground at his feet. Then one man fell from the roof of the Land office with an arrow in his back, another man shoots at Jim from the restaurant roof, and Stew shoots that man. A shot rang out from a window in the hotel. Jim fell to the ground, hit in the leg. Hanna saw him fall, and she yelled, "JIM!" Hanna hears a shrill whistle; Anna's horse came running by her as she made it to the street. The horse ran down the street, and Anna ran out to Jim. The horse stops at Jim, "grab the stirrup, Uncle Jim," said Anna. Jim reached up and grabbed hold of one stirrup. Anna dragged him into the alley with her horse. Then, she helps Jim up onto her horse, and Anna puts a pigging string around Jim's leg above the wound. "He got you good," said Anna, "don't worry, I'll get you out of here." "They will be coming, Uncle

Jim, you be ready," "I'll try to find them before they get here," said Anna, as she ran to the other end of the alley and disappeared. Jim waited. Hanna, Missy, and Kate all started trying to work their way to Jim before the other men got there.

They hear more gunfire back at the Mill. Hanna gets to Jim first, "Where's Anna?" asked Hanna in a panicked voice. "She's close by somewhere," said Jim. "How bad are you hurt?" asked Hanna. "I think it went through," said Jim. They both hear a whistle like a whippoorwill, and Anna's horse starts walking forward to the back end of the alley. "Where's this damn horse going?" asked Hanna, as she was following along behind them. The horse turns left, and they realize that they were behind the doctor's office. They hear a short whistle, and the horse stops dead still at the back door of the office. The doctor comes out and helps Hanna get Jim inside. The horse takes off running, and Hanna locks the door. After about thirty minutes, Anna rides up to the Sawmill, dragging one man by a rope; he was still alive. "This is the last one," said Anna, "take him to the Sheriff." "Oh, yeah," "y'all haven't seen me." Charles stepped out into the open. "Oh, hi, Dad, bye, Dad," said Anna as she rode off in a gallop.

As things calmed down and everyone started to come out, Hanna helped Jim walk out of the doctor's office. J.C. Chanler and two of their ranch hands came riding in from South of town with two more men from the gang tied up. The Sheriff took them and put them in jail along with the other one that Anna caught. The sheriff told his deputy to get a wagon and help load up the dead and wounded. As the deputy, Charles, Chanler, Stew, and Thomas were loading the bodies into the wagon, the deputy asked if they had Indians helping them fight. Chanler laughed, "Why do you ask?" "Well, there's one, two, three, four, five bodies shot with arrows," "that would be my cozen Anna," said Thomas with a smile. "Whose Anna?" asked the Deputy. "My daughter," said Charles. They loaded up thirteen bodies and had three in jail. Once the men in jail were told they were facing multiple attempted murder charges, they began to sing like canaries. They were hired by Guttery to put the King's Land Lumber Mill out of business one way or the other. Of course, they claimed at first that they were only trying to scare the Evens into shutting down. But with Jim having been shot, and one of the Mill workers shot. That story was not going to stand up; the men were sent to trial and then to the State Prison. Mr. Guttery was found after a few days and brought to the Courthouse in Salem, Oregon. After being charged with multiple counts of assault and attempted murder, Mr. Guttery was sentenced to hang. But as he was being led out of the courtroom, he tried to take the gun from the bailiff and was shot by the guards at the door.

When Hanna and Charles returned home that night after the gun fight, Anna was setting up waiting for them. She knew she would be in trouble, but when Hanna came in, she said nothing. Charles walked over to her, leaned down, kissed her head, and said, "Go to bed." The next morning, after breakfast, Hanna told Anna to get her things, that they would be taking a ride. After saddling up their horses, Hanna rode off, and Anna followed her. "Where are we going, Mama?" asked Anna. "We're just riding, honey," they rode for a few more hours. Finally, they stopped, "let's rest here," said Hanna, "thank God," said Anna. They sat on a log, "This is a nice place," said Hanna. "Where are we?" asked Anna. Hanna looked around the area. "I don't know for sure," said Hanna, "I think we might be lost," "What?" said Anna, "It's ok," said Hanna, "I'm sure you can find the way out of here." "You're so much smarter than me or Charles," "but momma, I don't know where we are," said Anna. "Neither do I," said Hanna, "Ok, Momma, I'm sorry, I should have listened and stayed home." "No, honey, all we have to do is find North, then go in the opposite direction back home." "But how, Momma? I don't know how." "Do you know how, Momma? "Anna started to cry." "Why, are you crying?" asked Hanna, "I know you're not scared, you weren't scared yesterday." "But I was helping my family, I helped Uncle Jim get off the street and to the doctor," said Anna.

"That's true, honey, I'm glad you did that," said Hanna, "but why do you think your Uncle Jim walked out into that street where he could be shot?" "I don't know, he just did," said Anna, "your Uncle Jim knew I was on the roof of the dress shop and had the main street covered." "But what he didn't know was, I saw you running around shooting arrows into people, and I had left my post to go find you because I was scared you would be shot." "Because of you, your Uncle Jim got shot," "because I wasn't there to cover him," "I've always covered him, and he's always covered me." Anna cried more, "So it was my fault Uncle Jim got shot," said Anna. "No, it's my fault," said Hanna, in a loud voice, "because I love you more than I love him." "I let him down for the first time ever." "It's killing me, I just want you to understand that 'every action has a reaction,' I told you to stay home so I wouldn't be worried about you and be distracted from what I needed to do." "Not because I didn't think you could help, I know what you can do, Anna, I thought you." "But because you don't know yet how to be part of a team," "I'm sorry, Momma," said Anna. "I'll never disobey you again, Momma, I promise."

"Ok, honey, now let me teach you how to find your way home," said Hanna. "The sun comes up in the East in the mornings, and it goes down in the West, we need to go South." "But I can't see the sun, Momma," "see that green moss on that tree growing around the bottom," asked Hanna. "Yes," said Anna, "look closely, which side is the moss the highest on that tree?" asked Hanna. This side pointed Anna, "that's North," said Hanna, "we want to go South." "Which way should we go?" asked Hanna. "The other way," said Anna, pointing South. "Let's get going," said Hanna, "it will get dark before we get home." "Then what," asked Anna, "we follow the moon and the stairs."

Six months later, Mr. Guttery's Lumber Company went up for action; it seems it was purchased by an investment Company (EP&W) to be managed and operated by Mr. Tom Wagner. The new company signed a contract with Kings Land Lumber Company to help fulfill all the back orders left by Mr. Guttery. Anna learned to find her directions even in the dark of night and agreed to use her skills to help the Evens family as a teammate, and not by showing off. She went to her uncle Jim's house to see him; she told him she was sorry about him getting shot and that it was her fault." "Jim smiled, "No, honey, it's my fault, I didn't know how many were left out there, but I knew the longer it went on, the more chance it would be that our family would get hurt." "But momma left her post because of me," said Anna. "No one thought a man would be in the hotel window," "we could talk about ifs and buts from now on until the end time," said Jim. "I'm just glad we all made it out alive." "I'm also glad to know there will always be somebody to protect this family in the future." Jim hugged her and kissed Anna's head, "It's all about family, now you go train me a horse that's as smart as that one you have," said Jim.

After about two months, Jim was all healed up from his gunshot wounds. Anna was working with a new three-year-old horse for her uncle Jim; she wanted this one to be special. Jim told Hanna what he had told Anna when she came to see him: "Hanna, I love you, you, my sister, we've always looked after each other," said Jim. "But if Thomas, Stewart, and you were in trouble, I'd try to save you all, but I would save my boys first." "Because you and I are grown, we know the risk, we chose to take the risk." "Don't you ever choose me over any of our kids, yours or mine," said Jim. "They are the future of this family, not us," Hanna said, hugging Jim. "You know Anna takes after you," said Hanna. "I know," said Jim, "that's why you felt that you had to protect her like you always have me." "Then Jim laughed, she took out more outlaws than any of us," said Jim, "they never knew what hit them, did they, Sis?" "Nope," said Hanna, "we Evens girls are something else." When Hanna made that statement as a joke to her brother, she never knew that one day those words would be tested again.

As time went by and the Kings Land Ranch organizations continued to grow and prosper, things got quiet for the most part. It had been three years séance the big gun fight in town, and that day had been all but forgotten. Anna was now a young woman, but still a cowgirl and horse trainer. Lizzy, Missy, and Sissy all had children now, as did Patina and Stew. The Evens family was growing fast. Matt and Sara now have seven grandchildren and two great-grandchildren. That spring, Lizzy decided to have a girls' day out in town. She invited all her sisters and nieces to lunch at the diner; she had reserved the banquet room there. Seems they never got to spend time together without the men around. A woman's reunion of sorts, Sara had to watch the grandchildren, and Hanna's youngest chose to stay in the valley. But Hanna, Anna, Missy, Sissy, Ezy, Patina, and Lizzy were there. They had a wonderful time laughing and talking about the men and the crazy things their kids did. It was so nice just to be together as one group of women, the Evens women, all prominent in their own rights. But not all were respected and liked by everyone in town that day.

In the salon, there was a group of men who had all seen or felt the raft in one way or another of the Evans women. Some had been fired or laid off by the Evens, either from the ranch or the lumber operations. A few of the men had seen the women gathering in town outside the café. This started a conversation about them, as they thought the high and mighty Evans women. As the men drank and talked trash, and the women and their families, the talk got stronger. As they continued to drink, they got braver and madder. One of the older men said, "We should teach them a lesson and put them in their place." "Yeah, that's right," said another man, "we should show them that the men run this town, not a bunch of women." A spark had been made, and the liquor inside them had started to burn. One of the men saw the girls coming out of the restaurant across the street, "Here they come yelled the man. The older man and four younger men jumped up and headed to the door.

They stood on the porch of the saloon, the older man yelled, "Look at the Evens queens." He walked off the porch onto the street, and the others followed. Anna turned to face them. Hanna grabbed her arm, "ignore them," said Hanna. One of the younger men yelled, "There's Miss Lizzy, the sawmill bitch. Lizzy stopped and turned to face them, as did the other women. Anna stepped out front, "Sounds like you boys need to go sleep it off," said Anna. "Come here, little girl, I'll take you to bed," all the men laughed. Anna put her hand on her gun. "Anna, don't," said Hanna. Missy had already moved to a clear spot and had her hand on her gun. The women were lined up on one side of the street, and the five men on the other side. Hanna pulled out a silver dollar. "Here, have another drink," said Hanna as she tossed it to them. One of the men said, "You think because you have money you rule this town." "I think we need to teach you, Evens, that men run this town." Hanna puts her hand on her gun, Anna hands her spare gun to Sissy, and Hanna hands hers to Lizzy. Some of the townspeople had started to come out into the street, and the air was getting thick. "Look, guy, don't do this," "whatever we've done to make you mad, we're sorry," said Hanna. "Not me," said Anna, "or me," said Missy, "Patina, get behind me," said Hanna. "Look," said Hanna, "you don't want to die in the street. Your brother Jim is not here to protect you; we saw him leaving town," said the older man. "Y'all want to act like men, ride like men, talk like men, but can you fight like a man?" One of the younger men went for his gun, and six of the seven women were shot. Anna, Missy, Ezy, and Hanna shot twist, in the blink of an eye, five men died without firing a shot. The seven women stood there, Anna, Hanna, and Missy reloaded their guns, "somebody get the Deputy," said Hanna.

There were no tears, no remorse, all the men had cleared leather with their guns, but had no time to fire a shot. Stupidity had killed them all, they just didn't know what they were facing. Every single woman in that group had faced death before, they had overcome and survived it. They thought they would scare the women and make them run off crying. The story is still told around town, and those who saw it happen still can't believe the grit the seven women showed. Although fearless, they still tried to talk the men down; they didn't want to fight them, but were given no choice. The people who risk it all for a dream or a chance are richer in life than all the others. When the settlers left their homes in the 1800s to head West, they all had the same questions on the back of their minds. "What if we don't make it?" But they also had the same dream, "But what if we do!"

In the spring of 1898, Jim sat in front of a news reporter, his hair had grayed, and his face was wrinkled like old leather. Still a good-looking man, with broad shoulders and piercing eyes. "Mr. Evens, they say you and your family built this town," said the reporter. "The Pruitt's built this town," said Jim, "I like to think we helped make it grow." "They say, you're the fastest man with a gun the northwest has ever seen," said the reporter. "Maybe, but only because they haven't seen the fastest gun yet," "that person is not a man, it's a woman," said Jim. "Who is she?" asked the reporter. "Can't tell you that," said Jim. "Why," asked the reporter, "well, because when word like that gets out, there are others who come that want to try them," said Jim. "Is that why you killed so many men?" asked the reporter, "men calling you out?" "No," said Jim, "I don't do that, I don't kill for sport or fun." Jim chalked up a little, "Yes, I've killed a lot of men in my life, but I never wanted to." "I killed my first man when I was sixteen, on the way here from Kentucky, they tried to kill our wagon boss," said Jim. "I've killed so many men since then, Bandits, Robbers, Indians, and Rustlers more than I could ever count." "All in the name of Justus or survival," said Jim, "but I'll let God be the judge of that when the time comes." A young man came running up to Jim wearing a Deputy Badge, all excited, "Sheriff Even, come quick, the Banks are being robbed." Jim jumped up and ran to the Bank. The reporter ran after them. The three bank robbers came running out of the bank, shooting their guns. Jim shot all three of them in the street. Jim walked to his office with his head down. The reporter followed him. As the reporter walked in, Jim was on his knees. "Sheriff, you, ok?" asked the reporter. Jim turned with tear-filled eyes, "No, son," said Jim, "Every time I have to kill, a part of me dies too."

P.S. God Bless the Dreamers who had the courage to tame the unknown and fight to survive:

Back Cover

King's Land Ranch

The Legacy

The author Marion Dees is sixty-seven years old. A construction worker for most of his life. In November of 2020, due to health problems caused by COVID, he was unable to work with years of life experiences around people from all walks of life and a deep love of the Western States. He began to reflect upon his travels across the country and the people he met. Also, the places he had seen and visited over the years. To keep his mind busy during these times, he started to write books about the things he saw. However, his stories are fictional with some actual facts, much of the liberation has been taken. However, like this story, they are based on actual locations and times that reflect the kind of events that could and did happen during the periods of his books. He has been back working since August of 2021 in construction, but is still writing his stories in his spare time. This book is the seventh book he has published. He hopes the readers will enjoy their journey back in time as much as he enjoyed writing it.

Made in the USA
Coppell, TX
15 March 2026

73934520R00154